THE FATHER OF LOCKS

Andrew Killeen was born and lives in Birmingham. He studied English at Corpus Christi College, Cambridge, and has spent most of his career working with homeless and disadvantaged children.

In his spare time he makes music, and can occasionally be found performing as a singer, musician and DJ. He supports Birmingham City FC, as karmic punishment for sins in a past life.

The Father of Locks is his first novel.

Andrew Killeen

The Father of Locks

Dedalus

Map of the World as known to Ismail al-Rawiya drawn by Matt Killeen

Published in the UK by Dedalus Limited
24–26, St Judith's Lane, Sawtry, Cambs, PE28 5XE
email: info@dedalusbooks.com
www.dedalusbooks.com

ISBN 978 1 903517 76 5

Dedalus is distributed in the USA by SCB Distributors,
15608 South New Century Drive, Gardena, CA 90248
email: info@scbdistributors.com   web site: www.scbdistributors.com

Dedalus is distributed in Australia by Peribo Pty Ltd.
58, Beaumont Road, Mount Kuring-gai N.S.W. 2080
email: info@peribo.com.au

Dedalus is distributed in Canada by Disticor Direct-Book Division
695, Westney Road South, Suite 14, Ajax, Ontario, LI6 6M9
email: ndalton@disticor.com   web site: www.disticordirect.com

First published by Dedalus in 2009
Father of Locks copyright © Andrew Killeen 2009

Printed in Finland by WS. Bookwell
Typeset by RefineCatch Limited, Bungay, Suffolk

CONTENTS

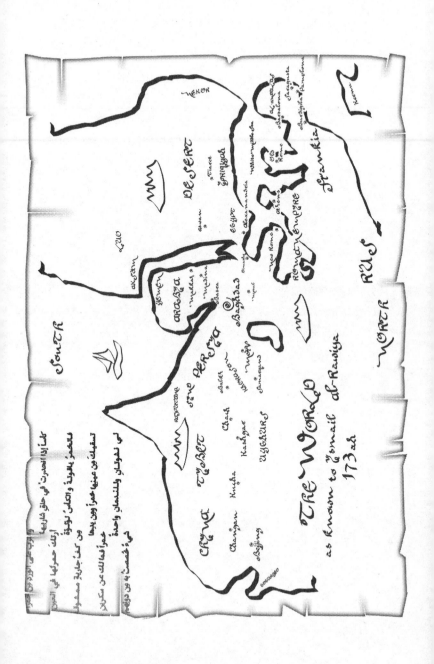

Prologue

The Tale of the Witch and the
Jeweller's Daughter

Once there was a jeweller, who was known for his good fortune. He was an attractive man, blessed with quick wits, a strong body, and a full and luxuriant beard. He could catch fish simply by putting his hand in the river, and find water by pushing a stick into the ground. His name was Ali, but his neighbours called him al-Mubarak, the Lucky One.

Al-Mubarak did not rely solely on his luck. He worked hard and prospered, and the fame of his merchandise spread throughout the land. Amirs and Shaikhs travelled to his shop to purchase tokens of love for their concubines or catamites. When it came time for Ali to take a wife, he married the most beautiful girl in his town. She had hair soft as spring rain and eyes as bright as lightning.

A year after they wed, she fell pregnant. When al-Mubarak learned that his wife was with child, he began to weep. His wife said:

"Husband, why do you not rejoice at this news? Have I offended you in some way?"

He looked up from his tears and answered:

"No, wife. I weep because God has favoured me better than I deserve. There are many who never know the happiness of wealth, love and fertility. I pity them, yet I believe it is harder to have such things and see them taken from you. Now I weep for fear that God will test me as he did the Prophet Ayyub. Would that I could protect my family from disaster and disease!"

The jeweller's forebodings proved to be well-founded; for his wife died giving birth. (We are from God, and to him we return.) The baby survived, but instead of the son he had hoped for it was a sickly girl.

9

Devastated by his loss, the jeweller poured his love and sorrow into the girlchild, whom he named Nadiyya, meaning Delicate. Against expectation she thrived, and grew to be more beautiful even than her mother, with skin like silken sheets and eyes as dark as hunger. Al-Mubarak's brothers and cousins brought their handsome sons, offering them as prospective husbands for the girl, but he turned them all away. Nobody was good enough for his daughter.

The jeweller became obsessed with finding her a husband who would be able to keep her safe from all harm. Having refused all the young men of his town, he began to travel further afield, in search of prospective sons-in-law. His business suffered, and in time he had to sell his shop. With nowhere to call home they trekked from town to town, selling trinkets from a cart.

In summer they slept under the stars, but winter was hard. Al-Mubarak found lodgings for his daughter, but could not afford to sleep indoors himself. So it was that the girl came out one morning to find that her father had frozen to death on the street in front of her door. (We are from God, and to him we return.)

As she was weeping over his body, a merchant by the name of Khalil happened by. He had just returned from a voyage which had brought him vast riches, and was on his way to the masjid, to give a share of his gold to the poor. He sent one of his servants to discover the cause of the girl's distress. When he learned of her misfortune, he thought:

"Surely God has put this girl in my path as a test of my charity. I shall take care of this orphan, and bury her father with all due ceremony."

Khalil had the jeweller's body washed and wrapped in rich cloth. He ordered his household to put on mourning weeds, and they prayed over the body before placing it in the grave. For the next three days, no work was done, and the women of the huram wailed and tore at their clothes as if the stranger were one of their own. That was the end of Ali al-Mubarak, the Lucky One.

The merchant Khalil took the jeweller's daughter into his

house, a spacious mansion of broad halls and pleasant gardens. He had fallen in love with her dark eyes before she had even stepped across his threshold. However he waited for four months and ten days, as if she were a widow, before offering her the brideprice: a heavy ring of gold, in which was set a sapphire the size of a ram's testicle. They were married with great feasting and revelry, and two hundred guests attended the celebration.

Al-Mubarak's life had ended cruelly, but some of his good fortune lingered. In death he had finally found the son-in-law he had been seeking. Khalil treated the girl as if she were a rare orchid, and tended to her every need. His attentions to her brewed bitter jealousy in his first wife. She had never borne him a child, and when her younger, prettier rival conceived, envy turned to hatred.

The first wife began to dream that Nadiyya had died, by accident or from illness. In the morning she would wake to find her husband gone from her side, and in her grief she would pull at her hair till it lay on her pillow, like a rebuke.

At last she sent her maid to buy poison, saying that she could hear rats in the garden. The first wife of Khalil the Merchant dug a hole in the skin of a sour orange, and impregnated the fruit with the venom. Then she sent her maid to take the orange to Nadiyya, saying:

"My new sister may think that I have been cold towards her. Let her accept this gift, so that there can be the beginnings of love between us."

The maid went to Nadiyya, where she sat in the garden with Khalil, under the shade of a fig tree, and spoke as her mistress had directed her. Khalil's heart filled with joy, and he cried out:

"Now we can live in harmony! Let us share this gift between us, as a token of the peace in which we shall live!"

But Nadiyya disdained the bitter fruit, and Khalil ate it alone. That evening he lay with his first wife, because he was pleased with her gesture. In the depths of the night he began to buck and puke. His screams brought his slaves to the chamber, but it was too late. Khalil the Merchant opened his bowels and died. (We are from God, and to him we return.)

The first wife saw what she had done. As the smell of sickly shit filled the room, she turned and walked away. She passed through the vestibule and onto the street, alone and unveiled. By the time anyone asked where she had gone, she had already waded into the river, to her thighs, to her waist, to her neck. When the dirty water began to fill her mouth she panicked and began to struggle, but her clothes were heavy and dragged her down to the mud.

We are from God, and to him we return.

Nadiyya was left in possession of his estate, and the Eunuch brought her the keys to the house. In the merchant's bedroom she opened a cedarwood chest to find it full of gold dinars. Every day his slaves would come to her for the household expenses, and she would take money from the chest and give it to them, before carefully locking it again. In this way time passed, and Khalil's child grew within her, swelling her belly.

Eight months after the death of her husband, Nadiyya gave birth to a girl, as beautiful as her mother and grandmother before her. The labour was difficult, and for weeks afterwards the jeweller's daughter lay close to death. When at last she recovered her strength the slaves begged her to give them money, as the household was in much debt. It was not until she opened the chest that she realized the merchant's treasure had dwindled to a few coins, and there was not enough to pay their creditors.

Nadiyya knew no way of acquiring wealth other than to marry a rich man. So she sent the Eunuch into the town to find her a husband. However, the men of substance wanted virgin brides, and nobody was interested in the pretty but impoverished widow.

She complained of her problems to the wetnurse, as she suckled the baby girl. The wetnurse looked at her for a long time, as if making a decision. Then she spoke.

"Mistress, there is a woman in this town that might help you. Her name is Qamra, and she is a witch. If you wish I will take you to her, but her services may cost you dear."

Eagerly the jeweller's daughter begged to be introduced to the witch. So it was that the two women set out after nightfall, with no escort and only a small lamp to guide their way through the dark streets. They came at last to a small hut on the edge of town, and the wetnurse said:

"You must go in alone, or the witch will not speak to you."

Nadiyya entered the hut. Inside she was dazzled by the blaze of sixty-six candles, and at first could not make out the huddled shape seated on a carpet. Her eyes cleared though as she sat down, and the jeweller's daughter beheld the face of the witch. Nadiyya had imagined her as an old crone, but Qamra was a young woman, who would have been attractive were the left side of her face not scarred, as if she had been burnt by fire. The witch addressed her.

"You seek a husband who will keep and protect you. That is no easy matter. What payment have you brought me?"

Nadiyya produced the ring which Khalil had given her, the one with a sapphire the size of a ram's testicle. Qamra took it and squinted at it in the candlelight, before secreting it in her robes. Then she took a disc of lead, and scratched into it three symbols. The jeweller's daughter could not read, but knew these were no letters of Arabic. The witch passed her the disc.

"Put this under your pillow, and sleep on it for three nights. On the morrow after the third night, your husband will come to you."

At those words the sixty-six candles all went out at once, and Nadiyya stumbled blindly from the hut in terror. For a month she hid the disc in a jar, too frightened to use it. But in the end, she reflected that she had spent her bride-price on it, and it seemed disrespectful to her husband not to make use of it. So she placed it under her pillow, and tried to forget what she had done.

Four days later, there came a banging at the door in the middle of the day. The Eunuch opened to see a tall figure silhouetted by the sun. The man at the door gave his name as Nuri, and said that his horse had gone lame in the street. He would pay for refreshment and a farrier to look at his animal.

This sudden apparition sent the whole household into a frenzy, like a termite's nest poked with a stick. Nadiyya ordered a curtain hung across the vestibule, and food and drink brought to the visitor. She sat behind the curtain and conversed with him, refusing all payment, while her stable boy treated the horse, which had merely caught a stone in its hoof.

Nuri returned the next day, and the day after, and the day after that. Each afternoon he sat on one side of the curtain, and Nadiyya on the other. They talked, and sang each other songs, while the slaves brought sherbet and sweetmeats. After sixty-six days of visiting, he offered her a bride-price: a chain of gold twice as heavy as Khalil's ring, studded with six rubies, each the size of a ram's testicle. Nadiyya considered that she had got good value from the witch, and accepted his offer.

For several years they lived in happiness. Nuri never spoke of his business, although he would sometimes disappear for weeks at a time. He took possession of the keys to the house, the slaves and the livestock. Nonetheless there was always gold in the cedarwood chest, and the jeweller's daughter wanted for nothing.

The wetnurse remained in the huram long after the child was weaned, looking after the daughter of Khalil the Merchant. Then one afternoon she took the girl to the river, to fish for minnows. Her friend came and sat with her, and the two women gossiped. When next they looked around, the little girl was gone.

The women ran up and down the riverbank, calling her name. Frantically, the wetnurse plunged into the river, fearing the child had met the same fate as her stepmother. However, there was no sign of the girl, and the nurse's friend begged her to return to the bank before she was swept away.

Weeping with shame the women returned to the house to take the grim news to Nadiyya. The jeweller's daughter felt her blood turn cold. Unveiled she ran into the street, shrieking and begging for help. Her neighbours came out of their shops and houses, and milled around, asking each other what was wrong.

Soon Nuri rode up on his horse. When he was told of the girl's disappearance, he organized the neighbours into search parties, scouring the town. Then he rode to the river and persuaded the fishermen to drag the riverbed with their nets.

All was to no avail. That night Nadiyya and Nuri held each other tight, and made desperate, unhappy love.

The next morning the people of the town returned to their occupations, but the girl's stepfather continued his search. Every day he rode further afield, following rumours and reports. The jeweller's daughter waited anxiously for his return, but each day he came in shaking his head sadly.

As days turned to weeks Nadiyya began to be troubled by a slow, thudding sound from the walls, as if the house had a beating heart. She told Nuri about it one evening, but he said to her:

"I hear nothing. Listen —"

They fell quiet, and she realized he was right. The house was silent. Nuri told her:

"You are tired, my love, and wracked with grief. You must rest more, then these strange noises will cease."

And he gave her opium, to help her sleep. However the next day the beating returned. Now it seemed to pulse and echo, like the thud of a drum in a deep valley. Again she told Nuri on his return, and again he pointed out that the house was silent. He told her:

"Perhaps some vermin has made its home here. I will arrange for the ratcatcher to visit."

But the next day the noise was unbearable. It felt to Nadiyya as if her brain was battering at the inside of her skull, in a bid to burst free. She went to the Eunuch and begged him to help her find the source of the din, but he told her:

"The master has the keys."

She seized his arm and dragged him after her, as she followed the sound through the courtyards of Khalil the Merchant's sprawling mansion. At last they came to a small wooden door, which led to a storeroom. Nadiyya begged the Eunuch to open it, and reluctantly he battered at the lock with his cudgel until the frame splintered and the door burst open.

It was dark in the room, which had no windows. As her eyes grew used to the gloom the jeweller's daughter saw what she thought was a pile of rags. She drew closer, and realized it was her daughter, bound and gagged, red eyed and filthy. The little girl tapped on the floor with one foot. This tiny sound, magnified and reverberating in the mother's ears, was what had drawn her to the room. Then a gasp from behind her caused her to turn round.

In the doorway stood her husband Nuri, knife in hand. At his feet lay the body of the Eunuch, his life bleeding and whistling out of a gash in his neck. Nuri laughed at the expression on her face, a harsh, heartless laugh.

"That look of surprise marks you out as the hypocrite you truly are. You sought a husband by magic. What kind of man did you think would be summoned by the twisted charms of witchcraft?"

Nadiyya was too frightened to speak, and her husband continued.

"I too once asked the help of Qamra the Witch, and in consequence I was possessed by a Ghul. It was the evil spirit within me that answered your call. The Ghul must feed on the blood of children, or both the spirit and my body will die. All these years I have only been waiting for the child to ripen, like a side of beef hung at the butcher's shop, while I hunted elsewhere for my prey.

"Now you have discovered my secret. But you will be the last human being ever to do so."

The jeweller's daughter watched, helpless, as the door slowly closed. Then the darkness was complete.

This much I can tell you. Only God knows all.

One

The Tale of the Thief in the House of Wisdom

It was a Golden Age.

As a nightmare fades in the mind of a man blinking awake, so the dark days of violence and bloodshed seemed scarcely real now that peace dawned across the Land of Islam. From the flood plains of the Nile to the bitter deserts beyond the Oxus, the Abbasid dynasty had prevailed over its foes. And all true believers bowed the knee to the young and handsome Khalifah, the Successor to the Prophet of God, the Commander of the Faithful: Harun al-Rashid, the Righteous One.

Of course the Holy War against the Unbeliever went on, as it would until the Day of Judgement. Every summer the warriors marched to war against the Christians of the Roman Empire. But they were civilised people, the Romans, People of the Book, and it was a civilised war that was waged against them, in the Golden Age. There would be raids across the border, some minor scuffles and sieges, a few small towns would change hands. Then the combatants would exchange prisoners, and everyone would return home to tend to their harvests.

The Roman Empire was like the serpent that continues to writhe after being cut in two, still dangerous but slowly bleeding to death. Its western half had long since rotted into anarchy. Even the city of Rome itself had fallen, and the empire that bore its name was ruled from New Rome, or Konstantinopolis as it was sometimes known.

There were those who said, in the markets and bath houses, that Christianity rose again in the west. They said that a yellow haired barbarian called Karlo sought to subjugate the warlords and have himself crowned Emperor in Old Rome.

However, to most true believers, he was no more real than the monsters or spirits with which storytellers frighten children.

The glory of the Golden Age was made manifest in the Khalifate's glittering capital. The great city of Baghdad was a mere quarter of a century old, and bristled with the arrogance and pustulence of youth. Everywhere it shucked its seed, pro-liferant and unchecked. Every day new citizens arrived, drawn by the lure of power, wealth and opportunity. Not only true believers but Jews and Christians and Mazdaists came, from Athens and Aswan and Samarqand, from the banks of the Indus and from the Kingdom of Yemen beyond the Empty Sands. Artisans and artists, doctors, astronomers and scribes, whores and mystics, peasants and princes, schemers and dreamers, the hopeful and the hopeless came to Iraq to bathe in the light of the Golden Age.

To the south of the city lay the suqs of Karkh, the bustling markets that sprawled over a square mile of land. Trade was brisk, and Faruz the Costermonger strained to hear his cus-tomer over the pitching and haggling of the other stallholders. As he leaned across to listen, he did not notice the slight figure who slipped three apples from his barrow and hid them under his patched tunic. No matter. Faruz had already made fifteen dirhams that week. If his business continued to thrive, he might be able to take a second wife before winter came. The thought of lying between two women, each competing to please him, made him smile. Even for a simple dealer in fruit, it was a Golden Age.

The thief in the patched tunic, a young man of some fifteen or sixteen years, headed north through the crowded streets, picking his way over the wheel ruts and the donkey shit, scampering across boats to traverse the canals that blocked his way, ignoring the shouts of the bargees. Ahead loomed the walls of the City of Peace, the height of seven men. The youth leaned against a well, munching one of the apples, and watched the traffic through the Kufah Gate.

The City of Peace was the germ from which Baghdad had grown so rapidly and violently. The Righteous One's grand-father, al-Mansur the Victorious, had himself marked its limits,

18

trailing ashes behind him as he traced a two mile circle on the ground. Then he had oil poured on the ashes and the circle set alight, so that his vision leapt into life, a city of fire in the night.

This infamously thrifty man, who commanded an empire but darned his own robes, spent twenty tons of gold on making his dream a reality. A hundred thousand craftsmen laboured for four years to create the perfect metropolis on the banks of the Tigris. Now Baghdad lay at the crossroads of the world.

In the shadows of the walls of al-Mansur's Round City, the young thief contemplated the soldiers of the Guard. He watched as they stopped and quizzed incomers, before the heavy wooden door slid up into the gatehouse and granted admittance. He caught glimpses of the iron armour beneath the black robes, glinting in the sunshine. He studied the heavy swords hanging by their thighs. These were no cheap thugs like the Shurta, the City Police, who were mostly recruited from the gutters, and would be committing crime if they were not paid to prevent it. The men in black were highly trained soldiers, the Khalifah's personal regiment.

Their function was not to defend against foreign invaders, here at the heart of the empire. The greatest threat to the Khalifah came from within; fanatics and assassins were a constant menace. Yet even that danger was subdued in the Golden Age. The revolution that swept the Abbasids to power had almost wiped out the Umayyad clan, who had reigned for a century before them. Only the young prince Abd al-Rahman had escaped, and he was now struggling to establish a tiny kingdom at the edge of the world, in the land called al-Andalus.

Inside its borders, the Land had recovered from the fevers that had convulsed it and threatened its very existence. Now it stretched like a cat, luxuriating in the ease and fecundity that came with peace. The dissidents and heretics, the Alids, the Kharijites, the Zindiqs: all were silent, or at worst confined to shabby small conspiracies of desperate men.

Nonetheless the Guard patrolled the circumference of the

City of Peace, and buildings and market stalls crowded the base of its walls. Anyone attempting to scale them, even after dark, would be quickly spotted. The thief must find another way in.

While he mused, a father and his son passed by. Ishaq was excited. It was his eleventh birthday, and his father was taking him to visit his uncle Musa. Musa was not a real uncle, but his grandfather's cousin. However he was very rich, and they always ate well when they visited him. Since his mother had died, and they had moved from Ukhaydir to the new city, there had been many days when there was no food on the table, and Ishaq went to bed hungry.

Ishaq's father Ibrahim did not share his excitement. He pretended he was nervous, but in truth he felt guilty. He would have tried to prepare the boy for what was to come, if he could have found the words. Instead he gave a thin smile and gripped his hand tightly. Life had been hard since they came to Baghdad. Uncle Musa could open doors in the capital, help him to a post in the civil service. From the moment the old man described Ishaq as beautiful, Ibrahim knew he had no choice. For some there were sacrifices to be made, to be a part of the Golden Age.

The ragged young man threw the apple core away, and stepped forward. The flow of traffic through the gate had been disrupted by a fat man in a red turban trying to drive a train of mules into the city. The animals, having halted while their owner negotiated with the guards, were reluctant to start moving again. Slaves ran around whipping the beasts and shouting, while those waiting to gain entrance cursed and spat.

The young man saw his chance. He worked his way through the throng and put his shoulder to a mule's behind, slapping its flank. A slave boy looked at him quizzically, but the youth winked and tossed him an apple. The boy accepted the bribe solemnly and said nothing.

With much complaining the beasts lumbered back into motion. They trudged through the long passageway under the outer wall, and across the open ground that led to the inner fortifications. The second wall was even higher than the first. Its massive iron gates had been found on the site of an ancient city. No craftsman of the present day could have forged them, even in a Golden Age; and it was said that Jinni had created them by magic, at the command of Sulayman ibn Dawud, King of the Jews.

The youth slipped through in the wake of the procession, then dodged away as they passed through the second gate. He crouched in the shadows and considered his next move.

Beggars were forbidden in the City of Peace, and his tattered clothes would soon attract unwanted attention. Besides, his appearance was unusual in other ways. Beneath the dirt and suntan it was apparent that his skin was pale, almost white. This unearthly pallor made his dark eyes all the more striking. He needed to find a refuge until sunset.

The building across the street was modest by the standards of the Round City. Its portal was of plain wood, studded with black metal. Above the door, however, was an alcove, decorated with brightly painted stucco.

There was nobody around. The youth scampered across the street and leapt up, grabbing the edge of the alcove. With a strength that seemed unlikely in his slender arms, he hauled himself up and slithered into the recess. Here he was invisible to all but the most assiduous observer below. He pulled out the last of the apples and settled down to wait.

Inside the building Muti'a inhaled carefully. She needed enough breath to carry her through the long first phrase, but not so much that her voice became strained. The slave girl opened her mouth, and hit the first note with an easy purity that even she herself found thrilling.

This was perhaps the most important song she would ever sing. If she could persuade Ali ibn Isa that she was worth the twenty thousand dinars that was her asking price, she could look forward to a life of comfort. The Khalifah's friend was a man of culture, who appreciated artistry and treated his musicians well. Besides, the gossip was that his sexual demands were straightforward, and that he was quickly satisfied. Muti'a was hopeful that that part of her duties would be not too onerous. Even for women, or at least for a few lucky ones, the reign of Harun al-Rashid could be a Golden Age.

Outside the last rays of the sun warmed the youth in his hiding place. Rather I should say, warmed me; for I remember the cool stone on my back, and the crisp sweetness of the stolen fruit as I bit into its flesh. I must confess that I was that pale thief – yes, I was young once, however strange that seems now. I find it hard to believe myself. Yet how many of us, as we look back to our past, really recognize ourselves in those callow, distant adolescents whose decisions have set the course of our lives?

You may be cross with me, perhaps, and feel that I have deceived you. You may ask, how could I have known the names of the costermonger, of the boy and his father, and of the singing girl, let alone their innermost thoughts? I could not, of course; and I did not. But what I say is true, nonetheless. I am al-Rawiya, the Teller of Tales.

As twilight fell I slipped from my perch and dropped to the ground. If my presence in the Round City during the daylight hours was risky, after dark it was potentially lethal. I flitted between the grand buildings, bare feet almost silent on the dirt. Fortunately the only other denizens of the evening streets were rowdy groups of men with lanterns, whose noise and light gave me warning of their approach. It was easy to duck into cover as they passed by.

Inside its walls, the City of Peace was not infested with the shanties that pullulated in the suburbs. Here there were only mansions and masjids, built by wealthy men to flaunt their importance. I knew that these strongholds guarded gold and jewels far beyond any hoard I had ever seen; but it was wealth of a different kind that I sought. I ventured on, until the Palace of the Gilded Gate came into view.

The Gilded Gate lay at the heart of the Round City, just as the Round City lay at the heart of Baghdad; and Baghdad itself at the centre of the world. The Umayyads had ruled from Dimashq, close to the holy cities of Makkah and Madinah. By moving his capital east, al-Mansur had not only distanced himself from the old regime, he had changed the very nature of the Khalifate. Here, in the fertile Black Lands between the rivers, far from the savage deserts where God spoke to his prophets, was the very womb of civilisation. Here the first city had been built, the first laws written down, the first canals dug. Here the brooding passion of Arabia met the haughty hedonism of Persia. The two cultures scrapped and coupled like mating dogs, and from this clash was begotten the Golden Age.

The primacy of the Gilded Gate was now purely symbolic. The Khalifah himself no longer lived there, preferring to make his home in Blissful Eternity, his pleasure palace by the Tigris. Yet the vast dome of al-Mansur's citadel, a hundred cubits high and one thousand across, still dominated the city, watching over the Ummah, the Family of Islam, like a stern but protective father. But it was power of a different kind that had tempted me to risk my life. My destination lay elsewhere.

In the light of the waxing moon it was hard to find my way. The streets and alleys twisted deceptively, and all the buildings began to look alike. The crude map, sketched onto parchment, that I drew from my tunic was hard to read. I tried to keep the dome in sight, navigating by it as if by a star, and after a long, nervous hour I found the place I sought.

It was a plain, square edifice, distinguished only by a slender tower, like a minaret, at the far end. Amid the ostentation of the Round City it looked like the ugly, stunted runt of the litter. But the name over the door, painted in elegant calligraphic script, spoke to me of magic and wonder: The House of Wisdom.

The door was locked and the windows shuttered, but I planned to use a different entrance in any case. I skirted the building until I reached the base of the tower. Then I began to climb.

The City of Peace was for the most part constructed of costly materials, marble, glass, sandstone and alabaster. The House of Wisdom, in contrast, used the same dried mud bricks as the poorer houses beyond the circular walls. This made my ascent much easier. My toes wriggled into tiny crevices, my fingers scraped away mortar to find a better grip.

Before long I was high enough above the street to crack my bones if I fell. However, I was also high enough that when a man passed by below, I remained unnoticed.

If he had looked up, he would have seen me, clinging like a lizard twenty cubits up the wall. But he did not, and he walked on. To stay still was harder than to move, and my fingers ached as I tried to hush my breathing. I started climbing again before he was even out of sight, hands shaking with the effort.

I could not stop again, and I could no longer look down. Finding the holds, testing my weight, battling the pain and the urge to ease it by just letting go, took all my concentration. If anyone else passed, I would have to take my chances.

At forty cubits my fingers at last felt the ledge of a window. However this was the moment of the greatest danger. I tried to pull myself up, and found that my muscles had frozen. I had to hang for a moment, find a still point amid the agony and fear, then move slowly and by small stages until I could grip the sill with both hands. Finally I heaved my aching body through the window, and tumbled onto the timbered floor inside the tower.

For several minutes I lay there in the darkness and silence, enjoying the relief and the sensation of being alive. Then I sat up and looked around.

The room was circular, occupying the full width of the tower. Opposite me was a hole in the floor, that must lead to a staircase or ladder. At first I thought the wall that curved round the room was panelled in wood. When I got to my feet and looked closer, I saw that the panelling was in fact hundreds of hinged doors. Each was around the height and width of my hand.

I traced my finger across one of the doors. It was marked with three symbols. It had been a few years since I had seen such letters, but as I traced them with my finger the learning came back to me. For a moment I was a child again, studying the strange shapes with Hermes the Kritan, and their names sounded like an incantation: Alpha. Beta. Gamma.

Every door had a different combination of three Greek letters. I selected one with the symbols Sigma, Alpha, Pi, and

24

examined it carefully. Below the Greek letters was a row of different signs. Recognising these required a more difficult and painful remembrance, but in time it came to me. It was a Latin alphabet, but with most of the letters missing.

I checked a number of doors, and found that although the Greek symbols were different on each, the Latin letters always followed the same sequence:

CDILMVX

When I touched one I found that it receded slightly into the wood. There was a sound of delicate metalwork shifting inside, a sound I was familiar with from years of picking locks. The symbols, then, formed some kind of password, granting or denying access to the mystery within, to the secrets that had drawn me half way across the world and into terrible danger. But what was the key that would open the box?

Something about the Latin letters tugged at my memory, something that linked the symbols selected. Then it struck me. They were not letters at all, but numbers. C was one hundred, D five hundred, and so on. I recalled that Greek letters also had numerical values, although these did not change according to position. In the Latin system a numeral coming before a larger number was subtracted from it, not added to it. So VI was six, five plus one, but IV was four, five minus one.

I was close to unravelling the knot. I returned to the first door I had inspected. If I remembered the Greek system correctly, Sigma was two hundred. Alpha, the first letter, was of course one, and Pi was eighty. Two hundred and eighty one.

I turned my attention to the Latin numerals. Two hundred was CC: I pressed the letter "C" twice, carefully. Eighty became "LXXX", fifty and three tens. Last, I touched the letter "I", once only, to represent the final digit. My fingertips knew the lock had been sprung before the door slowly swung open.

It was too dark to see inside the compartment. Groping in the hole made my fingertips itch, and I half expected to feel the sharp prick of a scorpion tail, but instead I touched a cylinder of odd, soft material.

Carefully I drew it from the cavity, and took it over to the window to examine it in the moonlight. It was a scroll, but felt like no parchment I had ever encountered. It was lighter, more flexible, and rustled as I unfurled it. Memories of the Greek language were now flooding back, as I read the words on the scroll:

"Phainetai moi kisos isos tieoisin . . ."
"To me he seems the equal of God,
    that man who sits with you,
his face so close to yours
    that he can taste the sweetness of your voice . . ."

It was true, then. Here, in the tower of the House of Wisdom, locked away even from the scholars who were admitted to the library below, were hidden the lost books of the ancients. With this theme, and denoted by the letters Sigma Alpha Pi, what I held in my hands had to be the work of Sappho of Lesbos. If so, the words I was reading had been written over two thousand years ago.

Sappho, a Greek aristocrat who had lived on the island of Lesbos in the White Middle Sea, was one of the most important figures in the history of poetry. Her passion for both men and other women drove her to pour out her feelings in verse, to use the forms of sacred hymns to speak of longing, lust and loss; to become the very first poet of love. However, her work had all but disappeared, surviving only in fragments.

The scroll that I held now could not be two millennia old, though. The miraculous substance on which the verse was scribed was clean and white. I recalled other rumours, of secret techniques imported from China, by which rags were transformed into a new kind of parchment, called paper. If the medium was new, that meant that the lost books were not only being preserved, but transcribed, copied.

My heart was beating faster than it had when I was scaling the wall. Somewhere, within the room, must be the text I sought, the one that I had risked my life for the slightest chance of reading. I began to scour the panels for the combination I needed: Alpha. Rho. Iota.

So rapt was I in my search that I did not notice the walls grow brighter, as a glow emerged from the hole in the floor. It was only when I heard footsteps on the stairs that I realised someone was coming.

Quickly I shoved the scroll back into its place. I looked around the room, but there was nowhere to hide. My hands seemed to hurt at the very thought of it, but I had no choice. I climbed back through the window, and hung from the sill.

I contemplated working my way back down the tower, but the descent would be even harder than the climb. For the first time it occurred to me that I had made no plan to escape from the House of Wisdom, had never thought past the moment when I would behold the occult texts. Then a voice from above interrupted my despairing thoughts.

"So, my young friend, you can hang there until you drop, and shatter your skull on the street below. Or you can come back in here and face me. Which is it to be?"

Two

The Tale of the Eunuch, the Wazir and the Chief of Police, which includes, The Marvellous Adventures of Ismail al–Rawiya

As I dragged myself back into the room two pairs of hands helped me. However, their intent was not benign, and once I was inside they handled me roughly. I could not see who pinned my arms behind my back, but when the man in front of me spoke I recognised the voice that had addressed me earlier.

"Well, lad, this is a strange place for a thief to ply his trade."

He was a heavily built man of middle age, holding a burning torch. I guessed that he had once been physically powerful but the muscle was now turning to fat. His robes were splendid, dyed orange and green and embroidered with gold thread. The impressive effect was marred, though, by the pustules that peppered his face, as if the acne of adolescence had become a lifelong affliction. His voice was the high-pitched croon of the eunuch.

The pimpled man looked at me as if waiting for me to speak, but he had asked me no questions and I was not inclined to give answers. He huffed at my silence and said to my unseen captor:

"Bring him."

I was forced over to the hole in the floor and thence to the staircase. Along the way I caught glimpses of the man who was holding me. He looked like a northerner, perhaps a Khazar. I assumed he was a slave, a bodyguard, judging from the long sword that hung from his side. Certainly he was strong, and I did not resist him.

At the bottom of the stairs a heavy door stood ajar. We passed through it into a short corridor, and the pimpled eunuch locked it behind us with a golden key. He pushed open another door ahead of him, through which we emerged into the main library of the House of Wisdom. Here the Arabic scrolls stood on wooden shelves, row after row filling the huge hall. When he closed the portal through which we had entered, I noticed that it seemed to form part of the wall, complete with shelving. From inside the library it was invisible, unless one knew where to look.

However I had little opportunity to examine these wonders before I was shoved outside. For the first time I considered attempting an escape. If I could slip from the Khazar's grasp, I was confident that I could outpace the two bigger men. Unfortunately he tightened his grip, and my wrists were sore by the time our short journey through the empty streets had come to an end.

We arrived at a great house not far from the Gilded Gate. Its facade was ornate, and the broad doors swung open at our approach. Somebody was watching for the return of the master.

Once inside, servants rushed to attend to the eunuch. They escorted us through the vestibule to a courtyard, and across a fragrant garden. At the far end was a room, with a roof and three walls but open on one side to the cool, perfumed air.

In this pleasant snug were two men, sitting on farsh rugs. Slave girls knelt at their feet, with golden goblets of wine and platters of fruit. The atmosphere was relaxed, but the men reeked of power. One was a sharp faced Arab with a steel-grey beard, the other, younger man, a lean, handsome Persian in his early thirties. It was he who greeted my captor.

"Here comes the Speckled One! Have you found the text which proves me right? And do you have the thousand dinars which you owe me in consequence?"

Then he noticed me, and rose to his feet.

"In the name of God! What apparition have you brought to astound us, Salam? Is this pale urchin a spirit, that you have summoned as a witness in your cause?"

The eunuch, whom he had called Salam, and also the Speckled One, mimed that he was out of breath, and sat down on a third rug. He signalled to a slave for wine, which he slurped theatrically before speaking.

"It is a curious tale, mighty Wazir, and one that I thought might amuse you. As I approached the House of Wisdom, I heard a rattle, as if dust were raining down the side of the building. I looked up, to see this strange creature scaling the tower like a fly. While I watched, he disappeared through the window into the Chamber of the Ancients.

"Since I had Ilig with me, and knew the thief to be alone, I had no hesitation in ascending the tower and apprehending the creature. He appears to be human, but has spoken not a word. What shall we do with him?"

The Persian seemed amused by the situation. Salam had called him Wazir, meaning minister of state. It was possible this was a nickname, but the cool authority with which he spoke suggested he really did hold that high rank.

"His courage and skill, in reaching the Chamber, seem to be matched only by his misfortune. What ill luck that our wager should take you to the library after dark, just in time to catch him; and worse luck that he should be caught by a man who happened to be entertaining both the Wazir and the Chief of Police!"

The old Arab, whom I assumed must be the Police Chief, snarled impatiently:

"Why do you waste our time with this nonsense, Salam? The boy is a thief, cut off his hands and throw him out on the street to bleed to death."

The eunuch gestured. Two slaves seized hold of my arms. This freed the bodyguard Ilig to step away and unsheathe his sword. I had held my peace while I watched where my destiny led me, but I had to speak now, or haemorrhage my life in the gutters of the City of Peace.

"The Sharia states that two eyewitnesses must swear an oath before the amputation of hands. Since I took nothing from the tower, there has been no theft, and can be no witnesses."

This pronouncement was followed by a stunned silence. Then the hush was broken by howls of laughter from the Wazir. His hilarity seemed to enrage the Police Chief further.

"You dare to quote the Sharia to me! Do you know who I am, boy? I have been appointed to keep the peace by the Khalifah himself, the Commander of the Faithful. In this town I *am* the Sharia."

The slaves stretched my left arm till my shoulder cracked, and I felt the cold touch of the Khazar's sword on my wrist as he aimed his blow. He raised his weapon to strike, and I cried out:

"Would that I could save myself, and save you, from this waste!"

The Wazir leapt forward, and seized the bodyguard's wrist. He was no longer laughing, and his face was so close to mine that I could smell his minted breath as he spoke.

"Tell me where those words come from, boy. Or I let him cut."

"The Ode of Tarafah, my lord. From the Mu'allaqat, the Seven Hanging Odes of the Jahili."

He stepped back, but signed for Ilig to put his sword away.

"Ibn Zuhayr, with your permission, I would like to question this miscreant further."

The Chief of Police nodded sourly. The Wazir sat down on his farsh and contemplated me, while the Speckled One gulped his wine.

It had been an insane gamble, but I had nothing to lose. And, praise be to God the All-Knowing and All-Powerful, it was, after all, a Golden Age, and a ragged youth could catch the attention of the masters of an empire by quoting poetry. And the masters of an empire would recognise that poetry, because for them there was no purpose to the empire and the power and the wealth if they could not surround themselves with beauty and brilliance, and the poetry they knew meant as much as the swords they commanded and the women they fucked.

And that was really how it was.

"The Chamber of the Ancients is a hard place to penetrate.

31

Surely, you could have risked less and gained more by burgling some wealthy merchant?"

This was not the right question, and I gave no answer, making the Wazir work to understand, even though it annoyed him.

"What then, *boy*, gave you the wings to scale the tower? What were you after?"

This was the right question.

"I wanted to read the "Peri Poietikes" of Aristutalis."

The handsome Persian face was immobile for a moment. Perhaps his eyes widened very slightly. Then he shouted with laughter, falling backwards and beating the floor with his fists. Ibn Zuhayr, the Chief of Police, did not join his merriment, but seemed resigned that the matter had spiralled out of his jurisdiction. Salam the Speckled One, who I gathered was the least important of the three, decided it was politic to join in the joke, and shrieked his eunuch titters.

At last the Wazir calmed himself, and, wiping his eyes, addressed me again.

"Oh, the solemn gravity of youth! Very well, boy, I am intrigued. What is this sprite with white skin and black eyes, that wears rags and risks his life to read Greek philosophy? If you tell me who you are and where you are from, I may spare your hands."

And so I did.

The Marvellous Adventures of Ismail al-Rawiya

I do not remember my original name, the one my parents gave me. Perhaps they never bothered. From somewhere comes the word Mau, but you should call me Ismail.

I was born in a land called Kernu. I could not tell you where it is. Later, when I found my way to civilisation, I saw maps, charts of the whole known world. My birthplace did not appear on them.

Kernu was beyond the world, and felt like it too. It was cold, and battered by fierce winds, and constantly raided by someone called the Wolf King. Living was thin. My earliest memory is of scaling the cliffs by our home to gather samphire and steal gulls' eggs, while my father yelled at me below. I think I could climb before I could walk.

My father was a Christian priest. Holy men of the western church are required to be celibate, although I am living proof that they do not always observe their vows. Whether he was expelled from his order I could not say, but I remember very little praying, and a great deal of drinking and cursing.

He did at least teach me some hymns, in the brief periods of geniality between hangover and violence, and to read and write a few words. When I could escape from him, I would sit alone on the clifftop, singing to myself, and I was happy. I think I may have learnt songs from my mother too, but my memories of her are uncertain. Do I truly recall that soft voice comforting me, or is it only my yearning? She died when I was very young. I suspect my father was responsible for her death, one way or another.

Most of my childhood in Kernu seems like a dream, but the incident that snatched me from that life is as sharp as yesterday. I can see the brown skins of the strange men standing in our hut, hear their guttural shouts. I can feel the strong arm around my waist as they carried me away. I must have been about five years old.

I do not know how much of the argument I understood at the time, and how much I discovered later, but the strangers were traders from distant Nekor. Somehow they had found their way to Kernu in search of tin, which was mined in the region. As they did not speak the local tongue, they had been brought to my father, who communicated with them in fractured Latin.

He promised them tin, and took in payment jugs of wine, a luxury almost unknown in savage Kernu. He got as far as borrowing a cart with which to take the wine inland, so that he could trade with the miners. But when the brown-skinned men returned a month later, the cart was still at our door, there was no tin, and a great deal of the wine had gone.

They were understandably angry, and told him they would

take me instead, and sell me as a slave, to recoup their losses. My father made some effort to protect me. He swung a fist, but he had been drinking himself blind every day for a month. The trader ducked his blow contemptuously, and kicked him in the stomach. The last time I ever saw my father he was on his knees retching. It was a comfortingly familiar pose.

My new owners were brothers, Shahid and Shahib. Once on board their ship they threw me in the hold, and set sail immediately, in case my father roused his neighbours against them. (It seems unlikely that he took the trouble, and if he did, they would not have come to his aid.) The traders were rough but not unnecessarily cruel. I had the impression they did not really know what to do with me.

Being knocked about was normal for me, and I adjusted to my new environment with equanimity, finding a place out of the way where I could curl up to sleep. The next morning when the brothers awoke I was singing.

My childish voice was high and sweet, and the sound delighted Shahib, who was very fond of music. When he approached me I shrank away from him, but through gestures he encouraged me to sing more. By our next landfall they had come to treat me more as a pet than a captive; like a songbird in a cage. They decided I would fetch more money in the civilised lands of the south, and when they journeyed on I was still on board the ship.

And so it continued as we meandered along the coast of Frankia. They were an odd couple, the brothers. It was years before I realized that most merchants dwelt in comfortable houses, only setting out to trade in the calm seasons. Shahid and Shahib lived almost entirely on their dhow, wandering aimlessly on the outermost fringes of the world, following rumours of opportunity and their own whims. There was talk of a family back home in Nekor, but the tone was not affectionate.

Shahid was the older, a lean, taciturn man who bossed and fussed over their dispirited rabble of a crew. Shahib was plump and childlike. It was he who gave me the name Ismail. When they had struck a big deal, Shahid would bring a whore onto the ship, as a treat for himself and the crew. Shahib would disappear onto the land. On one such occasion he was chased back by angry peasants, and we had to weigh anchor hurriedly, chucking the whore overboard as we sailed away. By then I could follow their conversation, but not enough to understand what exactly it was that Shahib had been doing with the goat.

They were kind to me in their way, kinder than my father had been, and they kept putting off the day when they would sell me. I was young enough to learn quickly, and by the time we reached the Straits of Gibel Tariq I spoke only Arabic. My original language was lost to me, save for scraps and echoes.

They seemed reluctant to enter the White Middle Sea. They were not sociable men, and were happier haggling with barbarians than conversing with their peers. However, the crew had been depleted by desertion and disease. I made myself useful scrambling around the rigging, but they needed fresh men.

I was at the top of the mainmast when I noticed the sinking ship. Even in the rolling swell I could see how it listed to one side, and pick out the waving sailors on board. Shahid wanted to leave them to their fate, saying that they were probably Christians anyway. Shahib, on the other hand, insisted that God would punish us if we did not help our fellow seamen. His argument appealed to the superstitions of the crew, and unusually his will prevailed.

We changed our course, and soon could hear the grateful shouts from the stricken craft. The Christians dived into the water as we approached. We threw ropes over the side to allow them to clamber up onto deck. That was when they pulled out their weapons.

Ironically, it was because we had been far from civilization for so long that we fell for the trick. There were no pirates in the wild Western Sea. The crew fought like maniacs, but to no avail. Shahib fell to a sword which pierced his plump flesh. Shahid's brain was crushed by a cudgel.

I was taken prisoner, and that night I understood for the first time how fortunate I had been in the Nekorite brothers.

The pirate captain claimed me as his prize, and in his cabin he raped me at knifepoint. He was careless, though. Perhaps he thought he had nothing to fear from a child. As soon as we came within sight of land, I slit his throat with his own knife while he slept. Then I squirmed through the porthole and dropped into the sea.

I had been living on a ship for almost two years, and had become a capable swimmer. However the shore was a long way off. I struggled through the heaving water, choking and gasping while the waves slapped my face and dunked my head, but seemed to get no closer. My sodden clothes weighed me down, and I shed them as I went. Even so I could feel my strength ebbing. My last thought as I slipped beneath the surface was that this was a kinder fate than life as a pirate's catamite.

That I survived was a miracle. Certainly I seemed wondrous to the villagers on whose beach I was washed up, white skinned and naked. Some thought I was a marid, a water spirit, and wanted to throw me back. Then I began to mutter unconsciously, and they decided instead to take me in.

I had come to the coast of Ifriqiya, and fallen among Berbers. They were simple people, but practised Islam after their own fashion, and the headman spoke Arabic. After they had nursed me back to health, I told him of my adventures. He nodded solemnly, and said he knew of someone who could help me.

A week later a tall man in black robes came into the hut where the villagers had placed me. He was a Badawi, an Arab of the desert. He looked me over but said nothing, ignoring my greeting and questions. Then he reached down, and, with strong hands, bound my arms and legs together. I was a slave once more.

Three

Concluding The Marvellous Adventures of Ismail al-Rawiya, And, The Tale of the Eunuch, the Wazir and the Chief of Police

The Badawi handed over gold to the villagers, and took me away with him. He rode a magnificent black stallion, but I was tied to the back of a mule. Our progress was slow, therefore, as we trekked eastward along the coast. He was so oblivious to my voice that I wondered whether he was deaf; until, at last, he acknowledged my increasingly desperate pleas to be allowed to relieve myself.

So we continued, until I lost count of the days. I tried to engage the Badawi with songs, stories and conversation, but he ignored all my efforts, and in the end I settled into the same sullen silence as my owner. All day we travelled, and every night he bound and gagged me before setting camp. At least he abstained from the foul practices of the pirate captain. Whether this was a matter of morality or of taste, I could not say. Perhaps the villagers had told him of my revenge on my violator.

Finally we arrived at the city of Tiaret. I had visited the ports of western Andalus during my time with the brothers, but never before had I seen a place of such wealth and splendour. The great ramparts seemed to reach to the sky – although, of course, they are nothing to the walls of the City of Peace. As we passed through the streets I was stunned by the clamour of voices, babbling in a hundred different tongues. There were turbaned Muslims, Jews in skullcaps and bare headed Christians. I saw not only camels for the first time, but also elephants, and, in cages, lions.

Our destination was the slave market. The Badawi spoke to several dealers, and I was poked, pushed and probed by rough fingers. At last an agreement was reached, and money changed hands. The Badawi shoved me onto a bench, next to a dozen bedraggled women and children, and walked away. I never even knew his name.

I had already learned the bitter lesson, that life can be hellish for the slave of a cruel master. I therefore decided to take a hand in choosing my fate. Since leaving the village I had eaten only the Badawi's scraps, and my wrists and ankles were covered in sores where I had been bound. As a succession of scowling villains examined me, it was easy to let my tongue loll stupidly, to squint and drool, and generally make myself into a very unappealing specimen.

I am not sure what it was about Hermes that made me choose him. Despite common prejudice, it is not possible to discern sexual preference from physical appearance. I could not be certain he was not a pederast, or a violent bully. He was old, and physically frail, which reassured me. However I think there was a glint of intelligence in his eyes, and an air of innocence in his demeanour, and it was on these that I staked my future.

As he came near, peering myopically at the slaves, I called out the only Latin phrase I could remember from my father's rituals:

"Miserere mei, et exaudi orationem meam . . ."

"Have pity on me, and hear my prayer . . ."

He looked over in my direction, then shook his head as if hearing things. I called out again:

"Miserere mei, et exaudi orationem meam!"

The old man stood in front of me, staring as if a dog had just spoken. He addressed me in Latin, then in what I guessed must be Greek. I shook my head desperately, and he made to move away. I did not want to lose this fish now that I had hooked him, and called out in Arabic:

"Please, master, buy me. I can read and write, sing songs and tell stories. You will not regret the purchase!"

The slaver smacked my head so that my ears rang, but the old man said:

"I don't know why you punish him. He does a better job of selling himself than you do of marketing your wares. How much is this one?"

Having heard me boast of my literacy, the slaver had doubled my price, but the old man haggled like a veteran of the suq. Before long, he took hold of the rope that bound me and led me back to his home.

My luck had turned again. Hermes the Kritan was a gentle soul. He had been a slave himself, taken as a child when the island of Kriti was invaded by Muslim exiles from Andalus. For most of his life he had worked as scribe and secretary to a merchant in Alexandria, until he was given his freedom on his master's death.

However, my good fortune went beyond having a benevolent master. For Hermes had a plan, by which he hoped to earn enough to end his days in comfort. His idea was to purchase promising young slaves, teach them to read and write, and sell them on for the higher price that educated boys attracted. I was to be his first subject.

At first he was annoyed when he discovered my promised literacy consisted only of a basic knowledge of the Latin alphabet. However I learned quickly, and he soon regained his enthusiasm for the project. He taught me both Arabic and Greek letters, and when we were not studying I served him, cooked for him and ran his errands.

I had never been so happy. Although I had enjoyed sailing with the brothers, their lives were narrow and dull. The long days on the cramped dhow were only varied by visits to drab fishing ports to barter with barbarians. Tiaret, on the other hand, was a cosmopolitan city. The Amir promoted a policy of religious tolerance, cannily recognizing the economic benefits this brought. The city was a regional nexus for both trade and intellectual thought.

It was the latter that thrilled me, even more than the colourful riches of the suqs. The written word opened doors onto the whole world, and other, infinite, imagined worlds. I devoured learning like a caterpillar in a cabbage patch. But it was poetry that was my greatest passion. Poetry was the philosopher's stone, which transmuted cruel reality into something strange and beautiful.

Cruel reality was to reassert itself, however, and show me a different side of kindly Hermes. My fellow pupils never appeared, as had been the plan. Then there were the occasions when we had to lie on the floor in silence until the creditors went away. Gradually I realized that the Kritan, for all his intelligence, was an idle dreamer who was hopeless with money. One evening, after I had been with him for three years, he called me to him.

"My son," (for so he had taken to addressing me), "the evil day is upon us, when I have to sell you. A pity, for I have come to rely on you, and we have only just started on the Epigrams of Agathias Scholasticus, which I was looking forward to reading with you. However, money is short, and I have no choice. Unless, that is, you would perform a service for me . . ."

I did not understand why he would ask this of me, his slave, nor why he tugged on his beard so nervously.

"Master, I will do anything you require of me."

"Good, good. Then come with me."

We headed out into the twilit streets. The fear had begun to grow in me that he planned to pimp me to a deviant for sex, but it seemed out of character in the old man. Instead we arrived at an impressive house on a quiet street. Hermes spoke again.

"A friend promised to lend me some gold, but he has had to leave town on business. He will not mind if you hop over this wall and bring his strongbox to me. You will find it in the room with the yellow door. Here is the key."

I nodded, but Hermes grabbed my arm.

"And mind you make no noise. His wife is ill, and if you disturb her, he will be very angry with me. Go only to the room with the yellow door."

Clambering over the wall presented no difficulty. I found myself in a courtyard, where rows of washing hung to dry. Ducking through the sheets and robes I came to a portico which sheltered a wall with three doors. Identifying the yellow one was tricky in the half-light, but the key slid easily into the lock. The room was bare inside, but for a small chest in the corner. I picked it up and headed back.

When I reached the wall I faced the problem of how to get the chest, which was heavy for its size, over. In the end I managed by leaping up, hooking one hand over the edge, and swinging the box up to rest it on the top. I then climbed up myself, dropped the chest into Hermes' arms, and slipped down after it. We scurried away into the night.

The loan was a generous one, and for several months we lived well. Eventually, though, the creditors came back, and we had to seek further assistance. In fact, over the ensuing years, we received a steady stream of loans and gifts from Hermes' charitable friends, of coin and carpets and jewellery. Unfortunately, they were very busy people, and I never met any of them in person. Collecting the bounty always necessitated a night-time visit to their homes.

After the first such visit, they were too busy to remember to leave keys, so the Kritan, with some embarrassment, taught me how to pick a lock using crooked needles. They were also very unfortunate in their sickly wives. On the few occasions when I accidentally disturbed the household, they were quite annoyed, and we had to leave in a considerable hurry.

I was not a fool. Nor was I naive; in my eleven years, I had seen more than most see in a lifetime. I knew what was really going on. But the air of innocence that had first drawn me to the old man was compelling. We carefully maintained the fiction of the beneficent friends throughout a crime spree that was discussed everywhere in Tiaret, except between the two people responsible for it.

Hermes had forgotten his plan of educating slaves. His talk now was all of Baghdad. Word of the wonders of the new city had reached Ifriqiya, and the idea was irresistible to a dreamer like the Kritan. I had begun to write poetry of my own, and he hoped that I would find a wealthy patron among the aristocracy of the Khalifate.

However, we continued to live from hand to mouth. No money was set aside, no arrangements were made that would carry us through Egypt, across Sinai and beyond Palestine to our Eden in Iraq. The generosity of Hermes' friends became increasingly hard to access, their wives increasingly restive and irritable.

It could not last. But then, what can? We were in the suq. Hermes was negotiating the sale of a silver goblet, which had been donated by a nephew of the Amir. I was examining my reflection in the back of a shiny copper pan hanging on the stall. I had become very concerned about my beard. This growth, although invisible to the casual observer, occupied a great deal of my time, as if I could encourage its development by staring at it from different angles and counting the hairs. Then a voice rang out:

"Thief! Thief! That goblet belongs to my master!"

Sometimes, when I remember that afternoon, Hermes ran too. He was slow, and old, and had been increasingly unwell, but I grabbed his hand and dragged him after me. We ducked down an alley, but he knew that they would soon be upon us.

"Leave me. There is no sense in both of us being caught. You have been like a son to me, Ismail. I give you your freedom and appoint you my heir. Take anything you can carry from my house, and leave the city. Go to Baghdad. Live the life of which we dreamed."

I hesitated, but he nodded, and I fled.

Other times I recall running alone. When I remember it that way, I do not feel bad. There really was no point in both of us losing our lives, and I had more of it to lose than the old man. I am sure he would have said those things, that it was what he was thinking. But it was a very long speech to give when being pursued by an angry mob.

Ransacking the house is very clear in my memory. My heart was pounding and my ears straining for the first sounds of approaching vengeance. I knew where the treasure was hidden, but in the end I took only food and a couple of scrolls. Manuscripts in those days were more expensive than jewels or carpets. Each work we had read together had to be sold for the next to be bought. However, I had copied out some of my favourite passages to practise writing, and it was with these, and the Satires of al-Nabighah, that I headed east.

It took me a thousand days to reach Baghdad. I walked most of the way, although occasionally I begged a ride with a camel train, or on a cart. I sang for coppers, told stories and jokes, and wrote letters for the illiterate. At other times I stole, when I had no other way to eat. I was given the name al-Rawiya, the Teller of Tales. And as I grew closer to the city, the rumours grew more enticing. They told of the wise and cultured Khalifah, of the unimaginable luxury of his court, of the fabulous rewards to be won by poets who find favour there.

And they told of the House of Wisdom, the most magnificent collection of manuscripts since the Great Library of Alexandria. They told, too, of the tower. They said it housed lost writings of the ancients, looted from the ashes of the Great Library itself. Some even said that there were books of the Athenian Aristutalis, who is called the Philosopher, the First Teacher, and who was tutor to al-Iskander the Great. I dared to dream that these might include the "Peri Poietikes", his legendary work on the art of poetry.

I came, great Wazir, as one besotted with love or hashish. I was drawn as the moth is drawn to the candle. And if God wills that I am burned by the brightness of the flame, then better that than to live in darkness. I do not beg for my life, great Wazir. That is yours to take, or to leave alone. I beg only that, if I am to die, I might have a few hours in the tower, to consume a last feast of learning before the end.

★ ★ ★

After I had finished, there was a silence. When the Wazir spoke, he addressed not me, but the eunuch.

"Well, what an entertaining sprite you have brought before us, Salam. It must be brave, to have scaled the tower of the House of Wisdom. It must be clever, to have unlocked the secrets of the Chamber of the Ancients. And it is a pretty one, too. So what do you say, Speckled One? Do we release this alien being, to run wild in the sewers of the city?"

The eunuch licked his lips with a dry tongue. I realised in a flash of understanding that his position in society, his very life, depended on his ability to give the right answers to questions

43

such as these. The Wazir knew that too, and clearly delighted in teasing him with ambiguous problems and conflicting hints.

Salam drank noisily from his goblet, stealing time. However he was given respite from his dilemma by a servant, who came bowing his apologies, but urgently sought the ear of the Wazir. While the Persian walked away in muttered discussion with the newcomer, the Police Chief shifted irritably.

"Chamber of Ancients! Load of nonsense, anyway. If Fadl ibn Rabi has his way, those books will be freely available to anybody who wants them, and I must say I agree with him."

The eunuch was glad to change the subject.

"Because the Holy Quran commands us to penetrate the secrets of heaven and earth?"

Ibn Zuhayr looked at him distastefully.

"No, fool. Because the easiest way to prevent lawbreaking is not to make things illegal unless you have to."

The eunuch ignored the insult, and seized the opportunity to try out an argument before having to commit himself in front of the Wazir.

"You must agree, though, that the boy cannot be pardoned. For if we allowed theft to go unpunished, order would collapse and we would be no better than beasts."

"If I might remind you, esteemed master, there was no theft from the House of Wisdom."

Salam's pimpled face purpled with his rage that I dared to interrupt him.

"Do not offer me that false coin, boy! You have just stood there and admitted to a notorious career of burglary in front of three of the most important men in the land."

"But the Sharia states that the criminal who repents should not face mutilation."

Even the Police Chief smirked at this. Apparently he had been more riled by Salam's presumption, in ranking the three of them as equals, than by my continued quoting of Holy Law. I did not sense he liked me any better, but he was amused by the eunuch's discomfort.

Whatever Salam's final opinion might have been, it was no longer important when the Wazir returned to us.

"Speckled One, I believe you owe me a thousand dinars. I would be grateful if you would fetch them immediately, in coin of gold."

It took no magic to read Salam's thoughts, as he contemplated mentioning that the wager had not yet been settled, then realised it would be wiser to keep silent. Instead, he scuttled away to arrange the matter with his steward. The Wazir turned to me.

"I have decided you may keep your hands, Ismail al-Rawiya. I have a job for them to do."

The household slaves seemed to be accustomed to rapid changes of status, and responded quickly to this new situation. They let me go and brought me a stool and a cup of water, although Ilig the Khazar sheathed his sword only reluctantly, and scowled at me as he did so. My arms had been stretched for so long that they stayed sticking out at my sides for several minutes. By the time I was able to put shaking hands around the cup Salam had returned with a leather bag. The Wazir took it from him.

"So you like poetry, boy? Then I shall send you to visit a poet. We shall discover how long your enthusiasm lasts, when you encounter the real thing."

He hung the bag around my neck, and my knees sagged under the weight of the gold. The eunuch shifted uncomfortably, but said nothing. Ibn Zuhayr leaned back and sneered. The Wazir was oblivious to their reactions.

"Take this to Abu Nuwas, at the Garden of Delight. Tell him Ja'far the Barmakid is buying his freedom, and expects his attendance in return. Tell him to present himself to me at the house of Salam the Speckled One. You are to stay with him until he does so."

I bowed to indicate that I understood. The Persian turned away, but I spoke again.

"With respect, mighty Wazir – how do you know I will not simply disappear with the money?"

The Police Chief growled at my impertinence, but the Wazir smiled sardonically.

"Because you ask me the question, which you would not

45

do if you intended to rob me. Because I believe that you are no fool, and that would be the act of a fool. And because I am Ja'far ibn Yahya al-Barmaki, Wazir to the Khalifah, and there is not a flea that farts in this city without my knowledge. And if you ever cross me, you will pray for Shaitan to come for your miserable soul, because all the torments of hell will be a blessed relief after what I will do to you."

Four

The Tale of The Ring of
The All-Seeing Eye

I did not ask where, or what, the Garden of Delight might be.
I guessed that I was being tested, and that finding my way was
part of the test. However, I had only arrived in Baghdad that
morning, and all my efforts had been directed on locating the
House of Wisdom.

Instinct told me that I would not find it within the walls of
the Round City. I had secreted the gold under my tunic, in an
attempt to look less like a brazen thief, but even so I met with
considerable suspicion from the guards on the Syria Gate.
When I showed them the hand-written pass from the Wazir,
they were no less suspicious, but terror outweighed their mis-
trust. I grinned with satisfaction as the huge iron portal
groaned open, just to let through a slender youth in patched
clothes.

The pass commanded loyal citizens to offer me every assist-
ance, so I asked the guards on the outer gate for directions.
Grudgingly they pointed north-west, and I headed off towards
Harbiya.

This was a residential area, where many of the Abna had
made their homes. The Abna, which means the Sons, were
veterans of the revolution which had brought the Abbasid
family to the throne. Mostly easterners, hard men from
Khorasan and Kandahar, they now formed the military class of
the regime, and it was from their numbers that the Khalifah's
guard was drawn.

Despite their high social status, and the fact that the original warriors were now old men, Harbiya still felt like a
garrison town. Even at this hour of night, it was lousy with
beggars, whores and rowdies. Bent over by the weight of the

bag, I squeezed it against my ribs so that the coins did not jangle, and kept my head down. I did not think the Wazir's orders to assist me would carry much weight with the good citizens of Harbiya, at least not when compared to twenty pounds of gold.

War is a lucrative business for the victors, and most of the Abna had built splendid mansions with the loot of their conquests. Others though, less fortunate or more profligate, lived off their army pensions in boarding houses that resembled barracks. The Garden of Delight, despite its enticing name, was one such lodging.

As I approached, my heart was racing. I was to meet a real poet! I did not know the work of Abu Nuwas; before paper became common, it took decades for literature to permeate through the vast Islamic empire. However, I had heard his name mentioned in Kufah, where he had studied. He was one of the leading lights of the Muhdathun, a new wave of experimental, iconoclastic writers, who had converged on the court of the young Khalifah.

I pictured myself engaging him in philosophical discussion, impressing him with my wit and erudition, perhaps even earning his praise for my own verses. With these happy thoughts I hammered on the door of the Garden of Delight.

A small window opened in the door, and I could just make out a pair of eyes peering at me through the slot. The morose voice that belonged to them, however, was curt and unfriendly.

"We want no beggars here."

"I am no beggar. I have come to see Abu Nuwas the poet."

This did not meet with the welcome I had hoped for.

"We want none of your sort either. Bugger off."

The window closed, and did not open until I had banged on the door for several minutes.

"I thought I told you to bugger off!"

"I bring a message from Ja'far al-Barmaki. If Abu Nuwas is there you had best let me in."

As I hoped the name of the Wazir inspired the same fear I had seen in the guards. The slot closed again, but this time the door swung open to admit me.

I entered a courtyard, lit by flaming torches. A gang of rough-looking men stood or squatted on the sandy ground, armed with knives and cudgels. They were bare-headed, like Christians. The tension was palpable.

Behind me, the door was closed by a tall Pashtun. However, it was one of the gang who addressed me.

"Since when did the great Wazir use street urchins as messengers?"

He was a hulking man dressed in Syrian garb. At the centre of his face, instead of a nose, there was an ugly scar and a single dark hole. I ignored him and turned to the Pashtun.

"If you are master of this house, tell me where I can find Abu Nuwas."

The Pashtun, who had a long, mournful face that suited his gloomy voice, gestured to where a staircase led up to a second storey landing, open to the courtyard.

"Up there, first door along. Much good it will do you though – he's barricaded himself in."

The man with no nose was visibly angry that I had not answered him, but the name of Ja'far made him tread carefully.

"What news, then, from the Barmakid?"

The Christian thugs all stared at me. I decided this would not be a good moment to reveal that I was carrying a fortune round my neck.

"The words of the Wazir are for the poet's ears only."

The Syrian gave up trying to elicit information from me, and waved at the door.

"Then you might as well go, boy. If Abu Nuwas has not paid me what he owes by dawn, we will smash into his room. You can come and give your message to him then – or at least, to what's left of him."

I noticed him glancing towards a closed door at one corner of the courtyard. If he had not been so terrifying I would have thought he was nervous. The Pashtun raised his hands.

"I've told you, Thomas. If you damage my property you will pay for it, or answer to my brothers in the Abna."

Thomas, the Syrian, scowled, scratching at the scar where his nose should have been.

"And I've told you, Ghilzai, I have no quarrel with the Abna. It'll be worth the price of a door to restore my reputation. This business is costing me dear. Why should anyone else repay their debts, while that cocksucker is laughing at me? I need to make an example of him."

The Pashtun made no reply. There was a silence, then Thomas spoke again.

"He's gone very quiet. Are you quite sure he hasn't got out through the window, Ghilzai?"

"I am certain. The gap is too narrow for the poet's big head."

I had seen and heard enough. I told them that I was returning to Ja'far for further instructions, and the Pashtun opened the door for me with some relief.

Once outside, I did not head back towards the Round City. Instead I prowled the perimeter of the Garden of Delights. At the corner, I found a window. It was shuttered, but I could hear voices within. The first to speak I recognised as Thomas, speaking in rough Greek.

"You should not have come. There was a messenger from the Wazir here just now. You put us all in danger."

The second voice was high, with an accent I could not place.

"The traitor followed me! The oathbreaker spoke to him. I need your help to get out of the city. I am beginning to think this is all a trick."

When Thomas spoke again, he sounded conciliatory.

"Have no fear. Abu Murra has the Bottle. If you have the Name, you can unleash the power of the Fire."

Intriguing though this conversation was, it clearly had nothing to do with the poet. I continued round the corner, looking for the room the Pashtun had indicated. The windows on the second storey were unshuttered. Counting along, I identified the opening which I reckoned belonged to the room at the top of the stairs. It was indeed narrow, but I am thin. At least, I was in those days.

The climb, however, presented a different challenge. It was one thing to scale a sheer wall, but another entirely to do it weighed down by a sack of gold. After a moment's thought, I unwrapped the turban from my head. Then I tied one end of the long material securely around the neck of the bag.

My first throw fell short, causing the bag to slam against the side of the building and thud back down to earth. Relief that it had not burst open, spilling golden coins everywhere, was quickly replaced by fear that the noise would attract attention. I froze for a moment, listening for shouts and footsteps, but heard nothing.

On the second attempt I swung the bag a couple of times on a length of my turban rope, before launching it upwards. The momentum carried it to the second storey, and through the narrow window.

I tugged on it a couple of times, and it seemed to have snagged. Quickly I grabbed hold of the material and hauled myself up hand over hand, as if I were back in the rigging of the dhow. It took me only a few seconds to ascend, but just as I came to the window, the rope came loose and I began to fall.

I flung one hand through the opening and managed to cling on as my turban fluttered to the ground. It had been untied from the bag of gold. For the third time that long night I found myself dangling from a window ledge, and my muscles shrieked their complaints. Once again I heaved myself up and tried to wriggle through.

The aperture was tight even for one of my slight build, and entering was harder because I could not push with my legs, which flailed uselessly in the air outside. I scraped my face and shoulders, and was bleeding by the time I flopped onto the floor. The room was lit by a single lamp, which blinded me for a moment, so that I could not see the source of the drawling, husky voice which greeted me.

"This is indeed a night of miracles! First God the All-Merciful overlooks my many transgressions, and causes the window to bring forth a bag of money. Then the same munificent crack gives birth to an angelic youth. All I need now is for it to start gushing wine and I shall never leave this place."

The voice had a slight lisp, a weakness in pronouncing "r" sounds. As my eyes adjusted to the light in the room I saw a man reclining languidly on a farsh, long legs stretched out in front of him. He wore only qamis and pants, and held the Wazir's gold in one hand, and a limp wineskin in the other. I sat up.

"I believe there are several men in the courtyard who might have their own views on when and how you leave this room."

His startling blue eyes glittered with amusement.

"The Newborn talks! Truly it is a prodigy. But do not speak of those tedious men. Generally I adore Christians, for their liberal attitude to wine, and their willingness to lend money. They will insist on having it repaid though, and interest is such a bore. They should pay more heed to the words of their prophet, who told them to give to the needy without expectation of return.

"But that is enough theology. Let us instead discuss how you came to pop so lusciously through my window, and how we can pass the time together."

He leaned toward me with a salacious leer, and I got to my feet.

"I am a messenger from Ja'far al-Barmaki, who sends you one thousand dinars. He commands me to say that he is buying your freedom, and expects your attendance at the house of Salam the Speckled One."

The poet sighed.

"Like all powerful men, the Barmakid is so demanding and impatient. Sometimes I wish I was back in the desert with the Badawi. Then I remember the stink of the camels, the long dry days, and the endless boasting and farting, and think better of it.

"Still, I seem to be out of wine. Perhaps it is time to leave this heavenly bower."

He threw the empty skin into a corner of the room, and stood up. I had thought Ja'far handsome, but he would have looked plain next to the poet, who was perhaps the only man of whom I would have used the word "beautiful." When

I met him, he claimed to be thirty-two, but was probably a little older. Half Arab and half Persian, he had inherited the best features of both nations. High cheekbones framed a long nose and muscular mouth. His full lips curved in a sensuous half-smile, suggestive of both intelligence and cruelty. However, most striking was his long black hair, carefully teased and oiled into tresses that tumbled from his bare head like snakes. It was this that had earned him his name: Abu Nuwas, the Father of Locks.

The room was small and bare, and what furniture there was had been piled up against the door. The poet now began to clear the exit, carelessly hurling benches and tables to either side. I moved to help him. His response was to stand back and leave me to do the work, while he tugged on his boots and pulled a long embroidered coat over his underwear. I noticed, however, that he tucked the bag inside his coat, and picked up a long, thin package from the farsh.

By the time the barricade had been removed, there were scuffling noises from outside. Obviously the Christians had heard our labours, and gathered outside the room in readiness for our exit. Abu Nuwas put his ear to the door, then called out.

"How good of you to bring your friends, Thomas. I may not be able to see to all you big rugged men at once, perhaps you could bend over and wait in line for me?"

Even through the door I could hear the ruffians snarling like dogs.

"Don't make things worse for yourself, scribbler. Give me my money, and I might let you off with a beating."

"A beating sounds delightful. However, I have the means to pay you. If you can control your urges and not jump on me as soon as you see me, then I shall come out and discuss the matter with you."

There was no audible response from outside. The poet looked at me and raised his eyebrows.

"Well, boy, we are both without turbans; perhaps we shall pass for Christians."

He opened the door and stepped through. I followed him.

Thomas and his gang stood along the narrow landing, on both sides of the door. A couple of men waited below in the courtyard. Next to them was the Pashtun, watching anxiously in case any harm came to his boarding house. The Syrian raised his eyebrows when he saw me emerge from the room, but spoke only to Abu Nuwas.

"Where is the money, then?"

"Money, Thomas? Such tawdry stuff. I have for you something better than mere money. Oh, do not growl in that bestial fashion! It puts ugly lines on your pretty face.

"This ring on my finger is of great value in itself. The cabochon of ruby is set in finely wrought gold. However, its true worth is not apparent to the casual observer.

"This ring was given to me by Yahya ibn Khalid al-Barmaki, father to our illustrious Wazir. It comes from the highlands of Tibet, where icy mountains scratch the firmament, and the holy men summon demons, by chanting and playing trumpets made from human bone.

"One such demon is trapped within this ruby. To the man who approaches it with an open mind, it will show him his heart's desire. This is why it is called the Ring of the All-Seeing Eye. Gaze into its depths, and see what wonders you may behold."

Suspicion and fascination battled on the Syrian's face, and he leaned over the ring on the poet's outstretched hand, peering and squinting.

"I don't see – BASTARD!"

Abu Nuwas had suddenly bunched his fist and driven the stone up into Thomas's face. The Syrian staggered backwards, clutching his disfigured nose and cursing. The poet swung the package he had collected from the farsh, shedding its wrapping in the process. I was astonished to see that it contained a sayf, a long, straight, highly polished sword.

Behind me the ruffians had begun to respond to the abrupt outbreak of violence. One of them shoved me out of the way as he passed, slamming me into the wall. Abu Nuwas had slashed the chest of the nearest thug with the sayf, and turned to face this new threat. As the point of weapon jabbed at the

Christian, he halted his charge and stepped backward. Without thinking what I was doing I threw myself behind his knees, causing him to trip over me and fall from the landing onto the courtyard below.

"The prodigy becomes more marvellous by the minute!"

Abu Nuwas's shouted praise for my intervention distracted him from Thomas, who had recovered from the punch and was glaring hatred from his watering eyes. He advanced on the poet waving a butcher's cleaver with disturbingly practised movements. I tried to shout a warning, but nothing came out. However Abu Nuwas must have seen my look of alarm, because without even turning towards the Syrian he jumped from the landing, his coat flying open as he fell, as if he had sprouted wings. Thomas stopped on the edge, contemplated the drop, and turned back toward the stairs.

There were still four men in the courtyard. Of those one was the man I had tripped, who was lying very still. Another was the Pashtun, who was a wise enough old warrior to know a pointless fight when he saw one, and stay well out of it. That left two men to bar our exit. If you had asked me why I had taken the side of the Father of Locks so wholeheartedly I would have struggled to give an answer. In truth he was something of a disappointment to me. Instead of a high-minded discussion of aesthetics, I was stuck in a brawl over a debt he was quite capable of paying. However I was prone to gambling heavily on impulsive decisions, in those days.

My new ally had landed heavily, and was dancing around trying to test the damage to his right foot without putting too much weight on it. This allowed the two Christians to come from either side of him. Although the poet wielded his sword with surprising skill, he was in trouble. I launched myself from the landing toward the nearer of his attackers.

I was small and barefooted, but caught his head with my midriff as I fell, hurling him to the ground with a satisfying crack. I jabbed my elbow into his throat. While he rolled around in pain, I jumped to my feet and looked for Abu Nuwas.

The poet's injured foot was hampering his movement. The

Christian danced around him, swinging a heavy cudgel which he barely managed to dodge. Thomas was now lumbering down the stairs, and soon Abu Nuwas would be outnumbered again. Seeing the danger, he waited until his enemy had heaved a meaty stroke that threw him off balance. Then he rolled underneath the club, spiking the ruffian's thigh with his sayf. As the Christian fell, Abu Nuwas staggered to his feet and limped towards the exit, bellowing at the Pashtun.

"Unbolt the door, Ghilzai! Open the door!"

The Pashtun looked appalled as he realised that neutrality was no longer an option. Thomas was now pursuing Abu Nuwas across the courtyard, threatening all manner of vengeance if the door was opened. I noticed a finely woven prayer rug in an alcove, and snatched a knife from one of the fallen thugs.

"Unlock the door, Pashtun, or I slash this carpet to ribbons."

The furious landlord moved to seize me, but I dug the knifepoint into the rug, and he froze. As I had guessed, his sole concern was to keep his property safe. Reluctantly, he turned and began to draw back the bolts. Thomas howled, but had managed to get between Abu Nuwas and the door.

"I won't forget this, Ghilzai, and you can threaten me with the Abna all you like. As for you, scribbler, I'll chop off your pox-riddled organ and choke you with it."

He launched a fierce assault on the poet, and sparks flew as the sayf and the cleaver clashed. I was unable to intervene. The Pashtun would have torn me apart as soon as I ceased to menace the prayer rug. Abu Nuwas was moving with more freedom, however, and began to taunt the Syrian.

"Pox-ridden, you say? Your mother should see a physician, then, it was she who gave me the disease. You need to get your son looked at as well, I've probably passed it to him by now."

Thomas responded as the poet must have hoped, with a wild swing at his head. Abu Nuwas dropped to the ground and grabbed a handful of sand, which he hurled at the Syrian's face. As Thomas clutched at his eyes the pommel of the sayf rammed into his stomach, bringing him to his knees.

Abu Nuwas headed straight for the door. For a terrible

moment I thought he was about to abandon me to the wrath of his enemies. Then he paused, with his sword aimed at the landlord's throat.

"Well, boy, are you coming? I believe they have a vacant room here, if you wish to stay."

I scampered after him. As I left the courtyard I glanced back at the door in the corner. It was ajar, and I thought I saw eyes staring at me from the darkness.

The poet's legs were long and my feet quick, and after a couple of streets it became apparent we had escaped. We slumped against a wall to catch our breath. I recovered first, and asked him the question I had been burning to ask since the fight in the courtyard.

"Why didn't you just pay him the money?"

"Pay him the money?"

Abu Nuwas snorted with contempt.

"Where would I be if I went round paying my debts? What would happen to my reputation? You might as well ask me to give up drinking, or blaspheming, or sodomy!"

There was no answer to that, so I tried another approach.

"So now we go to the Wazir?"

This time he laughed at my naivety.

"No, boy, we are not going to the Wazir. Ja'far al-Barmaki is a cultured and intelligent man, but he has a dreary obsession with duty and responsibility. Whatever he wants me for, it will assuredly not be fun."

"Where, then, are we going?"

"Where else would we be going? We are young, and good-looking, and free, and have a small fortune in gold coins. You and I, boy, are going to a monastery."

Five

The Tale of Three Gentlemen and a Musician, which includes, The Tale of Iblis, the Father of Bitterness

"Welcome, brothers, to the Abbey of Saint Pachomius!"

The monastery to which Abu Nuwas escorted me was indeed an interesting establishment. My memories of my upbringing in the Western Christian Church were vague, and I had long considered myself a Muslim. However I was certain that even in the Eastern Church, novices did not usually wear so much make-up. I also had not imagined that monks and nuns would mingle quite so freely, and believed that traditionally they tended to wear rather more clothes.

This indulgent institution was on the very fringes of town. Abu Nuwas had managed to find a bargee still punting along the dark Northern Canal, and a gold coin was more than enough to persuade him to convey us most of the way. The barge travelled little faster than walking pace, but it was a relief to sit down for a while. As we drifted along I explained to the poet, to his great amusement, how I had come to be the Wazir's messenger.

Despite my having told him my name was al-Rawiya, he continued to call me al-Walid, the Newborn. I was annoyed by the implication that I had not existed until he deigned to notice me, but my annoyance only seemed to encourage him. To divert him, I asked him about Ja'far al-Barmaki, and he was shocked by my ignorance.

"You have never heard of the Barmakids? You truly are a Newborn, like a babe playing with lions, surrounded by dangers you do not understand.

"The Barmakids, boy, are the second family of the Khalifate,

58

after the Abbasids. While our glorious ruler struts around being magnificent, they quietly get on with the business of running everything. They are administrators to their bones. Before the coming of Islam, they were the hereditary wardens of an important Buddhist temple, over in Balkh. They saw which way the wind was blowing though – converted to the true faith, and grabbed the tail of the Abbasid revolution. They soon made themselves indispensable to the new regime.

"Ja'far's father, old Yahya al-Barmaki was Wazir to Harun's father and brother during their reigns. Now Ja'far serves Harun, although the old man is never far away from the crucial decisions. There's another son as well, Fadl ibn Yahya. Fadl's a worthy fellow, but rather dull. I think Harun finds Ja'far more fun to be around."

I was not sure whether I should have made more of an effort to conduct the poet to the house of Salam, but short of bashing him over the head and dragging him there, there was very little I could do. Besides, the Wazir's instructions had been to take him the gold, pass on the message and stay with him until he presented himself. The first two I had done, and the third I was obeying by accompanying him to the Abbey of St Pachomius.

We were greeted at the door of the monastery by a plump, cheerful monk. Despite his age he had reddened his graying hair with henna and his eyes were ringed with kohl. There was a little embarrassment about an outstanding bill, but this was quickly settled with a handful of coins. I noted that there were some debts which Abu Nuwas chose to repay.

When he saw the bag of gold the fat monk became positively effusive. He showed us to a room where three men sat around drinking wine. In the centre of room two novices, a boy and a girl, were listlessly breaking their vows of celibacy, to cheers and jeers from the onlookers. In a corner musicians played a tired ghazal.

"Who's the gosling, Abu Ali?"

The speaker was pudgy and weak eyed, with a smile that seemed a little too eager and a nervous half laugh in his voice. The man who sat across from him was more attractive,

fine-featured to the point of gauntness. There was a third
drinker, but he ignored our arrival. Instead he listened intently
to the music, although from the scowl on his face it gave him
scant pleasure.

At first I looked around for the Abu Ali that the plump
man was addressing. It took me a moment to realize that he
was walking to Abu Nuwas, whose close friends rarely used
his nickname. The gosling, of course, was me.

"His name is Ismail al-Walid, the Newborn. He is the
miraculous offspring of the moon and a window, and you are
to keep your grubby hands off him, Father of Madness."

Abu Nuwas sprawled on a vacant farsh, and indicated that I
should join him. I sat carefully upright on the edge of the rug.
The pudgy man whom he had called Abu'l-Atahiyya, Father
of Madness, passed a jug of wine over. His gaunt companion
joined in the banter.

"Does that stricture only apply to our fat friend? Are my
grubby hands free to roam where they will, Abu Ali?"

He was lean to the point of emaciation, but handsome in
the delicate way which was in vogue at the time. Abu Nuwas
waved the jug at him.

"I have nothing to fear from you, Abbas. I know your
pecker doesn't lean that way. Besides, are you not still
consumed with love for the delicate Fauz? How is your Tyrant?
I was deeply moved by your last ghazal:

"When Fauz walks, her girls around her,
      She walks as if on eggs and glass.
I heard she cried from fright on seeing
      A lion's image cast in brass . . ."

Abbas' hollow cheeks flushed at Abu Nuwas' teasing, and
the Father of Madness joined in.

"Don't tell his adoring public, but the real Fauz is a saggy
wife with three ugly kids. After Abbas deflowered her, the best
she could do in marriage was an oil merchant. Yet still he
churns out that whining verse about his unrequited passion
for the dainty virgin Fauz . . ."

This was too much for Abbas.

"Fuck off, Seller of Jugs! Don't you have some jugs to sell? Or is there not some rich man willing to toss you a coin for some arse-licking doggerel? For a jug seller to look down on an oil merchant's wife, the world must be turned upside down."

It dawned on me at last who the two men were, both of them renowned writers. Gaunt Abbas was famous for his verses of chaste love, whereas Abu'l-Atahiyya, the chubby Father of Madness, was a master of madih, poetry in praise of the high-born and wealthy. My head twitched from side to side, watching their faces, as I tried to keep up with the verbal sparring. Abbas was still riled by others' mockery, and turned on Abu Nuwas.

"As for you, Abu Ali, how is your Tyrant? How is the Father of Bitterness? Have you heard, Ibrahim, the latest story he is spreading around, in a desperate bid for notoriety?"

The last question was addressed to the scowling man across from us, who had not acknowledged us. Despite the annoyance the music seemed to be causing him, he was more vexed still to be distracted from it. He shook his head. Abbas pushed on regardless.

"Then I shall tell you. It is not enough for people to believe that his words are whispered to him by a captive Jinn, as they say of the rest of us poor scribblers. No, he is trying to start a rumour that he gets his inspiration from Iblis, the Father of Bitterness, the Devil himself!"

The older man, Ibrahim, shrugged, but Abu'l-Atahiyya shifted uncomfortably.

"Such talk is dangerous, Abu Ali."

"What, do you fear that to talk of the Devil is to summon him?"

"This is no subject for jest. The Khalifah is indulgent, particularly of you, but he has imprisoned me for heresy in the past."

Abu Nuwas did not answer, instead taking a long draught of wine straight from the jar. He passed it to Abbas, but the skinny man had not finished badgering him.

"Is that what the gosling is for, Abu Ali? Is he for Iblis? Are you going to sacrifice him, so that you can use his blood to summon the Devil?"

"It won't be his throat that's bleeding, either, but the other end."

These were the first words that Ibrahim had uttered since we entered the room, and they did not endear him to me. I began to wonder what further depravity I might encounter, in this temple of perversion. Abu Nuwas' response was as close to serious as I had yet heard him.

"I have always thought that Iblis has been given a bad name unfairly. Surely his refusal to bow to Adam was simply a rejection of idolatry?"

Up until now I thought I had been following their raillery, but this reference was beyond me. Abbas must have noticed my puzzlement.

"Your gosling looks confused. Does it speak?"

"Speak? It reads Greek philosophy, Abbas, and is probably smarter than you. However it was raised by wolves, or sharks, or something, and has never been schooled in the true faith."

It was true that there was much I did not know about Islam, which I had adopted unquestioningly as the religion of civilisation. The Nekorite traders taught me nothing of their faith, and Hermes the Kritan was a Jew, in name at least. We had studied the Sharia law for practical reasons, but I had never heard the myths that these men would have learned as children.

"You should educate him, Abu Ali. You are so learned in these matters."

Abu'l-Atahiyya turned to me, the first time anyone had addressed me directly since our arrival.

"Did you know, boy, that your debauched master was once a pious scholar? He was the youngest hafiz in Basrah – memorised the entire Quran before he was ten! Tell him the story, Father of Locks. Nobody tells it better than you, obviously because you know the protagonist so well. Tell us all the story."

So he did.

Before the world began, there was only God. In His wisdom He created light, then from the light He fashioned angels. The angels all fell down and began to worship Him. However they did not do so through choice, but because such was their nature, and they could do nothing else.

In his wisdom God desired to be worshipped by a being of consciousness and free will, that adored Him because it understood his divinity. He therefore created fire, which itself makes light. From the fire He shaped the Jinni. And He made the Earth, and placed the Jinni upon it.

At first the Jinni were grateful to their creator, and gave Him praise and thanks. But in time they became intoxicated by their own power. They began to fight among themselves to determine who was the greatest, and the Earth screamed with the scorching of their battles.

When God heard the screams of the Earth, He called to Him the most devout and upright of the Jinni, who was called Iblis. He commanded him to go among his people, and bring them back to the ways of righteousness. Iblis did as God willed, and when the Jinni did not heed his calls, he blasted them with flames so fierce that they burned even these beings made of fire.

As he pacified the Jinni, pride began to creep into the heart of Iblis. He considered that he must be the favourite of God. But God, in His wisdom, had decided to create a new race of beings, which would have the free choice of the Jinn, but without their supernatural powers.

He sent the Angel Jibril to the Earth, to take soil from which He might mould His new creation. But the Earth begged to be spared, saying:

"If this being offends God, then I will suffer, just as I suffered for the sins of the Jinni. Surely God cannot have intended for you to harm me, by stealing my very substance from me?"

Jibril, who by his nature could do no wrong, was confused by the Earth's pleading, and returned to God empty handed.

So God sent the Angel Mika'il. Again the Earth begged, and again the Angel returned empty handed. Finally God sent Azra'il, the Angel of Death. When the Earth pleaded with him, he answered:

"It is not for us to wonder why the innocent suffer. When God commands me to take, I take, and there is no reasoning in the universe that can persuade me to disobey. But to ameliorate your loss, I will take only a little from each land."

So the Angel of Death took some black mud from the lands of the south, and some brown sand from the centre of the world, and some white clay from the countries of the north, and took them to God. And from these God created Man.

The first Man was called Adam. By the standards of our times he was a giant, being sixty cubits in height. God breathed life into him, and for forty days he lay immobile and insensate as the dirt from which he was made. Then, from the top of his head downwards, the dirt turned into flesh, and the mud became his blood. When the process was complete, he sneezed, and praised the name of God.

At this God was pleased, and ordered all creation to bow down before Adam. The ranks of the angels fell to their knees, for they could do nothing other than obey. The stars and the moons made obeisance to Man, and so did the Earth, and all the creatures of land and sea and air. Even the proud Jinni bowed down.

All except Iblis, who stood with his head held high. And God said to him:

"Why do you not prostrate yourself before this being that I have created?"

Iblis replied as follows:

"How can this thing be greater than I? It lives and dies, and has an immortal soul, but so do I, and the others of my kind. Do we not also think, and converse, and have children that we love? Do we not also choose how we live our lives, and suffer the consequences of our choices?

"Yet we have powers that this being can only dream of. We can fly, and make ourselves invisible, and bend reality to our will. We can be as large as a mountain or smaller than an ant. How can we be inferior to him?

"Further, this Adam is made of dirt and muck, of dull, unresponsive earth, home to blind, slimy, crawling things. We Jinni are beings of fire, of subtle, dancing flame, which gives both heat and light. Surely we are of a higher order?

"Above all else, You have taught us that there is no God but You. How can You ask us to bow down before this Man, as if he were another Creator? I abase myself to You, and to You alone."

With that Iblis the Jinn prostrated himself before God. But God was angry, and said:

"O haughty, clever Iblis. You try to trap me with my own words? I banish you to the scorched wastelands of Jahannam, where you shall eat nothing but the bitter, thorny fruit of the Zaqqum tree, and it will boil and gash your innards for time without end. And to Mankind I give the ability to enslave your people. They will call them Afarit, the Strong Ones, but they will enchain them with symbols and incantations, and make them carry out their wishes, for good or ill."

Iblis replied:

"I submit to Your will. However I ask one boon. Before I go to Jahannam, let me visit the Earth for a little while. I will tempt and confuse these Men, and they will turn away from You, disobey and deny You, for they are weak and foolish creatures of mud."

And God answered him:

"You shall have your boon. You may walk the earth until Judgement Day. And any men that you succeed in distracting from submission to My will shall be your companions, and go with you to Jahannam for all eternity."

So it was that Iblis of the Jinni became the Great Shaitan, the Tempter who whispers in the ears of men, in the hope that they will fall for his lies and join him in perpetual suffering. For this reason he is also known as Abu Murra; the Father of Bitterness.

★ ★ ★

"I'm not sure I like this friend of yours, Abu Ali. His

punishment is not lessened, the more it is shared. Is he not merely a spiteful loser?"

"Ah, Abbas! Beware, I shall tell him what you said about him. Besides, does he not have reason to feel aggrieved? It is galling, as we all know, to have to grovel and scrape to those of lower intelligence."

Abu'l-Atahiyya looked terrified at these near-treasonous comments, but at that moment the lethargic rutting of the young novices came to a shuddering halt. The girl sat up without covering her nakedness. She was slim and pretty, but her face was vacant, possibly drugged, and I felt only sadness when I looked at her. Besides, I was trying to remember where I had heard the name Abu Murra before.

Abu Nuwas, who had now been given a goblet of wine, waved it at the couple.

"Such fine entertainment – this is indeed a perfect evening. Wine, wit, the company of three gentlemen and a musician . . ."

If I was disgruntled not to be counted amongst the gentlemen, this was nothing to the reaction of the surly Ibrahim.

"I am as much a gentleman as you, Abu Ali, you lisping fop. And my verse is the equal of yours."

"When did you become so grouchy, Ibrahim al-Mosuli? You used to be able to take a joke. Play us a song, al-Mosuli. These butchers have got that tune pinned to the floor, they only need you to come and slit its throat."

Ibrahim smiled mirthlessly.

"Well, since we are discussing your friend the Father of Bitterness, you might like to hear my latest composition. It's a setting of a lyric of yours, on precisely that subject."

The other two poets clapped and shouted their approbation. Ibrahim al-Mosuli walked over to the musicians and took the lute, putting a halt to their desultory busking. After a muttered discussion the drummer started to beat a lively pattern. The tunbur joined in, its long, thick strings thumping out a ground. Over this al-Mosuli began to pick a complex progression, wild, forlorn, yet somehow sly and knowing in its harmonic sophistication.

The mizmar player was listening with a look of furious concentration. As he picked up the sequence he joined in with a wailing phrase, like the cry of a desperate lover. After a couple of repetitions he took the reed from his lips, grinning with satisfaction. Al-Mosuli nodded at the vastly improved sound the band was making, then began to sing, in a high, sonorous voice that seemed incongruous coming from his grey-bearded face.

I gave rapt attention to the words of the song. It was my first encounter with the poetry of Abu Nuwas. I expected the traditional lament for a lost love, but instead the lyric was teasing, an unsettling combination of lightness and shocking blasphemy:

> My sweetheart was sulking
>   His letters stopped coming
> I called on the Devil
>   And said to him, weeping,
> "How could you forsake me?
>   See how I'm hurting!
> I'm worn to my bones
>   With tears and not sleeping,
> The worry has caused
>   My elan to start drooping.
> I've done what you asked of me –
>   All of it, everything –
> Spat on your enemies,
>   Never stopped sinning.
> So make his heart burn for me
>   (to you, that's nothing)
> Or I'll turn away from you
>   I'll start repenting!
> Give up music and poetry
>   Even stop drinking
> I'll read the Quran again
>   Spend long nights studying
> Go as pilgrim to Makkah
>   Give virtue a fling . . ."

It was not three days later
My boyfriend came visiting
Begged for forgiveness –
The change was astounding.
After such misery
Joy is abounding
With the boy in my bed
And Iblis as my king . . .

As the last notes of the song died away, Ibrahim al-Mosuli launched a new theme. The band, revived by the challenge of keeping up with him, watched his fingers on the lute strings, then began to accompany him. The mizmar player, who had had little to do during the singing, improvised a melody that caused al-Mosuli to laugh with sheer pleasure. He was transformed by his music, almost unrecognisable as the taciturn man I had first encountered.

I reflected that Hermes might forgive my desertion, if he could see me now. Only my second night in Baghdad, and I was sitting with poets and musicians! It was true that the surroundings were seedier, and the conversation more coarse, than I had envisaged, but their intelligence and learning were unmistakable.

Then I noticed the sapphire eyes of Abu Nuwas fixed on me. Abbas and Abu'l-Atahiyya were deep in a muttered discussion, and his attention was on me alone. When he offered me the wine jug, I hesitated; it had been a seemingly endless night. I could hardly believe it was only a few hours since I had lain hidden in the alcove, eating an apple. Suddenly I felt tired, and wondered where I might go to sleep. However Abu Nuwas grabbed my hair and tipped the wine into my mouth, so that I had to swallow it or choke.

"You are right to think twice, boy. The common horde make these decisions lightly, as if they are of no consequence: what shall we eat, what shall we drink, whom shall we fuck. But the man who lives the life of thought knows that each choice is critical. At every moment you are gambling your life, staking eternity, on your understanding of the world.

"The fifth Surah of the Holy Quran teaches us that wine is an abomination. Yet an earlier Surah talks of the vine as one of the blessings of God, because it provides intoxication. The hadith describe the day the ban on alcohol was announced, and tell us the streets of Madinah ran red with discarded wine. The poet al-Asha was on his way to convert, but turned back when he heard of the ruling, preferring damnation to sobriety.

"But we are also told that the Quran has existed perfect and complete since before the world began. How can wine be permitted one day, and forbidden the next? Does the word of God change according to his whims?

"The forfeit for those who fail to untangle these paradoxes is nothing less than agony for eternity, with no hope of redemption. Yet still scholars argue over the meaning of the Quran, and which of the Sayings are genuine. If God truly is a merciful and loving God, why could He not transmit His word to us in a way that permits of no ambiguity? Is He not also an all-powerful God?

"We must play His game, be rewarded for success and punished for failure. Yet we are not told the rules of the game. All we are given is scraps and shreds, as if we are overhearing knowledge not meant for us. Then we must piece together the truth, or lose everything. What cruel father is this, who lays such traps to confound us, His children?"

He interrupted this learned discourse to force on me another mouthful of wine. I was sick from drink and exhaustion, and did not resist. His voice lulled, a charm tightening around me.

"You may decide to take the path of caution, and abstain from anything which might incur the wrath of God. But now another fear arises. What if there is no God, after all? What if this little glimmer of light is all we have, all we can ever know? Then the only right way to behave is to gorge on sensual experience, to seek out variety tirelessly and inventively. And the greatest evil would be to cower timidly, wasting your span preparing for an afterlife that does not exist.

"Most people do neither of these. They compromise and

equivocate, neither ascetic nor aesthetic. They can only live thus because they are somehow numb to the agony of awareness. Somehow they go for years at a time without thinking of the single most important fact in their lives; that those lives will end, and that that end could come at any moment, without warning or preparation. When forced to confront it, they assume that, if they mean well and muddle through, then all will be well in the end.

"But that gentle blindness is not for us, those of us who are condemned to wonder, to question, to try to answer the unanswerable questions. We must make our choice, and endure the consequences, like Iblis, with our heads held high.

"Perhaps, after all, we are not meant to use our reason, but instead to trust our intuition. Perhaps the only true guide – the only thing that matters – the only thing that exists is love."

He leaned towards me, his lips close to my face, breathing liquorous fumes. The memory washed over me of the rough hands of the pirate captain, his suffocating weight on my immature body, and I sprang to my feet. Abu Nuwas tumbled over, to the sound of coarse laughter from the other men. He got up staggered towards me, crooning with a mixture of mockery and menace.

"How could you refuse me? Both God and the Devil command you to submit to me!"

He was much bigger than me, and his strength frightened me. Fortunately the wine was wearing him down, and he was having trouble staying upright. I dodged around the room, evading his clumsy lunges, until I could make a break for the door. Flinging aside the curtain I dashed out – only to run straight into the muscled torso of Ilig the Khazar.

"Come with me. The Wazir does not like to be kept waiting."

Six

The Postman's Tale, which includes, The Tale of the Righteous Ones

Abu Nuwas sulked all the way back to the city, like a child whose plaything has been taken from him. He goaded the Khazar relentlessly, with comments on his parentage and cheap jibes about the length of his sword, but the bodyguard had said all he was going to say. I was still shaken and angered by the poet's crude attempt to seduce me, and seethed in silent resentment. So we were a merry crew as we trudged through the barren streets in the hour before dawn.

To my surprise Ilig did not conduct us to the Round City, and the house of Salam. Instead he led us east through Zubaydiya and over the northernmost bridge across the Tigris. One secret of the ancients that had been lost was the building of arch bridges. In Ifriqiya I had seen many stone viaducts still standing from the days of the old Roman Empire, six hundred years or more before. The bridges across the Tigris however were all pontoons, planks laid across a line of moored boats. The timbers creaked under our feet, and swayed slightly as we crossed.

The North Bridge took us to the exclusive district of Rusafah, on the east bank. Although outside the symbolic centre of Baghdad, this was a less constricted neighbourhood, where lavish mansions sprawled over generous acres. Here we were led to an imposing residence, through a magnificent courtyard with fountains and caged birds, and into an ante-room. Ilig left us here, and Abu Nuwas and I sat wordless on a bench. For some reason I was reminded of the slave market at Tiaret.

The walk must have sobered him up, because after a while he broke the silence.

"Go on then, boy. Say it."

"Say what, Father of Locks?"

"That you saved my ungrateful skin at the Garden of Delights, and deserved better of me than to force myself on you."

I pondered for a while what I assumed to be an apology, or as close as I was going to get.

"I do not say that, Father of Locks. However I do say this: I don't know what the Barmakid has planned for me, whether I am a slave, a prisoner, an errand boy, or something else. But I am no man's catamite. The last villain who violated me was food for fishes before the next sunrise. I would rather die than submit to such treatment again. Believe me, though, if that becomes necessary I will not be going to Jahannam alone."

Abu Nuwas looked at me for a while, then nodded. At that moment a servant appeared, and we were led into an adjacent chamber.

Ja'far al-Barmaki was not in the room. Instead there was an old man, a Persian, studying a scroll. A pile of similar parchments lay on a table beside him. The richness of his robes and the huge jewel in his turban spoke of wealth and power, but even in rags this man would command obedience. Sharp eyes glinted from below bushy eyebrows, and his beard was long.

He did not look up from his scroll as we entered, and in the end Abu Nuwas spoke first.

"Good evening to you, ibn Khalid."

The old man took a few moments to look us over before replying.

"Good morning, Abu Ali. And you, I presume, are the boy Ismail al-Rawiya?"

I nodded nervously. Abu Nuwas seemed nervous too, but ventured a question.

"Where is your son, ibn Khalid? I had expected to see Ja'far."

"My son has retired to bed, as he has a busy day ahead of him, managing the affairs of the entire civilised world. I agreed to see you on his behalf, before I go to my diwan."

This, then, must be Yahya ibn Khalid al-Barmaki, father to Ja'far the Wazir. The old man wrinkled his nose as he scrutinised us.

"You stink, poet. And your presence was requested several hours ago."

Abu Nuwas made to answer, but instead Yahya addressed me.

"What happened, boy?"

I related the events in the Garden of Delights, and our visit to the Abbey of St Pachomius, in terms of careful neutrality. I decided it would be wise not to give any details of what went on at the monastery. When I had finished, Yahya al-Barmaki shook his head.

"If it was up to me, Abu Ali, I would throw you into prison, if for no other reason than to preserve the morals of the Ummah. However, my son considers you useful, so instead I have a task for you."

"But – with respect, ibn Khalid, I understood that debt had been paid! Your son promised me – after the last time . . ."

"Shall I tell the Khalifah, then, that you refused to assist his minister? I am sure he will be disappointed in this lack of loyalty from his so-called friend."

Abu Nuwas looked thoroughly miserable.

"But you cannot ask me to leave Baghdad, not now! Everything I have worked for – my reputation, my patrons –"

"No, you will not need to leave Baghdad. This task will not be like your others. However Ja'far seems to think it will suit your particular talents – whatever they are."

Yahya paused, as if waiting for further objections from the poet. When none was forthcoming, he went on.

"The Devil has been sighted on the streets of the city. My son would like you to . . . look into it."

Abu Nuwas seemed about to laugh, but the sound was strangled in something close to fear.

"If anybody else had said such a thing to me, ibn Khalid, I would have thought that they were mad, or joking. Or drunk."

"I can assure you, Abu Ali, that I am sane, serious and sober.

I would not be wasting my time with this matter, if I were not deeply concerned.

"A hooded man was seen lurking in Sharqiya. It is a poor district, but tightly knit, and strangers attract attention. When he was challenged by a respectable widow, he told her he was Iblis."

"And that is causing you concern? A foolish old woman claims a stranger told her he was the Devil?"

"No, poet. What causes me concern is that the stranger then hurled a bolt of fire, which destroyed three houses before the blaze was finally extinguished."

Yahya ibn Khalid allowed these words to sink in, before he continued.

"The hooded man disappeared in the confusion, and now all of Sharqiya is in uproar. Only the widow spoke to the stranger, but several witnesses saw him cast the spell which caused such devastation. And we cannot afford disquiet in the streets, not while our visitors are in town."

"Visitors?"

"So you are not as well informed as my son believes. Well, you will hear soon enough. Every beggar in Karkh will know about them by sunset."

"But why me?"

The Barmakid's smile was cold.

"I ask myself the same question. My son is clever, but some day he will trip himself up with his cleverness. Still, he is old enough to make his own mistakes. A child can be told, but a man must face the consequences of his choices.

"Besides, are you not considered to be something of an expert on the Great Shaitan?"

Abu Nuwas made no response. Yahya stood up.

"Go home, poet. Get some sleep, wash yourself, cover your head, try to look like a true believer. After the call for midday prayer, go to the Sharqiya Watch House and ask for al-Takht. He is the Captain of Police who reported the incident. Al-Takht is not a dull thug, like most of his profession; he can read the streets like a sailor reads the weather."

Abu Nuwas turned to leave. I looked around desperately,

74

wondering what I was meant to do. Yahya noticed my confusion.

"Ah yes, boy, I had forgotten about you. Ja'far commands you to assist and accompany Abu Ali al-Hasan ibn Hani' al-Hakami, known as the Father of Locks, until the successful conclusion of this matter. You are to regard yourself as his apprentice, and he as your master. You will comply with any instructions he gives you which are consistent with the law and with conventional morality."

The Barmakid stared pointedly at Abu Nuwas as he said this latter part, then turned back to me.

"If you obey these instructions, Ja'far graciously permits you to remain alive and free."

He returned to his scroll, but I did not move. He looked up again irritably.

"Yes?"

"With respect, ibn Khalid, if I am to be of help, I must eat and sleep."

He paused. I had the distinct impression that he was about to order me to go with Abu Nuwas, then thought better of it.

"You may use the Hall of the Barid. Congratulations, boy; you have just become a postman."

★ ★ ★

Abu Nuwas stumbled away muttering that he would meet me at the Watch House. I wandered through the palace of the Barmakids, marvelling that nobody challenged me. However it was a public building as much as it was a private residence. Dawn was breaking, and already petitioners had begun to gather outside, seeking the patronage of the mighty Barmakid clan, hoping to be favoured financially, legally or politically. Everywhere servants rushed around, carrying dishes or parchments.

At last I managed to stop a serving girl who pointed me the way to the Hall of the Barid. This was a long, high room, with sleeping mats along one side. There was only one occupant, a man of around forty years who was winding his turban around his head. He looked at me quizzically.

"New, are you?"

"Actually, I don't know what I am."

And at that it all came out, my journey to Baghdad, capture in the Chamber of the Ancients, the Wazir, the poet, and all the rest of it. If the man was surprised at my rambling answer to his simple question, he did not show it. He was an excellent listener, nodding and gasping in all the right places, and something about his frank, plain face invited confidence. When I had finished, he stroked his beard thoughtfully.

"So you're the new hobble for the Father of Locks."

"Hobble?"

"Hobble, lad. A length of rope used to tie a horse's legs together to slow it down. Our friend Ja'far ibn Yahya likens Abu Nuwas to a swift but hot-tempered stallion. Says he needs a hobble so the rest of the team can keep up."

"He doesn't seem that brilliant to me."

"Don't be fooled by the drunkenness, the lisp, and the other affectations. He's got one of the sharpest brains in the city. He's not what you'd call a regular in the service, but Ja'far likes to employ him for occasional, particularly tricky tasks. I think the Wazir considers it proof of his own cleverness, to use and manipulate such a maverick mind."

"What happened to his last – hobble?"

The man stared sympathetically at me.

"A good question, lad. They tend not to last very long. Abu Nuwas has an appetite for risk that most find unpalatable. Sometimes fatally so."

I must have looked alarmed, because he tried to reassure me.

"Still, you're very different to the usual sort. In the past Ja'far has used men of middle age, stolid and unimaginative, hoping they would rein in the poet's extravagance. Perhaps he has a new plan. And you've joined the Barid without even knowing what it is?"

I understood that he was trying to change the subject, but I needed to learn whatever I could.

"Sit down, lad. I'm going to teach you how to rule an empire. You say you journeyed here from Ifriqiya?"

"It took me nearly three years."

"And you have not seen even half of the Khalifate. You could keep going all the way to China without leaving the Land of Islam. Different peoples, different languages, different cultures. Now, how do you think our masters keep the peace, enforce the law, arbitrate disputes?"

"Well, there are governors . . ."

"Think, lad! When you were in Tiaret, where did the people go for judgment?"

"To the Amir."

"Correct. The men who rule the nations of the Khalifate are the same people who always ruled them. The Amirs, the Shaikhs, the kings and princes. Do you think Harun al-Rashid is interested in disputes over cattle between Mongolian herdsmen who don't even speak Arabic?

"No, the governors are there for one thing only: to collect taxes. That revenue pays for the infrastructure of the empire, and most particularly the armies that hold the empire together. You see the beauty of it? The subjects pay their taxes, and those taxes pay for the soldiers who keep them subjected, and who come to collect if they're slow in paying.

"And the profits of this elegant racket permit the Abbasids, the Barmakids, and all their flunkies, parasites, concubines and half-wit second cousins to live in a decadent luxury that the Caesars of Rome would have considered excessive.

"It is a delicate equilibrium, however. The subjects are also taxed by their own, local rulers. It only takes a governor to squeeze his province too hard, perhaps because he is taking the cream off the top before passing it on to his master, and the people might decide that there are worse things than the Khalifah's armies. Baghdad needs to know what is going on, in Bukhara and Antioch and Alexandria, without waiting for the governor's bland reports about how terribly well he is doing.

"And that's where you and I come in, my friend. We are the Barid, the postmen. The Khalifah cannot openly send spies to check on his top officials. Such lack of trust creates more conspiracies than it prevents. But nobody can refuse entry to the messenger, with important letters from the Commander of the Faithful.

"Of course we do carry mail. There are post stations with fresh horses all across the empire. That journey from Tiaret, that took you three years? I could do it in three weeks, if the urgency was great enough. But we get everywhere, and we talk to everybody. And then we come back here and talk to Ja'far al-Barmaki."

"So we only spy on our own officials?"

The man laughed.

"They're the only real threat to the peace of the Khalifate. The Romans are too weak to mount any serious offensive. As long as the Emperor's mother keeps her grip on the balls of her feeble-minded son, there's no chance of them trying to regain the lands we liberated from them.

"I suppose the Emperor of China could raise an army which might rival that of Islam. But between our lands and his lie the empty wastes of Qyzylqum, which blaze in summer and freeze in winter. Any expedition seeking to cross it would face grave difficulties.

"There are other dangers within our borders though, beside corrupt governors. We have to keep our ears open, maintain contacts amongst the heretics, particularly in Makkah and Madinah. There is always some fanatic seeking to overthrow the Abbasids, to put an Alid on the throne."

"What is an Alid?"

He looked at me incredulously.

"You truly do not know? Such political naivety could be terminal, in a member of the Barid. The Alids are the descendants of Ali ibn Abi Talib, who was married to Fatimah, who was the daughter of the Prophet – you have no idea about any of this, do you? I'd better tell you the whole story."

So he did.

The Tale of the Righteous Ones

Aisha bint Abi Bakr was playing on the swing with her friends when her mother called to her. The girl ran to the house, thinking that dinner must be early tonight. Instead her mother tugged a comb through her hair and told her that she must go and wash, for she was to be married that day.

Vaguely Aisha recollected her betrothal, three years previously, although she had barely understood it at the time. All day long, serious beards had come and gone, waggling at each other. Then she had to hold the hand of a nice old man. She only really remembered it because that evening there was feasting, and she had been allowed to stay up until she drifted to sleep in a torchlit, noisy tent.

Before that, she had apparently been promised to a boy of good birth from a local tribe. His family had broken off the engagement, though, after the trouble in Makkah. This Aisha did not remember at all, but only knew from the stories of the women. Instead of being a disgrace, however, the broken engagement was a blessing. Because her father, Abu Bakr, had been free to give her in marriage to his best friend, the most important man in the history of the world.

Muhammad ibn Abd Allah al-Hashimi al-Qurayshi, peace be upon him, was the Prophet of God, chosen to be the messenger of the Last Testament. For over a decade now the Angel Jibril had been visiting him, bringing the Word, pure, perfect, and eternal. All mankind needed for salvation was submission, *Islam*, to God's will, as dictated to his Apostle.

This was not a new religion but a reclamation of the only true faith, the faith of Adam and Nuh, of Ibrahim and Musa. The Word had been given to the Jews, but they had perverted it in their sinfulness. Isa ibn Maryam brought it to all men, but his followers twisted his meaning, calling him the Son of God and dividing the one God into three. And finally had come Muhammad, humanity's last chance to listen.

Not everybody welcomed the chance. The Prophet's tribe, the Qurayshi, governed the city of Makkah, and within it the Ka'bah, the most sacred shrine of the Arabs. This brought them not only prestige but profit, as the trucial zone around the shrine made it an important trading post. When Muhammad preached against idolatry and false gods, most of the Qurayshi felt that he had turned against his own.

Things had got so bad that Abu Bakr fled to Aksum, taking his daughter with him. Only now that the Prophet had settled in Madinah could they return to Arabia, and the marriage take place.

Aisha had been chosen by God to be his Apostle's wife. The Angel Jibril had brought visions of the little girl to his dreams. Abu Bakr, though, was worried about engaging his young daughter to Muhammad. He was concerned that he and the Prophet were brothers by oath, and that the marriage would be incestuous. The Angel came again, reassuring them that God had sanctioned the union.

On the day of the wedding, Aisha's playmates were frightened by the imposing man with his cloak and staff, and ran away. However Muhammad called them back, sat on the floor with them and joined in their games. So the Prophet played with the children as the sun declined, until it was time for the husband to take his wife to bed.

The marriage was happy on the whole, although not without occasional troubles. Even the favourite wife of the Chosen One was but a woman. There was the time when she left her husband's camp to look for a lost necklace, and returned to find the caravan had moved on without her. She was rescued by a man named Safwan, only for evil slanderers to claim that she had slipped away deliberately to meet him for sex.

Muhammad was troubled by the allegations, but the Angel visited him to inform him of Aisha's innocence. Jibril also told him that those who accuse honourable women must produce four witnesses to the adultery or face eighty lashes and never be believed again. The slanderers received the punishment they deserved.

Then there was the time the Christian concubine, Maria al-Qibtiyya, bore a son to the Prophet. Muhammad spent much time with her, sharing dishes of honey, of which Maria was very fond. Consumed with jealousy, Aisha and another of the wives told him that the honey made his breath stink. The Angel warned him of the deception, however. The Prophet did not visit Aisha for a month, and she was duly chastened.

Despite these difficulties, it was to Aisha's house that Muhammad retired when he realised the end was near. And it was there that God took back His Prophet, peace and blessings be upon him. He was sixty-two years old, and passed away with his head in his young wife's lap, in the ninth year of their marriage.

And that was when the trouble started. Muhammad had named no heir. His son by Maria had died in infancy, as had all his children except his daughter Fatimah. On his deathbed he had asked for writing tools, so that he could record the name of his anointed successor. But Aisha chased off the attendants who brought them, telling them not to worry a sick old man with such things.

The Prophet's legacy was not only religious, but also political. By the time of his passing all the tribes of Arabia had come under his sway, either by conversion or by conquest. In addition there was the not inconsiderable matter of his personal wealth, his slaves, land and property. A great deal depended on the events of the next few hours. Aisha immediately sent a messenger to her father Abu Bakr, who was a couple of miles away in the small town of al-Sunah. However, while she was busy, Muhammad's body was snatched from her house, carried away by Aisha's greatest rival for his affections.

Fatimah bint Muhammad was the only child of the Prophet to survive to adulthood and give him grandchildren. Her mother was Khadijah, Muhammad's beloved first wife. Indeed, while she lived, Khadijah was Muhammad's sole wife; he refused all other offers of marriage, even for reasons of charity or alliance.

Fatimah herself was married to her father's cousin, Ali ibn Abi Talib. Loyal and devout, she had reason to consider herself to be the leader of Muslim womanhood. Recently however she had faced a rival in her father's child bride, to whom he had gone to be nursed through his final days. By claiming his body for washing and burial, the Prophet's daughter was asserting her position at the head of the Ummah.

As Fatimah's household wailed around the corpse, Aisha's messenger reached Abu Bakr. The old disciple, who still bore the scars of the beating he had received when he first preached the Word on the streets of Makkah, knew what had happened. He knew before he saw the dust kicked up in the distance by the messenger's horse. He knew from the stillness that had descended on the mud huts and olive trees. The animals, the birds, even the wind seemed to have fallen silent. So he merely nodded, when the sweating rider climbed down from his mount and gasped out the grim tidings.

Now, men have fought and died over what happened next. You can read a hundred different accounts of the events of that tempestuous summer in Madinah, and no two will be exactly the same. But this is my story. I had it from my grandfather, and he had it from his grandfather, and he was that sweating horseman who broke the news to Abu Bakr; or so he always claimed to his family. Whether this is the true story, nobody knows for certain, and anybody who might have known is long dead. But this is how I heard it, and this is how I tell it.

Nobody had discussed what would happen after the Prophet's death, as if to speak of it was somehow to wish for it. Abu Bakr, however, was a man and a warrior, and it fell to him to care for the well-being of the Ummah. He had lost his best and oldest friend as well as his leader, but the time for mourning must come later. He called for his horse and hurried back to Madinah.

On his arrival more bad news awaited him. Abu Bakr's right hand man was Umar ibn al-Khattab, a fierce zealot who had fought at his side through the difficult years. Now word came that Umar had gone mad with grief, and was rampaging around the city. Abu Bakr found him in the market place, brandishing his sword and raving.

"The liars are saying that the Prophet is dead! He is not – cannot be dead. He has gone into the wilderness for forty days, like the Prophet Musa. He will return! By God, he will come back and cut to pieces those who said he was dead!"

Gently Abu Bakr took the sword from Umar's hand, and gripped his shoulder.

"Do you remember, my friend, the words of God, that his Apostle relayed to us? 'Muhammad is no more than a Messenger. Other Messengers have passed away before him. If he dies, will you turn your back on their message?' The Prophet is gone, my friend. God's work is still to be done."

And Umar ibn al-Khattab, veteran of a score of battles, threw his arms around his friend's neck and wept like a baby.

The tremors from the Prophet's death were still spreading through the city. The elite of Islam were the Sahaba, the Companions who had come from Makkah with Muhammad. They were a tiny minority though. The dramatic expansion of the faith over the previous decade had been dependent on the new converts of Madinah, known as the Ansar. Abu Bakr heard that the Ansar had gathered at the Saqifah, a tribal meeting house, to choose their next leader. If they elected one of their own number, then the Companions would be irrelevant to the future of the true faith.

Abu Bakr and Umar crashed into the assembly at Saqifah. While Ali and Fatimah saw to the body of the Prophet, the warriors argued over the soul of the Family he had created. Many of the Ansar viewed Islam more as an Arab unification movement than a religion, and could not see why their own tribal chiefs should not be candidates for the leadership. There seemed no way forward other than dissolution, and a return to idolatry and constant warfare.

Then the impetuous Umar seized the hand of Abu Bakr, and loudly declared him Khalifah ar-Rasul Allah, Successor to the Prophet of God. In the stunned silence that followed, other allies stepped forward and swore allegiance. Now any rivals for the succession would have to declare their challenge openly, or fall into line. One by one they yielded, and pledged loyalty.

However there was another potential Successor, who was not present at the assembly. Ali ibn Abi Talib was the Prophet's cousin, and his son-in-law, and father to his grandchildren. Ali seems to have filled the void in Muhammad's life left by the sons he had lost. Moreover, he had been one of the first to accept the new teaching, and had fought heroically as captain of the Prophet's bodyguard. When Muhammad fled Makkah, Ali had risked his life by sleeping in his cousin's bed, covering his escape as the blades of the assassins closed in.

Ali was not pleased to hear that the succession had been decided without him having even been consulted. He and his followers, who were called the Shi'at, or Faction, of Ali, were in no position to challenge for power. On the other hand, nor were they prepared to acknowledge the new regime. They simply stayed out of the way, licking their wounds. This withdrawal became increasingly embarrassing for Abu Bakr, who was struggling to assert his authority over the fractious tribes.

Finally, Abu Bakr sent Umar to the house of Fatimah, to negotiate a deal. Fatimah, though, was smarting that her father's huge estates had been claimed by the Khalifah, who had remembered Muhammad saying that "Prophets left no inheritance", and had taken it all for the Ummah. Worse, she had watched the smirking Aisha be awarded a pension for life, as had the other wives, whilst she, the daughter, was left with nothing. She refused Umar entry to her house.

Not for the first or last time, Umar lost his temper. He broke through the door by force. Fatimah, pregnant with the Prophet's grandchild, was standing in the way. She was trapped against the wall, and lost the baby. She never recovered, dying two months later.

Ali was no coward, but after that night he had no stomach for the fight. Although he had never feared to risk his own life for the true faith, he was reluctant to venture the lives of innocents. He pledged allegiance to Abu Bakr.

The first Khalifah ruled for only two years of constant warfare. First he had to convince Arabia that Islam had not ended with the death of Muhammad. That could only be done by a show of military might. Abu Bakr subdued the tribes, then took Iraq from the Sassanid Persians, and Syria from the Romans.

Unlike the Prophet, his Successor was careful to nominate his own heir, before sickness and death put an end to his brief reign. Umar ibn al–Khattab's ten years at the top were marked by relentless conquest, as the Land of Islam exploded across the world, swallowing the ancient nations of Egypt and Persia. The fiery old warrior lived simply, like a man of God, but was hated by many. In particular his discrimination in favour of Arabs aroused resentment in the increasingly complex empire. At the age of sixty he was stabbed to death by a Persian slave.

Still Ali was ignored when it came to the succession. Uthman ibn Affan, the third Khalifah, was another of Abu Bakr's cronies, and one of the first to swear allegiance to him at Saqifah. And still the Family of Islam grew. Over the twelve years of Uthman's reign, the empire spread to the east and the north and to the west: into Ifriqiya and Andalus, Sistan and Tabaristan, Sindh and Khorasan. But Uthman had always been less of a presence than Umar or Abu Bakr, and did not have the iron in his soul needed to keep control of his vast dominions. He was finally murdered by rebels under the leadership of the son of Abu Bakr – who, in the strange way things turn out, was now an important figure in the Shi'at of Ali.

Ali seemed to be the only one who could hold the Ummah together, and effectively became Khalifah simply by outliving all his rivals. However, he was nearing sixty himself, and had always been reluctant to see people die to advance his claim to power. By the time he ascended to the throne Islam was disintegrating into civil war. It was a period that became known as the Fitna, a subtle word that means both Secession and Persecution, Tribulation and Purification.

Despite his qualms, Ali ibn Abi Talib had to go to war once more. His wife's old rival Aisha had raised an army against him. Her pretext was that he had failed to punish the murderers of Uthman, but in reality she sought to put her favoured candidate on the throne. God had forbidden the Prophet's widows from remarrying. Aisha had therefore formed an alliance with two of her brothers-in-law, but there was no doubt who was really in charge. Now in her forties, Aisha commanded her own troops from a litter on the back of a camel.

The armies met near Basrah. Ali tried to negotiate a truce, but a dawn raid by Badawi lancers triggered a chaotic conflict. It was the first time Muslim had openly fought Muslim, tribes divided against their own. The Shi'at of Ali triumphed, at what became known as The Battle of the Camel. When Ali's troops identified and hamstrung Aisha's mount, the Mother of the Faithful tumbled from her litter and out of the struggle for power. Aisha spent the remainder of her life in pious retirement. She devoted herself to recounting tales of her life with the Prophet, and perhaps a quarter of all the Sharia derives from sayings dictated by Aisha bint Abi Bakr.

Those who were opposed to Ali needed a new claimant on whom to fasten their ambitions. They settled on a relative of Uthman, a man called Mu'awiyah. The prospective Khalifah was an Umayyad, a member of an aristocratic family who were kin to the Prophet. However the Umayyads had fought fiercely against Islam before belatedly converting. The Fitna was now a civil war between the traditional ruling class of Arabia, and the surviving Companions, who claimed their status from their early conversion.

The final clash of the First Fitna was the Battle of Siffin. There, amid scenes of escalating chaos, the two forces skirmished ineffectually, sat down at parley, and finally agreed to submit the matter to arbitration.

This extraordinary outcome was Ali's worst and greatest moment. The gentle Khalifah preferred to have wise men arguing over his right to power, rather than warriors fighting over it. In making this choice he had saved the lives of thousands but condemned himself to death. Many of his followers believed that Islam had lost its way, that wealth and conquest had distracted its leaders from the true faith. They had taken Ali's side because they thought he would return Islam to its roots. His meek capitulation at Siffin disgusted them, and they marched off. They became known as the Kharijites, Those Who Walked Away.

And it was a Kharijite assassin that finally ended the life of

Ali ibn Abi Talib, three years later, striking him down with a poisoned sword during public prayers. You may believe the official story that it was a conspiracy aimed at simultaneously wiping out all potential leaders of Islam, and that only the attempt on Ali succeeded. You may believe, if you have been paying attention, that there were other parties which might have had an interest in the death of the Prophet's cousin.

Either way, the next Khalifah was Mu'awiyah of the Ummayyads. His family were accustomed to authority, and knew how to hang onto power. To give them their due, they also knew how to run an empire. The Land of Islam stabilised and grew fat, even as those first four Successors, Abu Bakr, Umar, Uthman and Ali, were remembered as al-Rashidun, the Righteous Ones. But the Alids, the descendants of Ali, live on, and as long as there is a wild-eyed fundamentalist, or a sharp-eyed politician, in the Holy Lands, the regime will always be at risk from the Shi'ites.

* * *

"But Harun al-Rashid is of the family of the Abbasids, not the Ummayyads."

"Good lad. You have been paying attention after all. But that is a story for another day. You look exhausted. If you ask the household servants they will bring you food."

"Thank you. Might I know the name of the man who has shown me such kindness?"

"My name is al-Mithaq. Yaqub al-Mithaq. I will see you here again. But in the meantime, take care around the Father of Locks."

Seven

The Tale of the Visitors

"I hope this lateness is not a habit with you. I have been waiting for almost an hour."

Rest had given Abu Nuwas back his brazen swagger. In fact I had seen him arrive only moments before I got to the Watch House, and immediately begin pacing up and down with exaggerated impatience. He was now more respectably dressed, wearing a green turban and a matching robe, although his black locks snaked intractably out from underneath his headdress.

It was true that I was late. After talking to al-Mithaq, my head buzzed like a bee-hive with so many thoughts that I thought I would never sleep. However exhaustion must have taken its toll, because the next instant I was woken by the wailing of the call to prayer, from the minaret of the masjid that adjoined the palace. I found waiting for me a fresh set of clothes, plain and worn but clean and respectable, a bread roll and a cup of water.

There was also a small brass key. It unlocked a door in the corner of the room, and a second door at the end of a long corridor which opened onto the street. Obviously this was to permit members of the Barid to come and go without the knowledge of the household servants; although I guessed that unseen eyes scrutinised everybody using the private entrance.

Finding my way out of the Barmakid's palace was the easy part. Disorientated by my nocturnal meanderings, I made the mistake of crossing the Tigris by the same bridge as the night before. This meant that I had to pass through Harbiya and walk three quarters of the way around the walls of the Round

City before I arrived in Sharqiya, an impoverished neigh-bourhood east of Karkh.

I decided not to argue with my new master, but instead led the way into the Watch House. This was little more than a single room providing shade from the heat of the sun, although at the rear was a row of doors leading, no doubt, to cells. At the centre of the room were three thickset men, squatting on their haunches. They wore identical blue robes, although their garments were grubby and moth-eaten. A heavy truncheon lay on the floor by each of them.

"Good afternoon, gentlemen! Would you tell us where we might find your captain?"

The men glanced up grudgingly, and one of them grunted: "Out."

His mate nudged him, and our informant turned his attention to the fistful of arrow shafts being waved at him. He selected one with the appearance of profound thought, examined it quickly and threw it to the ground cursing. The remaining arrows were proffered to the remaining police-man. He seemed much happier with his choice, yelling and scooping up a handful of copper coins from the floor.

I looked at Abu Nuwas, who was smiling cruelly, turquoise eyes glittering. Unfortunately, even on our brief acquaintance I already knew him well enough to guess what this meant. I realised, to my horror, that he was about to say something provocative, perhaps involving the policemen tugging his shaft, and that violence would probably ensue. Now I understood what al-Mithaq had been trying to tell me, about how quickly the Father of Locks wore out his hobbles.

Just as he opened his mouth to speak, we were interrupted by a bellow from the doorway.

"What have I told you miserable scum about gambling on duty?"

I was surprised to see that the booming voice came from a short figure in the doorway. Although stocky, the newcomer was no taller than me. He wore the same blue garments as the gamblers, but his were neater.

He bustled into the room, kicking the behinds of the bigger

men as they gathered up their truncheons and scurried out onto the street. Any one of them could have floored him, let alone three together, but they allowed him to scold them as if they were naughty schoolboys. When they had gone, he faced us, breathing heavily from his exertions.

"You're the men the Wazir has sent? You're not what I was hoping for. Frankly, I'm rather disappointed."

The crazed look had left my master's face, and he responded to this dispiriting assessment with a low bow.

"I am Abu Nuwas of the Barid, and this is my servant Ismail al-Walid. Do I have the pleasure of addressing al-Takht, Captain of Police?"

It seemed we did indeed have that pleasure. Al-Takht was curt in his speech, although his methodical approach suggested a well-organised mind. I formed the impression that nature had given him little patience with fools, while society had cruelly decreed that he spend a great deal of time in their company. Consequently he lived most of his life in a state of simmering annoyance.

Our arrival did little to lighten his habitual distemper. The look of glum resignation on his face, as he contemplated the lisping fop and the scrawny white boy before him, was eloquent. More articulate than any scholar, it adduced our arrival as the final, conclusive evidence of his theory, that the universe had been constructed purely to vex him. He sighed.

"Come on, I'll take you there."

We could probably have found the street where the fire had raged, even without the Police Captain's help. A sooty smog still hung gloomily over the place, and the stench of smoke was heavy in the air. The mud brick walls of the ruined houses remained standing, although they were scorched black and sodden from the water used to extinguish the blaze. Their roofs had collapsed, however, the timbers burned through, and the wooden doors and shutters had been incinerated. Through windows that gaped like the eyeholes of a skull, we could see that the houses were gutted to their bones.

"The hooded man stood over there."

Al-Takht indicated a spot across the street.

"When the old woman approached him, he hurled the firebolt – or whatever it was – at this building in the middle. The blaze soon spread to the neighbouring houses. Fortunately the building was empty, and nobody was hurt."

"Could it have been a flask of oil?"

Al-Takht looked wearily at my master.

"Have you never knocked over an oil lamp by accident? Or thrown one in anger? A small quantity of oil could not have caused this devastation. Besides, it would need to have been already lit. If the stranger had been carrying a burning lamp in daylight, somebody would surely have remarked on it."

Abu Nuwas nodded in acknowledgement.

"Who lived in the house?"

"A dyer and his family. Only been here a year – went back to their village last month, couldn't get enough work in the city. House has been unoccupied since."

"So there would seem to be no purpose to the arson?"

"Unless to cover the stranger's escape. Or for sheer love of destruction."

We examined the damaged buildings. Usually fire needs to grow stealthily, before it dares to rage. Yet this conflagration had blossomed in an instant, watched by a street full of witnesses. Its ferocity must have been terrifying; no wonder the locals were willing to believe in a supernatural explanation.

"Is the man deaded?"

Our examination was interrupted by a small boy, four years old at most. His accent was coarse, but he stood fearlessly in front of us, eyes intense and bright, and repeated his question.

"Is the man deaded?"

Abu Nuwas seemed nonplussed by the child's boldness.

"What man?"

"Is the man deaded?"

The boy's face had the earnest gravity of the very young. My master tried to assert his superiority.

"Do you even know what that means, child?"

"Yes I do. Deaded is when you go to sleep and you don't wake up. Then everybody cries and washes you and puts you in a hole. My granny is deaded."

He finished proudly, as if inviting us to admire his granny's achievement. Al-Takht was impassive, although I thought I detected a glint of amusement in his eye. Abu Nuwas tried to rid himself of his interrogator.

"No, child, the man is not deaded – dead."

"Why?"

Like a cunning general the boy had switched his line of attack, causing consternation in his foe.

"Well . . . Because he wasn't there."

"Why?"

"Because he went away."

"Why?"

"Because he couldn't make enough money."

"Why?"

"Because there are too many dyers in Baghdad – in the name of God the Infinitely Patient, I don't know!"

The bright eyes were implacable.

"Why?"

Abu Nuwas clearly had no experience of dealing with small children. Much as I was enjoying his discomfort, I decided to come to his rescue.

"Because a magic horse with wings made of gold and silver flew down and carried him away, back to his family, so that he was safe from the fire."

The boy pondered this explanation for some time, before a solemn blink indicated that he deemed it satisfactory. He turned back to Abu Nuwas.

"Is the lady deaded?"

"Ahmad! Leave the gentlemen alone."

The man who bounded across to us was bow-legged and long-armed, and hairy as an ape. He swept up the child with a single huge hand. The boy Ahmad giggled, and although the man chided him his pride and love were evident. Al-Takht greeted the ape-man familiarly.

"Peace, friend Ghassan. Your boy was just browbeating an agent of the Wazir."

Ghassan laughed.

"An agent? Some day Ahmad will be Wazir himself. Don't

believe those old crows, like Umm Dabbah, who tell you the son of a Porter cannot rise to the top! Ahmad is cleverer and braver than all of their sons put together. You have heard of the Chamberlain, ibn Rabi, the most important man in Baghdad after the Wazir? His grandfather was a slave who tended a water-wheel."

Al-Takht had been smiling at the ape-man's words, but now he grew serious again.

"It is Umm Dabbah we need to see. Where might we find her?"

Ghassan the Porter waved a hand northwards, and we took our leave. The Police Captain explained.

"Umm Dabbah is the widow who spoke to the stranger. She lives alone – there was a son, but he went off to fight as a mercenary in al-Andalus, and never came home. She's an evil-minded old busybody, but the women look up to her, because of her skill with cosmetics.

"She is always spreading stories of one kind or another. If I had her account alone of the apparition, then I would never have troubled my masters. But several people saw the hooded man. And you have seen for yourselves the devastation he caused. Whatever he is, he is a threat to my city – to my neighbourhood – to my Sharqiya."

We heard Umm Dabbah before we saw her. She was sitting by a well holding forth to a group of women.

"So they snatch children, and carry them off to their temple. There they cut the poor little things' throat. As the blood drips down they catch the precious drops in a bottle. Some of it they drink themselves, then they carve the Afrit's name on a tablet. It's the name that summons the Afrit, see, and the smell of children's blood lures it into the bottle. Once it's in the bottle, gorging itself on the blood, they put the stopper in. Then it can't get out, see, and they make it obey their evil commands . . ."

She trailed off as she saw us approach. She was a large woman, dominating the group as much by her bulk as with her strident voice.

"Who does, Umm Dabbah? Who does these terrible things?"

She peered at the policeman suspiciously. The eyes above her veil were tiny for her size.

"You know, al-Takht. You and all the authorities, but you won't admit it. You hide their crimes, and deny their guilt. But I know. I've worked at the palace, you know, and seen all kinds of things."

"Whose crimes, woman? I am friend to no criminal."

Despite being only a few feet apart, they were bellowing, as though they could convince each other by the loudness of their voice. The effect was rather exhausting.

"You know who, al-Takht. Witches, that's who."

Abu Nuwas gave an involuntary snort of derision. The woman turned on him.

"And who are you, coming round here laughing at respectable women? You have the look of one of them. Is that how it is, al-Takht? Does a warlock have to follow you round, now, to make sure you keep their filthy secrets?"

The Police Captain was bubbling like a vat of boiling oil, but managed to keep from exploding.

"This man is the representative of the Wazir, minister of state to the Commander of the Faithful. And I have never turned my back on a crime, not for money, nor for religion, nor for politics; nor even for friendship. So if you would be so kind, Umm Dabbah, then the Khalifah Harun al-Rashid, in the person of his properly delegated agents, would like you to tell us about the man that you saw."

She gazed at him for a moment, and her veil moved as if she was chewing. Then:

"He was tall, but sort of stooped. Like he used to be a soldier, but now he carries a great burden. He stood there by the well, wearing a hood that concealed his face.

"Nobody comes round here, unless they have kin in the neighbourhood. I thought he must be looking for someone, so I went up to him. I know everybody round here. First thing I noticed was his eyes. Big, bulging things they were, pointing in different directions. And his skin – it was black. Not dark like a man of Aksum or Sind, but pure black, like nobody I've ever seen.

"I asked him who he was. He looked at me as if from a thousand miles away, and said:

" 'I am the Father of Bitterness.'

"He brought his hand down, and sparks of red burst from his fingers. The dyer's house erupted into flame, as if it was a gateway to Jahannum. The neighbours threw buckets of water, but it only made the blaze worse.

"And when we looked round, the hooded man had vanished."

Umm Dabbah's mouth kept moving, although she stopped talking and stared intently at al-Takht, waiting for his response to her story. The other women watched too. Finally, the policeman spoke.

"So if witches are summoning a Jinn, why does the Devil appear?"

The heads of the women swung round to see how the widow would respond. She got to her feet, slowly and with dignity.

"You may mock me, Nasr ibn Nasr al-Takht, Captain of Police. Just because you can read and write, you may sneer at me as an ignorant gossip. But evil attracts evil, as any woman can tell you. And Iblis is of that kind, the Jinni, the Afarit, as anyone of learning could tell you. And your mother, may God the All-Merciful forgive her sins, would have slapped you round the ears for treating me in such a way. And she would never have looked down on a respectable woman like me, so be careful how you talk to me, Captain of Police."

There was a pause and she seemed to be finished, but Umm Dabbah turned once more to administer the killer blow.

"And if you want proof that children are being stolen by witches, you need only go to Karkh, and talk to the merchant Imran ibn Zaid. Ask him what has happened to his little girl, who disappeared from his own house. Ask him where his daughter is, Captain of Police, before you impute dishonesty to a poor widow."

Al-Takht was so choked by fury that he could not speak. I guessed that the references to his mother touched on a long-buried shame. Umm Dabbah sat back, with a satisfied air. Abu Nuwas, however, stepped forward.

"Thank you for your aid, Umm Dabbah. But poor widows who accuse others of witchcraft would do well to avoid practising it themselves – even for their own protection."

It was Umm Dabbah's turn to look aghast. As we left she bent towards the other women, speaking in hushed tones and with frequent glances at our departing backs. No doubt the mysterious strangers, sent by the Wazir, were being woven into her conspiracy. Al-Takht had recovered his composure enough to recommence grumbling.

"Now she truly will believe you are a sorcerer."

"How did you know she was using magic?"

Abu Nuwas tried to act stern with me, but was clearly pleased that I had asked.

"Really, boy, you must learn to use your senses, or your career in the Barid will be painfully brief. She reeked of frankincense. What would she have been using it for but to purify talismans against evil spirits?"

"Perhaps that is why she claimed the stranger was the Devil, so she could sell amulets to her neighbours."

Both the men seemed surprised by the simplicity of my suggestion, but al-Takht shook his head.

"Umm Dabbah has lived in this neighbourhood as long as there has been a neighbourhood here to live in, and has never stopped interfering in other people's business. Some day she'll get her tongue cut out. But she does not have the imagination to invent a conversation with the Devil. If I know her at all, she is telling the truth, at least as far as she understands it. If I know her at all, she is frightened."

Abu Nuwas and I exchanged a glance. It spoke of shared amusement at the policeman's eccentricities, but also an acknowledgement that his word carried weight. What struck me most, though, was that for the first time the poet had looked at me as an equal. Now he addressed me directly.

"Well, boy, we have the scent of our quarry now. And it seems the trail leads to Karkh."

Al-Takht decided to accompany us. Despite his affected

acerbity his curiosity must have been aroused. Abu Nuwas, on the other hand, was suspiciously quiet and serious as we walked slowly westward. I wondered whether his belligerence was the product of boredom, and contempt for the slow wits of those around him. The challenge of the Wazir's mission gave him something to gnaw at, like a dog with a bone.

My thoughts were interrupted by shouts from ahead. We turned a corner to find crowds lining the street, jostling to see something further down the road. The policeman forced his way through the mob with his club, muttering about idiots with nothing better to do than stand around gawking. However the onlookers closed ranks behind him, and Abu Nuwas and I were left stranded.

The lanky poet stretched his neck in a bid to find out what was causing the commotion. All I could see was the backs of the malodorous throng. I was determined not to miss out, and scrambled up the wall of a low building behind me. Hands reached out to grab me as I neared the top, and pulled me up onto the roof where a rabble of ragamuffins already sat, swinging their legs against the wall. I looked down – then I understood what Yahya the Barmakid meant about visitors.

A procession was working its way down the street. Black-robed Guardsmen were clearing a path, making enthusiastic use of their long cudgels, but it was not the Khalifah who had drawn the spectators. Nor was it any of his household, nor his ministers or family. They were neither Arabs nor Persians, the men parading toward the Kufah Gate, but instead beings so strange to the ordinary citizens of Baghdad that they might as well have come from the moon.

They were mostly bare headed, and wore strange clothes, long garments of unfamiliar cut and hue. And they were white, the first people I had seen of my own colour since passing through the Straits of Gibel Tariq. At the head of the train were two men in grey robes. The top of their heads was shaved, so that their hair grew in a ring like a crown. One carried a cross, the other a red banner that hung down to three jagged points. Stitched onto it was a depiction of a flaming yellow sun, dripping tears of flame down the cloth.

Behind them walked a man in magnificent vestments of white and gold. He seemed to be the focus of the procession. His importance was underlined by the servants on either side of him, who carried a silk canopy on sticks to shield him from the sun. He wore a peculiar hat shaped like a diamond, and carried a long stick similar to a shepherd's crook, except that it was tipped with silver.

After this spectacle came the animals. A number of horses with embroidered caparisons must have been the transport which conveyed the moon-men to Baghdad. There were also mules and donkeys with packs and saddle bags, attended by Arab servants.

The strangest sight of all came at the rear of the train, where three figures walked behind the baggage. One was a beardless man in black robes. The whole front of his head was shaved, but the back was left to grow long, and hung a span below his shoulders. Beside him was a giant, taller than Abu Nuwas and with a bulk to match. This ogre had a red beard, and his hair was of the same hue where it stuck out from his round helmet. He carried an enormous double-headed axe, and the gasps from the crowd were audible as he passed.

It was the third figure that held my gaze, however. She was female, and young, and wore a long green dress but no veil. Her hair, cropped short, was the colour of wheat at harvest time, and her eyes the colour of the sea in spring. Her face, naked to the stares of the whole city, was a soft oval with plump, pale lips. If you asked me to guess her age, I would have thought it to be about the same as my own. If you asked me to guess what she was thinking, as she walked between the shouts and speculation of the Baghdad mob, I could not have told you, for her face revealed nothing.

The boy next to me pointed at her and made some gibe about her needing no veil because she was a freak; there was no risk of anybody lusting after her. He noticed my own white skin just as I smacked him round the back of the head, toppling him from the roof. The boy, who himself had a blotchy birthmark on his cheek, picked himself up from the dirt and hurled a stone at me, but I dodged it absent-mindedly and stared transfixed at the retreating back of the wheat-haired vision.

It was not love, or even lust, that drew my gaze toward her. Rather I admired her beauty as one might admire the stars on a summer night, or rose tinted clouds at sunset. I never dreamed of touching her, but could have sat looking at her for days, and would have gone without food and water to do so.

I was shaken from my reverie by a shout from below.

"Put your eyes back in their sockets, boy, you're going to need them."

Abu Nuwas stood below. The crowd was dispersing, and he had managed to find al-Takht. I jumped down from the roof, and my stone-throwing adversary scurried off when he saw me with a policeman.

"Who were those people?"

Again, it was al-Takht, not Abu Nuwas, that answered my question.

"They've been waiting outside the city for a week while we made arrangements for their arrival. Kept it secret though. You can see the reaction they provoked. Imagine what it would have been like if the mob had had time to get themselves worked up. Those people were the ambassadors of Karlo, King of the Franks: the man who would be Emperor of the West."

Eight

The Tale of the Deserted Camp

The house of the merchant Imran ibn Zaid was a marked contrast to the hovels of Sharqiya. It stood south of the suqs, on an avenue of ostentatious mansions. Even in such grand company, it refused to be outdone. The long façade was lavishly decorated, and quotations from the Quran were painted over the door.

We were admitted to a courtyard, where the harsh-faced, red-nosed merchant sat under a canopy sipping sherbet. Beside him a slave girl wafted a large fan of cloth soaked in water. However we were offered no such comforts. The three of us stood in the blazing afternoon sun, while Imran ibn Zaid addressed us imperiously.

"Who sent you?"

Abu Nuwas allowed al-Takht to answer.

"The Wazir, sir. We understand your daughter has gone missing."

"That is none of your business! It is a private matter within my household. I asked for no interference from the City Police. Some foolish slave must have reported it without my permission."

I noticed a woman standing behind the merchant, in the shade of the portico. She watched our faces as he spoke, her dark eyes above her veil brightened by quick understanding. Al-Takht persisted with his questioning.

"With respect, sir, if the child has been abducted . . ."

"Abducted? Who told you that? Nobody could have got into or out of this house to take her. Do you take me for a man who cannot protect his huram? My daughter was last seen in this house, and by God she must still be here

100

somewhere. I'll beat it out of the slaves, sooner or later. Now get out."

And that was the end of our audience with the merchant. Abu Nuwas had not uttered a word, but his gaze darted around the courtyard, as if committing it to memory. We were escorted politely but inexorably to the door, which banged shut behind us.

"I wonder what that was all about?"

Al-Takht pondered the poet's question.

"He's guilty of something. I don't believe it has anything to do with his daughter, but there's something in his house he doesn't want us to find? Oh, well – we can't go breaking down the doors of wealthy men, especially when he is the victim. Besides, we have no reason to believe this has anything to do with the hooded stranger. Come on, it's a long walk back to Sharqiya."

Before we reached the end of the avenue I heard the sound of bare feet running towards us. I turned to see a female figure chasing us down the road. As she approached, I recognised the deep brown eyes of the woman from the courtyard.

"Stop! Wait! I need to talk to you . . ."

The poet and the policeman watched expectantly while she recovered her breath. When she spoke, her voice was like cool rain at the end of a drought.

"My name is Layla bint al-Bazza. I sell fabrics – I have a little shop near the Basrah gate. Ibn Zaid's wife is one of my best customers. I am often at their house. I was there the day the little girl disappeared."

Al-Takht nodded, and Abu Nuwas said:

"Tell us what happened."

"It has been ten days now. She was playing in the courtyard of the women's quarters. There should be no safer place! The nurse was watching over her, but had to go to pass water. When she returned, the child was gone.

"The doors of the house were locked. Even if anyone had got in, they would have to pass through the main courtyard; somebody would have seen them.

"The girl is called Najiba. She is six years old, but small for

101

her age. She always greeted me merrily, with a 'Peace be upon you, Layla,' and some new song or jest she had learnt. I must go now. If the merchant knows I am speaking to you, he will be angry, and I will be barred from his house. But if there is anything I can do to help Najiba, I will do it."

"We will find the girl, Layla bint al-Bazza, I give you my word."

The girl and both men turned to stare at me when I blurted this out. Then I could see from her eyes that she was smiling.

"Thank you. I believe you will."

She was about to go, then said:

"One more thing you might need to know. There was a man hanging around the house, for a couple of days before. An old man, with skin as black as night, and strange eyes that seem to look all around you. Thought it might be useful."

With that she raced off back to the house. I could see the shape of her long, strong legs through her robe as she ran, and found myself hoping destiny would lead me to the shop at the Basrah Gate. Al-Takht stroked his beard thoughtfully.

"So the Father of Bitterness has been here, after all. Still, the merchant did not want any help from the police, and chasing demons is your job, not mine. So if you have no further need for me, I shall return to Sharqiya. And if Abu Murra wishes to cause any mischief there, he will have to get past me first."

He stomped off. Abu Nuwas was smiling, but this time I did not share his amusement. The policeman's mention of the Father of Bitterness, Abu Murra, had reminded me where I had first encountered the phrase.

"Master, I overheard something at the Garden of Delight that might be important. Thomas the Syrian was talking to another man, who was hiding in a room there. The other man was angry with the Syrian, accusing him of trickery. And Thomas said, 'Have no fear. Abu Murra has the Bottle. If you have the Name, you can unleash the power of the Fire.' "

I did not know whether he would mock me, or take me seriously. Nor did I know which would be more frightening. His face revealed nothing.

"I see. And you believe this is relevant, because . . .?"

Suddenly I found my teeth rattling against each other, and I could not speak. Abu Nuwas answered his own question.

"Because it reminds you of the stories of Umm Dabbah, of tales of murder and human sacrifice. Of spirits of fire called Afarit, evil Jinni who can be enslaved, and made to grant wishes. Of the rituals used to summon and bind these spirits. Rituals which use the blood of children . . ."

I knew there were others around, but the street felt cold and empty. The words of the old woman pounded in my ears. The Name, by which the Afrit is invoked and controlled. The Bottle, within which it is imprisoned. I tried to shake the chill from my skin.

"But master, surely you are not giving credence to the foolish talk of an old gossip? Spells, Jinni, wishes – this is the stuff of children's stories."

"You call the Jinni children's stories, boy? Are you disputing the truth of the Quran? The holy book teaches us that God created the Jinni from smokeless fire, that they will be saved or damned on the Day of Judgement just like men. The seventy-second Surah is named for them. King Sulayman, we are told, was given Jinni to serve him, and they built him shrines and statues and fetched treasures from the deep sea –"

"Hey, Abu Ali!"

A man calling from horseback interrupted him, causing me to jump.

"I've chased halfway round the city looking for you, you elusive devil."

The man leaned forward in his saddle, and I saw that it was Abu'l-Atahiyya, the pudgy poet I had met at the monastery. His breathless shout seemed to break the enchantment, and the street came back to life around us.

"I have been sent to tell you that Ibrahim ibn Mahdi is ten years old today. You had best be at Blissful Eternity by sundown, in your finest garments. Bring the gosling!"

He clopped away, and I saw that Abu Nuwas was gritting his teeth.

"Bad news, master?"

He sighed.

"Ibrahim ibn Mahdi is the little brother of our beloved Khalifah. His birthday will be the cause of great feasting and celebration. And I will be expected to be there, being witty, improvising verses, and acting scandalously without causing an actual scandal. It will be such hard work."

"But, master . . . is that not how you make a living?"

"Indeed, boy. And those that want to see me suffer for my sins might reflect that the punishment sometimes precedes the crime. Of course it will be a marvellous opportunity for advancement. One smart remark tonight could make me rich; although I hope he doesn't want to fill my mouth with gold coins again. It's undignified and uncomfortable, but you have to pretend to be terribly grateful.

"On the other hand, though, one smart remark might also lose me my head. It is a coincidence, is it not, that this happy event comes at the same time as the Frankish embassy? Al-Rashid is making a point. We can only hope he is playing munificent monarch, not ruthless despot. God the all-merciful save us from the whims of princes!"

"And what about the Devil?"

"The Devil will have to wait, since royalty has come calling. To be frank, I find Iblis considerably less frightening than Harun the Righteous. Now, we must try to prepare you for the feast."

I had visions of being marinaded and roasted, but it transpired that I had only to be washed and dressed in more appropriate clothing, and we set out for a bath house in Rusafah. I was glad to have been invited to the feast. This was less because I was curious to meet the rulers of the civilised world, than because I was ravenously hungry.

After the Abbey of St Pachomius I was wary of visiting a bath house with the poet, but the hammam to which he led me was a respectable one, in a fashionable part of town. The water was hot, the steam dense, and it was pleasant to sweat and scrub the dust of the road from my body.

In the cool room we met again the poets Abbas and Abu'l-Atahiyya, also preparing for the feast. They sat amid a gang of aristocratic young men, who shouted abuse and scraps of verse at each other. I noticed that wine was being served, discreetly but illegally. There was also a boy of around my age, who simpered and giggled at all the men's jokes. Abu Nuwas sat near him, throwing him glances and outrageous compliments, causing him to bat his eyelids shamelessly. I was nauseated and oddly a little jealous.

Everybody knew the Father of Locks, and everybody deferred to him. Even in the company of the other distinguished poets, he was the undisputed pack leader. It was not only his entourage who seemed to collude in his self-importance; the bath boys, waiters and scrubbers fawned on him, neglecting the princelings and plutocrats, and other patrons pointed and whispered when he passed.

I watched Abu Nuwas borrow money from one of the youths to pay for our bath, and wondered what had happened to the Wazir's gift. My master, it appeared, was penniless again. How he had managed to blow the remainder of a thousand dinars in the few hours that we had been apart was mystifying. It was more money than Ghassan the Porter would see if he lived as long as Methuselah. I guessed the poet's creditors were many, and swooped like magpies at the first flash of gold.

I sat quietly listening to the aristocrats trying to impress Abu Nuwas while we waited for clothes to be delivered. One young man, giddy with forbidden drink, called out a teasing couplet.

"The Father of Locks becomes truly perverse
    First Christians, now white boys, his taste just gets worse."

My master's response was immediate.

"Don't give Abu Ayyub more wine
    He never knows when he's crossed the line.
In his cups he'd swap his best racehorse
    For that stinky old donkey of mine."

In the laughter that followed I hardly heard what

105

Abu'l-Atahiyya said, and it was only when all eyes turned to me that the full horror of his words sank in.

"Your gosling writes poetry, doesn't he, Abu Ali? He must recite some for us."

I looked pleadingly at Abu Nuwas, hoping he would spare me. Instead he smiled wickedly.

"Yes, Newborn, give us a few lines."

Reluctant as I was to be at the centre of their circle, I reflected that if I wished to be considered a poet, I would have to expose my endeavours at some point. I took some deep breaths and decided that I might as well commit myself wholly. I launched into the prelude to a qasida, the most prestigious form in Arabic verse:

> "Wait, friends, I know this place, I swear –
>   Stay your horses, let us tarry here.
> This is where we camped, so long ago;
>   Now the dust of the desert has scoured it bare.
> The firepits now stand cold and black,
>   In the place where I held my love so dear.
> Just as our love now burns no more
>   And chills with every passing year . . ."

I trailed off. They were sitting in silence, some with open mouths. For a moment I feared that they were appalled by the drivel I was uttering. Then Abu'l-Atahiyya, the chubby Father of Madness, spoke.

"Well, technically it is impeccable. Is it truly your own, boy?"

A few heads nodded. I realised that their astonishment had nothing to do with the quality of my poetry. Seeing my white skin, they viewed me as some kind of dancing bear, and were amazed that I could achieve mere competence. Most, however, looked to Abu Nuwas, waiting for his verdict to guide their opinion. He stared upwards for a long time, as if he was finding his speeches written on the ceiling.

"Not bad at all. I suppose you have at least seen a campfire, not like our friend the Seller of Jugs."

Abu'l-Atahiyya gave a sickly smile, but his face paled, and I understood that these jibes really hurt him. The Father of Locks pressed on, heedlessly.

"But you write what you think you should, not what you feel you must. Form should be the midwife to creation, not an infanticide strangling it at birth. What are the three movements of the qasida, Newborn?"

I answered with some defiance. This was schoolboy stuff.

"The nasib, the prelude, where the poet laments the loss of past love, usually symbolised by an abandoned encampment. The rahil, the theme, where the poet exults in the nomadic life, describing at length the admirable qualities of his mount, his horse or camel. The madih, the panegyric, where the poet praises his tribe or his patron."

"And you know that, and I know that, and anybody whom it is worth your while addressing knows that. Leave it to be known, and it is one less thing you need to say. The qasida was developed by the Jahili, the Arabs of the desert in the days of ignorance, before the coming of the Prophet. It spoke of what was important to them. Now, its value lies in what is shared, and goes unspoken.

"Observe the metalworker who makes his model in soft wax, and builds his mould around it. When the mould is complete, the wax is burned away, and replaced by molten gold. So let the forms of the ancients be to you. When I told my old teacher Khalaf al-Amar that I wanted to write, he told me that I had to memorise one thousand poems of the Jahili first. Six months later I informed him that I had done it. 'Very good,' he said, 'now forget them again.' "

"Then let us hear a qasida of yours, Father of Locks, so that we can learn how it should be done."

There was a stunned hush at my impertinence. Abu Nuwas unleashed a piercing glare, although I sensed he was not displeased.

"Very well then, Teller of Tales. I shall give you a qasida of mine."

When Abu Nuwas recited his own verse, I understood how skilfully Ibrahim al-Mosuli had used music to capture the cadences of his voice. I immediately recognised the sinuous melody of his lines, the teasing lilt. However the poet's performance had a depth and complexity that the musician had missed. The words of his qasida echoed around the dripping stone of the cool room.

> "Sit down in the dirt where the camp once lay
>   The traces now whispered away
> Ill-fated stars turned the fire we shared
>   Into dust with which zephyrs play.
> I have unclasped the necklace of lust –
>   Just one glass, warmed by morning sun's ray –
> Perfect pearls on a thread of fine words
>   The bubbles soar skyward. They
> Are too delicate to be touched or felt
>   And like dust, they drift away.
> The boy hid his charms beneath sacred robes
>   Like a bride on her wedding day
> So sweetly he sings of the wine he brings
>   Shaitan must possess him, we say.
> A saint, had there been one among us
>   Would for love have been tempted astray."

Much as I wanted to dislike him, I had to admit it was dazzling. The shocking twists of phrase, both honouring and mocking the traditional form, said more in a few lines than other poems five times its length. I wondered whether I would have to admit defeat to him publicly. Then one of the aristocrats, mimicking the enraptured look on the poet's face, let out a long, slow, noisy fart, and the tension collapsed into laughter.

I was glad to slink back to the shadows, but Abu Nuwas leaned towards me.

"Still, boy, yours was good, of its kind."

I nodded gravely, and accepted the compliment. After all, it had not escaped my attention that after hearing my verse, he had not called me Newborn, but addressed me by the name I had earned for myself, in my years of wandering: al-Rawiya, the Teller of Tales.

Nine

The Tale of the Khalifah's Feast, which includes, The Tale of the Poet and the Three Boys, and, The Tale of the Horn of Hruodland

Al-Khuld, The Palace of Blissful Eternity, was Harun al-Rashid's preferred residence in Baghdad. The Gilded Gate, built by his austere grandfather, had too much of duty and too little of pleasure in its design for any of al-Mansur's successors. Blissful Eternity lounged along the riverbank, between the City of Peace and the Tigris, away from the stink and striving of the general populace. The river gate, leading to an enclosed private marina, allowed for graceful arrival; and, when the city became too much, for discreet escape.

While the noble guests drifted in by water, Abu Nuwas and I walked the short distance from the hammam. The expensive clothes he had ordered for me were uncomfortable, and I itched with embarrassment too. As we were leaving the baths a slave had brought a small basin of scented water. I was about to drink it, when Abu Nuwas intervened, showing me how to dab it on my skin. I could still hear the snickers of the young men.

I was therefore eager to distract the poet from my humiliation, but also genuinely troubled by something he had casually let slip.

"Master, you said one smart remark might cost your head. Are you really in danger tonight?"

"Do not underestimate the power of poetry, boy. Every line spoken or published is a political act. Words have the power to sway men's hearts, and minds; to make their progenitors wealthy, or dead. And poetry is the memory of the Arabs. The common people cannot read or write, but they can remember rhyme and verse, and pass it on to others. The Umayyads were no more decadent that the current regime, but they fell because they neglected their reputation. If you learn nothing else from me, learn this: what is important is not what actually happened, only what people think they remember happening.

"Those rich men, who pay Abu'l-Atahiyya to write verses in their praise; you think they do so purely from vanity? They hope to influence how they are viewed, both at court and in the suqs. Perhaps most of all, they hope to be thought of as great men, even long after their deaths. It was the Khalifah al-Mansur who built Baghdad, and laid the foundations for the current peace. But it is Harun al-Rashid about whom all the poetry is written. Who do you think will be remembered, in a hundred years time, or a thousand?

"And just as poetry can redeem, so it can condemn. There are hacks who live by writing satires about important men; and then make those important men pay, to ensure the verses about their vices are never published.

"Only a few years ago the poet Bashshar was beaten to death by the Khalifah's Guard, and his body thrown into the Tigris in a sack. Admittedly though that may not have been for anything he wrote. The horny old toad may have just fucked the wrong man's wife or daughter. And I myself came close to execution once, thanks to an ill-judged jest.

"It was a few years ago, when I was new to the city. The Khalifah took it upon himself to visit me late at night. This was particularly inconvenient as I had picked up three charming, if somewhat rough, boys from the back alleys of Harbiya. We had just finished dining and were getting down to dessert, as it were – no, I must tell you the story properly.

The Tale of the Poet and the Three Boys

It is a sad thing, to dine alone. Sadder still, when the fare is as fine as that which lay before me on the evening in question. I had not been long in Baghdad, but earlier that day I had met the young Khalifah for the first time. Harun's coronation feast was barely cold, and everyone was clamouring for an audience with him. However, Ja'far al-Barmaki got me my chance, in return for certain tasks which I had performed for him among the Badawi of the Empty Quarter.

The Khalifah was delighted by the freshness of my wit, and had rewarded me richly. I had been half starving since arriving in the city, and blew some of my new wealth on a fabulous meal, which I ordered cooked for me and brought to my apartment. Then I sat down, and looked at the meats and the breads and pies and the stews, and felt lonely.

I did not live in fashionable Zubaydiya, back then, but in a draughty hole in Harbiya. I wandered out onto the street, and I did not have to go far to receive offers of company, of many different kinds. As soon as I saw the three youths, though, I knew with whom I wanted to share my good fortune.

They were around your age, Newborn, and skulked sullenly by the bridge where the Sarat Canal cuts across Madinah Road. They did not speak to me, but looked at me with suspicion. When I offered them food and wine, though, their greedy eyes came to life.

They were mean spirited, and illiterate, and cared nothing for me, only for what I could give them. But also they were young, and lean, and hard, with clear skin and white teeth. I took them home with me.

It was a delightful repast. If they truly had not been with a man before, then they approached the novelty with considerable enthusiasm. I teased them with treats, demanding that clothes were shed and kisses given in exchange for each morsel. Eventually the food was forgotten, and we all four sprawled on a soft rug together.

The first was called Hakim, and he was the most eager of the boys. He could scarcely wait for me to undress him, and nipped at me hungrily. His zabb, when I freed it, was short and stubby, and burst out in joy as soon as I clasped it in my hand.

The second was Hakam. He did not push himself onto me,

but turned away coyly. From behind I drew down his pants to reveal wide hips and plump white buttocks like twin moons. I reached round, to find his snake was small and shy. When I pierced his hole, however, I entered with ease, and the serpent awakened and stretched, expressing pleasure in our union.

Hamid was the third. He neither sought nor fled my attentions, but stared at me from dark eyes that spat anger. I bowed my head humbly before his power and beauty, laying a trail of kisses along the ridges of his chest and stomach, until I came to a tall, proud member, which I worshipped with my tongue and my heart.

While thus engaged I was surprised to discover that Hakam had wriggled under me and taken my own zabb into his mouth, heedless of its recent plunge into his cave. Hakim, not wanting to be left out, set about applying his best efforts to my backside. And that was how we were disposed, when God's representative on earth walked in.

Harun had suffered one of his nocturnal glooms, and come in search of the droll poet who had given him such amusement earlier that day. My servant Iyas tried to turn him away, but who can deny the Khalifah? The Righteous One was not pleased by what he found.

"What is happening here?"

This was possibly the stupidest question I had ever heard.

"What is happening here, Commander of the Faithful, is beyond questions and beyond answers."

Fortunately for me, Harun, who is nothing if not capricious, decided to make a joke of the situation.

"Father of Locks, I shall have to appoint you my Minister for Pimps and Whores."

Unfortunately for me, I had drunk a great deal, and could not resist taking the joke too far.

"I gratefully accept the appointment, o Khalifah. In which capacity have you come to petition me? Are you pimp or whore?"

Harun's face darkened, and he stormed out without a word. The youths grabbed their clothes and scattered as Masrur the

Swordbearer loomed into view, accompanied by two Palace Guards. The Swordbearer is the Khalifah's personal bodyguard, a giant black man who is rarely far from his master's side.

I was dragged through the streets, naked as I was, towards the Gilded Gate. It was late, but there was no lack of spectators to jeer along the way. I had no idea what danger I was really in, but in fact the Khalifah had ordered Masrur to chop my head off once we reached the palace. If I had known that, I might not have given such a cheery response to Salam the Speckled One when he saw my plight, and therefore might not have lived to tell this tale.

"In the name of God, Abu Ali, what have you done?"

"Nothing, Speckled One. I showed the Khalifah my finest lay, and in return he has gifted me his finest robe."

As witticisms go, it was pretty weak, but it saved my life. Salam knew that I had worked for the Barid, and thought Ja'far might like to know I was in trouble. The Wazir hurried to the Khalifah to plead on my behalf. At first Harun was obdurate. It was only when Ja'far told him that I was still joking along the way to my execution, that he decided my value as entertainment was worth the occasional insolence. The reprieve came just as we arrived at the Gilded Gate.

I heard the messenger tell Masrur that the death sentence was repealed, and found myself shaking.

"Would you truly have killed me, Swordbearer, for a few ill-chosen words? I have done you no harm."

Masrur shrugged.

"I carry the Khalifah's sword as his right arm might do, and I obey him as the arm obeys the wishes of the heart. I bear you no ill will, poet, but does your hand argue with you when you use it to write your verses? No more would I question the orders of my master."

★ ★ ★

By now we were arriving at al-Khuld. I had been impressed by the mansion of the Barmakids, but compared to Blissful Eternity it was a mere hut. In a city where few buildings had even a second storey, the Khalifah's palace seemed to soar to neck–aching heights. Etiquette demanded that the Gilded Gate remain the tallest structure in the city, but the designer of al-Khuld had exaggerated its stature through cunning use of columns and terracing.

In some ways it resembled a fortress, its crenellated walls being studded with bastions and towers. However the structure was too delicate to withstand any assault. The stone and brick was carved to look as light as spun sugar, and painted in exuberant red and gold. The whole seemed both vast and ephemeral, like an illusory palace created by a Jinn in a story.

The gates through which we entered were high enough to ride in on horseback. They opened onto a paved yard, with stables to one side. From here silent attendants guided us to a long, torch-lit corridor, with black–clad Guardsmen standing at intervals along the walls.

The corridor led to a small garden, and here we were left in no doubt as to the importance Harun placed on impressing the western barbarians. At the centre of the garden was a tree, glittering in the moonlight. As we crossed the garden I realized that the trunk of the tree was made of silver, the rustling leaves of beaten gold, and plump gems hung like fruit from its branches. Two lions were tethered to the base of the tree, to deter anybody who considered plucking the precious drupes.

At the other end of the garden was the entrance to the Great Hall. Along either side of this cavernous space guests sat on intricately woven prayer mats, talking quietly. At the end a silk curtain hung across the room, separating us from the royal presence. As we walked through the centre of the hall I noticed the poets Abbas and Abu'l-Atahiyya. I also saw Ibrahim al-Mosuli, who was directing the musicians by waving his hands expressively. However there was no time to greet them, as the attendants ushered us toward the curtain.

Here we were met by a fat man with a harassed demeanour. I heard Abu Nuwas call him al-Fadl, and remembered al-Mithaq talking about the Wazir's brother. I decided to try out my courtly manners.

"It is an honour to meet you. I have already made the acquaintance of your distinguished family."

The fat man stared at me as if I were a slug in his salad. Abu Nuwas quickly came to my aid.

"You must forgive the boy, Chamberlain. He popped into existence from a magical window only yesterday, and is ignorant of the ways of the world."

Still looking askance at me, the fat man waddled off to see whether we were to be admitted. Abu Nuwas hissed to me:

"Idiot! That is not Fadl ibn Yahya, the Barmakid. That is the Chamberlain, Fadl ibn Rabi. You have just mistaken him for one of his greatest rivals, and doubtless offended him gravely. Two minutes at court, and you have made an enemy of one of the most powerful men in Baghdad. Smart work, boy, smart work."

I felt sick with anxiety. I had met so many people in the last two days I had no faith at all in my ability to remember who was who at court, even if my life depended on it – as apparently it did. The Chamberlain reappeared, and beckoned us through a gap in the curtain. On the other side we were stopped by a huge black man, who carried the biggest sword I had ever seen, a blade the length of my body and nearly as wide. He addressed Abu Nuwas in a voice that rumbled like thunder.

"Best behaviour tonight, Father of Locks. We have visitors."

Masrur the Swordbearer patted the poet's clothes, and then mine, as if knocking off dust. It took me a moment to realize he was checking for concealed weapons. Then he stepped aside, and finally we were in the presence of Harun the Righteous, Successor to the Prophet of God, the Khalifah ar-Rasul Allah.

The Khalifah sat cross-legged on a pile of expensive rugs. He was tall and elegant, with long limbs and slender hands. His face was surprisingly soft, with brown eyes, a small mouth, and chubby cheeks like those of an infant. However his eyes blazed with awareness of his power.

"Welcome, Father of Locks! What clever words do you have for me, to gladden my spirits on this happy day?"

Abu Nuwas fell to his knees and touched his forehead to the ground as if praying. I did the same, determined not to

115

make any more embarrassing, or possibly fatal, errors. Then he sat up, and stroked his beard as if thinking, although I am sure he had prepared the verses earlier.

> "Bounty and Beauty could not agree
>   And debated their claims over thee.
> Said Bounty, 'His right hand is mine,
>   For its giving so kindly and free.'
> Answered Beauty, 'Then I take his face,
>   For its elegance, form and symmetry.'
> They parted as friends once again,
>   Because each one had spoken so truly."

Harun al-Rashid clapped his hands.

"Very good! Then I had best not disappoint Bounty, by acting the miser when offered such generous praise."

He threw across a bag of gold, which, like the poet's verses, he must have had ready. The whole exchange had an almost ritualistic air about it.

"It's all nonsense, you know."

The interruption came from a young boy, sitting beside the Khalifah. I guessed him to be the little brother, Ibrahim ibn Mahdi. His childish voice aped the languid sophistication of the adults.

"It's all nonsense. My birthday was last month. We are only celebrating now because Harun wants to flaunt his magnificence to these Frankish apes."

He glanced jealously at me.

"I hate politics. I wish I was a poet, like you, Abu Ali."

Harun laughed indulgently at this, but an elderly woman sitting behind him tutted.

"What talk is this, from a prince of the House of Abbas? A poet? You might as well aspire to be a porter, or a street sweeper."

Abu Nuwas accepted this denigration of his calling gracefully, making a low bow.

"As ever, the Mother of Islam speaks good sense. You should take heed of your stepmother's words, little prince."

I looked at the old woman. Even I had heard of the famous al-Khayzuran, mother to the Khalifah, and an influential figure at court. Her hair was greying, but her face was still strong with the beauty for which she was legendary. She was thin, and nearly as tall as her son; her name meant "The Reed." She made to speak again, but a guttural voice intruded.

"No, let the boy be a poet! And while we're about it, turn al-Khuld into a brothel so the Commander of the Faithful can pimp his daughters and wives. Then we can abandon the pretence that there is any dignity left in this charade of a monarchy."

I could not believe that anyone would dare abuse the Khalifah's family with such crude mockery, and looked round to see where the voice was coming from. An extraordinary figure was stomping towards us. He was dwarfishly short; his head would only have come up to my waist. His thickset body was twisted and deformed, so that his back was hunched and he walked with difficulty. An angry, warty, black-bearded face adorned his head, which was of normal size but seemed disproportionately large for his stunted body.

I waited for the Khalifah to order his bodyguard to seize this vile intruder, but instead Harun seemed amused.

"Are we sunk so low, then, Buhlul? Is there no chance of redemption?"

"Poets! Musicians! Your grandfather would have had all these wittering fops castrated and sold into slavery. Then he would have sent the Christian pigs back to their so-called king without their heads. Now he was a *real* Khalifah . . ."

Harun shrugged in mock resignation.

"You see the burden that I have to bear, Abu Ali? Come to visit me tomorrow. We shall have a pleasant evening, without any of this tedious formality."

Abu Nuwas prostrated himself once more, then got up to leave. I gathered that the invitation also constituted a dismissal, and rose too. As we walked away, my master muttered to me.

"Is it necessary for me to warn you, never to talk in front of the Khalifah in the way that Buhlul does? As the court jester, he has licence to speak freely that is not granted to the rest of us. If you or I said such things, our deaths would be slow and extremely painful."

"I hear and I obey, master. I suppose the poor man deserves pity, being crippled like that."

"Oh, don't waste your sympathy on Buhlul! He has done very well for himself. And don't underestimate him either; he has the ear of the Khalifah, and while he may be a Fool, he is not an idiot."

Flunkies escorted us towards vacant seats in the main hall. Abu Nuwas continued my education.

"The bodyguard, Masrur, he's another one. He likes to pretend to be a bit slow, but he's as sharp as his sword, and Harun's man to the death. Watch yourself around him; he'll cut you in half without blinking if he thinks you're any kind of threat to his Khalifah. In fact, you'd best just keep your mouth shut until we're safely out of here."

We were placed by the Frankish delegation. As they were the guests of honour, I assumed this represented kudos for my master; indeed, I saw Abu'l-Atahiyya staring at us enviously from near the door. The Franks themselves had their own concerns. The two men in grey looked uncomfortable on their rugs, and the red haired giant would not sit at all, but stood against the wall scowling. I nearly fell over when I saw that the white girl squatted at his feet, still shamelessly unveiled and gazing around the room with open curiosity.

The leader of the embassy, the man who had worn the diamond-shaped hat, seemed at ease with his surroundings though, and soon engaged Abu Nuwas in conversation.

"I believe you are Abu Ali ibn Hani al-Hakami? They tell me you are a poet. I have some modest pretensions in that direction myself."

"I am he, my lord – but you have the advantage of me."

"My apologies. I am Angilbert, ambassador from the court of Karlo, King of the Franks."

"Your Arabic is excellent, my lord ambassador."

"You flatter me. I spent some time in Egypt in my youth. We are not all primitive peasants in the west, you know."

As they spoke Fadl ibn Rabi strutted towards us, looking

for a seat near the visitors. Abu Nuwas turned to me with a vicious grin.

"See, boy, how our friend the Chamberlain seeks the pleasure of your company once more . . ."

Angilbert raised an eyebrow.

"Is this young man, then, an intimate of the honourable ibn Rabi?"

"Indeed he is. Since the moment they met there has been a special bond between them."

My chagrin was brought to a merciful end when we were interrupted by slaves bringing golden basins of scented water. This time I did not try to drink it, but allowed them to pour it over my hands to cleanse them, as I saw them doing for the other guests. Abu Nuwas gave up teasing me, and continued to demonstrate that he could be not only diplomatic, but even charming when he chose to be; or had to be.

"I will confess, my lord ambassador, that a man of your taste and learning would come as something of a disappointment to the ignorant masses of Baghdad. They imagine all Franks to be savage troglodytes, little better than animals. Your friend here is much more what they would be expecting!"

He indicated the red haired man. The giant appeared oblivious to the discussion, but as I looked at him I realised with a shock that the white girl sitting at his feet was staring directly at me. Angilbert was amused by the poet's comments.

"Then I must disappoint you further. Gorm is not a Frank. He is a Rus, from the icy north. His people are celebrated warriors, and he helped keep us safe on our difficult journey."

The white girl had not dropped her eyes when I looked back at her, but held my gaze with a bold effrontery that would have marked her as a whore, had she been Muslim. At last we were interrupted by servants, finally bringing the promised feast. Since arriving in Baghdad I had eaten only a couple of apples and a bread roll, and I found it difficult not to drool openly at the wonders laid before us.

There were chickens roasted in saffron, and a stew of lamb with rice and tomatoes. There were stuffed vine leaves and marrows and eggplants. There were dishes of delicate black roe, pastries filled with sweet cheese and honey, and cakes of crushed sesame flavoured with orange and cinnamon. To drink, however, there was only clear, cold spring water; the Khalifah did not take wine in public.

I made myself eat sparingly, knowing from my years of wandering not to suddenly gorge an empty stomach with rich food. Besides, I was painfully aware of the stare of the yellow-haired girl, and did not wish to appear gluttonous in front of her. My master continued to engage the ambassador in conversation. It occurred to me that Ja'far's intelligence service might have alerted him to Angilbert's poetic aspirations. It would be typical of the wily Wazir to have placed a writer, rather than a diplomat, next to the guest of honour, to put him at his ease and draw him out.

"Perhaps, my lord ambassador, you would honour us with a sample of your verse?"

"Alas, even if my feeble efforts were adequate for this great occasion, they are written in Latin. I lack the skill to render them in Arabic with any vestige of poetry remaining."

"Might I ask, then, what is your theme?"

Angilbert blushed slightly, and for the first time I sensed his embarrassment was genuine, rather than the false modesty of courtly manners.

"I must admit I have the temerity to attempt epic poetry, in the style of the Greek Homer or the Roman Virgil. I am currently working on a lay commemorating the Battle of Orreaga, and the death of Hruodland, Governor of the Breton Marches."

"I can only regret my ignorance, that the fame of that battle has not reached my ears."

"Then, in lieu of a poem, might I tell you the story of those tragic events?"

And so he did.

In the year of our Lord seven hundred and seventy seven, or, as you would count it, one hundred and sixty years after the Prophet left Makkah for Madinah, there came a merchant to the court of King Karlo. Despite the continual wars between the Franks and the Saracens, it was not unusual for Arab traders to cross the mountains separating Andalus from Aquitaine in search of profit. However it was almost unknown for a Muslim to penetrate as far into Frankia as this man had done. When he requested audience with the king, Karlo was intrigued, and agreed to see him.

Once he stood before the king, the Saracen revealed his true identity. He was no mere merchant, but Sulayman al-Arabi, Wali of Barsalona. He had come to seek the aid of Karlo in his struggles against Abd ar-Rahman, the Falcon of Andalus.

Abd ar-Rahman was a scion of the Umayyad dynasty, and would have been Khalifah one day had his family not been overthrown by the Abbasids. During the revolution he had fled Syria and escaped to the west, hunted all the way by Abbasid agents. Finally he landed on the shores of Andalus, where he proclaimed himself Amir of Cordoba, and called on all Muslims loyal to the Umayyad cause to join him.

Sulayman was not happy at this turn of events. He had been content to pay taxes to the Khalifah half a world away in Dimashq, but to have this upstart prince on his doorstep demanding his allegiance was a different matter. The Wali considered asking the Abbasids for help, but even if they could spare an army, it would take years for them to arrive. Instead he conceived a daring plan, to make alliance with the barbarians across the mountains.

Karlo was keen to seize this opportunity, but at the time was heavily committed to his war against the pagan Saxons. It was not until the following year that he was able to muster a force and invade Andalus. I was nineteen years old, and thrilled at the prospect of leading a troop against the Saracen with my king. Hopes were high as we assembled at Burdigala.

The intention was that we would march on the city of

Saraqusta, strategic key to the whole of the north of the peninsula. The governor of the city, Husayn al-Ansari, was part of Sulayman's conspiracy, and was supposed to surrender quietly. Unfortunately, by the time we got there, things had changed.

The self-styled Amir of Cordoba, Abd ar-Rahman, had caught wind of the plot, and sent an army to subdue the troublesome north, under the command of his trusted friend Thalaba ibn Obeid. To the surprise of all concerned, the rebels defeated the Amir's army, and captured ibn Obeid. Now the conspirators began to wonder whether they needed the barbarians after all. When the king arrived at the gates of Saraqusta, he found them barred against him.

We laid half-hearted siege to the city while fitful negotiations took place. After a month of deadlock and boredom, Sulayman and Husayn decided to give us money to go away. Word of the offer was brought to the king: one hundred thousand dinars in gold and ibn Obeid as hostage.

Karlo was rapidly losing enthusiasm for the whole adventure, and decided to accept. However, he planned to take more than had been offered. Believing the Franks to have been placated, the Wali came out of the city to supervise the transfer of the tribute. Karlo threw him in chains and took him hostage too. We left as hastily as we could without appearing to flee.

Almost immediately the retreat began to go wrong. Firstly we were ambushed by Sulayman's men, who rescued him and took him back to Saraqusta. In truth we put up little resistance; capturing him had been more an act of petulance than anything. Then we came to Pamplona, city of the Vascones. Here my king made the mistake that was to lead to the greatest disaster of his reign.

The Vascones live in the mountainous regions that separate Andalus from Frankia. They are nominally Christians, but practise many strange rites of their own, and speak a tongue that has nothing in common with the other languages of the west. Fiercely independent, they accept the rule of neither Frank nor Muslim.

These mountain people had caused Karlo much bother

over the ten years of his reign. Since he found himself in their territory with an army, he decided to teach them a lesson. I suppose he thought it would give justification to what had been a largely futile expedition. The walls of Pamplona were pulled down. Some of the wilder elements of the army seized the opportunity to vent their frustration at being denied a proper battle, and took the punishment too far. There was looting, rape, a few murders. We left behind us a burning city, and a people who burned more furiously still.

There were few safe routes through the mountains that separated us from the safety of home. Karlo decided to take the one known to the locals as Orreaga. This pass was so narrow that to traverse it we had to march in extended column, with the head of the army several miles ahead of its tail. The baggage, including Sulayman's gold, was placed under the protection of the rearguard, which was commanded by Hruodland, Governor of the Breton Marches.

Hruodland was a big man, loud, confident and hearty. He was fond of hunting, and always carried with him the horn which he used to call his hounds, and also to rally his troops around him in battle. This instrument was not made from the horn of any animal, but skilfully fashioned from brass. Hruodland claimed it had been made by the ancient Romans, and passed down through his family for generations.

He was an experienced general, but getting the baggage train over the rough ground of the pass proved difficult, and the rear fell further behind the main body of the army. I myself had been placed at the head, so what happened next I can only tell you from the accounts of the few who survived.

The leader of the Vascones was a man called Otsoa, the Wolf. Hearing of the depredations suffered by Pamplona, and perhaps more pertinently of the cartloads of gold and other booty we were taking back, he had gathered a troop, and even now the mountain warriors were stalking us. Lightly clad in sheepskin jerkins and leather helmets, they remained unseen as they worked their way along the slopes faster than we could negotiate the valley below.

Otsoa realised the rearguard had become detached from the

rest of the force, and saw his chance. That night the Vascones fell upon Hruodland's camp, slaughtering men and animals and carrying off loot in the confusion of darkness. The governor sent a message to the kng informing him of the raid, but the mountaineers had been careful to cut off communications. The messenger perished along the way with a spear through his chest.

When dawn came Hruodland surveyed the carnage in the valley, as the dead were hastily buried under cairns of stones in the grey light. Having received no orders from the king, he decided to fight back. He sent companies of warriors up the slopes in search of the raiders. However, the heavily armoured Franks had no chance of catching the mountain people on their own ground. Those who came back, came back bleeding and beaten; and the main army had pulled still further ahead.

Hruodland marshalled his men and pressed on. He also sent more messengers to Karlo, but none survived to carry word to the king. Throughout the day the ambushes continued. Not daring to stop, the Franks piled the bodies of their fallen comrades onto the baggage carts for later burial. By afternoon the corpses were too numerous to be carried, and were left behind for the wolves and eagles.

That night nobody slept, and Hruodland gathered his captains for a crisis meeting. They had realized their messages could not be reaching Karlo, but Eggihard, Mayor of the Palace, had an idea.

"Your horn, Hruodland! It could be heard along the valley, and would alert the king to our desperate situation."

Hruodland shook his head fiercely.

"What, and drag the others back into this deathtrap? No, I will not summon my king unless I can warn him of the dangers we face."

By morning the rearguard had been reduced to half its original strength. The raiders now did not bother to conceal themselves; their silhouettes could be clearly seen on the bluffs and ridges as javelins rained down on the Franks. Again Eggihard begged Hruodland to blow his horn, and again the general refused.

Finally, at midday the showers of javelins ceased. However, it was replaced by a rhythmic drumming sound. To their horror, the Franks realized it was the sound of swords rattling on shields, as hundreds of mountain men emerged from concealment all around them, walking slowly down the slopes to the surrounded rearguard. For a third time Eggihard asked his general to blow his horn, and Hruodland realized that all was lost if he did not.

The sound rang down the pass, piercing, keening, echoing from the rocky slopes. But the king was too far away to hear. The Vascones closed in for the kill.

Karlo did not realize what had happened to his rearguard until he was back in Burdigala. A few survivors, who had managed to hide among the rocks and somehow evaded capture or death, brought news of the disaster. He dismissed them gruffly, waving them away, and they left his presence hurriedly fearing they had offended him. It was only when a sudden sob erupted from him that I realised he was not, as first appeared, deep in thought.

It is the only time I have seen my king weep.

Ten

The Tale of the White Ghost in Blissful Eternity

"A moving account. I would wager a sum equal to the stolen gold, however, that by the time you have completed your epic, the enemy will not be a rabble of Christian bandits. I suspect they will have transformed, as if by magic, into a vast horde of well-armed Muslims, of – what was that charming word you used? – Saracens. Will you take the bet, my lord ambassador?"

Caught up in the story, I had not noticed the arrival of Ja'far al-Barmaki. Seeing others around me jump when he spoke, I guessed that had been his intention. Angilbert, however, was unperturbed.

"Ah, my lord Wazir. I am sure you will understand that my king commands my services as politician as well as bard. I could not risk incurring such a heavy debt."

"Your honesty does you as much credit as your tact. With a hundred victories to boast of, you choose to recount your master's sole defeat. What became of the conspirators?"

"Husayn al-Ansari's confidence in the Wali of Barsalona was shaken by his clumsy handling of their rebellion, and further damaged by his foolishness in allowing himself to be captured. The Falcon of Andalus exploited this division between his enemies with the cunning for which he was famed. When he secretly promised Sulayman's title and lands to whoever got rid of him, Husayn wasted no time in poisoning his former ally and pledging allegiance to the Umayyad."

"You say, 'was' famed? It is true, then, that Abd ar-Rahman is dead?"

Angilbert smiled.

"As I am sure your agents have told you, my lord Wazir, the Falcon died some months ago. His son Hisham has succeeded him as Amir of Cordoba – and, no doubt, as rival claimant to the Khalifate. It seems, does it not, that we have an enemy in common?"

Angilbert gestured to an empty space on his farsh. Ja'far sat beside him, and they continued their conversation in low voices. As if to prevent them being overheard, Ibrahim al-Mosuli's musicians struck up a bold tune. The girl who had been singing was replaced by a young man with a strong yet graceful voice. Ibrahim was still directing his band, and when he and the vocalist exchanged a brief smile I noticed the extraordinary resemblance between them.

The yellow-haired angel-whore seemed to have disappeared, so I dedicated my attention to methodically devouring every scrap of food still within my reach. Abu Nuwas, to my surprise, was flirting with the singing girl. He fixed her with his blue eyes and whispered to her while she blushed and tittered. It was like watching a snake hypnotise a rabbit.

Ja'far was the first to leave, vanishing as unobtrusively as he had arrived. It was only when the delegation rose to depart that I realised what had been niggling at me all night. The beardless man with the half shaven head, whom I had seen with them on the street, had not been present at the feast. I tried to draw my master's attention to this, but he refused to take his eyes off the singing girl.

The ambassador's exit was the signal for the other guests to stand up. I noticed one of the Frankish priests offering an egg to Fadl ibn Rabi. This seemed odd given the great feast we had just consumed. Still more odd, however, was the sight of the Chamberlain slipping the egg into his sleeve. He bumped into me as he left, and glared at me as if he could poison me with his eyes, like the basiliscus snake.

I assumed that I would return to the Hall of the Barid, but instead my master and I were escorted to a small room on the second floor. Spending the night alone together in such close proximity made me a little nervous, particularly when Abu Nuwas sent a slave in search of wine. I wished I had pilfered a knife from the feast, in case I needed to defend myself.

However, it soon became apparent that the poet had other plans for the evening.

"Where are you going, Father of Locks?"

"Is the Newborn jealous? You need only pout those tender lips, and I shall stay by your side. No? Then I shall go to Muti'a, my pretty singing girl. Besides, there are few dangers as rewarding as sneaking into the women's quarters in a royal palace. The risk of terrible punishment adds spice to the joy of coupling."

"The Khalifah seems to favour you. Would he really begrudge you a slave girl?"

"She is no kitchen maid, boy. These singers change hands for vast sums of money. It is like smuggling a donkey into his stable to cover his prize mare. And don't be fooled by that regal charm. Harun al-Rashid is master of an empire, successor to the Apostle of God, and a ruthless bastard with those who don't show him the proper respect."

"I did not think women to be your taste, master."

"Are you sure you are not jealous? You seem very reluctant for me to go. Since you ask, it is my rule not to deny myself gratification, in whatever form it comes. Granted, if you offer me the choice, I would probably prefer a beautiful boy to any other companion, but there is a myriad of paths to ecstasy. Old, young, male, female – as long as it is breathing, I will seek pleasure in its arms. In fact, even death need not be an impediment to love . . ."

He gazed at me seriously for a moment, then laughed uproariously at my shocked expression.

"You disappoint me, boy. I had believed you to be a philosopher, who could think beyond conventional, unreasoning morality. What harm can be done to a body from which the life has departed? Of course they must be fresh, while the bloom is still in the cheek and the flesh still soft. But the dead are amenable lovers, if a little passive. It is not unlike fucking a Chinese girl."

He left cackling, and I could only hope he was making fun of me.

With the rare luxury of a room to myself, I settled down for a welcome rest. However I would not have survived the years on the road if I were a heavy sleeper. Even the gentle footfalls that entered my room in the still of night woke me immediately.

At first I thought it was Abu Nuwas, returning from his assignation. I pretended to be asleep, hoping he would be sated or too drunk to bother me. Then I realised something was wrong. The steps were too stealthy, the breathing too hushed. Even if he were sober my master would not take such trouble to keep quiet. I dared to open my eyes a slit.

A figure was leaning over me. In the darkness all I could tell was that he was too short to be Abu Nuwas. I braced myself to roll away if he struck, swearing to myself that I would never again leave myself so defenceless, even in the Khalifah's Palace. However he hovered, as if uncertain.

I lashed out, grabbing his shirt as I twisted, hoping to swing him across me and roll onto his head. It was a clumsy move which could have been disastrous against a skilled opponent, but my attacker seemed surprised and fell easily. We writhed in a tangle, but I managed to get myself on top, pinning down his shoulders with my chest and seizing his wrists.

It was at this point that I realised two lumps the size of pomegranates were pressing into my ribs. My assailant was female! I leapt away, and she sat up. The light of the moon caught her white skin. It was the Frankish girl.

We stared at each other for a moment, breathing heavily from our tussle. Then she said something in Latin. I shook my head, as much in befuddlement as refusal. She tried again, this time in Greek. At first I did not understand. Whether it was the years since I used the language regularly, her heavy accent, or the extraordinary nature of what she said, she had to repeat it twice before I grasped her meaning.

"I've come to rescue you."

"Rescue me? From what?"

Now she appeared as confused as me. She was dressed as an Arab man, in shirt and pants, but with no turban, so that her yellow hair gleamed like gold. I had torn her shirt during our fight, and found it difficult to stop glancing at the curve of breast this had revealed.

"From the Saracens. From slavery."

"But I am not a slave."

Before each sentence she looked away and her mouth moved. I guessed she was silently trying out the words in an unfamiliar language.

"Then come away with us!"

"But this is the greatest city in the world! Why would I want to go anywhere else?"

We were struggling to communicate, and not only because of our unpractised Greek. I watched her mentally assemble her next speech.

"For the sake of your immortal soul. You will burn in hell if you stay with these heathens."

"I think the people round here would say the same about you. How can you go about with your face on full view like that? Do you have no shame?"

"You don't cover your face."

"But I am a man."

"You are a boy, who is frightened of the body of a woman. I shall show my face if I choose. Perhaps I shall show you my breast, as well. Then you might die of fright."

She put her hand to her torn shirt, and I was unable to speak.

"But if you die now, you will go to hell with the other heathens."

The girl lowered her hand, and I breathed again. In truth, when I merely looked at the shaded hollow beneath her collarbone I felt like I was choking. If she actually had exposed her breast, her dire predictions might have come true. I found my voice.

"Are all Frankish women as immodest as you?"

She made a plosive noise of contempt.

"I am no Frank. The women of Frankia are whimpering mice, like your Saracen girls. I am Hervor, a woman of the Rus. My father is raising me to be a shield-maiden."

I did not know what a "shield-maiden" was, but I was busy

trying to remember where I had heard of the Rus. Then it came to me.

"So the warrior Gorm –"

"Is my father."

She must take after her mother, I thought. There was very little resemblance between the pale beauty and the red-haired giant. However before I could find out more we heard footsteps outside. Hervor stood up.

"I must go. You will not come with me?"

I shook my head.

"Then tell your friend that if he seeks the secret of the Name, he must stand before the demon with the wings of an eagle and the head of a dog."

I do not know whether I was more dumbfounded by these strange words, or by the kiss she planted on my forehead.

"Farewell, boy. Don't worry though, I will come back to save you."

Suddenly and unexpectedly she smiled, an impish grin that transformed her serious face, and caused my cheeks to flush.

"And next time, I really might show you my breast."

With that she was gone, like a ghost in the night. An instant later, Abu Nuwas lurched into the doorway.

"If anybody asks, I have been here all the time."

He hurled himself onto the farsh and began to snore immediately. I tried to go back to sleep myself, but I was haunted by thoughts of a teasing smile, and dreams of a pomegranate breast.

★ ★ ★

I woke at the first sallow glow of dawn. Abu Nuwas still lay grunting and twitching, but I got up and headed out. I had a rendezvous at the Basrah Gate.

I had resolved that, since my master appeared in no hurry to delve into the mysteries that faced us, I would take action myself. The trail in Sharqiya led nowhere, so looking for the merchant's daughter seemed as good a place to start as any. Besides, it gave me the excuse I needed.

If the girl Najiba had disappeared from within her father's

house, then I must enter the house to look for her. Getting in was no problem for me. But any burglar will tell you it is always safer to have inside information; and for that I needed Layla bint al-Bazza.

It was only a short distance to her shop, but first I had to find my way out of al-Khuld. I had thought the name of the palace to smack of arrogance, of what the Greeks call "hubris", in using the Quran's description of Paradise to denote a place of fleeting earthly pleasure. However, as I wandered around seemingly endless gardens, sparkling with diamond dew in the early light, Blissful Eternity felt like an appropriate description.

The serpent had crept into my Eden, though. Much as I looked forward to seeing Layla, I could not escape a creeping sense of guilt. I told myself that I had not invited the Rus girl to my room, that she was clearly insane, that the moment I felt her warm body against mine I had jumped off her as if stung. That I had no evidence that Layla even remembered me, let alone expected my fidelity. It was all to no avail; I could not escape the sense that I had somehow transgressed.

Nonetheless, I was shivering with excitement when I arrived at the Basrah Gate. Layla's shop was ideally placed, on the border between Sharqiya and Karkh, at the confluence of two major roads. I wondered how a woman, particularly one so young, had come by such valuable property. It was a busy time of day, when the sun finally gave warmth as well as light, and the crossroads was a popular meeting place for household slaves to gossip and joke while out buying provisions. I had to elbow my way through the bustle to reach the comforting quiet and darkness of the shop.

"I was hoping you'd come."

There was a faint emphasis on the word "you", and a crinkling around her eyes that suggested a smile. This was enough to lighten my spirits and dispel the gloom that had been dogging me since al-Khuld. I told her of my plan to break into the merchant's house. Not only did she draw me a map of the building, but she also agreed to help me search. Her business relationship with the merchant's wife had become a friendship, and it was not unusual for her to spend the night there.

When all was arranged, there was a moment of silence, and our eyes met. I longed to ask her a thousand things, who she was, where she came from, what her dreams were, but there were too many questions fighting for answers. Then a customer came into the shop, and my spirits sank once more. As I left, though, she put a hand on my shoulder.

"Please – what is your name?"

"Ismail. Ismail al-Walid."

I did not know why I told her the name that Abu Nuwas had given me, instead of the one I had won for myself. Perhaps it just felt good on that new morning, in that new city, to be the Newborn, al-Walid. It felt like anything was possible.

She nodded, and the skin around her dark eyes crinkled again with pleasure. I was smiling too, as I emerged blinking into the sunlight. It was a long time before sundown, and I wondered what I was to do next. It seemed unlikely that my master would be awake for some time yet, and I did not know whether I should return to al-Khuld, or meet him elsewhere.

Eventually I reasoned that Ja'far ibn Yahya had told me I was free, so I might as well enjoy my freedom. I would spend some time exploring the suqs of Karkh, then go back to the Hall of the Barid. I hoped that Yaqub al-Mithaq, the friendly postman who had taught me so much, would be there; I found his solidity reassuring in the crazy whirl of Baghdad.

The markets were teeming now, and not only with servants on errands. Respectable wives handled and sniffed the merchandise, yelling at stallholders for their outrageous prices. Wealthy merchants strode past, with serious faces and heads full of business. Newcomers to the city could be quickly identified by their wide eyes and open mouths; the pickpockets, fortune tellers and hustlers closed in on them like wolves circling their prey. Ibn Zuhayr's men, with their blue robes and wooden clubs, were on patrol, but those who could afford it came with their own protection: bodyguards, chaperones and purseholders.

At first the suqs seemed utterly chaotic, but in fact each alley specialised in different merchandise. One entire lane was given over to sellers of honey, an astonishing variety of sweetness in hues of amber and ochre. I sated my eyes with the riotous rainbow colours of the Boulevard of Clothiers, which stretched across the whole square mile, with endless silks, brocades and fabrics hanging along its length like the banners of an army. On Spice Row I rejoiced in the fragrances that drifted from the baskets and jars: bitter nutmeg, warm cinnamon, delicate saffron, sharp ginger and rich coriander.

Best of all, however, was the side alley where the booksellers set up shop. The odour of parchment was more delightful to me than all the perfumes and scented oils the suq had to offer, and I wandered up and down in a kind of besotted longing for the priceless manuscripts: the Surahs and Hadiths, the histories and fables, and of course the poetry. There, within my sight but denied to my touch by the suspicious stares of the stallholders, were the odes of al-Qays and Labid, of ibn Kulthum and ibn Shaddad.

As well as the classics, the Muhdathun, the new wave, were represented too. I saw at least a couple of scrolls tagged with the name of the Father of Locks, and I watched a matronly woman chatter excitedly to her friend as she bought an ode by gaunt Abbas, the poet I had met at the monastery:

"Oh, the elegance of phrasing in his verse! And of course, the purity of his love, the aching of his unfulfilled longing for Fauz. So much more proper than some of the filthy stuff that passes for poetry these days. My rawi reads it beautifully, such emotion in his voice. You must allow me to send him round to you . . ."

I mischievously contemplated telling her what I knew about the real Abbas and Fauz, how their love had not been as pure as the poetry suggested, but I was in too good a mood to want to shatter her illusions. Besides, I doubted she would believe me. The manuscripts may have been beyond the means of most Baghdadis, who would not have been able to read them in any case; but the verses they contained were repeated and memorised throughout the city, and sordid truth could never compete with the legends they propagated.

Despite stuffing myself the previous night, I was growing hungry again. I supposed I could get food at the Hall of the

Barid, but I was tempted by the aroma of the grilled fish and meats, the pastries and patties hawked by market vendors. It occurred to me that if I was not a slave I really should be getting paid by somebody, even if it was just a few coppers.

Then I remembered the egg which the Frankish priest had given to ibn Rabi. Stealing it had been easy. As the revellers left the hall I made sure that I got under the Chamberlain's feet, then when he bumped into me I simply lifted it from his sleeve. It had been an act of childish mischief, but I was glad of it now that my mouth was watering.

I pulled the egg from my belt. A tentative shake suggested it was hard-boiled, so I began to pick off the shell. And it was halfway to my mouth before I noticed the writing, a brown scrawl on the white.

How the Franks had managed to inscribe a message on the inside of an egg was a question nearly as baffling as why they had bothered. The writing was in Arabic, a string of eight characters written as if it was a single word, but having no meaning I had ever encountered. There were none of the marks which had recently been introduced to indicate vowel sounds, and without any context it was impossible to make sense of it. I attempted to read it out loud, guessing at the vowels.

"Ghihafa . . . at . . . tighasa . . . Ghihafa at-Tighasa."

"Do you give names to all your food, or just the boiled eggs?"

I wheeled round, to see Abu Nuwas grinning at me mockingly. Beside him stood al-Takht, the Police Captain. Red-faced, I shoved the egg into my mouth and tried to eat it in a single swallow. While I choked and spluttered, the poet slapped my back.

"Come, boy, we must go to Harbiya. Another child is missing."

Eleven

The Tale of the Red Cloth

My bright mood had evaporated, and was replaced by irritation.

"How did you find me?"

"Really, Newborn, you are nothing if not predictable. I guessed you would dream up an excuse to visit that silly drudge, whose charms, bafflingly, you find more to your taste than my own. Still, I am impressed with your invention. Breaking into the merchant's house is an excellent idea."

Al-Takht winced at this, and pretended he had not heard. Abu Nuwas continued.

"Learning from the girl that you had already been and gone, I reasoned that you would most likely be drawn to the suqs, and thence, being a healthy young man, to the smell of food. And here I find you, talking to your breakfast."

Reluctantly, I decided to confide in him.

"Master, do you know the words Ghihafa at-Tighasa?"

"Yes, Newborn, it is the name of your egg."

I told him about the Franks, and the Chamberlain, and the mysterious writing. As I spoke, he looked at me with growing concern.

"And you ate it, boy? Have you never heard the tales of magicians and demons keeping their soul in an egg? Perhaps you have consumed the soul of the Afrit, and now it possesses you. Or you may have summoned the spirit, by speaking its Name out loud."

My face must have reflected the horror I felt, until Abu Nuwas burst out laughing.

"Forgive me, Newborn. Writing on the inside of a boiled egg is an old spy's trick. A mixture of alum and vinegar will penetrate the shell without leaving any external marks. The only question is why our Frankish friends are passing secret messages to ibn Rabi. And, of course, what that message means."

I had been debating whether to mention to him the nocturnal visit of Hervor, and the demon with the wings of an eagle and the head of a dog. His teasing had decided me. I said nothing more as we walked to Harbiya.

The home of the Abna seemed a different place during the daylight hours than it had on that crazy evening when I had first met the poet. Its more rambunctious citizens were presumably still asleep, and the neighbourhood maintained a tone of genteel respectability. It was surprising therefore to see grown men and women running through the streets as if from a fire. Al-Takht stopped one man as he passed.

"In the name of the Khalifah, tell us where we can find the veteran Abd al-Aziz."

The man had to catch his breath before replying.

"That's where I'm going! He's at the Blue Masjid. He's dragged his neighbour in front of the Qadi. Reckons he took his boy!"

He set off again and we followed, even the barrel-like policeman breaking into a gentle trot. When we arrived at the Blue Masjid the courtyard was crowded, and al-Takht had to use his cudgel to force a way through. At the end, by the minbar, we found the source of the excitement.

Two elderly men were engaged in a furious row. One was an Arab, who was waving a double-pointed sword, and was only being restrained from using it on the other by the intervention of a plain woman of middle years. The other man was taller, thinner, and dark-skinned. He appeared fearful, but smacked his right fist into his left palm in obscene defiance. As we approached the Arab with the sword was yelling.

"You don't fool me, Babak ibn Bundar! You might fool all these others, but I know what you are, you filthy pervert. Give me back my grandson unharmed, and your death will be swift and easy."

Babak ibn Bundar, the black man, replied in an odd, high voice:

"The only person making a fool of you is yourself, Abd al-Aziz. I don't know where your grandson is. If you were truly concerned, you would have taken greater care of him in the first place."

This enraged Abd al-Aziz still further, but the woman holding him back spoke impatiently.

"Don't be a fool, father! If you kill him here – in this holy place–"

For a moment the veteran slumped in her arms, and I could see through the bluster to the tired old man that he really was. His daughter spoke again, loud enough for everybody to hear.

"The Qadi will settle this matter. He is from the city of Madinah, where he studied under the great scholar Malik ibn Anas himself. He will find the truth about what happened to my son."

Abu Nuwas leaned across to whisper to me.

"This should be interesting. Imam Malik is a brilliant man, but also a stubborn curmudgeon with a strong anti-authoritarian streak. He dared to issue fatwas against al-Mansur the Victorious! The Khalifah had him flogged, but later begged for his forgiveness.

"Harun has invited the Imam to his palace, but Malik won't shift from the holy city. Instead he is supposed to have sent his wisest pupil. Let us see what happens when the scholarship of Madinah has to sift through the sleaze of Baghdad."

I was intrigued to discover that, although Baghdad had a police force to keep the peace, it seemed that crime was dealt with there in the same way it was dealt with everywhere else: the plaintiff would drag the accused down to the masjid, accompanied by the whole neighbourhood, to have the matter decided by the Qadi.

A hush settled on the crowd, and my master fell silent too, as the pupil of Imam Malik emerged from the rear of the masjid. I had pictured a white-bearded sage, but instead a young man appeared, little more than two decades in age. He had a beard, but it was deep black, and sprouted oddly, as if he

138

had hung a small, hairy fruit from his chin. Despite his youth and eccentric appearance, he walked into the courtyard with supreme confidence, eyes almost closed, as if his penetrating intellect made sight unnecessary. He seated himself on a prayer mat.

"Who seeks the judgement of Muhammad ibn Idris al-Shafi'i?"

There was a pause, which suggested I was not the only one for whom al-Shafi'i did not conform to expectation. Then Abd al-Aziz started shouting again.

"My grandson was snatched from the street three days ago, by this deviant son of a donkey. Forty years a soldier, fighting for the true faith, and this is how I am treated! I marched with Abu Muslim, from Merv to Makkah –"

"You speak as if you are the only man who was ever in a battle! I lost my eye at Talas river –"

Babak ibn Bundar was pointing at his right eye, which I now realised had been replaced by some sort of glass ball. The effect was disconcerting, as his false eye lagged behind his real one when it moved, so that he seemed to look at everything twice. Al-Shafi'i raised a hand, and astonishingly the old men fell silent.

"All Muslims are equal before God, and before the law. You will both receive a fair hearing. Now, you, the accused; how do you answer this charge?"

Ibn Bundar stood upright.

"I deny it utterly. He's never liked me. I've always been perfectly civil to him, yet he seems to take offence at my mere presence in his neighbourhood – as if he owned the whole of Harbiya. And the way he talks about his military service! You'd think he overthrew the Umayyads single-handed.

"This is all because of the time I questioned his account of the battle of Talas river. Because I was there, and from the rubbish he talks about it I would swear he was not. He has never forgiven me for daring to disagree with him. Since then he has just been looking for an excuse to accuse me of something."

Abd al-Aziz was bubbling like a pot, but the Qadi nodded impassively, encouraging further disclosures from ibn Bundar who, it belatedly dawned on me, matched the description Umm Dabbah had given, of the hooded man with black skin and strange eyes.

"And he boasts about that family of his, as if they were the family of the Prophet. I mean, the daughter, he even called her Fatimah, where is her husband then? Died a martyr at the siege of Samalu, they'll tell you. Well, Samalu was nine years ago, and that grandson is no more than seven, at most. You work it out, then tell me what's going on. Because I don't know, and it's none of my business."

"I am sure you have nothing to worry about. You only need to say where you were when the child disappeared, and that will be the end of the matter."

The old man's initial relief at the Qadi's words was replaced by increasing horror, which he then tried badly to conceal.

"Where I was? Of course I can – I mean to say, why should it be for me, to prove where I was? Does he not need some evidence of my involvement? If, that is, there's anything to be involved in. I mean to say, that boy, he runs wild on the street day and night. Anything could have happened to him."

Al-Shafi'i closed in on his prey.

"Well, if there is any problem, we could –"

"Problem? There is no problem. I mean to say, who could call witnesses to their whereabouts all day long? A man needs his privacy. A man must pray, and void his bowels, and . . ."

Ibn Bundar was spared trying to think of any more things that a man might admit to needing privacy for, when, to my surprise, Abu Nuwas walked to his side.

"If I might be permitted to speak, learned Qadi?"

Al-Shafi'i was not pleased by this intervention, and did not deign to address my master directly.

"Who is this man?"

Al-Takht stepped forward reluctantly.

"Wise Qadi, he has been appointed by the Wazir to look into the . . . into this matter."

He had obviously decided not to complicate things by mentioning supernatural apparitions. Al-Shafi'i took the interruption as a challenge to his authority.

"It is not the place of the Barmakid to involve himself in the judgement of such matters. If the veteran is condemned he may petition the Wazir for mercy; but the child's family have a legitimate grievance, and a right to have their case heard in public.

"In my court, I will not tolerate novelty, nor innovation, even if such practices purport to derive from reason, or common sense. Everything we need to know is contained within the holy Quran, or the Sayings of the Prophet (peace be upon him!) God is the one who judges us. For man to believe he can improve on His laws is arrogance worthy of eternal damnation."

"You will agree, learned Qadi, that it is neither novelty nor innovation for the accused to be represented by somebody with legal training?"

Al-Shafi'i gazed coldly at the poet for a long time. I had the impression he was searching for a reason to disagree. Finally he spoke.

"I will hear what you have to say."

I remembered Abu'l-Atahiyya telling me my master was a hafiz, one who had memorised the Quran. However I did not understand why he was taking it upon himself to defend the one-eyed man. Nonetheless, he pressed on.

"Surely, wise Qadi, if there is no evidence against Babak ibn Bundar, he should be asked to swear an oath affirming his innocence. Then, unless there are grounds to disbelieve him, the court must accept his word."

Abu Nuwas was right. Even I, with my meagre grasp of the Sharia, knew that much. But surely, he could not have failed to realise that ibn Bundar might be the mysterious stranger seen at the site of the other disappearances? I began frantically trying to signal to my master to look at his eyes, by means of spastic hand gestures and wriggling of brows.

"You are correct in law, agent of the Wazir. Babak ibn Bundar, will you swear the oath?"

Abu Nuwas bowed deeply.

"I am indebted to you, learned Qadi. If you would excuse me for a moment, my servant appears to be having some kind

141

of fit. Allow me to take him to one side and administer treatment."

The treatment, administered as soon as we were out of sight in a back room off the courtyard, was a stinging slap around the head.

"Shut up, you fool! Do you think you are the only one who has seen his eye? If that pompous judge and the Harbiya mob get the idea that he is a demon or a witch, they will have him stoned before sunset. That will bring us no closer to understanding what has happened, nor to finding the children."

It was the first time Abu Nuwas had shown any concern for the fate of the innocents, and I held my tongue. We returned to the courtyard, where a Quran had been produced and ibn Bundar was taking the oath.

"I swear by God the All-Knowing and at the peril of my immortal soul that I am innocent of all the charges which have been put to me before this court."

He looked around defiantly, his diverging eyes taking in the whole crowd at once. The onlookers were muttering, wondering whether the entertainment was nearly over.

"Then, learned Qadi, if there is no evidence against this man —"

"But I do have evidence!"

Those spectators who had started to drift away hurriedly returned to their places and sat down. Abd al-Aziz was pointing a trembling finger at his neighbour.

"My grandson had a red cloth, which he used to staunch his blood when he was hurt in scrapes and scuffles — which was often, as he is the son of a warrior and the grandson of a warrior. If that man has upon his person a square of crimson fabric, a span along each side, then he has taken my boy."

This caused a sensation among the crowd, two of whom leapt forward and began to search ibn Bundar. Almost immediately they tugged something red from his sleeve. The cloth fluttered to the ground and lay there like a bleeding corpse.

"But — I mean to say, that is my kerchief! I have had it for months! He could have seen me using it — knew that I had it —"

142

Ibn Bundar's bleated protestations could hardly be heard over the excited chatter of the assembled citizens. Al-Shafi'i reasserted his authority, with an air of self-justification.

"Abd al-Aziz, can you produce two witnesses who will swear that the cloth belongs to your grandson?"

The veteran scented victory.

"I am one – and my daughter another –"

"But two women must act as witness in place of one man! This is insufficient testimony!"

Abu Nuwas was shouting now as well, as events threatened to stampede out of his control. Al-Shafi'i looked at him in icy triumph.

"As you well know, agent of the Wazir, that Surah refers specifically to the witnessing of business loans. If this woman of the true faith is willing to testify, I will accept her word."

I thought I saw Fatimah glance at her father before looking down and nodding her assent. Al-Shafi'i settled on his mat as if that was the end of the matter, but Abu Nuwas had not given up.

"Wise Qadi, might I be permitted to question the witnesses?"

The young judge ignored him, and my master took his silence as permission.

"Abd al-Aziz, who was your commanding officer at Talas?"

The veteran bristled.

"What does this have to do with my grandson? By whose authority do you interrogate me?"

As he replied, Abu Nuwas looked toward the crowd, who were eagerly awaiting the next development.

"But I understood that you were proud of your military record. What reason would you have for refusing to answer?"

The old man stared at him and scratched his neck for a long time before responding.

"I fought at Talas in the regiment of Sayf al-Din, of the tribe of Quraysh."

"Thank you. Fatimah bint Abd al-Aziz, did you buy this cloth for your son?"

The woman seemed as unsettled as her father by this shift in approach, and her reply was hesitant.

"Yes . . . yes, I did."

"From where did you buy it?"

"I don't remember. Karkh . . . the suqs . . . I don't remember exactly."

"So it was not a significant expense? Not a costly purchase, that you would recollect making?"

Fatimah was becoming increasingly nervous.

"No, no. It is just an ordinary piece of cloth, which I gave to the boy . . ."

Abu Nuwas picked up the red rag, and stared at it intently. The silence in the courtyard became unbearable. Finally he spoke.

"This fabric is Sichuan weave. It is only produced in western China. Admittedly, there it is common stuff, but to arrive in Baghdad it must have travelled thousand of miles, and would be as expensive as silk. How, then, could you have picked it up, almost without noticing, in the suqs of Karkh?"

Fatimah looked at my master, then at Abd al-Aziz, who glowered through his thick brows. The hush was so deep that a cat could be heard mewing outside the masjid. Then –

"I'm sorry, father, but this madness must stop. I have only seen that cloth before in the possession of our neighbour Babak ibn Bundar. And I am grateful to you, whoever you are, for exposing the lie before I swore a false oath, and risked damnation."

The furious reaction of Abd al-Aziz was drowned out by the clamour of the crowd. I am sure I saw money change hands; if wagers had been placed on the outcome of the trial, they were now paying out. Babak ibn Bundar looked more relieved than jubilant, and skulked off before anybody could stop him. Al-Shafi'i stood up to formally proclaim the accusation disproved, but he was inaudible and increasingly red-faced.

Abd al-Aziz was escorted away by al-Takht, still complaining vociferously.

"You will all regret this mistake, releasing that son of fifty fathers. I tell you, he is guilty! He lives on his own – has never married – never even has a whore! Yet strange noises come from that house – voices, chanting, Iblis knows what manner of evil . . ."

As the crowd dispersed, I contemplated Abu Nuwas with new respect.

"Master, how do you know so much about weaving?"

"Weaving, boy? I know nothing about weaving. Do I look like a woman, or an artisan?"

He chortled gleefully at my confusion.

"I do, however, know about liars. Abd al-Aziz scratched the back of his neck every time he mentioned that cloth. I asked him about Talas to test my theory, as I was pretty certain that he was lying about being there. And sure enough, he scratched as if infested. Then it was a simple matter of making the woman think she had been caught out. She was obviously less comfortable with deceit than her father."

"But – what if she had held her nerve? What if she knew about weaving herself?"

Abu Nuwas shrugged.

"I guessed she would be more comfortable with a sword in her hand than a needle. And I was right, wasn't I? When I am wrong, then you may stand there looking appalled at me, and say, 'But Father of Locks, what if?' Now close your mouth and open your ears, boy. Our police friend is back."

I stared at him, uncertain whether to be impressed or appalled, as Al-Takht came over to us.

"The grandfather knows nothing of any real use. Apparently the child has been running with a gang of street kids, who call themselves the Raiders. The old man was all in favour, thought it would toughen the boy up. Three days ago, he didn't come home. As far as I can tell, he's only blaming his neighbour because he doesn't like him."

"But he looks like the man Layla saw."

Al-Takht looked at me for a moment before answering.

"I am not so sure. Umm Dabbah is not the most discerning of women, but she was clear on one point. The man had black skin – 'not dark like a man of Aksum or Sind, but pure black, like nobody I've ever seen.' There are thousands of dark-skinned men in Baghdad. The Khalifah's grandmother was from Somalia, and his father al-Mahdi was of the same complexion as ibn Bundar. We cannot accuse him simply for being black."

"But his eyes – surely we could just take him to the woman, ask if he is the man –"

This time I had clearly gone too far. Al-Takht exploded.

"I take no orders from catamites! Ibn Zuhayr commanded me to assist your master. If he wishes me to arrest Babak ibn Bundar, then that is what I will do."

Before he could answer, we were interrupted by a dishevelled policeman, who nervously tugged at al-Takht's sleeve.

"Captain – you'd better come back to Sharqiya – you're needed."

The unfortunate man took the full brunt of his Captain's wrath.

"Can you dribbling cretins not cope for a single day without me? What's the matter, have you lost your balls or something?"

The policeman winced, but persisted desperately.

"No, Captain – it's Ghassan the Porter – his little boy Ahmad –"

Al-Takht was at the door of the masjid before his man had finished the sentence. Abu Nuwas and I hurried after him.

The Police Captain's legs were short, but he powered ahead of us furiously as we crossed the city once more. I was surprised that a man of his rank did not have a horse, as would a Captain of the Guard. However it seemed that the Shurta were not so privileged, and al-Takht was a man accustomed to walking. Abu Nuwas loped beside him, and I scurried in their wake, too breathless to ask questions.

The house of Ghassan the Porter was tiny, only raised above the status of a hovel by constant, desperate and exhausting effort. It was clean and orderly, but a strange smell lingered, like heavy spice. His long, hairy arms gesticulated wildly, his eyes red from weeping.

"He has been gone since morning, my lord! Even if he had

146

wandered off, he would have come home to eat before now. He must be hungry –"

Ghassan's face distorted, and his words froze. Al-Takht shook him.

"You must tell me what happened, or I cannot help you."

The porter sucked in breath.

"My wife, she was out to fetch water – the well at the end of the road there, where you talked to Umm Dabbah yesterday. She saw a friend of hers, and stopped to talk. She let go of the little boy's hand, my lord. I've told her she's not at fault. She often did, on the street outside our house."

Ghassan's wife was older than him, certainly too old to bear any more children, and I wondered how they had come to be wed. She too was red-eyed, and seemed distracted with grief, staring into an imaginary distance. She did not react to being discussed, but tipped her head to one side, as if listening to echoes of movement. Ghassan addressed Abu Nuwas defensively.

"It's a friendly neighbourhood, my lord, and everybody round here knows my Ahmad. But when she next looked around, he was gone. Nobody saw nothing, master. And with all the talk, my lord, of witches snatching children, and the Devil, and all –"

The ape-man was convulsed by silent sobs, and we left before he cried out in his pain. Outside, al-Takht inhaled deeply.

"Agent of the Wazir, I hope you have one of your clever tricks to play now. If not, might I ask that you look for this child, the son of my friend and neighbour, while I go and organise my men?"

Abu Nuwas nodded, and the Police Captain left. My master and I drifted down the street in uncomfortable silence, peering around. Twilight was settling on the city, the shadows lengthening and distorting, and our efforts were futile. Soon we arrived at the charred remains of the buildings destroyed by the hooded stranger. It was here we had spoken to the boy Ahmad, only the day before. I shivered.

"Is it possible, master? That the children are being . . . sacrificed?"

"I don't know, boy. One disappearance is an accident, two a coincidence; but three begins to look like a hunt."

Just then a sharp wind blew up, cutting me to the bone, even through my costly clothes. At the same moment a dark hulking shape loomed at us out of the gloaming.

Without thinking I stepped behind Abu Nuwas, and I noticed that he reached for a sword he was not carrying. Then I looked at the stranger's face and recognised the spiteful, terrified eyes of Umm Dabbah.

"He has come! He has taken the boy! Protect me, my lord . . . if you have power you must protect me!"

She clutched the poet's arm as she spoke. Gone was the resentful suspicion she had displayed the previous day; darkness was closing in and fear was overwhelming her. He tried to calm her.

"Who has come, Umm Dabbah?"

She shook her head, desperately.

"He has come for the Name . . . she opened the Door That Should Not Have Been Opened. Ten hungry men! Shall I be saved, if I can find ten hungry men?"

Abu Nuwas could form no words. Umm Dabbah's eyes seemed to clear, and she noticed the confusion in his face. With an indrawn breath like a mirror shriek, the old woman turned and fled.

For a moment we stood dumbfounded. Then we raced after her. In the instant we hesitated, though, she had vanished into the crazy alleys of Sharqiya.

Abu Nuwas pointed me along the south road, and ducked down a side street himself. I trotted in the direction he had indicated, painfully aware of the slap – slap – slap of my feet echoing off the houses. As I approached a crossroads I slowed and quietened my gait, fearing to startle the old woman. So when I turned the corner, I nearly ran into the back of the hooded figure which strode ahead of me.

At first I thought it must be Umm Dabbah, but I quickly realised the old woman was a good cubit shorter. I padded like

148

a cat after the tall figure, keeping to the shadows, trying to catch a glimpse of the face under the hood without being seen myself. At the next corner he paused, and glanced furtively around. I saw huge, aberrant eyes in a dark face. And my heartbeat was scarcely slowed when I saw it was Babak ibn Bundar, the glass-eyed veteran whom my master had defended in court.

The old man scurried off around the corner. I followed him as swiftly as I dared. His presence in Sharqiya, so close to the scene of another abduction, was enough to condemn him, even if he had not been acting so suspiciously. Every few paces he looked around him. Several times I had to duck into doorways, and if he had two good eyes I am sure he would have spotted me.

After a few blocks of this stuttering pursuit, he arrived at a long, low building, and tapped at a small door. I saw a spyhole open to examine him, before he was admitted. The door closed behind him, and I was alone on the street.

It was clear that knocking on the door would be futile. Whatever was going on inside, casual visitors were not welcome. I strolled around the building nonchalantly. All the windows were shuttered, and there were no other entrances. Then, at the rear, I noticed a peculiar thing.

At the level of my feet, there was a gap in the wall, perhaps a cubit long and a little over a span in height. The hole was covered by a crude grille of iron. From somewhere inside the building I could hear a rhythmic sound, like a muttering or moaning.

There was nobody around. I squatted down to examine my find. I reckoned I would be able to wriggle through the gap, if I could get the grille off. I tugged at it uselessly, then looked for signs of corrosion that I could exploit. There were none.

Something did not make sense. For the iron to be free of rust it would have to be relatively new, but the building was rough and weathered. My fingers ran around the edges, feeling for the join. The grille had been stuck over the gap fairly recently, using some form of mortar.

I picked up a sharp stone from the ground and scraped it

against the mortar. The cement crumbled easily. Encouraged, I worked vigorously at the join, and soon the grille was loose like a rotten tooth.

So intent was I on my work that I nearly missed the sound of footsteps until it was too late. Someone was coming. Hurriedly, I rubbed dirt on my face and slouched against the wall with my hand out like a beggar. Then I realised that I was still wearing the expensive coat Abu Nuwas had given me for the feast. I stripped it off, and, with only a moment's regretful hesitation, scrunched it into a ball and sat on it, just as a man came round the corner.

Fortunately, my white skin must have convinced him that I had some horrible disease, because he muttered a charm against the evil eye and hurried away. My heart was pounding; my hasty disguise would not have survived closer inspection. When I was calm again, and certain that nobody else was around, I got up.

The coat was ruined, and I left it in the dirt. The grille, however, came away in my hands with only a little force. I noticed that there was no floor on the other side at street level, but I had come too far to turn back now. Checking for one last time that I was unobserved, I squeezed through the gap and dropped into the darkness.

Twelve

The Tale of The Great Demon Time, Devourer of All Things, which includes, The Tale of the Game of Four Divisions

I fell some six cubits, landing with a thump on cold, hard earth. The impact knocked the wind from my body, and I had to lie still for a moment while I regained my breath.

I was in a dim corridor. The only light came from the hole through which I had entered, now high above my head. At one end of the corridor a stairway led upwards. At the other, the passage turned sharply, and I could not see what lay beyond.

The air was hazy, and reeked of incense and candle wax. The rhythmic sound I had heard earlier came from around the corner, and was now clearer. It was the sound of a dozen voices, repeating, in a slow monotone, a string of meaningless syllables:

"On Ma Tri Mu Ye Sa Le Du
On Ma Tri Mu Ye Sa Le Du . . ."

The chanting was punctuated unpredictably by long, resonant chimes, apparently operating to a rhythm of their own, and an animal grunting and bleating. All this must have covered the noise of my clumsy entrance, as nobody had come to investigate. I crept towards the corner.

Peeking around I saw an underground chamber, lit by braziers. The men and women intoning the gibberish sat on cushions with their back to me. They had shaved heads and wore red robes.

Babak ibn Bundar stood in front of them, also clad in red, and with his eyes closed. In one hand he held two thick cymbals which dangled from a single leather thong. From time to time he clashed the rims of the cymbals together, and this produced the chimes I had heard. The animal noises emanated from a young goat, tethered to a butcher's block. All of this was unsettling; but what really caused my hair to stand on end was the indigo-skinned monster watching over the scene.

The beast was human in shape, but with fangs like a tiger's and a third eye in the centre of its forehead. It wore a crown made of five human skulls, and trod corpses beneath its clawed feet. In one of its six hands it held a bowl of blood, also made from a skull.

My fear was hardly lessened when I realised that the monster was a painting on a wall hanging. The illusion of movement had been created by the smoke from the braziers, and a faint rippling of the cloth. Other banners hung beside it, decorated with horses and dragons and tigers, but none was as detailed and lifelike as the three-eyed monster. There were also strange symbols carved into the walls, crosses with four crooked arms.

The chanting was increasing in intensity now, slowly building in tempo and volume. Ibn Bundar passed the chimes to one of the seated figures, and picked up a knife with a long blade that curled like a snake. The goat took fright, and began to writhe and whine.

"On Ma Tri Mu Ye Sa Le Du
On Ma Tri Mu Ye Sa Le Du . . ."

As the incantation reached a climax, some of the seated figures began to break into spontaneous shouts and wails. The animal, too, seemed to scream as the knife descended. Then it was silenced.

The chanting fell back to a whisper. Ibn Bundar bent down behind the block, and I could not see what he was doing. When he stood up again, he held an inverted skull in both hands. He put it to his face and tipped it back, and the blood ran down his face and into his beard as he drank. I must have let out an involuntary gasp, because his real eye darted in my direction, the glass orb following slowly after it. I pressed myself against the wall, but too late. He lowered the skull, pointed in my direction, and let out a hideous, wordless howl from his bloodstained mouth

I turned and ran. Behind me I could hear the thud of twenty bare feet. There was no time to leap for the hole and try to squirm back out onto the street. I headed for the stairs.

At the top of the stairs was a door, bolted on my side. I flung back the bolts, and tried to wrench the door open. But it was locked. I tugged at it helplessly, then hands seized me from behind and threw a red cloth over my head.

I was carried by my wrists and ankles, back down the stairs and along the corridor. I could hear the black man's thin voice directing them.

"Here, over here. Get rid of that animal, and tie him to the block, while I decide what we do with him. I mean − Yes, I know, I'm thinking! Shut up a minute."

The stone of the block was cold against my back, and I could feel the goat's blood soaking my shirt. Absurdly, I found myself thinking that Abu Nuwas would be cross, that I had ruined the expensive clothes he had given me. The cloth was pulled from my head, and I looked up into the frightened face of Babak ibn Bundar.

"God's death! He is a spy from the Barid."

The block had a metal ring screwed into each corner with a length of rope tied to it, and it was with these that I was secured. The shaven headed acolytes had gathered around, peering down at me. Some had the symbol of the crooked cross embroidered onto their garments.

"Why did you come here, boy?"

I sensed that ibn Bundar was not really interested in the answer to this question. I shouted something useless, about how they would all be caught and executed, and it would be better for them if they let me go. Ibn Bundar shoved the red cloth into my mouth to shut me up. I managed to bite one of his fingers, crunching down to the bone, before one of the acolytes tied a rope around my head to secure the gag.

The black man nursed his injured digit, and the fear in his voice was outweighed by cruelty.

"He interrupted the ritual. Maybe Mahakala sent him to replace the sacrifice."

An awkward shuffling suggested that some of the acolytes were nearly as unhappy with this suggestion as I was.

"But, master, if we kill him –"

"Fool! If he survives to tell the tale, we are all dead. Take your places. The demon will come to us, and with his power we can take on anybody who wishes to do us harm."

The acolytes shuffled away. I jerked at my bonds, but they held. The chanting began again, uncertainly at first, then with increasing conviction.

"On Ma Tri Mu Ye Sa Le Du
On Ma Tri Mu Ye Sa Le Du . . ."

Ibn Bundar, eyes closed, shifted his grip on the knife. I sensed he was trying to steel himself for the deed. The incantation, however, was driving him inexorably to the climax of the ritual. I tried to shout; the rough cloth of the gag scratched the back of my throat and made me want to retch. In the distance I thought I heard a crash, but the mounting clamour in the chamber made it impossible to tell. The black man opened his eyes, and the real orb was as cold and empty as the false one. He raised the knife to strike.

Then the chanting was disrupted by the clatter of boots and gruff shouts. A woman screamed. Ibn Bundar dropped his weapon as two burly figures in blue slammed him against the wall, knocking the painted monster to the floor. The next person to stand over me was a scowling al-Takht, followed by Abu Nuwas, clutching his sayf and grinning like a maniac.

"No, don't untie him! I'll cut his throat myself for what he did to that coat."

With a sigh al-Takht signalled to one of the guards to release me. I sat up, rubbing my wrists and ankles. Everywhere the acolytes were being bound and marched away by men of the Shurta.

"How did you find me?"

Al-Takht looked like he had just drunk sour milk.

"It seemed scarcely possible, but perhaps you are as foolish as your master after all. What, did you really imagine your progress through Sharqiya was inconspicuous? Ducking and dodging down the streets . . . One-Eye here might not have noticed you, but everybody else in the area did.

"Fortunately, one of my halfwit constables managed to recognise you from the Watch House, otherwise they'd probably have given you a good kicking in a back alley somewhere, just for looking suspicious. Instead, he sent a boy to tell me that a member of the Barid was acting funny on my turf, and watched you while you broke into this house.

"I found your master, and rounded up some men. When we'd all arrived and you hadn't come out, we decided to come in after you. Good thing too, by the looks of it."

He surveyed the room's peculiar trappings.

"At least we've got our man. So it was human sacrifice after all? I never thought I'd see the day that Umm Dabbah was right about anything, even by accident."

"Babak ibn Bundar – he was a witch, then?"

The Police Captain picked up the picture of the three-eyed monster.

"Certainly looks like it."

"Bon."

We both looked puzzled at this apparently meaningless interruption from Abu Nuwas. It sounded as though he was mimicking the cymbal chime.

"I never thought to see it in Baghdad, but this is Bon. It is the religion of the Tibetan mountains. They believe that if the gods were all benevolent, we wouldn't need to placate them with prayers and sacrifices. Many of the deities of Bon are fierce demons who hate humanity. It is a world view that fits the evidence rather better than most others, in my opinion."

Al-Takht tutted at this blasphemy, but my master took the picture from al-Takht and contemplated it thoughtfully.

"Bon is not really a religion as we understand it. Rather it is a system of secret magical rites to protect against demons, and at the deeper levels to bind them to the service of master practitioners. This handsome blue gentleman is Mahakala, The Great Demon Time, Devourer of All Things."

The Police Captain was eyeing him suspiciously.

"How do you know so much about it?"

Abu Nuwas shrugged.

"I have travelled to the East. As has Babak ibn Bundar. Did he not mention being at Talas? That was a battle against the armies of the Chinese, fought in the land of the Uyghurs."

Al-Takht watched ibn Bundar being led from the room.

"Well, we shall see what this apostate has to say for himself. For his own sake, he had better have kept those children alive somewhere. My men all know Ghassan the Porter, and they are not renowned for their gentle natures."

★★★

On the way back to the Watch House, I voiced the doubts that had been nagging at me since my rescue.

"Master, I don't think the Bonists –"

"Bonpo. Followers of Bon are called Bonpo."

"I don't think the Bonpo killed the children."

Abu Nuwas stopped walking and stared at me.

"Well, you have changed your opinion. Why is that?"

"When ibn Bundar suggested sacrificing me, the others seemed shocked and uncertain. If they'd already murdered three children, I don't think they'd have any qualms about doing it to me."

"Then it may be that the children are still alive somewhere. In any case, al-Takht now has grounds to hold ibn Bundar."

"Is the practice of Bon prohibited, master?"

"No, the good people of Baghdad are free to damn themselves for eternity in whichever way they see fit, provided they are born into their errors. But abandoning the true faith is another matter. Ibn Bundar was a Muslim. The penalty for apostasy is death."

This explained why he was prepared to kill me for intruding

156

on their rites. When we next saw him, however, in the cell of the Watch House, the murderous fit had passed from him. He slumped against the wall, shattered and defeated. It seemed he had had an accident, or a series of accidents, along the way: his one good eye was bruised, he was covered in cuts and he held his right hand in a way that suggested some fingers were broken.

"Tell us where the children are, and I will make your end as swift and painless as I can."

Al-Takht began the interrogation, his arms folded and his face impassive. Ibn Bundar looked up helplessly.

"Children? I don't know what —"

The police thug standing over him had kicked him in the stomach. Ibn Bundar gasped for breath, desperately trying to speak.

"Why would I lie to you? I mean, I am going to die any-way. I told you, that grandson of Abd al-Aziz, anything could have happened to him. And I don't know about any other children."

The policeman went to kick him again, but Abu Nuwas stopped him.

"Moron! If you kill him, we have no chance of finding the children. Bring him water."

The thug looked outraged at this suggestion, but al-Takht nodded, and he complied sullenly. When the prisoner had drunk, Abu Nuwas crouched close to him.

"Tell me everything."

So he did.

The Tale of the Game of Four Divisions

I was born in Merv, capital of the province of Khorasan. Merv is a city of warriors, standing proud in the fierce cold deserts on the other side of the Oxus. The walls are so high it seems that sunlight never reaches the streets. My father was a war-rior, and my mother was a woman of the Luo, a slave taken as loot from one of his many battles.

I was too young to take part in the Abbasid revolution, but as soon as I could shave I marched off to the land of the Uyghurs to fight for the Khalifate. In truth I had no idea where I was going, who the enemy was or what the war was about. I just wanted to fight alongside Abu Muslim.

Abu Muslim, like me, grew up in the darkest alleys of Merv, and he was the greatest warrior of his generation. Nobody ever talked about his parentage, at least not openly. The name by which he became famous – Father of a Muslim – revealed nothing of his family or tribe. The rumour whispered around Khorasan was that his mother was a soldiers' whore, and that he was born in a baggage train. Yet he rose to become head of an army that conquered an empire.

It was Abu Muslim who raised the Black Flag of revolution; he who led the unstoppable westward drive that blew away the Umayyads; he who found the surviving Abbasids, as they cowered in their safe house in Kufah, and first pledged allegiance to the new Khalifah. He was brilliant, ruthless, a man with a face and heart of granite, who cared for nobody but his troops. But the passion with which he loved them was so deep that dying for him was the least they could do. You say God chose the Abbasid dynasty to lead his people? I say it was Abu Muslim who anointed them.

We headed north and east, to where the city of Samarqand straddled the Silk Road. I knew nothing, then, of trade and politics and strategy. I was a wide eyed child in a new world, a boy desperate to be accepted by the men around me, men who swore and spat and boasted about how many men they had killed.

However one such man befriended me. He was a chubby, genial fellow from Sind. I noticed him because he did not loll around the fire with the others in the evening, but sat slightly apart, hunched over something invisible in the darkness. Reluctant as I was to leave the inner circle, in the end curiosity got the better of me, and I wandered over to see what was interesting him.

On the ground in front of him was a square piece of wood. It was criss-crossed with lines, which divided it into smaller squares. Dotted around this surface were a number of lumps of stone, which he was studying intently. I could guess at only one reason for this strange behaviour.

"Are you telling fortunes?"

He looked up at me and laughed.

"In a sense, maybe I am. I've seen you around. You want to be a real soldier?"

I was about to protest that I was already a real soldier, but instead I nodded and listened.

"Then you must learn that there is more to it than hitting people and bragging. Your education starts with this."

He handed me one of the stone lumps. It was carved into the shape of a tiny spearsman.

"You are playing with toys?"

He laughed again.

"This, my friend, is al-Shatranj, the Game of Four Divisions, and you will learn more about the art of war from these toys than from a thousand evenings of sitting with those grunts. Sit down, and I'll show you."

And so he did. He showed me how the stones represented the four divisions of the army, the infantry, cavalry, chariots and elephants, each moving differently across the grid. He taught me how they combined in both attack and defence, for they had to protect their leaders, the King and the Wazir. If the King fell, the battle, and the game, was lost.

I pointed out that nobody had used chariots for hundreds of years, but he insisted the detail did not matter, the principles of strategy remained the same. Before I realised what was happening, we were engaged in battle. Knowing only one way of fighting, I ordered my brave warriors to charge headlong at his centre. With almost regretful ease, the Sindi contained my assault, then crushed it with attacks from both flanks. I stared at the decimated remnants of my tiny stone army.

"Let's do it again."

Each evening when we made camp, the Sindi and I would sit playing al-Shatranj. Gradually his victories became less easy, the battles more bloody and complex. And each day, as we marched, he would school me in the more subtle arts of war. I learned that politics, money and intelligence were as significant as swords and arrows.

"You see the track we are following here? This is the old Silk Road. For a thousand years, camel trains have followed this route that links east to west, running from China to Egypt and beyond. Not much actual silk is carried, these days, not since the Romans stole the secret of making it for themselves. They quite literally stole it, in fact; their ambassadors took home silkworm eggs hidden in hollow walking sticks. But everything else that can survive the journey passes this way: textiles, jewellery, spices, knowledge . . .

"The Silk Road is not often the cause of conflict. Trade benefits everybody, and nobody wants to frighten off the merchants. But Islam has been expanding since the Angel Jibril first spoke to the Prophet Muhammad, peace be upon him, and it doesn't know how to stop. So a minor squabble between petty kingdoms now threatens to bring two mighty empires to war.

"Farghana sought the support of the Chinese in its war with Chach. The Chinese Governor of the area, Gao Xianzhi, besieged the city of Chach, and when its king sued for peace, promised him safe passage if he surrendered. He lied, however. The King of Chach was beheaded in front of the walls of his city.

"His son, the new King of Chach, escaped, and fled to Merv. Here he begged Abu Muslim to help restore him to his throne. Our wise leader decided that a grateful ruler in a key city on the Silk Road was worth the gamble. And this, my friend, is why you and I are hardening our soles on this long march."

I asked him once, why, with all his wisdom, he had not become a general but remained a common soldier.

"Ah, my friend, look at me. I am a man of Sind, neither Arab nor Persian. Who will take orders from me? Besides, he who sticks his head out of the ditch risks having it cut off. I prefer to watch history unfold from the safety of the ranks."

At Samarqand we joined up with the army of Ziyad ibn

Salih, nearly doubling our numbers. To my chagrin Abu Muslim himself turned back here, handing command of the joint force to ibn Salih. But learning the ways of the world, and the Game of the Four Divisions, helped to make up for this disappointment.

Ibn Salih led us north-east to the valley of the Talas River. Here Gao Xianzhi waited with a Chinese army augmented by the Qarluqs who lived in the Talas valley, as well as by his allies from Farghana. The Chinese were ensconced in a bend in the river, where they blocked the only crossing on the road to Chach. We did not have sufficient men to dislodge them, and they seemed disinclined to sally out from their fortifications and drive us away. I learned later that Gao hoped to avoid battle with a dangerous and largely unknown enemy.

For four days the armies glowered at each other across the valley. The only action was a series of skirmishes, duels and raids. Despite badgering our captain for a chance to fight, I was allocated only dull guard duty. The air felt sick, as it does before a storm. The Sindi, however, was curiously serene.

"You will see battle, my friend, have no fear. Ibn Salih is busy."

Whether he truly knew something or was just guessing, he was right. As I discovered later, ibn Salih had made contact with the Qarluqs, promising them independence if they turned against the Chinese. On the fifth day they attacked their former allies in the rear, throwing Gao's meticulous defences into disarray. At last my company was given the signal to attack.

We ran into the battle, yelling and waving our spears. After several minutes of running, however, we had found nobody to fight, and slowed uncertainly to a halt. Then somebody spotted the Chinese fortifications, and we set off again, our enthusiasm only slightly diminished.

By the time we arrived at the barricades they had been abandoned. We wandered around the ditches, ramparts and caltrops in bemusement, picking up any small objects of value that had been dropped by the retreating foe. Eventually our captain rounded us up and we headed on towards the river.

When we finally came across the enemy they seemed as surprised as we were. They were not Chinese but Farghana, and for a moment nobody was sure whether we were on the same side. Then they rushed at us. I hurled my long spear uselessly, and pulled out my sword.

It was all over in seconds. I killed one of them, a boy of around my age. When he came close to me I swung my sword, catching his hand. He dropped his own weapon as blood exploded from the wound, and I stabbed him several times until I was sure he was dead. I don't know which of us was screaming louder.

The whole experience had as little to do with my dreams of glory as it did with the Sindi's grand strategies. He was wrong, too, about the safety of anonymity. A Farghana javelin had impaled him before he could draw his sword. His dead eyes stared up at the empty skies. I took his pack, which held the game of al-Shatranj, and nobody disputed my claim. Again we milled uncertainly, before a voice shook us back to reality.

"You! Stop looting the dead, and gather your spears! The Chinese are retreating!"

It was true. Betrayed by the Qarluqs, Gao had decided to withdraw beyond the river Talas. However, he did not bother to discuss his plans with his Farghana allies, who were defending the river crossing. In the confusion they were unable to organise their own withdrawal, nor to get out of the way of the Chinese. Gao's second in command, Li Siye, ordered his men to chop them down if they blocked the retreat.

So it was that the great army of Chinese, Ferghana and Qarluqs destroyed itself, and we won a famous victory for minimal losses. Unfortunately for me, that was not quite the end of that bloody day. The commander of the Chinese reserve sent a message to Li Siye reproaching him for his cowardice in fleeing. Stung by these words, Li rallied a group of volunteers and made a stand to cover his general's escape.

The first I knew of this development was when a bullet from a sling hit my right eye, crushing the delicate orb. We had struggled across the river, along with thousands of other Muslim troops, and chased headlong in pursuit of loot and honour. Our leaders had for the most part lost control of the situation, and we simply blundered into Li's rearguard.

When the bullet hit me I fell to the ground shrieking. Between the blood and the pain it was hard to follow what happened next, but I guess my comrades must have fallen back and left me lying there. A few of the more courageous, or greedy, Chinese came forward to search my pack, and found al-Shatranj. Curious about these strange objects, which they thought must be some new form of divination or secret battle plan, they carried both my pack and me to their general. I passed out along the way, and by the time I regained consciousness I was a prisoner of Gao Xianzhi.

Thirteen

Concluding, The Tale of the Game of Four Divisions, and, The Tale of The Great Demon Time, Devourer of All Things

"I hope you are feeling better."

The voice spoke in cultured Arabic, with only a slight accent. I opened my eyes. My right eye was hard and sore, and covered by a bandage. I reached up to touch it.

"I advise you not to do that. I am afraid your eye was dead by the time you got here. We had to take it out, for fear that the rot would spread into your brain. We have replaced it with a globe of glass."

With my one good eye I looked around. I was in a tent, lying on something like a farsh which had been placed on a low platform. A man stood over me. He was Chinese, with the trimmed beard and long moustache of that land. He wore long silk robes trimmed with fur, and a tall, cylindrical hat.

"My name is Wang Wei. Please consider yourself my guest. I hope you will not make it necessary to treat you as a prisoner."

I croaked something at him, and he had water brought for me. The servants also carried in the Sindi's battered old pack. Wang Wei gingerly pulled out the square board and stone pieces that made up the game of al-Shatranj.

"Now, when you are ready, you will please tell me what this is."

I did not have the strength to refuse him, even if I could think of any reason why I should. I set out the stones on the wooden grid, and explained to him how they moved. At first he was suspicious, then disappointed when he realised I was telling the truth, then intrigued, as we casually fell into playing a game.

Wang Wei visited me every day, and interrogated me, gently and politely, about the Khalifate and its military power. I felt some guilt at giving intelligence to the enemy, but consoled myself with the thought that I knew very little of any value. If anything, I exaggerated the might of the Muslim armies, and perhaps I played a small part in convincing them that full scale war would not be in their interests. Increasingly the questions were only a pretext for the games of al-Shatranj.

I asked some questions too, and learned that we were in an army camp somewhere in the land of the Uyghurs. Ibn Salih had not advanced since the battle of Talas, and Gao had no intention of provoking him. It had begun to seem that the lands of the Silk Road were too barren, too distant from supplies and reinforcements, for either side to fight a real war there.

On one occasion Wang Wei brought with him a long embroidered bag. It contained a qin, a stringed instrument similar to the qanun. My captor played it with considerable skill and sang songs, which he told me he had composed himself. I asked him the meaning of the words and he told me, although he insisted they would lose all beauty in the transla-tion. Unlike the bravado and heightened emotions of our poetry, his songs described moments of stillness and calm:

> "Empty hill, no man seen
> Yet we hear men's voices.
> Sun returns to deep forest;
> Again glistens the green moss."

After a couple of weeks, I was summoned to the presence of General Gao. I had been well treated and was recovering quickly, so that I could walk virtually unaided, with an escort of guards around me. His tent was as grand as many a rich man's house in Merv, and he sat on a raised dais at the end of a long carpet. Wang Wei interpreted for him.

"So, what is this Game of the Four Divisions, of which I have heard so much?"

Gao Xianzhi did not look like his troops, being darker of skin and squarer of face. I learned later that he was not Chinese, but from Goguryeo, a kingdom far across the vast lands of China. He learned al-Shatranj quickly and enthusiastically, commenting only that it might be better if one could turn an opponent's captured pieces against him. I wondered if he was recalling the way his own allies had betrayed him in the Talas valley. He had an ivory board made for him, and pieces carved from jade and quartz.

Then word came that ibn Salih had withdrawn from the land of Qarluqs, and returned to Khorasan. Despite his stunning victory at the Talas River, he knew that the Chinese still outnumbered him, and would not be so easily caught out a second time. More importantly, however, among the prisoners captured was a maker of paper. The secret skill of turning old rags into a substance cheaper and lighter than parchment, and more durable than papyrus, was of far more value to the Family of Islam than shaky conquests in hostile lands.

The war was over. But when Gao marched back to Kucha, I went with him. Perhaps he would have let me go home, if I had asked. But life as the favourite of a provincial governor was infinitely preferable to poverty in Merv; and he did not insist on the other duties which a Khorasani man would demand from a young protégé. The Chinese were fascinated by my black skin, and treated me with respect.

I learned to speak some words of their language, although I never truly mastered the tones which distinguish between otherwise identical sounds of very different meaning. For example, while playing al-Shatranj one day, I tried to say that I had gained an advantage over Gao; what I actually said was that I had caught a carp. This caused enormous hilarity, and my inability to grasp what seemed childishly obvious to them endeared me to them all the more.

I lived in Kucha for four years. China was a land of wonders to me, and its scholars were capable of such feats that at times I thought they must possess captive Jinni. Among the other miracles I saw was a device crafted of wood and metal which told the hours of the day more accurately than any sundial; and a magical bar of iron, which, when placed in water, always pointed to the north.

But there was a sickness at the heart of the empire that was to destroy my new life. In the capital city of Chang'an, the Emperor Tang Xuanzong, who had reigned over forty years of prosperity, was growing old and foolish. He had fallen in love with his son's wife, the lady Yang, and forced them to divorce so that he could take her as his consort. He disarmed central China, ordering all spear and arrow points to be melted down. Then he withdrew increasingly from public affairs, devoting himself to pleasure with his young bride.

When a ruler is absent, scum rush to fill the gap like water seeping into a hole in the ground. Provincial governors like Gao, who already wielded enormous power, became virtually independent now that the Emperor had no armies to keep them in line. At court, Lady Yang's favourites gradually replaced competent and conscientious officials.

One such favourite was An Lushan. He was a sheep rustler from Bukhara who had run away to join the army in order to escape the law. Cunning and brave, he had risen through the ranks to become Governor of Manchuria. As his wealth grew he became obscenely fat, and his rivals in Chang'an thought him a fool. An Lushan had no qualms about acting the buffoon; on one occasion he allowed Lady Yang and her entourage to dress him up as a giant baby. However all the time he was using his reputation as unofficial court jester to conceal his ambition.

This dangerous state of affairs was held in delicate equilibrium by the Chancellor, Li Linfu. Chancellor Li was a shrewd and experienced administrator, who occupied a position similar to the Khalifah's Wazir. His sober influence balanced the excesses of Lady Yang, and kept in check her relatives and sycophants, particularly her dissolute cousin Yang Guozhong. When Li Linfu died, Yang Guozhong took over his office, and the Empire began to unravel. Yang's first act as Chancellor was to have Li's body dug up and beheaded for treason.

The new Chancellor was jealous and frightened of the provincial governors, and particularly An Lushan. He began to make unsubtle hints that the fat man was plotting treachery. The fact that this was true, and that he had spent ten years perfecting his plan to seize the throne, did nothing to lessen An's indignation at being accused. Yang had provided him with the excuse he needed.

An Lushan marched from his provincial capital of Beijing with over a hundred thousand men. Having no armies of his own, Yang recalled all the loyal governors. Gao returned to Changʾan, and I went with him. With no opposition, the Tibetans gleefully seized the Silk Road kingdoms that had been so hotly contested a few years earlier.

I can tell you little of the capital, or the vast plains of central China. All I saw were endless camps and councils of war. By the time we arrived, An Lushan had captured the eastern capital of Luoyang, and proclaimed himself the first Emperor of the Great Yen dynasty. Gao was ordered to defend Changʾan.

Despite Gao's efforts, Yang's military incompetence allowed An to capture the capital. The Emperor and his retinue fled the city. However, his guards had had enough. They stopped along the road, and refused to march another step until they were given the head of Yang Guozhong. The terrified Emperor complied, and the Chancellor was executed at the roadside. Unfortunately this did not satisfy the soldiers, who now demanded the head of Lady Yang. The old man refused, but his consort, seeing her world collapsing around her, hanged herself from a tree.

The Emperor Tang Xuanzong, consumed with grief, abdicated in favour of his heir. This was the turning point in the rebellion. An Lushan's obesity was making him increasingly unwell. He was nearly blind, and began to believe everyone was plotting against him. His ravings scared those around him, and he was murdered by a eunuch slave on the orders of his own son.

Nonetheless the anarchy in the Empire continued. I had no suspicion of how bad things were until the night a servant came to my tent with two horses and supplies for a long journey.

"General Gao Xianzhi orders you to take these mounts and flee the country. He thanks you for the gift of al-Shatranj and wishes you a long and prosperous life."

One of Gao's subordinates had accused him of embezzling supplies. In the fervid atmosphere of the court, allegation was as good as evidence. His subordinates offered to testify on his behalf, but he refused, fearing that they too would be accused. He was arrested and executed the day after I fled the camp.

I did not stop riding until I was a hundred miles from danger. That was when I found, stuffed into a saddle bag, the battered old game set I had inherited from the Sindi. Even the harsh wind in my face was insufficient to dry my tears as I galloped on.

I headed north-west, hoping to find the Silk Road and follow it back to the Land of Islam. The Empire I travelled across had been devastated by the civil war. Crops were ruined, villages burned, and hungry bandits roamed the countryside. I heard later that over half of the population died, in battle or from disease or famine, before order was restored.

The journey would have been dangerous for a Chinese man. With my poor linguistic skills and obviously foreign features, it was deadly. My supplies were soon gone, and in a starving land food was hard to come by. One of the horses went lame, and I killed and ate it. The second was still strong and healthy when we arrived at a range of hills, and I wept as I cut its throat.

I still believed that I would find the Silk Road on the other side of the range, and this kept me going as I struggled up the slopes chewing on rotten horse meat. However, the hills went on and on, each higher than the last. Finally I admitted to myself the truth. I was hundreds of miles too far to the south, and had wandered into the foothills of the Himalayan mountains.

It was too late to turn around. I knew I would never survive the journey back to China, and there was nothing there for me in any case. I aimed north, inasmuch as I could choose my direction over the difficult terrain, and pressed on.

When I saw the flags I thought I was hallucinating, or dead. They ran along a gulley that cut between two inclines, a row of identical orange banners hanging from sticks and flapping in the stiff wind. I staggered towards them and they seemed to form a path, leading me upwards, as if to heaven. I remember following the waving guides, which nodded at me as my feet dragged in the rubble. Then there is only darkness.

Later, I thanked Yeshe Torma for saving my life, and he answered that he had not. He said I had died on that day, but had been reborn. Certainly he nursed me with the milk of yaks, as if I were a newborn whose mother had died during the labour. He also said that it was not chance that had led me to him, but the gods, so that their ways could be preserved. He even claimed that he had been waiting there for me, that his divination had foretold my coming.

He was a small man, who seemed always to be smiling. I could not tell how old he was. His face may have been prematurely lined by the sharp mountain air, or his hair might have stayed black into old age. I questioned him once, and he simply asked me why I wanted to know. I could not think of an answer, and that was an end to the matter.

From the moment I was born into my new life, Yeshe Torma began to teach me the ways of Bon. The only language we had in common was Chinese, which was no more Yeshe's native tongue than it was mine. However I understood Bon as easily as if I were recalling something I had known long ago, but forgotten. He taught me about the spirits of the stones and rivers, and the gods of the household. He taught me about the sacred symbol of the crooked cross, the sauwastika. And he taught me about the terrible demons who, unseen, plague mankind. I thought about the blasted landscapes of China, over which I had ridden. And I decided that, although the demons themselves were invisible, it was not hard to see where they had passed by.

Later, he taught me the rites by which demons are summoned, controlled and turned against one's enemies. I am forbidden to disclose these secrets, and I will not, regardless of what you do to me. There are worse things in the universe than physical pain and death.

I lived for twelve years in the mountains with my teacher, and would be there still, if he had not instructed me to return to the west. I begged him to let me stay, but he told me that it was my fate.

"The old ways are dying in the mountains. From the west comes Islam, from south and east comes Buddhism. Now the King of Tibet has converted to the Dharma. You were sent here to learn Bon, so that you can take it to new lands, plant the seeds of knowledge in fresh soil. Return to the land of your birth, my son, and fulfil your destiny."

I trudged away down the old Silk Road. When I got to Merv I kept walking. After spending half of my life in the east, there was nothing for me there. I set myself to finding the captain of my old company. I finally tracked him down in the new city of Baghdad. It took some time to persuade him of who I was; he thought me long dead, and when he had last seen me I had been a youth with two eyes. In the end it was the Game of Four Divisions that convinced him.

I told a tale of long captivity by yellow devils, and as a veteran I was able to claim a small pension. I settled in Harbiya, where I dedicated myself to finding pupils worthy of the secret lore. Of the rites I will tell you only that we sacrificed animals, but I have never harmed a child in my life. Now I am to die. Whatever demon you have working for you, it is more powerful than any protecting me. I have failed my master, and failed in my destiny, and because of me the ancient teachings too will die. There is no torture you can inflict that would be worse than that knowledge.

* * *

Al-Takht was unimpressed.

"A pretty tale, but it will not help you. One of your acolytes has just confessed that you sacrificed the porter's son to your demon god."

171

I was relieved when Abu Nuwas led me away from the Watch House. I could not bear to look at ibn Bundar's battered face any longer. Even though he had tried to kill me, I could not escape the thought that it was my fault he was facing execution – if, that is, he survived questioning by the police.

"Do you think he killed those children, master?"

Abu Nuwas pondered before replying.

"In truth, I know little of Bon – its followers guard its secrets carefully. However I have never heard of human sacrifice forming part of the rites. I imagine the heavy handed approach of the police will produce the confessions it seeks, whether or not the suspect is actually guilty. Some of those acolytes were so scared, I think they would admit to stealing the moon from the sky if you put it to them.

"Still, let al-Takht go on believing he's got his man. It keeps him from bothering us, at least until the next child disappears.

"Now we must go to cleanse the filth of this shabby business from our bodies. I have to dress for an evening drinking with the Khalifah. You, on the other hand, must don your best burgling attire."

"You still wish me to search the house of the merchant ibn Zaid?"

Abu Nuwas looked at me in mock surprise.

"But you have an assignation with a young lady. It would be most ill-mannered to leave her unsatisfied."

I told him that I had clothes at the Hall of the Barid. This was a lie, but I wanted to test the extent of my privileges as a postman. Arriving at the Palace of the Barmakids I let myself in through the private door. I was disappointed to find that my friend Yaqub al-Mithaq was not there, but I found a household servant and demanded food, clothing and water to wash in. Almost instantly he reappeared with a dish of rice and broiled chicken, and a huge bowl of hot water.

The clothes took a little longer, but they too were eventually produced. They were plain and black, and not as fine as the ruined garments Abu Nuwas had given me, but they suited my purpose, consisting of a simple qamis, a short

tunic and thick pants. As an afterthought I asked for, and
received, a small dagger which I concealed inside my sleeve.
Not wanting to push my luck any further I dozed away the
hours till sunset, then headed out to Karkh, to meet with
Layla bint al-Bazza.

Fourteen

The Tale of the Shower of Petals, including, The Tale of the Cock and his Hens

She was waiting for me when I descended into the garden.

Getting into the merchant's house was nothing to me; I had often broken into buildings in search of gold, silver and jewels, but never for the promise of greater treasure than her company. I scrambled up a wall, using shuttered windows and the cracks between bricks, any irregularity my eager fingers could probe. The outer wall was two storeys high, but the upper level was only a facade. I swung myself over and dropped gently onto the flat roof of the outer rooms. From there it was a silent flit over the heads of the sleeping householders until I came to the women's quarters, and a feather leap down to the courtyard.

The moon was nearly full now, but even so I did not believe what I saw as she ran up to me. She was unveiled, and I beheld her whole face for the first time. She was a few years older than me, at the peak of her comeliness. Her mouth was so shapely it seemed to be have been coaxed from clay by a master sculptor, and still glistened wet from the touch of his fingers. The wide brown eyes that had first caught my attention had shadows under them, as if they carried some secret sadness, but were clever and generous.

I gasped at the sight of her naked face. She smiled, causing small creases to appear at either end of her mouth, and whispered to me.

"This is the women's quarters. Why would I wear a veil here?"

I was reminded of the danger I was in. If Imran ibn Zaid

caught me in the women's quarters of his house, he would rip me apart, and no qadi in the land would condemn him for it.

"Show me where it happened."

Layla gestured around the garden.

"She was playing here. The nurse was in the privy, over there. It opens onto the courtyard, so she could see the child most of the time."

I looked around. Ibn Zaid did well for himself, and for his women. A shallow pool at the centre cooled the air, and arranged in artful lines around it were roses and carnations, richly scented jasmine and beds of fragrant basil and coriander. The place seemed so calm, so soothing to the senses, it was hard to believe evil had come there.

"Where is the merchant?"

Layla pointed to the wall that separated the women's quarters from the rest of the house.

"Through there."

The door in the wall was secured with a heavy iron lock. Glancing nervously at the girl, I drew a couple of bent needles from my sleeve. I was ashamed to let her see my skill at house-breaking, but she watched with shining eyes and her mouth slightly open as I picked the lock, and kissed me on the cheek when the door swung open. I could hardly look at her as I spoke.

"Wait here. If you are found sneaking around the house . . ."

But Layla took my hand and led me through. Her skin was warm, her touch both reassuring and tentative.

The main courtyard was less ornate than the women's garden, but was elegantly laid out, with a well at the centre. This made me wonder whether there was a simple answer to the mystery after all.

"Could it be that the girl fell down the well?"

Layla looked at me as if her confidence was slightly shaken.

"How could she have reached it? Besides, we have examined it thoroughly, even sending the kitchen boy down on a rope to search the water, until there could be no doubt Najiba was not there. And then we did again several times after that, when we could think of nothing else to do."

175

Her use of the little girl's name shamed me slightly. This was not about my efforts to impress an attractive woman. A child's life might be at stake. I had to start acting and thinking like a serious agent of the state, not just worrying whether I looked like one.

"What happened when the nurse raised the alarm?"

"People came running, from all over the house. The steward was in the vestibule, arguing with the porter, so nobody could have got out through the front door. We searched every room; the windows were all shuttered and barred from the inside. Could somebody have come as you did, over the roof?"

I thought not. I was small and light, and an experienced climber. Anybody who managed to get over the high facade would then face the impossible task of carrying a six year old girl back across. They would need to be able to fly.

A light across the courtyard caught my eye. Somebody had lit a lamp within one of the rooms. I looked to Layla, who whispered:

"The merchant's chamber."

We crept over. There was a window onto the courtyard, from which the light was leaking. The window was shuttered, but one of the slats was broken, and allowed us to peer inside.

A woman stood in front of a long mirror. Although alone, she was fully dressed and veiled. Without taking her eyes from the mirror, she turned to both sides, putting one hand to her waist. She seemed to be admiring her reflection, although I thought her too heavily built to be attractive, with large, ugly hands.

As we watched she began to dance. At first she simply swayed her hips from side to side. Then she raised a hand above her head, elbow crooked slightly, and span so that her skirt swung around her ankles. There was no sound apart from the thud of her feet on the floor, but she danced as if hearing music which grew faster and wilder.

As she swirled, the hand at her waist crept towards her belly. To my astonishment she began to stroke her groin rhythmically, her whole body jerking in response. It was only when she

176

threw her head back and climaxed with a groan as deep as a lowing bull that I recognised the harsh eyes above the veil, and understood the truth. The "woman" was the merchant Imran ibn Zaid.

I was distracted from the bizarre sight by a tug on my hand. Layla pulled me away from the window and we scrambled back to the women's quarters. At first I thought someone was coming, but once we were in the rose garden she burst into fits of giggles.

"His wife is always complaining that her clothes are going missing! She has had the slaves beaten several times over it. No wonder he did not want you poking around the house . . ."

She did not let go of my hand as she recovered her composure. At last she became serious again.

"Have you had any luck finding the old man?"

I thought of Babak ibn Bundar, battered and broken in his cell at the Watch House.

"I don't know. Maybe."

She looked at me as if expecting more, but I found myself unable to talk about him. Layla faced me, and fondled the collar of my tunic with the hand which was not holding mine.

"You are very brave, coming here like this."

I wondered about that. Since arriving in Baghdad I seemed to have been at the mercy of forces greater than myself. I wondered whether I had made any choices at all, or whether my path was already determined for me, by God or Ja'far al-Barmaki. Her next words encouraged me not to contradict her.

"Such bravery deserves a reward."

We were the same height, and our faces were very close to each other. Mingled with the perfume of the jasmine I could smell her cinnamon skin and her honeyed breath. She tugged gently on my collar, bringing my mouth to hers. As she pressed her lips against mine, the deep eyes slowly closed.

After a moment she leaned back, and contemplated me.

"You've never kissed a woman before, have you?"

I jerked away from her. It was true, but I had not expected it to be so obvious. No respectable girl would look at me in my

177

years of journeying, and the diseased whores who were available held no appeal for me. She laughed at my hurt expression, a fresh, cleansing sound.

"It is no sin, to be young. I have only ever kissed one man, before you. I loved him truly, but he is dead now, so you may take the scowl from your face. We all have secrets, deep below the ground. Come, sit with me."

"But this is madness! If I am caught here –"

She was serious now, and the sadness under her eyes deepened.

"Then you wish to die in old age, without ever having lived? I did not think you were so ordinary, Ismail the Newborn."

She drew me down beneath the shelter of a rose bush, heavy with star-white blossom. Petals drifted down onto us as we reclined on the thin rug which she had lain there. She stretched out on her back, and drew my head toward her. I suddenly found I did not know what to do with my arms, uncertain of whether I could touch her and if so where. The result was that I collapsed on top of her. She giggled, shaking quietly under me.

"Lean on one elbow. Put your other hand on my cheek – there."

I stroked her face, and found the courage to lean forward myself and kiss her. After a couple of moments she pushed me away.

"That's nice, but don't press so hard. Here –"

Layla took my head in both hands, and craned her neck towards it, so that she could control the contact. She teased my mouth with little brushes and licks from her tongue and lips, before kissing me properly. When her mouth opened mine did the same, and our tongues were like beasts mating, writhing around and caressing each other.

My zabb was painfully stiff, and protruding through my pants. It ached for contact with her body, but I arched my back away so that it did not accidentally prod her. She wore no coat, only a green dress that hung modestly to her knees, over her pants and qamis. Now she sat up and pulled the green dress over her head. Only a thin layer of cotton separated me from her naked skin.

She lay back, and I bent over her, kissing with more confidence. She took my hand and placed it under her qamis. I felt the warmth of her belly, which was both firm and yielding.

The excitement was unbearable, and my hips jerked towards her in involuntary spasm, so that the tip of my tool brushed her torso through our clothes. Layla reached below, and eased down my pants. My zabb sprang free, quivering in the mild summer air.

The gentle kiss of the breeze on my buttocks sent thrills through my body and caused my skin to pimple. I would have exploded at the slightest touch, but then we were interrupted by a voice.

"What's that? Who's there?"

Layla and I froze. My zabb slowly declined, and the glow of a lamp intruded on our bower. I rolled away, pulling up my pants as Layla scrambled back into her dress. She stood up, while I shrank behind a nearby bush.

"It's only me, Wahb. I couldn't sleep and came out for some air."

A turbanned figure was waddling towards her.

"Then why are you skulking under the roses, child?"

Wahb had the typically wide hips of the fat old eunuch. The loss of sexual desire was often replaced by indulgence in other, simpler appetites.

"I was frightened when I saw your light. After what happened to Najiba – oh, Wahb!"

Layla flung herself onto the eunuch's neck, bursting into very convincing tears. In the process she spun him round, so that his back was turned to me. I had burgled enough houses to know when it was time to get out quick. I scrambled for the wall.

Fortunately getting out was even easier than getting in. The inner wall offered plants and decorative features to aid my swift ascent to the flat roof. Once there I waited until Wahb escorted the weeping girl inside, then carefully scaled the facade, hanging from the outer face before dropping lightly onto the silent street beyond. The fall stung the soles of my feet, but I was confident I had escaped undetected. That is, until strong hands grasped my shoulders.

"Got you, you filthy degenerate!"

I reached for the knife in my sleeve. Then in my mind I saw again the damaged face of Babak ibn Bundar. I had caused enough death for one day. Instead, I drove an elbow backwards, at the same time crouching slightly. As I had hoped, the difference in heights between me and my captor meant that I jabbed his groin. While he fell to his knees gasping in pain, I ran for my life.

My assailant recovered with terrifying rapidity. I was quick on my feet, but before I could get round the corner I heard booted feet pounding after me. I risked glancing back, and saw a giant shadow bearing down. I ducked down another alley, but my pursuer was gaining on me.

I turned again, running blindly now with my head down. So it was that I nearly rammed the wall before I realised I had turned into a dead end. I tried to clamber upwards, but felt a jerk on my ankles. As I crashed to the ground, a heavy body fell on top of me, pinning me down. It reeked of wine and river mud.

"Ah, Newborn, I have dreamed of this moment, but somehow this is not as I imagined it would be . . ."

My pursuer was Abu Nuwas. I spat in his face in fury.

"Get off me, Abu Ali, you disgusting pig!"

He sat up, laughing.

"So it is no longer 'master,' and 'Father of Locks'. Now the Newborn calls me 'Abu Ali', as if he were my equal!"

His facetiousness only enraged me further.

"Actually, I called you 'disgusting pig', as if you were my inferior. I have been risking my life to search for the missing child, while you have been carousing with royalty."

He gave me a sly look.

"Let me see if I can predict the outcome of your efforts. You found no trace of the merchant's daughter, but the shop girl revealed a few things to you, eh?"

I tried to maintain my pose of righteous indignation, but my astonishment at the accuracy of his guess made it impossible.

"Oh, don't look so surprised. I've seen the way she looks at you, and if I can't spot a girl with a bit of the devil in her, than I am not the man I am reputed to be. Besides, when you hopped over that wall you were blushing like a virgin bride."

"Then why were you waiting for me . . . master?"

Abu Nuwas jumped to his feet.

"Of course! I must tell you what I have discovered this evening. But not here. We must go somewhere more agreeable. And I must have wine."

We hurried through the quiet streets of Karkh, and along the way I told him more about the merchant's house. He nodded absently and offered no comment, until we came to an impressive residence at the southern end of the district. Here he banged on the door like a debt collector. A face peered over the edge of the roof.

"In the name of God the All-Merciful, what do you think you are doing, Abu Ali?"

"Let us in, Abbas! I have a tale to tell and a terrible thirst that threatens to choke me to death. If you do not satisfy my needs, I may expire here on the street."

Abu Nuwas fell to his knees and began to make awful retching and rasping noises. Voices could be heard from neighbouring houses. I could now make out the features of Abbas, the emaciated poet, as he hissed at us.

"What are you playing at? I have a woman here. Her reputation —"

"Are you ashamed of your friends, Abbas? Will you not introduce us to the lady? Perhaps I need to serenade her."

My master drew breath as if to begin singing, and Abbas realised he was not going to win.

"Wait there, Father of Locks. I will give you a drink, if you promise you will go immediately afterwards."

His head disappeared, and Abu Nuwas grinned at me. Moments later the door creaked open. A hand yanked my master inside, so I followed.

Abbas hauled him off to a small but richly decorated room off the main courtyard, and flung him onto a rug.

"Wait there, I will return with the wine."

I sat beside him. A veiled head peered shyly round the door.

"I heard Abbas call you 'Father of Locks'. Could it be that you are –"

Her voice was refined, but tinged with a childish excitement. My master rose and bowed.

"Indeed, my lady. I am Abu Nuwas, the poet. And you are?"

The woman danced into the room, clapping her hands in joy. If she had been about to disclose her name, she was interrupted by the return of Abbas, carrying a tray with a jug and three goblets. I thought he was going to drop the tray when he saw that the woman had joined us.

"My lady, what are you doing down here? It is not seemly –"

"Oh, don't be such a bore, Abbas. It is not seemly for me to be lying on your roof with you, doing what we have been doing. The greatest living poet hammering at the door, in the middle of the night, with a story to tell – you surely don't expect me to hide upstairs like a timid maiden, and miss all the fun."

She settled imperiously on a farsh. Abbas, whose temper had clearly not been improved by her description of Abu Nuwas, sat glumly beside her. He reluctantly poured the wine, and I was touched by his courtesy as he passed me a goblet and went without himself. The woman took command.

"Well then, Father of Locks. You have your drink, now tell us your tale."

So he did.

The Tale of the Cock and his Hens

I arrived at al-Khuld at sunset, and was taken to a garden planted with sandalwood and lavender, which I had not seen before. At the centre of this fragrant sanctuary was a pavilion. It had a domed roof and the walls were perforated by a hundred windows.

Within the pavilion was the Commander of the Faithful, already flushed and excited from wine. This Harun is a very different creature to the haughty monarch you see on public occasions. Our Khalifah never forgets that the Umayyads were thrown out for their decadence and deviation from the true path, and is careful to maintain his front of pious orthodoxy. However in private, with his friends, there is nothing he likes more than to get outrageously, slobberingly drunk.

Abu'l Atahiyya, the Father of Madness was there, and of course Ja'far al-Barmaki, who is perhaps Harun's favourite drinking companion. I was not unhappy to see the Wazir. His demands on my services are vexatious, but he is a good source of income, and he tempers the Khalifah's more dangerous whims. The music was led by Ishaq al-Mosuli, son of Ibrahim – I think you heard him sing at the feast last night? He is a young man with a fine voice, and all the charm Ibrahim seems to be losing in his old age.

My little singing girl, Muti'a, was performing as well. I was glad to see she was not foolish enough to risk even a wink in front of her master, but even with modestly downturned eyes she somehow made harlot promises. Standing against a wall, leaning on his giant sword as he silently watched everybody, was Masrur, the bodyguard.

Harun leaned forward enthusiastically on seeing me, almost toppling over.

"Peace, Father of Locks! You are late. We must devise some appropriate punishment for you."

Abu'l Atahiyya must have been the object of the Khalifah's mockery before my arrival, because he seized eagerly on this theme.

"Yes, he must be strapped to an ass, and paraded around town. All the while being beaten with reeds. By dwarves."

I gave him a hollow smile, promising myself I would make him suffer for this. If the suggestion had caught the Khalifah's imagination he would have insisted on it being carried out without a second thought. And Masrur would have seen it done, regretfully but implacably obeying his master's order.

Fortunately at that moment the dancing girls entered, distracting us all.

They were a gift from Ja'far to his Khalifah. There were seven girls, each from a different nation: a plump Chinese maiden, a statuesque Slav, a long legged black woman from south of the Great Desert, a pretty Turkmen, a dark-eyed Greek, even a pale Goth from distant Andalus. My eye was particularly caught, however, by the Hindu. She had a slim, boyish figure, with small breasts. Her flat stomach was bare, between a short top and loose pants. She noticed my gaze, and dared a sidelong glance from lustful, half-closed eyes.

Each was dressed after the fashion of their country, but their costumes were artfully designed to tempt. The tribal garments were enhanced by slits and thin fabrics, which permitted tantalising glimpses of buttock and breast. They danced sinuously to a seductive tune, competing for the attention of the Khalifah. There were many worse fates than being a concubine in his huram. They would live and eat well, and even if they found his attentions repugnant, he had so many women that they would likely soon be forgotten in favour of new pleasures, and would be left in peace.

It was a stimulating sight, and even my jaded member stirred its head in interest. Harun was delighted, and when the music climaxed, to the accompaniment of much frenzied jiggling, he beckoned the Goth girl to come and sit by him. The disappointed rejects sat by the musicians. I noticed the Hindu talking to Muti'a, and the two of them scrutinising me when the Khalifah was not looking in their direction.

Harun was getting drunker, and wanted to be entertained.

"Poetry! I must have poetry from my brilliant friends. Enchant my ears with your magic charms."

I reluctantly stirred myself, trying to dredge up some scrap of doggerel that might pass for spontaneous wit. I had wasted some of my finest pieces on the Khalifah when he was so inebriated that he would never remember them, and had every intention of using them again when the opportunity arose. However, Abu'l-Atahiyya beat me to the post, jumping in with a madih of his own. He was clearly still smarting from being placed by the door at the previous night's feast. (Oh, you were next to him, weren't you, Abbas? How gauche of me to dwell on it.)

I had no interest in listening to his effusions. We must all write praise of our patrons, but one can at least do it with taste and wit. Abu'l-Atahiyya simply piles up the praise like a farmer shovelling shit. Father of Madness, indeed! Do not mistake me, I value the friendship of the chubby old milksop. I have known him since the old days in Basrah. However, he needs to find some real courage, if he wants to be a real poet. I made the excuse of having to pass water, and wandered out into the cool garden.

It was true that there was pressure on my bladder, from the wine I had consumed. Unfortunately, when I exposed my zabb to the outside air, I found that the excitement generated by the dancing girls had not dissipated. If anything my tool hardened. Every time I thought the drawbridge was lowering, and my amber liquid might sally forth to dance with the leaves, the image of the Hindu girl's hard belly tantalised me, and the treacherous serpent sprang back to life.

As I stood, pants round my ankles and waving my zabb at the unfortunate sandalwood, a sultry voice caressed my ears.

"Hey, beautiful man. Don't waste that on a tree. Bring it over here – we need you to settle a bet."

I looked back towards the pavilion, and saw that the Hindu had accompanied Muti'a into the garden. The two women stepped from the bush behind which they had been spying, and advanced on me.

Fifteen

Concluding the Tale of the Cock and his Hens, And, The Tale of the Shower of Petals

"Wait a minute, Abu Ali. Have you knocked us up and intruded on our night of passion just to brag of your sexual conquests? Is all this a dirty story so you could have a cup of wine?"

Abbas had voiced my own concern at the increasingly implausible turn of events. I noticed that his companion, on the other hand, seemed quite aroused by the tale; her eyes had widened above her veil, and her breathing deepened.

"I've never known you to object to a dirty story before, Abbas. But let me tell you what happened, then judge for yourself whether it was worth the disturbance."

Abbas sat back, and my master went on with his tale.

★ ★ ★

I watched the girls slink across the garden towards me, and the naked desire in the Hindu's dark eyes stiffened my zabb still more. Muti'a the singer spoke first.

"Oh Father of Locks, this is my friend Dhanya. I was telling her about the splendour of your sword, but she did not believe me. I said it was the size of a cucumber, she insisted that I must be thinking of a courgette. We came out in the hope of settling the argument. Well, little sister, do you concede that I was right?"

The hussy Dhanya came up and took my zabb in her hand, weighing it as if it were indeed a vegetable.

"Then you must have very small cucumbers in the Black Lands. In my home country of Rajputana, we grow cucumbers as big as my arm."

Muti'a sauntered over and stroked my denigrated tool, as if to console it after Dhanya's insults.

"But you must admit, little sister, that it is a strong, straight sword, which would penetrate deep into its victim."

The Hindu ran her finger along its length as if testing a blade.

"No doubt it would prick soft Arab flesh, but it would shatter against the steel of Rajputana."

She pressed it against her firm belly, and I shivered slightly. Muti'a pushed her away, and caressed my zabb possessively.

"At least you will allow it is a shapely instrument, that would play a fine tune."

Dhanya put her lips to the tip of my zabb and blew gently, while pressing her fingers along its length as if it were a flute.

"It plays sweetly enough, but its tone is not as rich and deep as the instruments of Rajputana."

They started giggling. I had had enough, and pulled away from them both.

"Whether it is flute or sword or vegetable, I do not recall taking it to market to be weighed and measured and manipulated! As for you, dancing girl, if the zabbs of Rajputana are so much better, I suggest you go avail yourself of them."

I made to pull up my pants, but Dhanya stopped me. She pressed herself against me, twisting my locks around her fingers where they dangled from my turban.

"I am the property of Ja'far al-Barmaki, and most likely will never see Rajputana again. Now that the Khalifah has not chosen me, I do not know what my fate will be. Perhaps the Wazir will keep me for himself, perhaps I will be sold to a rheumy old man with foul breath and stinking armpits. Whatever happens, this may well be the last time I ever make love to a beautiful man, with oiled hair and brilliant eyes, to whom I give myself freely and for my own pleasure.

"So fuck me, Father of Locks. Fuck me as if this was also your last chance for ecstasy."

She stripped off her clothes and stood naked before me, scented and bejewelled as she had been prepared for the bed of the ruler of the world. Her breasts were small but rounded, tipped with hard pink nipples, and her mound had been shaved and powered. She lay upon the grass, and as I knelt beside her I noticed Masrur the Swordbearer watching us from by the pavilion. He shook his head in gentle reproach, and I knew that we were in no danger. One of his functions as bodyguard was to protect Harun from knowing or seeing what might cause him distress. I am sure it would distress him sorely to have to order my execution.

And so we discovered that the steel of Rajputana did, after all, yield to the sword of Arabia. The gates of the stronghold were opened, and admitted the conqueror, to great rejoicing. Muti'a watched our coupling with increasing excitement, contributing little kisses, nips and slaps whenever opportunity arose and to whichever body presented itself. And when the dancer was satisfied, she made way for the singer, and we discovered that there was, also, enough cucumber for two.

At last the three of us sat up and made ourselves decent, before returning, one by one, to the pavilion. I entered first, to see the Khalifah regarding me sternly. For a moment my blood turned to ice, and I feared that he knew of my dalliance in the garden.

"I had forgotten to punish you for your lateness, Father of Locks. I have decided that your sentence is to be a dozen lashes."

What drunken whim was this? Twelve lashes was a terrifying penalty for tardiness. I started to stammer an apology, but Harun interrupted me.

"However, I shall be merciful and will pardon you; if, that is, you can do as we do now."

I looked at the stony faces of Ja'far and Abu'l-Atahiyya in perplexity. Then Harun al-Rashid of the Abbasids puffed out his cheeks and began to cluck like a chicken. The Commander of the Faithful flapped arms bent like wings, squawked and pecked, before finally producing an egg from his backside.

It was the Khalifah's idea of a joke, obviously cooked up during my absence. I almost wished he had just had me whipped. It would have been less painful.

Abu'l-Atahiyya went through the same performance, brandishing his egg with stifled sniggers which, unfortunately, I suspected to be genuine rather than sycophantic. Even the elegant Wazir played his part, disdainfully but dutifully. When three eggs had been held under my nose, Harun folded his arms and looked at me in expectation.

I had no idea whether he really would go through with the punishment, but Harun al-Rashid was a man who approached his humour with grim seriousness. I had to respond in the spirit of the original prank. However I had no egg which I could pretend to lay. Then inspiration struck. I stood up, threw my head back, and crowed like a cock.

There was a stunned silence, during which everyone looked to the Khalifah. I had just insinuated that the most powerful man in the world was my concubine. It was entirely possible that he would have me killed.

Fortunately, the true implications of my act must have passed him by, because he rolled around on his rug bellowing with laughter. As soon as everyone was sure it was safe, they all joined in too. I spotted Muti'a and Dahnya, who had sneaked in unnoticed, gazing at me with the intimacy of our shared secret.

More wine was sent for, and consumed. This caused the Khalifah to experience one of the swift reverses of mood to which he was prone. Now that the hilarity of his jape had faded, he was suddenly depressed. He began to gripe to Ja'far on one of his favourite subjects: the oppressiveness of Baghdad.

"Oh, my friend, the stench! The city is well provided with public hammams – why can the rabble not wash themselves? Then there is the stink of the tanneries and the dyers, the droppings of the horses and donkeys and camels, the fetid water of the canals . . . And the heat, the awful stagnant, relentless heat. Sometimes, my friend, I think this place will suffocate me."

Harun had lain his head in Ja'far's lap, and the Wazir stroked his face. Sometimes I wonder about those two; they seem a little too close. If the Khalifah drinks in private, what other sins might he commit behind closed doors? The caresses did not stop him whining, however.

"And yet it seems I cannot escape. When I set out to build a new palace, in the fresh air of the Meadow of the Castle, God struck me down with illness, and I had to be carried home on a litter. Under the constant demands of work, and the heavy responsibility of leading the one true faith, I feel the weight of my people pressing down upon me, crushing me.

"Only here, in my Pavilion of Air, can I expand my chest. Only here, with my best friend Ja'far by my side, can I breathe, and laugh. Yet even here, sometimes, the darkness comes upon me. I try to live rightly, to be a good Muslim and a good ruler. Why does God punish me so?"

The Commander of the Faithful began to cry, big, gulping, baby sobs of wine-sodden weeping. His Wazir tried to comfort and distract him, as if he were a small child.

"Khalifah, if there is anything you require, any delight of touch or taste, we can have brought to you food or wine or women –"

"I am gorged with such sensual pleasures! I seek the simple joys that are not denied to the meanest of my people."

The agonised expression on Ja'far's face suggested he was having difficulty imagining what simple joys might look like.

"Sport, then! A horse race . . . archery . . . polo?"

Harun shook his head, which he had now buried in a satin pillow. I wondered how exactly he proposed to organise an archery contest between four inebriated men in the middle of the night, let alone a polo match. I supposed anything was possible when you were the master of the world. Ja'far made a supreme effort to imagine where poor people found solace.

"Perhaps, Khalifah, we should go up to the terrace and look out over the Tigris? We can contemplate the myriad stars in the firmament, watch the moon reflected in the water, and see the fishing boats bobbing like toys."

The Commander of the Faithful howled in misery.

"Then, Khalifah, you must cut off the head of your servant Ja'far, for I cannot find any way to please you!"

I am sure that the Wazir was speaking rhetorically, and that he knew his master well enough to be certain he would not be taken at his word. In some ways it was satisfying to see that Harun al-Rashid, who ruled nations of millions and commanded armies of thousands, whose every need was met and whose every wish gratified, could still be so unhappy. However his bawling was becoming tedious, and I felt the need to intervene.

"Why don't we venture out onto the streets of the city in disguise, and see how the common people live?"

Harun was sitting up. His face was still blotchy from tears, but his blubbering had ceased, and he was looking at me with shining eyes.

"Of course! In this way might the Khalifah lift his spirits, and also learn more about the people whom God has appointed him to lead. Thank you, my friend! You – bring gold for my friend Abu Ali. Five thousand – no, ten thousand dinars for my friend!"

Abu'l-Atahiyya was staring at me resentfully. I had doubtless earned ten times more for my offhand suggestion than he had been awarded for his carefully crafted panegyric. Masrur also looked none too pleased. It would be his responsibility to indulge this new caprice of his master's while ensuring that the Khalifah came to no harm.

Harun's depression had transformed to excitement about this new adventure. He had forgotten all about the odour of the working man, and was full of praise for their simple dignity, their honest toil, and other such atrocious nonsense. Now all was bustle and ado to prepare for our expedition. The dancing girls were chivvied away, with the exception of the Goth, who was led off to be prepared for the Khalifah's bed, whenever he decided he was ready for it. I bade a silent farewell to Muti'a and Dahnya, who had provided the only real fun of a rather strange evening, and arranged for my dinars to be delivered to my home. Even with the protection of the Swordbearer I did not fancy wandering the streets laden with gold.

Harun had sent for ordinary clothes, and somebody brought

a pile of shabby, patched garments which would normally have been worn by household slaves. We were all obliged to find a set that fitted us. Ja'far looked as if he would have held his nose if he dared, but Abu'l-Atahiyya had decided that if the Khalifah was enthusiastic, then so would he be. He pranced around in his costume, aping the bow-legged walk of a porter. Masrur looked exactly the same as he usually did; if he were dressed as a dancing girl, you would still notice only his bulk and his enormous sword. As for me, I have had on occasion to don a disguise while working for the Barid, so I shed my finery with only mild regret.

However, this was not enough for the Successor to the Prophet. He ordered maids from the hurram to come with cosmetics, and we were all decorated with fake spots and wrinkles and scars. Abu'l-Atahiyya found a crutch from somewhere, and tied up his left leg under his coat as if he had lost it in battle. By the time we finally staggered out through a side gate, Buhlul the hunchback would have been embarrassed to be seen with us, we looked so ridiculous.

The expedition was a fiasco. Masrur subtly guided us to one of the more respectable hammams, where the Father of Madness shamefacedly had to reveal his hidden limb when we undressed, and our make-up dripped from our faces. A couple of scarred, angry veterans looked like they were about to take exception to our outlandish appearance, before the Sword-bearer reared up behind us, causing them to think better of it.

In the cool room Harun decided to engage one poor bastard in conversation. The Khalifah's victim, a tailor from Basrah, obviously recognised his ruler, and was struck speechless in his confusion. Once again it was Masrur who saved the situation, engaging in a mime of extraordinary precision behind his master's back, somehow conveying to the tailor what was required. The terrified man stammered a few sentences about how much better life was under the enlightened leadership of the Righteous One, and Harun was satisfied.

Eventually the wine began to wear off, and the Khalifah tired of his adventure. We stumbled home, sobering up with unpleasant rapidity. When we arrived at al-Khuld I pretended to have a stone in my boot, and insisted the others go on ahead of me. In truth I was hoping to skulk off home and go to bed; I had had as much of the company of royalty as I could stomach.

However, as I leaned against the wall, fiddling with my foot and waiting for them to disappear round the corner, I heard a noise behind me, as if a lizard were scuttling down the wall. Caution made me withdraw into the shadows. I saw a rope hanging from a window of the palace. Then, as I watched, a lean figure slid down the line. At the bottom, he paused to look around before sloping away into the night. In the moonlight I could see him clearly.

You remember the beardless Frank, who you noticed was missing from the feast? It seems that he makes a habit of absenting himself without the knowledge of his hosts. I wondered what it was that drew him away from the comforts of al-Khuld. It had been a long evening, and I was tired, and worse, sober. However there was only one way to find out where he was going. I set off after him.

I did not have to track him very far. He circled away from Blissful Eternity before heading down towards the river. Even at this time of night the riverside was busy. The Frank was wearing a hood for concealment. However his pale, beardless face still attracted stares and comments from the stevedores and fishermen.

He walked down to the marshy beach, taking up a position below the Shammasiya bridge. I moved carefully round to the other side of the bridge, before ducking in between the moored boats that raised it above the water. I was able to crawl under the thick boards over which the traffic clatters, sloshing through the river water and squirming my way back to the side where the Frank was waiting. I was glad that I was wearing my commoner's disguise, as it would have pained me to have ruined another set of robes amid the mud and mould under the pontoon, but at least I remained unobserved and had a clear view as he greeted the boat that drifted up to the shore.

"Peace, friend."

The priest spoke in Greek. Fortunately I have picked up a little of the language on my travels, enough to follow the conversation. A harsh voice shouted back to him from the boat.

"Show your face, barbarian."

The Frank threw back his hood, and I could clearly see his peculiar hair, shaven at the front and long at the back. The man on the boat was similarly disguised, but he did not reveal himself in turn. He called out to the Frank again.

"Are you alone?"

I almost glanced around, to reassure myself that we were right beside one of the busiest bridges in Baghdad, with boats loading and unloading all around us. However, I knew what he meant by alone. Wise citizens did not pay too much attention to the business of the night sailors. Most were innocent fishermen, but those who were not did not welcome curious bystanders.

"I am alone, as agreed. Will you come ashore?"

The hooded man on the boat made no move to disembark.

"Have you brought the money?"

The Frank shifted his weight from foot to foot as if irritated.

"Have you brought the Brass Bottle?"

"You will have the Bottle when I have the gold. More importantly, you will have the knowledge of its use. If you try to open it without the secret – if you seek to cheat me, and take it by force – the Fire will destroy you."

The Frank was now jigging from side to side as if he were a nervous dancer at a wedding.

"I do not yet have the money. You should not have followed me, last time. You were seen."

The harsh voice drifted across the water.

"I do not yet trust you, barbarian. I have been betrayed before, by those in whom I put my confidence. First, by my Master, who made me bow to my inferior. Then by the men who bore me away. I will not be betrayed again."

"Wait! What was that noise?"

The noise was my stifled shout of shock as something – a rat, I hope – ran across my foot. I had been so caught up in the extraordinary conversation that I was unable to conceal my reaction. The surprise caused me to straighten up suddenly, bashing my head painfully against the bridge, then duck down again, clutching at my turban in agony. However this undignified spasm saved my life, as the timber above me exploded into splinters under the impact of a massive axe. I looked up, into the bloodshot eyes of Gorm, the red bearded Rus.

He was close enough that I could have kissed him, although I would rather have kissed a bear, and would have had less chance of having my nose bitten off. He roared at me, and while he struggled to tug his axe out of the plank with one hand, he aimed the other at my face. For all his strength, however, he was slow. I ducked under his punch and rammed his midriff with my aching head.

For an instant his stomach felt as solid as the timber, and I feared I had hurt myself more than I had hurt him. Then he exhaled in a long, slow moan, and staggered backwards. I dodged round him, cursing the lack of a sword.

The Frank had vanished in the few seconds our battle had taken. However his accomplice could not escape so easily. He was frantically pushing his boat out of the muddy shoals with a wide oar. I splashed out into the shallows and grabbed the edge of his boat.

Immediately my boots started to sink into the ooze. His response was to shove with even greater enthusiasm. As the boat slowly pulled away from the shore I clung on, but could not halt his retreat. Instead my feet were slowly pulled out of my boots, which had been irretrievably sucked into the riverbed.

Before I knew what was happening I was being dragged along behind the accelerating vessel, bare feet trailing through the filthy Tigris water. Had the Rus been able to retrieve his axe from the bridge then those feet would shortly have been no longer my concern, as I am sure he would have severed them. However his weapon had lodged there, and he had abandoned his struggles to recover it. Instead he waded after me and grabbed hold of my ankles, trying to pull me off the boat.

For a moment I was stretched as if on a rack. Then Gorm's efforts began to hinder rather than help the boat's escape. I hung grimly on, and slowly the Rus began to haul the vessel back toward the riverbank.

I saw the hooded man on the boat raise his hand, as if to throw something. Some primal fear caused to me to release the rail despite myself. As I crashed down into the black water he brought his hand down, fingers splayed, and the river erupted into flame in front of me.

The heat was immediately intense, singeing my dripping beard. When I plunged my head under the surface, I was then faced with the problem of being unable to breathe. Worse, I had very little choice as to which position I adopted, since Gorm still had hold of my ankles. Yet with my chest bursting and my vision blackening, I could still see before me the huge, bulging eyes, glittering in the blood-red light, that I glimpsed beneath the hood of the man on the boat.

I managed to poke my mouth above the water and snatch a breath, but Gorm's response was to release my ankles, stride forward and put one huge arm around my neck. With his improved grip, he tried to thrust my head into the fierce blaze that floated eerily on the river. However the sluggish current was carrying it away from us, so instead he shoved my head back under, and held me there.

I writhed around underwater, clutching at the barbarian's clothing. He was wearing a short tunic over long woollen trousers. In desperation I yanked down his pants, located one gruesomely red-haired testicle and squeezed as hard as I could. There was a brief race between my dwindling breath and his rapidly decreasing chances of fathering offspring, then he reached down with the arm that was not around my neck, trying to locate and remove my hand.

He was now distracted and in an awkward pose, and I seized my opportunity. I pushed upwards, breaking his grip and driving my head against his chin. My soggy turban was not the hardest weapon, but the impact was sufficient to cause him to stagger backwards. With his pants round his knees and up to his waist in water it took him vital seconds to regain his balance.

We faced each other across the wine-dark water, and I longed for my sword, or indeed any means of attacking him other than my aching head. I swung a couple of punches, but the giant Rus batted them aside like wasps and strode towards me. His intention seemed to be to seize me in a bear hug and crush me to death. I backed away but stepped into a hole in the river bed and fell. Once again I was floundering and gasping for air, and I could hear Gorm huffing with what I supposed must be laughter as he closed in for the kill.

Then I felt hands on my shoulders, not pushing me under but dragging me out of the water. A spear thrust past me, halting the approach of the Rus. He tried to grab the shaft, but the wielder was too quick, jabbing at his face and causing him to retreat warily.

I flopped onto the deck of the fishing boat as if I were part of the catch. Indeed, for all I knew I was about to be gutted and eaten. However, when I looked up into the friendly, ugly, cheerful, diseased faces of a couple of Baghdadi river fishermen, I knew I was safe. I vomited most of the Tigris onto the deck, and managed to splutter out a few words.

"Follow that boat!"

The fishermen looked bemusedly at each other.

"What boat?"

I hauled myself to my feet. The hooded man had vanished under cover of the blaze, which was now burning itself out. I could not even be sure whether he had gone upriver or down. I slumped back onto the deck.

"I am very grateful to you for saving me. But why?"

"Well, we don't know who you are, but you look like a true believer. As for that – thing, that was attacking you – well, we weren't even sure it was human."

My rescuer narrowed his eyes.

"Anyway, I do know who you are. You're the Father of Locks, aren't you? 'The wine was brought in by one with a cunt, who dressed like she had a cock' – that was one of yours, wasn't it?"

He leaned towards me conspiratorially, breathing fish fumes all over me.

"Gets me and the missus going, that one does. My mate Shuẚyb, he loves your stuff, he's memorised three of your poems . . ."

As my piscatorial admirer blathered on, I looked for the Rus. He must have beaten a hasty retreat when he realised he was outnumbered and out of his element. I persuaded my new friends to drop me back on shore, although they insisted I gave them a few lines before they would let me off the boat. Then I thought, I must share this new information with the Newborn. And even more importantly, I must have wine.

* * *

As if to illustrate his words, Abu Nuwas took a long draught from his goblet. I realised we were alone. The mysterious lady had been aroused by my master's tale of dalliance in the fragrant garden, and had dragged Abbas back to the rooftop at some earlier point in the story.

"So what, boy, are we to make of all this?"

"Besides the fact that you are irresistible to both sexes, and even the most impoverished labourer in the city recognises your face and can quote your poetry?"

Abu Nuwas looked at me suspiciously.

"You are becoming very impudent, Newborn. I hope you are not suggesting that I would embellish my account?"

"I mean, o Father of Locks, that we can only approach the truth through the stories we tell to others, and to ourselves."

"A slippery response, suitable to a Newborn babe. I shall let it pass, for now. But what of the strange meeting by the bridge?"

"Well, it seems that the Frankish spy must have been Thomas the Syrian's secret visitor."

"Indeed. And at that time, he should not have been in Baghdad at all. Now he skulks around the streets at night, for clandestine assignations with – whom?"

"According to Umm Dabbah, the hooded man claimed to be the Father of Bitterness. 'Abu Murra has the Bottle . . .' "

"He was betrayed by his Master, who made him bow to his inferior. That does sound like my friend Iblis. On the other hand, he is trying to sell his Bottle for gold. I have never heard it said that the Devil was short of cash."

"What does the Bottle contain, master?"

"I don't know, boy, but I have seen what it can do, and its power terrifies me. If primitive savages like the Franks get hold of it, then the peace of the whole world is threatened. A spirit of fire . . . a captive Jinn. Such things have not been seen above the surface of the earth for centuries."

I said nothing, but my face must have betrayed my scepticism.

"Unless you have a better explanation, I suggest you keep an open mind. After all, you saw the merchant's house. You said yourself that whoever took the child must have been able to fly . . ."

Sixteen

The Tale of the Boy in the River, including, The Tale of the Father of a Muslim

Abu Nuwas finished the wine and we departed the house of Abbas. As we left I could hear moans and gasps coming from the rooftop, and my master shouted obscene encouragement to our host.

At the river I refused an invitation to sleep at his house – offered more, I felt, in hope than in expectation – and crossed the Southern Bridge, heading back to the palace of the Barmakids. Already the Hall of the Barid felt more like home to me than anywhere since I left Tiaret. I was so relieved to turn the brass key in the small door that I impudently greeted the unseen observer who scrutinised me as I walked down the corridor.

I slept soundly, and was pleased when I woke to see Yaqub al-Mithaq sitting cross-legged nearby, darning clothes.

"Good morning, lad. I am glad to see you still alive and whole."

"It has been a near thing, at times."

I told him how I had nearly been sacrificed to the demon Mahakala, and of my other adventures since I had last seen him. At the end of my account he whistled.

"So you have been three days in Baghdad, and have already met the Khalifah? I have served the Barid for thirty years, and have never so much as set foot in al-Khuld. God has chosen an interesting destiny for you, my boy."

I felt that al-Mithaq owed me a story in return, and took the opportunity to ask about something that had been intriguing me.

"Ibn Bundar talked about a man called Abu Muslim. Who was he?"

Al-Mithaq sat back.

"Ah, now there is a question. I can tell you what he did, but I don't believe anyone can tell you who he really was. However, I promised to explain how the Abbasids came to the throne, and without Abu Muslim that would not be a story at all. If you have a little time to spare, I would be happy to recount it to you now."

So he did.

The Tale of the Father of a Muslim

It began in a prison cell.

The Agent was calm as he watched the door slam closed behind him, and heard the key turn in the lock. It was not the first time he had been arrested, and would doubtless not be the last. Already his masters would be agitating for his release; and they were important men, men of wealth and influence. Of course there was always a risk that the order for his execution would win the race against the order for his freedom. If so, he would die a martyr, working to save Islam from the decadent Umayyads who were perverting the true faith.

A noise from a dark corner of the cell caught his attention. For the first time he noticed that there was another prisoner there, chained by his wrists to the wall. He was a powerfully built Persian of middle age, wearing only a loincloth. His face was harsh and forbidding.

"Peace, my friend. Would you tell me your name?"

The Persian only growled at this greeting. The Agent tried again.

"We share a prison cell; perhaps we share the same enemies. At the very least we can pass the time together."

The chained man stared at the Agent as if looking into his soul. Finally he spoke.

"They call me Abu Muslim."

The Agent contemplated his cellmate with renewed interest.

"So you are the infamous Father of a Muslim, from Khorarasan? The most notorious revolutionary, heretic and highwayman in the Khalifate? Truly, I am privileged."

"I am not a highwayman. Did not the Prophet himself raid caravans to provide the Companions with food and supplies, in the early days in Madinah?"

"Yet they are to try you as a highwayman, and if convicted, as seems certain, you face crucifixion."

Abu Muslim's only response was to spit on the ground. The Agent was intrigued.

"So are you a new Prophet, then? Are you the Mahdi, come to warn of the day of judgement? What justifies your criminal acts?"

Abu Muslim stood erect in his chains.

"I am a warrior, not a scholar. I cannot tell you how to save the world. But like any honest man, I can tell what is wrong, and fight against it."

"And what is wrong? What are you fighting against?"

"Everything, my friend. Everything and everybody."

The Agent smiled.

"Perhaps, Father of a Muslim, we can help each other after all . . ."

The Agent was released the next morning. A few days after that, Abu Muslim was also freed, with no explanation and much to his surprise. Outside the prison the Agent was waiting for him, with two saddled horses.

They rode to Makkah, where the Agent led Abu Muslim into a room lit by smoky lamps and ringed by men wearing black. Here, he explained why he had saved him from death on the cross.

"The Umayyads are usurpers, and false Khalifahs. If you seek proof of this, you will see it all around you. They angered God by damaging the Ka'bah, the sacred shrine of the holy city. Since then, the Family of Islam has been sick at its heart. After years of victory, we have recently suffered defeats against the Christians, both the Romans and the Franks. Tax reforms have left the state bankrupt. The Arab tribes fight amongst themselves once more, as they did in the days of ignorance before the coming of the Prophet.

"The only cure for this sickness is to cut the diseased organ from the body. The Khalifah must be overthrown."

"You are Shi'ites, then?"

The Agent looked at the other men in the room before answering.

"We are the Hashimiyah. We hold the secret of the true succession of the Khalifate. From Ali it passed to his son Muhammad, and thence to his grandson Abu Hashim. Abu Hashim died childless, but named as his heirs the family of Abbas, the Prophet's uncle.

"The current head of the Abbasids, Ibrahim al-Imam, lives quietly on his estate in Humeima, but across the whole of the land of Islam we are working to elevate him to the Khalifate. We have many allies. The arrogance of the Umayyads has made them widely hated, particularly by converts to Islam, who suffer from the laws which discriminate in favour of Arabs. Converts like you, Father of a Muslim, and the people of your country.

"We want you to go back to Khorasan, Abu Muslim, to further our cause there. The risk is great, but the prize greater still. Will you join us?"

After years of discontent and aimless criminality, Abu Muslim had found his vocation. The conspiracy was already established in Merv, but under his direction the network was revitalised. He trained soldiers and spies, leading raids on tax convoys and destabilising the authorities.

He also spread propaganda, addressing secret meetings in crowded rooms, promising the coming of a new Khalifah, "from the Family of the Prophet." This phrase had been carefully devised to appeal to Shi'ites, who imagined that the candidate would be an Alid from the bloodline of Muhammad. All the while Abu Muslim was protected from arrest by a people resentful of their Arab governor, and their decadent rulers in distant Dimashq.

The decadent rulers themselves meanwhile were doing as

much to undermine their regime as the conspirators were. The young Khalifah, al-Walid, was cruel and lecherous. After only one year of his reign he was deposed and murdered by his cousin Yazid, but he too died a mere six months later. Yazid had named his brother Ibrahim as heir, but the throne was seized by another cousin, Marwan ibn Muhammad. He was to be the last Umayyad Khalifah.

Like an expert cook, Abu Muslim had brought his insurgency to the boil at the perfect moment. Khalifal troops were stoned and mocked on the streets of Merv, and the people talked openly of the coming of a new Commander of the Faithful, who would restore the integrity of Islam. When word came that Marwan was facing uprisings in Syria, the Khorasani made his move. Without waiting for orders from the Hashimiyah, he unfurled the Black Flag and called on the people to rise up. The revolution had begun.

Abu Muslim proved to be as brilliant a general as he had been an agitator. His makeshift army quickly defeated the governor's troops and captured his deputy. When the governor, who was eighty-five and had taken the job believing it would offer him a comfortable old age, got sick and died, nobody was sent from Dimashq to replace him.

Khorasan had fallen, but even if Abu Muslim had wanted to stop there, the revolution had developed a momentum of its own. Gripped by messianic fervour, the Army of the Black Flag rolled westward like a horde of locusts, growing in numbers as it went, drawing support from Alids, Kharijites, converts and convicts; all the disaffected and dispossessed of the Umayyad era.

Around the campfires at night the revolutionaries talked about the future. Many believed that the Day of Judgement was approaching, and that the "Khalifah from the Family of the Prophet" would be the Mahdi, the promised redeemer of Islam in the Last Days. Others argued they were fighting for paradise on Earth, where no men would be slaves and all possessions would be held in common. However every man agreed that nothing would be the same, once the Black Flag flew in the holy cities.

The Abbasids themselves, at their base near the Sea of Salt, were far away from their enthusiastic supporters. When word came of the insurrection the family were at risk from agents of Marwan, and had to go into hiding. Ibrahim the Imam was caught and murdered. The new leader of the Hashimiyah movement was his brother al-Saffah, the Spiller of Blood.

The beginning of the reign of al-Saffah, the first of the Abbasid Khalifahs, was not exactly auspicious. He was hiding in a cellar in Kufah at the time. The advance of the Army of the Black Flag was so rapid that he did not realise the city had been taken until eager revolutionaries found him and dragged him out. Eventually word reached Abu Muslim, who raced to the scene. Just as he had been the first to raise the Black Flag, he was the first to bend the knee and swear allegiance to the new Commander of the Faithful.

The proclamation of al-Saffah as Khalifah came as something of a surprise to the Army, most of whom were not privy to the details of the Hashimiyah conspiracy. Many had been waiting for the glamorous freedom fighter Abu Muslim to declare himself the lost descendant of the Prophet. Having come so far and killed so many people, though, most found it easier to accept al-Saffah as the promised saviour of Islam, and press on until the hated Umayyads were deposed. Besides, they trusted their general.

Marwan and his army, ragged and exhausted from putting down rebellions, turned to face this new challenge. The two forces met at the River Zab. The Umayyad's army was vastly superior in numbers, armour and experience, but the revolutionaries had never lost a battle and were possessed by a terrifying sense of destiny. Marwan's cavalry charged at the rabble, who formed a wall of spears. And the finest horsemen of Arabia died in their thousands, hurling themselves against the sharpened sticks of peasants.

Marwan himself escaped, scrambling away from the carnage when his army broke and the raging easterners poured through. He fled south and west, eventually being caught and slaughtered in Egypt. The new Khalifah invited his rival's surviving relatives to dinner, to a feast of reconciliation and peace. Before the first course was served his men rushed in with clubs and beat the Umayyads to death. The corpses were covered by a leather sheet as the remaining guests began to eat.

The metamorphosis of the movement, from religious reformation to political coup, was now complete. After storming Dimashq, the Army of the Black Flag returned to Khorasan. Many of the revolutionaries went home, dazed and uncertain of what they had accomplished. However others remained in military service under the new governor, Abu Muslim. He ruled the province as his own personal domain, but was always careful to pay respect, and taxes, to the Khalifah.

Al-Saffah warily tolerated this situation, but his suspicious brother al-Mansur constantly urged him to act. A popular, powerful demagogue, with a private army, posed a serious threat to the fledgling regime. From the moment the Spiller of Blood died of smallpox and al-Mansur succeeded him as Khalifah, Abu Muslim was doomed.

However, he was to perform one last service. Al-Mansur's uncle rebelled, claiming the throne for himself. In desperation the Khalifah turned to the governor of Khorasan, asking him to put down the rebellion. If Abu Muslim had truly sought power he could have stood to one side and allowed the Abbasids to fight among themselves, before making his move against the victor. Instead he tried to prove his loyalty by crushing the revolt and handing the uncle over to the Khalifah for execution.

Abu Muslim waited for reward, or at least for thanks. Instead al-Mansur sent an agent to make sure he was not cheated of his share of the campaign loot. This insulting distrust might have been put down to the Khalifah's stinginess, but the next letter from al-Mansur could only have been cunning provocation. It was a decree appointing Abu Muslim as Governor of Syria.

Superficially, this was an accolade from a grateful ruler. In practice, it would isolate Abu Muslim from his army and his loyal followers back in Merv, and put him in Dimashq where al-Mansur could keep an eye on him. The Khorasani declined his Khalifah's kind offer. After a correspondence during which the language of diplomacy became increasingly strained, al-Mansur summoned him to Iraq, where he planned to build his capital. They would discuss the matter face to face and settle their differences.

Abu Muslim, remembering what had happened to the last enemies of the Abbasids who were invited to peace talks, made his excuses. Then, unexpectedly, he changed his mind. In part this was because the Hashimiyah had given him meaning and purpose, and all the bloodshed and politics of the intervening years could never quite obliterate his faith in their cause. In part he was disturbed by a message in which al-Mansur swore to pursue him through fire and water if he disobeyed, and take revenge in person. Abu Muslim also took advice from his friends. What he did not know was that many of them were now in the pay of the Khalifah, and were sending him to his death.

Al-Mansur, who had not been raised as royalty, remained a nomad at heart. Even when staying at his palace he would often set up his tent inside his bedroom. On the day Abu Muslim came to him, he was camping near Kufah, looking for a site for his new city.

Al-Mansur's Wazir had been trying to dissuade him from murder, fearing reprisals from the easterners. As the moment approached, and Abu Muslim rode out from Kufah, the Khalifah's nerve failed. He greeted the general in his tent, but sent him away again.

"Go and rest, my friend. Bathe, for travel is a dirty business. Come back tomorrow."

Abu Muslim returned to the city. Once he had gone, the Khalifah was overwhelmed with embarrassment at his cowardice, and took it out on his Wazir. The unfortunate man endured one of al-Mansur's infamous rages, before being sent to summon the captain of the guard, wiping the spittle from his face as he went. Al-Mansur asked the captain what he thought about the situation with Abu Muslim.

"I am a mere servant, my lord. If you commanded me to

lean on my sword until the point comes out of my back, I would do so."

"Then will you kill Abu Muslim for me?"

There was no response. The captain stared at the ground. The Wazir pretended an anger he did not feel.

"Is something wrong, captain? Why do you not speak?"

The captain raised his eyes as if lifting a heavy weight.

"I will do as the Commander of the Faithful tells me to do."

The following night the governor of Khorasan came again to the tent of the Khalifah. This time there were no greetings. Al-Mansur stood up as he entered and immediately launched into a tirade, accusing him of treachery, trying to work himself up to give the order to the hidden guards. Abu Muslim could not understand the Abbasid's change in mood.

"Enough of your questioning. I have shown you nothing but loyalty, and I will answer before God."

Perversely, al-Mansur's guilt at the injustice he was committing gave him the fury to see it through.

"Still lying, you son of a whore? May God destroy me if I spare you now!"

He clapped his hands. This was the signal for the black-clad guards to dash into the tent. The old general fought for his life, but he was unarmed and outnumbered. He howled like a wolf as the swords cut into him again and again, his blood erupting onto their uniforms. Finally he was still, his body unrecognisable, a gory mess on the ground.

The soldiers were pale, shocked at what they had done. Al-Mansur ordered them to wrap the corpse in the ruined carpet on which it lay. They carried it from the tent and threw it into the river. There would be no grave to form the centre of the cult of Abu Muslim.

Meanwhile the Khalifah sent word to Kufah that the governor would be staying with him. A second tent was erected next to his own. The pretence ensured that word of the murder trickled out slowly, dogged by confusion and contradictions. The grief and outrage of Khorasan never bubbled over into widespread rebellion.

But to this day, when the radicals and heretics of the east seek popular support for the overthrow of the Abbasids, for the return of Islam to its original purity, for the equal sharing of wealth between all men, or for whatever other madness grips the mystics of those strange lands, they invoke one name, to give power to their cause: Abu Muslim al-Khorasani.

★★★

"Still spinning yarns like an old woman, Yaqub?"

"Ah, Father of Locks. I see your famous charm has not deserted you."

I was shocked to see Abu Nuwas in the Hall of the Barid. Of course, when I thought about it, he was a postman himself, albeit an irregular one. Nonetheless, I had considered the Hall my refuge, and was disappointed that he could let himself in. Al-Mithaq seemed to voice my thoughts.

"We do not often see you here, Abu Nuwas."

"No, Yaqub al-Mithaq. That is because I have my own house in the city, where I live in comfort with slaves tending to my every need. However, I came to the palace to inform Ja'far of the conspiracies that prowl the city at night. Yes, he does not need to set you to spy on this naïve young man to find out what is going on. When Christian barbarians are sneaking around plotting with hooded men who possess magical fire, I can be trusted to report it.

"(Why do you look so surprised, Newborn? Did you think it coincidence that he is always here when you are, quizzing you on your adventures and teaching you about politics? How touchingly innocent you are. He is both training you and watching over you. And over me, no doubt.)

"Since I was here anyway when I heard the news, I came looking for the Newborn. We must go to the Royal Bridge, immediately. They have found the veteran's grandson."

Abu Nuwas was in serious mood this morning, and strode so fast on his long legs that I had to scamper to keep up.

"Is the boy dead, master?"

"So I believe."

"Then why are we in such a hurry?"

"Because, Newborn, a murdered body is like an open bottle of wine. Leave it too long before sampling it, and its subtleties are lost. Also, the Khalifah, who seems unable to live without my company at present, has invited me to go hunting with him this afternoon. You will come with me, if only to ensure that I have somebody to talk to who is not entirely insane."

"Will the Wazir expel the Franks, now that he knows how they have abused his hospitality?"

I pretended to myself that I was asking this because of my concern for the safety of the Ummah, and not because of any interest I might have had in a certain yellow-headed lunatic. Abu Nuwas laughed coldly at my question.

"Much as it may surprise you, the Barmakid did not outline his planned foreign policy to me. He thanked me for the information, gave me some gold, and sent me on my way.

"However, I think we can make some reasonable assumptions about how Ja'far will respond. Firstly, he will not act rashly, out of anger. Politicians cannot afford emotions, and ambassadors are always engaged in spying, of one form or another. Our rulers tolerate a certain amount of clandestine activity, in return for the benefits that embassies bring. If they are clever rulers, they will make sure that the spies only learn what they want them to learn. And when you know that someone is spying on you, be it enemy or friend, it is better to let them continue than to cut off their sources and force them to send new spies, ones that you don't know about.

"Furthermore, you should not underestimate the significance of these Franks. They may be barely civilised, but their king is a distracting wasp, buzzing around two of our most dangerous foes: the Roman Empire, and the Umayyad Amir of Cordoba. Of course, if our interests ever cease to coincide, we will have to exterminate them, as you would a nest of wasps. For the time being, though, it benefits the Ummah if we work in harmony with them.

"Last, and most importantly, there is the pride of Ja'far ibn Yahya al-Barmaki. He will view this intrigue as a challenge to his intellect, and seek a way to turn it to the advantage of the Khalifate. I have never known him to take the simple course when a more devious one was open to him. In any case, he has already deployed his own secret weapon."

"What is that, master?"

"You and I, of course! Can you not hear that sound? It is the enemies of Islam, shaking in fear at our approach."

Abu Nuwas flashed me a wicked grin. I reflected that, if the hopes of the Ummah were dependent on a wine soaked deviant and a bewildered youth, it might be time to think about converting to Christianity.

Our arrival at the river darkened my mood. A crowd had gathered by the bridge. Policemen tried to disperse them with the implausible claim that there was nothing to see there, to which the natural response of the good citizens of Baghdad was, "What are you lot doing here then?" One blue-clad thug tried to block our way, but al-Takht spotted us and called us over.

He was standing in the sludge on the north side of the bridge, talking to a tall, thin police captain. At their feet was a muddy mound, covered in a dark cloth. As we approached he silently pulled the cloth from the mound.

At first, when I saw the bloated body beneath, I thought they had dredged up some undiscovered monster from the dark of the river bed. I had to stare at the misshapen flesh for some time before I could make out the young boy it had once been. His skin was puffed and bleached, and had been gnawed by fish or crabs, so that white bone was visible, and black holes gaped instead of eyes.

Abu Nuwas bent over the corpse while al-Takht spoke.

"Washed up against the pontoon sometime during the night. A washerwoman spotted him at dawn, and a couple of fishermen dragged him to the bank. Word spread fast, and every idler in Rusafa had come down here for a look before anyone thought to alert the police. If there was anything we could have learned from his position or clothing, it's too late now."

"He has obviously been in the river a few days. His throat has been cut. The wound is too straight to have been caused

211

by any animal. However it is also too ragged to have been made with a sharp blade."

Abu Nuwas looked up from his examination.

"Are you certain this is the grandson of Abd al-Aziz?"

Al-Takht nodded.

"Too old to be the porter's son. I summoned the veteran and his daughter at the same time that I sent for you. They identified him as their boy, as much by his clothing as by what is left of his face. The daughter struck me as a tough one, but she could have done with someone to look after her. The old man, though, he went charging off to haul ibn Bundar before the Qadi again, left her sobbing. I think some old woman took her away."

Abu Nuwas stood up, asking him to repeat what he said, demanding the loan of a horse to take him to the Blue Masjid, saying he had to stop them. However I was not really listening. I had been gazing round at the dull faces of the onlookers, wondering what pleasure they took from the grim scene in front of them. Then I saw that one pair of eyes was not staring at the grotesque cadaver, but directly at me. And they were not empty and bored, but frightened and fascinated and hateful.

The eyes were set in the face of a boy, his face marred with a birthmark splattered across his cheek. I remembered laughter on a rooftop, ribald mockery of an unveiled girl, a stone flying at my head. Then the face was gone.

Seventeen

The Tale of the Birthmarked Boy, which includes, The Tale of the Raiders

I could hear Abu Nuwas shouting behind me as I clambered up the riverbank, but I ignored him. I was not sure, and did not want to explain, why I was chasing the birthmarked boy. However the mere fact that he fled as soon as I noticed him justified my pursuit.

When I reached the top of the bank the boy had gone. I looked across the bridge, and up and down the road that ran alongside the Tigris, but there was no sign of the dirty green turban that topped his blemished face. Then a flash by the water caught my eye. In a bid to escape unseen he was crossing the river by jumping over the boats that supported the pontoon.

I raced to the bridge and dodged between the porters, mules and horsemen that thronged its wooden boards. Ahead of me I could see a green shape bobbing along beside the deck. Despite the difficulties of negotiating the traffic, I reached the other side in time to follow him as he turned away upstream.

"You! Son of a dog, stop there!"

He was heading up a strip of muddy beach, with the river to one side and the back of a row of houses to the other. No-one else was around. He turned when he heard me, and for a moment his eyes darted around like those of a cornered rat. Then he realised that I was alone, unescorted by policemen or lanky swordsmen. He swaggered towards me.

"Who are you to insult my parentage, you albino monkey? I am Mishal ibn Yunus al-Rafiq, son of a better man than you will ever meet."

As he spoke he pulled a short sword from his robes. It appeared to be old and rusty, but still sharp enough to deal death. I took from my sleeve the knife I had been given in the Hall of the Barid. Compared to his sword, it looked like an instrument for peeling fruit.

"I am an agent of the Wazir. I command you to come with me and answer our questions – about the death of the grandson of Abd al-Aziz."

Mishal laughed. I am sure he intended to be menacing, but, although he was growing a scraggy beard to cover his birthmark, his voice was still high and childish, and his laughter sounded like the cackle of an old crone.

"You command me? You are an agent of the Wazir, you bastard offspring of a whore and a leprous ape?"

I tried to summon an authority I did not feel.

"You have nothing to fear if you are innocent, and tell me the truth."

"Fear? What do you know about fear?"

He was close enough now to take a couple of swings with his sword, and I jumped back.

"I'll teach you about fear, lackey of the Barmakids."

And he let out a bellow, and charged at me. Like his shout, his charge lacked the conviction of his words. I sidestepped easily, and jabbed with my knife as he passed. I struck out with my words too.

"Fear, street rat? I have fought with pirates in the White Middle Sea, and battled bandits while crossing the Empty Quarter. So teach me what you know, street rat, I am eager to learn."

I ducked under his crude slash, and darted quick stabs at his belly, forcing him backwards. A blow from his sword threatened to sever my hand, and we separated. As we circled it was his turn to launch a verbal assault.

"You think you are the only one to have experienced suffering? I watched my friends and neighbours drop dead from the plague, one by one, all the time wondering who would be next. Then the disease took my mother, leaving me alone to fend for myself over the freezing winter that followed. I will face your pirates and bandits any day, rather than the cold and sickness and evil that stalk the city."

Mishal lunged again. I dodged, but that was what he was expecting. His left arm grappled me, pinning my knife arm to my side, and as we struggled we toppled to the ground. We were too close for him to use his blade, so he tried to bring the pommel up to my face. My free hand seized his wrist, preventing him from bludgeoning me to death. For a few moments we wrestled in the silt, grunting desperately.

Then he began to laugh. This time there was no counterfeit menace in the sound, but instead real hilarity, a puerile giggle that erupted from his stomach and convulsed his whole body. There was something infectious about the unexpected innocence of the sound, and I found that I, too, was chortling, shaking at the ridiculousness of the situation, two boys with barely thirty years between us battling to the death in the mud over God knows what.

He rolled off me, still cautiously pointing the rusty sword, but the point was shaking, and I knew he was helpless with laughter. I sat up and put the knife back in my sleeve. As soon as he could gather his breath he spoke.

"You know what, albino monkey? I like you. Have you really crossed the Empty Quarter? I would enjoy hearing that story some time."

He fell serious.

"And I wished no evil to the grandson of Abd al-Aziz, whom I counted as my friend and brother, and if you are truly seeking his killer then I will help you. Take my hand in peace, and I will tell you everything I know."

So he did.

The Tale of the Raiders

They should never have killed the Camel.

Of course, that's not where it started. Nor is it where it ended, if it ever has ended, or ever will end, before the Day of Judgement. But most of the rest of it was just people doing

215

what they had to do to survive. The imams teach us that God has decided our destiny for us, and usually that's the way it feels, on the streets of Harbiya. There aren't many choices, just necessity. But there was no need to kill the Camel. That was just greedy.

I suppose where it really started was when they built the City of Peace. That's how my father told it, anyway. A lot of soldiers came to settle here, not just from the Army of the Black Flag, but veterans of other campaigns as well. Old al-Mansur paid out a pension to anyone who could prove they had served in the revolution, or the Holy War. It must have grieved him sore, because every penny he ever spent was like pissing stones, but he was too smart to have starving warriors wandering the streets of his new capital.

Anyway, that wasn't the only living available to them. Some of them were very rich, and came to retire in comfort. Victorious soldiers never come home with empty packs, unless they squander their booty on gambling and whores. The best were recruited to the Khalifah's Guard, and for those still willing to march there were wars to be fought: campaigns against the Christians, and rebels to suppress, like Muhammad of the Pure Soul, or that Khorasani peasant who pretended to be Abu Muslim risen from the grave. For the truly desperate there was the city police.

Even so, there were still many in the city who knew no trade, no life other than fighting and killing. It was inevitable that they would try to find ways of turning those skills into a source of income. The Abna, those who had fought under the Black Flag, were already tied to each other by oaths of brotherhood. Soon they were forming into other bands, and swearing other, darker oaths, of secrecy and fidelity till death.

They were not all easterners, the young men who formed these gangs, these fityans. My father, Yunus al-Rafiq, was an Arab, from Najd, east of Madinah. Nor were they bad men. He was a warrior, my father, respected within his tribe. He had fought for the Umayyads at the Battle of the Zab. There was no shame in having been true to his allegiance and supported

216

the losing side, although it meant there was no pension waiting for him in Baghdad.

But robbery came easily to men of the desert, like my father. The tribes had always raided each other, for horses and camels and cattle, and then boasted of their exploits. And any caravan which crossed their territory without taking suitable precautions deserved to be taught a lesson, by having their goods confiscated. Anything else would be shameful.

These had been the old ways, the ways of the jahili, the ignorant ones before the Prophet brought us back to the truth. But the truth is a hard dish to consume in one sitting. Some were still digesting it after nearly two centuries.

There were no caravans to be plundered, in Baghdad. But there were merchants, and shops. In particular there were builders, and building sites, everywhere. Thousands of artisans came to create the Round City, from all over the Khalifate. When it was complete, many of them stayed. Al-Mansur gave land near his palace as gifts to his friends, family and women. It cost him nothing, but if they developed it they could grow rich on renting out the property.

As a result there was a frenzy of building. All around the walls of the capital houses sprouted like mushrooms. They seemed to appear overnight, and still it was not fast enough to satisfy the demand from new arrivals. The fityans soon learned that foremen would pay to ensure their precious materials were not stolen and sold to other builders. They applied the same principle to shopkeepers, and passed some of the gold to the police to ensure that they did not bother to interfere. Soon they could consider themselves guardians of their neighbourhoods, keeping the peace and protecting the innocent.

Some people are born to be leaders. Others are born lieutenants, and my father was such a man. What he lacked in glamour and imagination, he made up for in loyalty and diligence. The leader to whom he gave his allegiance was al-Malik, "the King", a handsome Yemeni who had fled to the new city after a mysterious scandal in his homeland, which he never discussed. Al-Malik had two other close friends. One was ibn

Nafi, a sharp-witted Badawi with a good head for numbers. The other was a man called Yusuf al-Jamal. Usually al-Jamal means the Beautiful One, but with this ugly, lumbering giant of a man everybody understood the name to carry its other meaning: the Camel.

Together the four of them assembled a group of disaffected young men, bound them by secret and terrible rituals which they invented to suit their purposes, and soon became the most powerful fityan in southern Harbiya. Al-Malik gave the orders, my father ensured that they were carried out, and ibn Nafi counted the gold. And those who refused to pay received a visit from the Camel. It was a boom time in Baghdad, and they quickly grew rich.

However, the Abna and the other veterans were not the only ones coming to the new city. Many of those who came did not follow the true faith. Of these, the worst were the Christians. Their perverted beliefs permit them things forbidden to decent folk: usury, gambling and intoxicants.

First came the monasteries. In the time of old al-Mansur, no respectable Muslim would be seen drinking wine, and it was banned from Baghdad. But the Christian monks petitioned the Khalifah, saying that they needed it for their disgusting rituals. Did you know, they claim to turn it by magic into the blood of Isa ibn Maryam, and then drink it anyway?

The old man granted them special dispensation, and soon everybody knew you could procure wine from the monasteries. The more pious establishments only shared it on feast days, but some were seduced by the opportunities for making money, and slid into degeneracy, becoming little more than drinking dens.

Nonetheless, the monks became very wealthy from the trade, and al-Malik decided that he and his friends should not miss out. When my father visited them, however, to warn them of the dangers of their cellar being raided by unscrupulous brigands, they told him that they already had protection. From the shadows stepped a villainous Christian, a man with no nose. His name was Thomas the Syrian.

My father was raging as he brought the news to al-Malik. He would have gathered his men and gone to battle with the Christians immediately. However, ibn Nafi counselled caution, and it was his advice that prevailed. Al-Malik feared drawing the attention of the authorities by brawling on the streets. The police were impoverished, apathetic, and easily bribed, but if the Khalifah sent his Guard to restore peace they would show no mercy. Besides, al-Malik knew that for all the Camel's intimidating appearance the big man was at heart timid and gentle. Against determined opposition his most powerful weapon might be exposed as a fraud.

So the Christians established their control over the wine trade, and then took to usury. Lending money at interest was illegal, even for unbelievers, but there were always men desperate enough with no other choice. Unable to enforce repayment through the law, Thomas hired Christian thugs to deter defaulters. Al-Malik and the Muslims, meanwhile, continued to protect the merchants and other businessmen from theft.

In this way years went by. The Khalifah al-Mansur died and was succeeded by his son al-Mahdi. My father married my mother, and I was the only offshoot of their union. I grew up around his gang. They were tough, confident men, warriors of the suqs, and I adored them, and wanted nothing more than to be like them. One of my earliest memories is riding on the back of Yusuf al-Jamal, as if he were indeed the beast after which he was named.

Al-Malik, the King of south Harbiya, never wed, and there was some talk that he preferred the company of men. Then, at the age of fifty, he fell in love. Fatimah bint Abd al-Aziz, the daughter of a boastful old veteran, came to her father's house to live when her husband was killed at the siege of Samalu. She was not beautiful, not even back then, but there was a strength and a courage in her that somehow touched al-Malik in a way no other woman could.

Al-Malik was wealthy, respected and still good-looking, despite the grey hairs in his beard. He was therefore astounded when the plain widow refused his hand, even at the lavish bride-price he proposed. He offered to double it, but she told him that money was not the issue.

"My father looks after me well enough, and relies on me to look after him in turn. I can never marry another man. I would always be comparing you to my dead husband, and I would not want to insult you or his memory by finding one of you to be inferior. However, I will take you as my lover, if you wish."

Al-Malik was at first dismayed at this extraordinary suggestion. Then he came to realise that he still loved Fatimah, and decided that if this was the only way he could be with her then he would accept it. Her father, so concerned with propriety and his reputation, was hopelessly indulgent of his headstrong daughter, and permitted the liaison to carry on under his roof, provided that they conducted themselves in the utmost secrecy. And when she fell pregnant, he presented the boy child to his neighbours as the son of her husband nearly three years dead, and waggled his bushy eyebrows, silently daring them to contradict him.

The boy had just turned two, and I was approaching my tenth year, when they found the Camel dead. He had been strangled and stabbed from behind, although which killed him, and whether there was one attacker or several, could not be determined. My father was furious, and confronted al-Malik.

"I told you we should have stamped on that Syrian scorpion years ago. Instead we have allowed him to become so strong, that now he seeks to supplant true believers. We must strike now, before he picks us off one by one."

But al-Malik shook his head slowly.

"We cannot be sure that Thomas is responsible. If he is, as you say, a scorpion, then we must tread carefully. I am making enquiries, and will act when the time is right."

The King stamped away, and my father saw ibn Nafi looking at him sadly. The old man spoke.

"Don't you know what's going on? Then you are the only one. Al-Malik murdered the Camel, or had him murdered. That lover of his, that Fatimah woman – he believed that

Yusuf was trying to steal her from him. Yes, I am afraid our King is losing his mind for love. Be careful, my friend. You may be next."

My father could scarcely believe what he was hearing. He dismissed it as an ill-judged joke from the old man. However, as the weeks went by, he began to notice al-Malik staring oddly at him. The King asked him peculiar questions about his whereabouts and movements. Then my father started to come across gang members in unexpected places. He wondered whether he was being followed. Finally he went to see ibn Nafi in private, and asked him what was happening.

"My friend, it is as I feared. Al-Malik's jealous suspicion has now fallen upon you. You must act quickly, before you suffer the same fate as the Camel."

Heartbroken, my father resolved to strike first. He arranged to meet al-Malik alone by the river, saying that he had news of great urgency and secrecy. I remember still the sorrowful look on his face as he hid a dagger in his sleeve, and kissed me goodbye.

My father never returned from that meeting. As I learned later, al-Malik knew of the planned assassination. Two of his men were hiding nearby, and when my father produced his knife they jumped out and struck him down. His body was found several days later, like the boy's, washed up against a bridge.

Al-Malik did not last much longer. He was poisoned the following month, probably by ibn Nafi, who had been in the pay of the Syrian for a long time. It had been easy for him to turn his friends against each other. At the same time he was warning my father of al-Malik's jealous rage, he was telling the King that my father plotted to betray him. The suspicion felt by each caused them to behave suspiciously. It mattered little to ibn Nafi who killed whom. Either way he had only to remove one more obstacle to become undisputed leader of the fityan; provided of course that he paid tribute to Thomas the Syrian.

Life became hard for my mother and I. My father had always spent money as if it would never cease to flow, as if it were as eternal as the Tigris. Nothing had been saved against lean times, and within a year or two of his death we had to sell our home and move into lodgings. The boarding house was dirty and crowded, and when plague came to the city in the summer heat it flourished in the foul conditions. I nursed my mother to the end, and dug her grave with my own hands.

The winter that followed was cold and hard. It killed off the plague, but also killed off many of the weakened survivors. I was still a child, but nobody would take me in for fear of the Christians. Somehow I scratched a living through the bitter months. I think it was only the hope of vengeance that kept me going.

However I was to be denied revenge against ibn Nafi. That spring he was cut down in the street, by an unknown hand. Most likely it was Thomas or his men, finishing the job they had started with the Camel. However there were persistent rumours that it was Fatimah bint Abd al-Aziz who struck the blow, avenging the death of her lover. Either way, there is only the Syrian left, to pay the price for my father.

As I grew older I began to gather my own fityan around me, street children and orphans like myself. We call ourselves the Raiders, as if we are horsemen of the desert swooping on an unguarded caravan. In truth we live by petty theft and intimidation, until we are old enough and strong enough to challenge the Christians.

When the grandson of Abd al-Aziz began to hang around with us, some of the gang objected. They said that he was too young, and his background too privileged. However I knew the truth: that he was in fact the son of al-Malik, who was once King of south Harbiya, and I was glad of his company.

I would be happy to blame the Syrian for his death, but I do not believe Thomas knew the secret of the boy's parentage, any more than he knows who I am. Recently he even tried to recruit us to help him. He was looking for the woman who knew the Name, or some such nonsense, and would pay well for information. I do not even understand what it was he wanted.

Then the boy disappeared. His grandfather tried to put the blame on that old crackpot ibn Bundar, and for all I know he might be responsible. All I can tell you is that the son of al-Malik was not with us on the day he vanished. When word came that his body had been found, I had to go and see it with my own eyes. And when I saw you with the police, I thought you must be an informer, and ran.

This much I can tell you. Only God knows all.

Eighteen

The Tale of The Royal Hunt

I found Abu Nuwas back at the Hall of the Barid, where he was waiting for me irritably. His annoyance was somewhat lessened when he heard what I had learnt.

"So my old friend Thomas is looking for the woman who knows the Name? That is interesting. What was it he said to the Frank? 'If you have the Name, you can unleash the power of the Fire.' There must be someone else, a woman, who knows the secret. Perhaps Thomas seeks to betray his accomplices, take the power for himself."

"Can we not have him arrested, and interrogated? He must know something about the death of the boy."

"I do not think you understand the influence that the Syrian wields. He could not rule the streets as he does without friends at court. Besides, as far as most people are concerned, the boy's killer is convicted and condemned."

"So they brought Babak ibn Bundar back before the Qadi, master?"

Abu Nuwas winced at my question.

"Indeed, and a ludicrous embarrassment it was too. The crowd gawping, the veteran demanding his neighbour's head on a stick, and the judge al-Shafi'i wiggling his ridiculous beard in smug vindication. At the end of it the accused was condemned to be beheaded. I tried to persuade them to take blood money instead, but then ibn Bundar announced that he was innocent and would rather die than pay them a copper penny. That set Abd al-Aziz raving again, and al-Shafi'i glaring at me as though he would condemn me too, if only he could find a reason. At last order was restored, and the execution is planned for tomorrow."

"Master, why are you so certain ibn Bundar is innocent?"

"Mostly because Abd al-Aziz and al-Shafi'i think he is guilty. When faced with difficult questions, it is not a bad rule to find out the opinion of fools, and then believe the opposite."

"But I thought al-Shafi'i was considered a man of great wisdom."

"Indeed he is, and therefore the worst kind of fool. When a clever man decides he has arrived at the truth, he is more blind to learning or evidence that the most ignorant bumpkin. But we have no time for such philosophical musings. We must go hunting with Harun al-Rashid; and I could not go hunting without my true beloved."

I was slightly embarrassed to be so described. To my surprise Abu Nuwas did not head down the corridor that led outside, but stomped off along the passageways of the Palace of the Barmakids. I ran behind him for a while, but eventually curiosity overwhelmed me.

"Master, where are we going?"

"To meet my true beloved. Ah, did you think I was talking about you? What delightfully complacent self-absorption you are beginning to display. We might make a poet of you yet. No, the friend of which I speak lives at the palace. This way; here we are."

We emerged into a courtyard where the air was pestilent with the stink of birdshit and the jangle of bells. A number of wooden poles, with triangular bars at the top like cripples' crutches, were fixed into the floor. Abu Nuwas called out.

"Hey, Salih! Where is my beloved?"

An old man emerged from a nearby colonnade, shuffling and snuffling towards us. He was bent of back and gnarled of hand, with a face so puffed that his eyes seemed to be at the end of deep holes, and his nose could hardly be distinguished at all.

"Eh, Abu Ali! You come round here after all these long months and expect your beloved to be waiting uncomplainingly? What kind of love is that, eh?"

I reflected that if the old man was my master's true beloved, then his usually high standards had collapsed like the walls of Yeriho. However his next words suggested otherwise.

"You are too severe, Salih. Cruel fate has kept me from my beloved; but now I am here to make amends. Where is she? Where is my beautiful Khalila?"

Salih, the old man, wheezed away grumbling. When, a few moments later, he returned, he seemed to be carrying something in a gloved hand, which he held carefully away from his body. As he came closer I saw that there was a bird perched on his wrist. It was a falcon, hooded and tethered. As the light fell upon her she stretched her wings, a full five spans across. Abu Nuwas made a throaty growl, almost sexual in its intensity.

"Ah, my beloved! But Salih, why is she veiled?"

"She cannot bear the sight of any human face but yours, Abu Ali."

As the old man spoke he raised his hand towards my master. Abu Nuwas pushed his finger against the bird's claws, and she stepped across onto his bare hand. Her talons dug into his skin, causing a drop of blood to roll down his arm, but he seemed not to notice.

"Let me look upon your face, my angel."

Abu Nuwas delicately untied the braces, as if undressing a lover, and drew the hood from the falcon's head. Khalila blinked her yellow eyes, and two beautiful, cruel faces stared at each other, in a mixture of hunger and fear that approximated love. Salih meanwhile transferred the leash to my master's wrist. At last the bird shook, ringing the bells on her feathered legs and breaking the spell. Abu Nuwas stroked her breast.

"Her keel is sharp, Salih. Have you been starving her?"

"She spurns food that is not from your hands."

The poet placed her on one of the perches while he pulled a leather glove onto his left hand, ignoring the wound.

"Come. It is time for us to hunt."

I did not know whether he was talking to me or the bird; but I suspected the latter.

Before leaving the palace we visited the stables, to borrow horses. Again this seemed to be an unquestioned privilege of the Barid. Abu Nuwas chose a fine-looking bay mare for himself, and was in the process of picking me out a pony when I was forced to make an embarrassing confession.

"But master, I cannot ride."

He stared at me as if I had admitted to – well, in fact I could not think of anything the debauched poet might consider shameful, except, apparently, poor horsemanship. At last he managed to speak.

"But – how did you travel here from Tiaret?"

"Mostly I walked. In Ifriqiya they still use wagons pulled by oxen, and where I could I sat on board. Sometimes I rode on camels . . ."

"Then if you can ride a camel, why not a horse?"

My answer did not come out audibly at first, and I had to repeat it.

"I am frightened of horses, master."

The laughter of Abu Nuwas was so raucous it disturbed his falcon, until her distress caused him to recover his composure.

"Well, well. I had thought you utterly fearless, Newborn. I am glad to discover that you have at least one human weakness."

In the end I consented to perch behind him on his mare, clinging to him rather more tightly than I would have done in other circumstances. We headed south out of the city, and Abu Nuwas geed the beast to a lively trot, relishing my misery. He still bore the falcon on his wrist as he rode, although he had replaced the bird's hood.

I had worried about how we would find the hunt, but my fear was short-lived. Even before we reached the outskirts of town I noticed the pleasure barges heading down the Tigris, brightly painted and crowded with aristocrats. By midday we were some thirty miles outside the city, but the road was as busy as the most bustling suq. Slaves and servants shouted to each other as they dodged round donkeys loaded with packs, and the horses from which their masters serenely surveyed the chaos. Everywhere packs of dogs barked and panted, straining against their leashes, long-eared hounds with slender legs and pinched stomachs. I wondered what we were hunting, that would not have fled long ago from such commotion.

"Master, is there really an abundance of game, so near to Baghdad?"

Abu Nuwas seemed surprised by my naivety.

"There will be now, if the Khalifah chooses to hunt here. You see that grove of cedars, down in the valley? Slaves have been working all night hauling cages of animals and birds out there, and beaters surround it, to stop them escaping. There will be no shortage of wildlife for the wealthy to slaughter."

We navigated to where the turmoil was most intense, and here we found the camp of Harun al-Rashid. An elaborate complex of tents had been erected, so that the Khalifah and his inner circle could be sheltered from the noon sun while they prepared for the hunt. Abu Nuwas and I dismounted to approach the royal presence. Harun was sitting in state, on a great pile of costly carpets, so we prostrated ourselves with full formality. He dismissed us with a vague gesture; I had the impression he was suffering for the previous night's adventures.

As we walked away, Abu Nuwas leading the mare and I keeping as far as I could from its huge, mad eyes and yellow teeth, a voice hailed us.

"Peace be upon you, fellow scribbler!"

It was Angilbert, the leader of the Frankish delegation, who was hauling on the leashes of a trio of slavering hounds. Obviously my master had been correct in his guess: not only had the embassy not been expelled after their escapades, but they were even guests of honour at the royal hunt.

"And upon you peace, my lord ambassador. I am glad you are joining us to sample the pleasures of the chase in the Black Lands. Let us hope it is as exciting as the fishing, eh?"

Abu Nuwas aimed this last comment at the Christian with the half shaven head. The priest, who had last been seen secretly meeting the hooded man by the river, was skulking uncomfortably at the rear of his party. Angilbert's face did not betray a flicker of guilt.

"Indeed, Brother Catwulf enjoys hunting in all its forms. That is a particularly fine bird on your wrist. From its size, it must be a female?"

While the ambassador adroitly diverted the course of the conversation, I studied the warrior Gorm, who was staring straight ahead. It occurred to me that he probably knew neither Arabic nor Greek. I supposed he used Latin to communicate with his Frankish masters. Then I noticed his daughter, the yellow-haired Hervor. She was dressed for hunting, in a man's shirt that left her arms as shamelessly bare as her face, and long leather pants. She had been staring at me, and when I looked at her she stuck her tongue out between pale lips. I was taken aback by this obscene gesture, but the shock on my face only caused her to shake with silent giggles.

My master had finished exchanging pleasantries with Angilbert, and led me away. Hundreds of men had gathered for the hunt, and now they began to spread out, forming a wide arc centred on the cedar grove a couple of miles away. Although nobody was directing this manoeuvre, the hunt seemed to be forming into an order of precedence, with proximity to the royal camp the measure of status and favour. Abu Nuwas took me to a position some two hundred cubits from the centre, a prestigious, but not presumptuous, station. I did not ask him how everyone knew their place. To courtiers, this kind of fine judgement seemed as natural as the flocking of birds.

I wondered how we would know when the hunt had started, but soon the chatter and bragging died away, and was replaced by a nervous hush. Then Harun al-Rashid emerged from his tent, surrounded by Guardsmen in their black robes. He climbed onto a grey stallion and sat erect in the saddle, allowing the onlookers to admire his fabulous hunting garments of green and gold.

The quiet was broken by strange sounds from a pavilion of the Khalifah's camp. It was a piercing noise, somewhere between a bird's chirrup and the yelp of an injured dog, but loud enough to stir birds from the trees and silence the hounds. Even the falcon Khalila shook her bells in unease.

A lean, slinking shadow slid from the tent, attached to a long rope held by a nervous Guard, and the source of the noise was revealed. It was a cat, half my height and nearly as long as I was tall. Powerful muscles moved under its dappled sandy hide as it prowled into the open ground ahead of the huntsmen; deep black lines ran like tears from its eyes to a whiskered muzzle, that yawned to reveal vicious teeth. Abu Nuwas muttered under his breath.

"What a show-off. He must really want to impress those foreigners."

Again the big cat emitted its peculiar yelp, which seemed to echo from the hills across the valley. The Khalifah spurred his stallion to a walk, and slowly the hunt came to life, advancing raggedly like a reluctant army. I clambered unwillingly back onto the mare.

"Was that a leopard, master?"

"Not quite. It is a beast of similar kind, which the Hindus call the Chita. It can outpace the fastest horse in pursuit of its prey. They do not breed in captivity, so must be captured as cubs and trained for the hunt. Only the very wealthy, and very ostentatious, own them."

Abu Nuwas had been scanning the skies. Now the vanguard of the hunt had reached the first trees, and a dove ascended suddenly, startled by their intrusion. My master freed his falcon from her leash and hood, still more lasciviously than before. While she roused and fluffed her feathers ready for flight, he spoke, in a distant singsong very different from his usual tone. He seemed to be addressing me, but his voice was low and he looked only at Khalila.

"I caught her myself, as a passager. On a high hill, where the swift autumn winds chilled the bones, I set my dho-gazza, baited with a fat pigeon. Her keen eyes saw the prey far below, and she was seduced. Khalila stooped, plunging to earth.

"She crashed into the net, bringing the dho-gazza down so that she was tangled in its mesh. I crept towards her. She battled against her capture, struggling for the freedom of the sky. Gently I withdrew her, though she scratched and bit in her passion."

Abu Nuwas thrust his hand out, and the falcon left him, beating her powerful wings as she fought her way upwards.

"I spent weeks manning her, caressing her with a feather

and soft words in a darkened room. When I brought her into the light, she shrieked at the sight of me and sought to flee. But in time she grew used to my face, my voice, my touch. At last she bowed her head before me to take food, exposing the back of her neck where a predator would strike to kill."

Khalila grew smaller as she ascended, climbing far higher than the dove, which looped dazedly above the grove.

"In the spring I flew her on the creance. Each day I paid out another turn of the reel, until the line stretched fifty cubits from my hand. Finally came the morning when I took her out untethered, and put her to the air. At first she noticed no difference. She circled at the limits of the creance, waiting for the tug that would mark the circumscription of her liberty. Then she understood, and soared away, disappearing with heartbreaking speed into the clouds."

The falcon, as if hearing herself talked about, suddenly dropped. She seemed to have stopped dead and fallen, except that the speed of her descent was too great. In an instant she was upon the unwitting dove. Inches from her prey she halted her dive, merely scraping the other bird's wing with her scything talons. The dove tumbled from the sky, while Khalila spiralled around her.

"She came back to the lure. She came, and I rejoiced in my heart. She spurned the wilderness for the certainty of my hand, and I was glad, because I had bent her to my will. But also I wept."

A shadow appeared over the falcon and the injured dove, as if a cloud had covered the sun. It was not a cloud, however, but a giant raptor with copper plumage, closing on the pair with menacing speed. I thought for a moment it must be a rukh, the monstrous bird of legend, which preyed on elephants. As it came near to Khalila I realised it was an eagle, but still a fearsome predator, twice the size of the falcon.

Khalila darted away, abandoning her prey to the larger bird. The eagle ignored the dove, which fell to the ground, and instead pursued the falcon, to a cry of horror from Abu Nuwas. Khalila was fast, but could not outpace the eagle's wide wings. I imagined the falcon, in the roar of the upper air, hearing the beat grow stronger and closer, the hunter fleeing for her life.

Then Khalila stooped, plummeting away from the eagle. The predator banked and wheeled, but already the falcon was skimming over the grass and back to the safety of her master's glove. Cheated of her kill, the eagle descended to where the dove lay bleeding, and put an end to its struggles.

As Abu Nuwas soothed Khalila, a sharp whistle came from behind us.

"Here, Hawwa! To me! Tch, she still refuses to come when called. There will be no eating left on that dove when she has finished ripping it apart. Still, my bird stole the prize from yours, eh, Abu Ali?"

It was Salam al-Abrash, the Speckled One, wearing a glove that covered most of his arm. I looked at my master's furious face, then involuntarily down to where his sword hung by his side. I thought he was about to murder the eunuch in front of hundreds of witnesses. Instead he turned his horse.

"Let us find somewhere quieter. Chitas and eagles! Is this sport, or a menagerie?"

We headed away from the royal party, and took a curving path behind the advancing hunt. As we drew further from the centre, the line became more extended, with lengthy gaps between groups of aristocrats. We began to see the beaters, servants with metal cymbals to stir up the game, and long spears to protect themselves in case the beasts came too close. Eventually my grumbling persuaded Abu Nuwas to drop me off his horse, and he rode on alone.

Walking was a sweaty business in the heat of the afternoon, but I found it far preferable to hanging on the back of a stinking horse. After the madness of Baghdad it was pleasant to be in the open air. The baying of hounds and the shouts of men were distant now, ringing round the valley. I almost convinced myself I was in the wilderness, rather than a few hours ride from the metropolis. It was not until I came across an irrigation canal running between the hills that the illusion was broken.

The canal was only a few cubits across, and I could easily

have jumped it. However it was a hot day, and the water sparkled in the blazing sun. I was wearing my plain Barid clothes, so I had no qualms about tying them into a bundle which I secured around my waist. First I dipped a foot into the water, but the chill sent shivers across my naked skin. Realising that this was no time for half measures, I leapt feet first into the canal.

The shock was at first agonising, then thrilling. My feet touched the bottom, and as I pushed up my head broke the surface. The canal was so shallow that I could stand upright in it. I gasped, snorted and bellowed as I tried to recover my breath. Then I pushed off and swam lazily along, enjoying the contrast between the icy water and the warm sunlight.

I had had little opportunity to immerse myself fully since arriving in Baghdad. It would be a brave man that bathed in the waterways of the city, where he would have to dodge the turds and other detritus chucked there by the good citizens. The water of the canal, although a little muddy, particularly where I had crashed in and stirred up the bed, was relatively fresh. Having no real interest in the hunt, I decided to follow the course of the canal until I tired.

In what seemed like no time I drew close to the cedar grove. Clumps of trees stood by the banks, and I could hear the squawking of strange birds, brought here to be victims of the archers and falconers.

And that was where I saw the demon with the head of a dog and eagle's wings.

Nineteen

The Tale of the Dog-Headed Demon

It was a statue, carved from coarse rock. The stone was worn by the weather of centuries and stained with mosses. I guessed it must have been there from the days of the ancients, the Assyrians or Babylonians.

The demon was twice the height of a man, but emaciated, as if it were starving. Two pairs of wings spread from its back, and a grotesque dog-skull leered above a narrow neck It stood atop a small hill that sloped away from the canal to my left, amid a small copse of cedars.

I pulled myself out of the water and cautiously approached the statue. As I came closer, I saw that someone stood beside it. I had no difficulty in recognising Brother Catwulf, the Frankish priest with the half-shaved head, who seemed to turn up wherever there was mystery and conspiracy. However it took me a little longer to distinguish the plump figure that climbed the hill towards him. It was Fadl ibn Rabi, the Chamberlain.

I concealed myself in the bushes, and listened to their conversation.

"Is it safe?"

The statue overlooked a clearing in the copse. The Chamberlain leaned against it, panting from his ascent. Brother Catwulf, when he responded, was calm.

"Have no fear. If we are discovered together we can easily claim that we were pursuing the same quarry. As, in a way, we are."

I was almost holding my breath, desperate to remain unnoticed and to catch every word they said. However I nearly let it out in a yelp when a warm hand slapped my bare behind. I span around, to discover that my assailant was the girl Hervor. She started to laugh, and I knocked her to the ground, desperately shushing her. As I lay on top of her, she put her lips to my ear, and whispered.

"I see you are not so frightened of my body now, boy."

I moved off her, suddenly aware of my nakedness. She leaned towards me again.

"Why must we be quiet?"

I was so seduced by her brazen intimacy that I nearly told her. The words were at my lips before I remembered that she was an emissary of a foreign power, and it was her confederate on whom I was spying.

"Because – so we do not frighten the animals."

Her eyes widened in surprise.

"And is it normal practice among your people to hunt unclothed, or your own personal preference?"

I tried to think of a clever response, but was disconcerted when her shameless gaze fell to my zabb, which had shrivelled to an acorn from exposure to the icy water of the canal. I mumbled an answer to both her question and her stare.

"I have been swimming."

At the same time as keeping the mad girl quiet I was desperately trying to listen to the men talking. The Chamberlain sounded testy.

"I cannot lay hands on that much gold at a moment's notice. It will take a week to arrange it . . ."

Hervor seemed unaware of their presence, although I found it hard to believe she could not hear them. Her eyes were still fixed on my zabb, and her mocking attention was not encouraging it to resume its normal proportions.

"Perhaps I too shall try hunting naked. I shall be interested to see what kind of game I catch."

With these words she stood up and pulled her shirt over her head. Her pomegranate breasts bore red berry nipples, and her soft belly centred on a succulent navel. My zabb began to stir, but I realised that she would be visible to the Chamberlain and the priest, if they happened to look in our direction. I dragged her to the ground. My arms encircled her waist, and

I stopped her mouth with kisses. As her lips parted against mine I felt some guilt that I was making such treacherous use of the lesson Layla had taught me in the rose garden. However I appeased my conscience with the knowledge that I was protecting the Land of Islam from Christian subversion.

She pushed my head down, and almost without thought, like an animal, I licked and sucked at the berry nipples. By now my acorn had grown to a mighty oak. Hervor ran one hand through my hair and with the other reached down and grabbed my zabb, demonstrating more enthusiasm than delicacy. The blood was raging in my ears, but I could still just about hear ibn Rabi.

"I need to know that you are not deceiving me. How does the oathbreaker know the secret of the Name?"

Then Hervor shoved me aside. For a moment I thought she had recovered her modesty, but instead she tugged off her boots and rolled down the leather pants, leaving herself utterly nude in front of me. I had seen women unclothed before, but never had I seen anything to compare with her slim white legs and triangle of golden hair at their juncture. I gawped like an idiot, mouth hanging open.

"Well, boy, what are you waiting for? Let's see what you can do."

Her habit of calling me "boy", when she was a year older than me at most, was annoyingly patronising. However, my witty riposte came out as a guttural croak, and I pounced on her. After a few moments of my thrusting optimistically in the general direction of her groin she rolled me onto my back.

"Wait – let me –"

She knelt with one leg either side of my hips, and took my zabb in her hand. As she leaned over me she guided its tip into her breach. I raised my hips, expecting to plunge into her as I had seen men do with whores during a childhood at sea and on the road. Instead she pressed me down with her hand. Slowly she eased herself onto my zabb, and every movement caused intense sensations bordering on pain.

When the whole sword was buried in her, she dropped limply onto me and lay there, the berry nipples pressing onto my chest. I wondered if that was the end of the business. Unsure of what to do I stroked her cropped yellow hair. Suddenly she revived, kissing me quickly and desperately. I ran my hand down to her hips, and she began to move.

I felt on the cusp of erupting, but each rise and fall was so slow that I never quite spilled over. The next wave though was a little quicker, and warmer, and softer, and the next better still, and pleasure was replacing the pain. Now I could have easily let go, but I was watching her face, listening to her breath, feeling her heart beat more rapidly as her body pressed against mine. She was utterly serious, eyes closed, frowning and biting her lip.

Then something opened inside her, and she moaned long and low, slumping back onto me. The change in pressure released me too, and I surged deep into her. The world melted as I put my arms around her. Far away I seemed to hear two pairs of feet running away through the undergrowth.

It felt as though the wind had changed. When Hervor wrenched away from me, my gasp sounded like the soul being sucked from the clay of my body. She grabbed her clothes and bounded off as if pursued by the Chita. I turned to see the flash of white flesh disappearing between the trees.

My zabb was shrivelling and sticky now, and felt cold. I heard an ursine grunt behind me. I glanced over my shoulder to see Gorm the Rus staring at me. For the first time I noticed that he had the same delicate blue eyes as his daughter. And there was an odd similarity between her look of lust and his glare of murderous hatred.

He was not wielding his usual weapon, but instead carried a long hunting spear. I supposed he had to pretend to have been pursuing game. The vision of him lumbering after a deer, roaring like a bear and waving a battle axe, was ludicrous enough that I almost laughed, but I quickly recovered my senses. Although he was some distance away the point of the spear was threateningly close.

Gorm was a wily old warrior, and did not strike blindly to kill, as would a common thug. He stood on guard, assessing the situation. Too soon though he reassured himself that his only adversary was small and bare, like a hairless monkey, crouching in terror under the scented needles of a cedar tree. He laughed.

"If you're going to fight the boy I really think you should undress too. Not only would it be fairer, but it would make it considerably more entertaining."

Abu Nuwas stepped out of the trees, his sword drawn, the falcon Khalila still perched on his gloved left hand. However, in the time it had taken my master to drawl his challenge, Gorm had considered and assimilated this shift in the situation. I too had a moment of heart-sinking and largely unwelcome clarity. I realised that when confronted with deadly peril, the poet relied heavily on taunting provocation, to distract and enrage his enemy. This had no effect whatsoever on Gorm, who could not understand a single word he was saying.

The Rus saw a man with a sword, still some distance away, and an unarmed enemy at the point of his spear. His course of action was clear: dispose of the distraction, then face the real danger. The choice would have been easy even if he had not just come across the distraction in question fucking his daughter. He drew back his spear to strike at me.

I do not know who the cry came from, whether it was my master or my foe, or whether it burst unbidden from my own lips as the sharp metal thrust at my gut. In the same instant Abu Nuwas jabbed his gloved fist toward the Rus. Swift as a shout the falcon hurtled towards him. There was a blinding pain as the point pierced my skin, but the spear faltered and fell. I heard screeching, and saw Khalila attacking Gorm's face with her vicious talons, while he tried to swat her away like a fly.

Now Abu Nuwas was racing toward him. Blood was splattering onto the grass from the cut in my stomach, but I had no time to tend the wound. I reasoned that if I was to be hunted like a monkey I would escape like one, and leapt for a limb of the nearest tree. From here I swung myself up to the highest branch that would hold my weight, and watched events unfold below.

Gorm's flailing arms had driven away the falcon, but Abu

Nuwas took up the assault, slashing at him with his sayf. The Rus dodged his blows with incongruous grace, and drew a long dagger from his belt. Khalila meanwhile flew up and perched in the same tree as me, where she stared at me, dispassionately assessing my potential as her next meal.

The two men now stood off and tested each other, with prods and feints. Abu Nuwas had the superior weapon, but Gorm had longer reach in his arms. Evenly matched, each studied his opponent, looking for a weakness or an opportunity.

When the assault came it was like lightning from a blue sky. The Rus lunged fiercely, but Abu Nuwas sidestepped easily, and swung his sayf at Gorm's unprotected side. However, he had fallen into a trap. Gorm, expecting the move, brought his left arm down like a club on my master's wrist. The sword fell from his hand. Abu Nuwas swayed away from the next slice of the dagger, but at the cost of overbalancing and falling on his back.

Gorm had him now, down and weaponless. There was no way I could have safely descended from the tree in time to save him, even if I were not injured and unarmed. In desperation I flung cones from the tree, and shouted uselessly at Khalila to attack.

My shouts were drowned out by deep howls that seemed to make the tree tremble. The bushes below me shook, and a creature burst forth. It was white, with a black devil's face, like a distorted skull. The bearded head was twisted to one side, and a massive single horn protruded from its forehead.

The beast bounded across the clearing. As it moved I saw that there were in fact two horns, that its unity had been an illusion. However they were vicious twin swords, a cubit in length. The creature was an oryx, favourite quarry of Arabian huntsmen.

Gorm turned, to see that the oryx was charging directly at him. Even the giant Rus feared being impaled on the sharp horns. He leapt aside, and Abu Nuwas rolled away from the beast's trampling feet, which barely missed him. Then the clearing was full of hounds, barking and baying, and I realised they were the source of the sound that had alerted me to the beast's approach. The oryx raced down into the hollow, pursued by the dogs.

After the animals came a squad of Guardsmen, armed with nets and spears, then three richly dressed men on horses. At the centre of the trio was the Khalifah himself, Harun al-Rashid, in his green and gold robes. He pulled his horse to a halt.

"Peace, Abu Ali! Are you trying to steal from me the quarry I have been pursuing for so long?"

My master pulled himself to his feet and made a deep bow of obeisance.

"Not at all, Commander of the Faithful. Your guest here had become separated from his party. I was merely trying to help him find his way."

He put an arm around the broad shoulders of Gorm the Rus, who stiffened, but was smart enough to make no move other than to nod his respect to the Khalifah. Harun gestured to a couple of Guards.

"Escort our honoured guest back to his countrymen."

As the Guards walked over Abu Nuwas turned Gorm to face him.

"Go carefully, my friend. I look forward with great pleasure to our next meeting."

The barbarian may not have understood his words, but he could not ignore the passionate kiss that Abu Nuwas planted on his lips. Gorm stared at him impassively, then uttered a single sentence in Latin simple enough that even I could decipher it.

"The next time we meet, only one of us will walk away alive."

With that he and his escort left. Harun al-Rashid smiled at his favourite poet.

"So, my friend, how goes your hunting?"

"Most enjoyably, o Khalifah. Might I enquire what has happened to your Chita? I thought it would soon bring down such laggardly prey as an oryx."

Harun pulled a face.

"The Chita does not like to hunt in wooded areas. Nor, it

240

appears, to chase quarry with such fearsomely long horns. I ordered it returned to its cage. Do you know, Abu Ali, I do believe that Chitas are not nearly as useful as they are impressive."

"I would hardly credit it, but if the Commander of the Faithful tells me so, then I must accept it as truth."

"And what success have you enjoyed, my friend? What quarry have you been chasing?"

Just as Harun spoke these words, the branch beneath me creaked and cracked. I tumbled downward, bouncing off the cedar's needles as I fell, and landed with a thump in front of the Khalifah. Mindful that Abu Nuwas had not told him of the battle, I concealed my bleeding abdomen by kneeling with my forehead touching the ground in obeisance.

Harun al-Rashid looked from the naked boy to the poet, and back again to the naked boy, and drew the inevitable, though erroneous, conclusion.

"I see. Then I shall leave you in peace, to feast on your prey."

He rode away, some of his Guard sniggering at the situation. Abu Nuwas remained in a deep bow until they had left, then looked over to me.

"How is your stomach, Newborn?"

I started to pull on my clothes, but he insisted on inspecting the wound.

"The point did not penetrate deeply enough to damage your organs. Wait here."

He disappeared into the trees, and returned leading his horse. When he rummaged in his saddlebag I expected him to produce a poultice or remedy. I was disappointed, though not surprised, when he pulled out a flask of wine. However, instead of drinking it, he splashed a hearty slug onto the cut. I gasped at the sting and the shock, and he laughed.

"A trick I learned in the desert. It prevents the wound turning bad."

He ripped my shirt into strips and bound the injury with some expertise. As he did so I told him of the meeting in the hollow; but not about the girl Hervor.

241

"At that point it became difficult to hear what they were saying. Something about the one who knows the secret of the Name. The Frank said . . . she painted the face of the one who opened the door . . ."

"It became difficult to hear? Did they move, or lower their voices?"

"No, it was – the wind, in the trees . . ."

Abu Nuwas looked at me oddly, but did not pursue the subject.

"So fat little Fadl ibn Rabi is plotting with Franks? I knew he was ambitious and ruthless, but I did not imagine him a traitor."

"Are you going to expose him?"

My master's mouth twisted.

"The politics of the court are like a maze of mirrors, with a monster at its heart. Not everything is as it seems. I shall pass the information to the Barmakid, and let him decide how it should be dealt with. Hey, Khalila!"

He whistled, and the falcon dropped from the tree onto his wrist. With the bird on one hand and the mare's bridle in the other he led the way out of the clearing. A thought seemed to strike him.

"Ibn Rabi speaks no Greek, as far as I know. What language were they speaking?"

"Arabic."

"Then Brother Catwulf speaks our tongue, but he talked to the hooded man in Greek. I had assumed that the Christian priest could not speak Arabic, but perhaps Abu Murra is a foreigner. When you heard Brother Catwulf at the Garden of Delight, what exactly did he say?"

I screwed up my eyes, struggling to remember.

"He said . . . 'The traitor followed me . . . The oathbreaker spoke to him.' "

"The traitor and the oathbreaker – fine company they keep, these Christian holy men."

We walked in silence for a while. My thoughts drifted to the yellow-haired girl, and my first experience of congress with a woman. It had been strange, certainly gratifying in the end, but awkward and uncomfortable too. It had also caused another physical response.

"Do you have any food, master? I am hungry."

The effect of my words on Abu Nuwas was extraordinary. He froze, staring into the distance, and gripped my wrist so hard it hurt.

"Hungry – of course – ten hungry men!"

"Master?"

"Umm Dabbah was looking for ten hungry men! We must get back to the city – she is in terrible danger."

He was climbing onto the bay mare as he spoke, and reached a hand down to pull me up. Reluctantly I swung up behind him, and we left the grove at a canter.

Light as I was, the mare struggled under the weight of two riders, and the sun was setting by the time we returned to the city. Abu Nuwas had ignored my frantic questioning, concentrating instead on nursing the horse through the journey. It was not until we dismounted in the darkening streets of Sharqiya that he deigned to enlighten me.

"I thought that the old woman was delirious, but there was sense to her raving. The Fifth Surah of the Holy Quran enjoins the feeding of ten hungry men as suitable expiation, or penance – for those who have broken an oath."

It seemed that Umm Dabbah must be the oathbreaker the men had been discussing. I was little wiser for this knowledge, but there was no time for further talk. We had arrived at the house of Ghassan, the porter whose son had disappeared. Abu Nuwas was hammering on his door.

"Umm Dabbah! You must tell us where she lives! I have to see her, now."

Ghassan was in no hurry to answer the door, but once he realised who we were he could not do enough to help, and agreed to show the way to the gossip's house. He raced barefooted ahead of us, stopping a couple of blocks away at a modest dwelling. Abu Nuwas shouted and banged, but the house remained silent. The neighbours, on the other hand, were beginning to take an interest.

"We have to get inside."

Abu Nuwas looked desperately at me as he spoke. Grudgingly I stood so that my body was between the door and the porter. Then I drew the needles from my sleeve. The lock was a crude one. I picked it so quickly that it must have seemed to the porter as though it just opened in my hands. The door to the house swung ajar, and the darkness within beckoned.

"In my saddlebag – there are flints, and a torch. Get them, now."

I obeyed wordlessly, recognising that my master was in no mood for banter. The porter, seeing him draw his sword, tried to avoid catching his eye in case he was ordered into the house, and came over to help me. However Abu Nuwas slipped through the door alone.

I was still not entirely sure what was happening. If Umm Dabbah had broken an oath, it did not explain why my master believed her to be in such peril. However, his agitation had infected me, and my hands shook as I tried to spark the torch. Ghassan had to steady me.

Once we had light, I entered the house. The porter hesitated, but came in after me. There was nothing unusual in the design of the building. A short passage led to a courtyard, ringed by rooms. Then, through a door that stood open, we heard a terrible scream, cut short by a gurgling noise.

I raced across the yard, and stepped cautiously into the doorway. Nervous footsteps suggested the porter had arrived behind me, but I did not look back. For the flickering light of the torch revealed Umm Dabbah, lying unveiled beneath an open window. Her heavy face was stained with red, and as we watched, blood bubbled out of her mouth and trickled down her neck. Kneeling over her, his sword dripping, was Abu Nuwas.

In his other hand he held something that flopped like a lump of dead meat. There was so much blood it took me a little while to realise that it was a human tongue. Abu Nuwas tried to speak, but I heard only Ghassan the porter behind me.

"Why is your master killing that woman?"

Twenty

The Tale of The Prisoner and the Guard

Abu Nuwas was struggling to sit the woman upright, but despite his strength, her dead weight was too much. Ghassan hurried over, but instead of helping he began to pull my master off her. I tried to restrain the porter, so that when the neighbours, alarmed by the scream, burst in, they found the three of us wrestling over a gory, mutilated body. Just then a belch of blood, exploding from her mouth, announced that Umm Dabbah had finally expired.

We were hauled out onto the street. Everyone was talking at once, but the porter was known and trusted by our captors. It was his voice which prevailed.

"I thought they were servants of the Wazir – it was al-Takht, the Police Captain, told me that, just after that fire, when Umm Dabbah saw – tonight they came knocking on my door like madmen – I thought they were helping to find my boy! I did what they asked, and showed them to the house of Umm Dabbah. Then the boy kept me outside, making a great fuss over lighting a torch, while that tall one went inside and murdered the woman. I should have known better than to think great men would care about the fate of my son . . ."

We were taken to the nearest masjid, and someone went to find a Qadi to judge the case. Abu Nuwas shouted for them to fetch al-Takht, but whether anyone intended to obey it was impossible to tell. A crowd was gathering, and nobody was deterred from expressing an opinion by such trivial concerns as not having been at the scene or knowing what had happened. The general view was that we weren't from those parts and looked funny, therefore we must be guilty.

Then our luck worsened. One of the bystanders was from

Harbiya, and recognised my master from the trial of Babak ibn Bundar. Before long we were dragged off again, trailing an ever-growing procession through the streets, until we arrived at the Blue Masjid.

Despite the lateness of the hour, the young judge al-Shafi'i was still hearing cases. When Abu Nuwas was brought before him he tried to disguise his look of triumph as the serene smile of the holy man.

"The good people of Sharqiya have saved me the trouble of having to summon you here. Now you must answer, not only for the aiding in the escape of the child-killer ibn Bundar, but also for murder – the murder of a witness who could have identified him as an evil warlock."

Once again the Qadi was seated on a prayer mat by the minbar, but this time it was my master and I who were held by burly Baghdadis in front of a goggling mob. Amid the hubbub it took a few moments for Abu Nuwas to digest the implications of the Qadi's statement.

"Ibn Bundar has escaped?"

Al-Shafi'i narrowed his eyes.

"Your feeble pretence of surprise does not fool anybody, poet. If you tell us how you managed to spirit him away from a locked cell, I may consider making the manner of your death a little easier."

Abu Nuwas struggled between his captors.

"Don't be stupid, man! I spent the entire day in the company of the Khalifah and his court. How could I possibly have been here, releasing ibn Bundar?"

"Whether it was your accomplices who freed him, or an evil demon summoned by witchcraft, I have no doubt that you are responsible. Why would you have argued so strongly for his innocence, unless you are a disciple of his foul practices?"

My master had to shout over the muttering of the crowd.

"I am an agent of the Barid, sent by the Wazir to look into these matters! The Commander of the Faithful will be angry, when he hears how you have treated me!"

At this the Qadi smiled.

"I do not fear Ja'far al-Barmaki, nor his master the Khalifah. My authority comes from God himself, and from his holy and perfect law. And I know who you are, ibn Hani al-Hakami. I have read your blasphemous verse, your cheap mockery of decency and morality, your eulogies to wine and sexual depravity . . ."

The more Abu Nuwas had to raise his voice to make himself heard, the more he resembled the dangerous lunatic the Qadi was making him out to be.

"But you have no evidence against me! You cannot condemn me for my poetry –"

Instead of shouting, al-Shafi'i lowered his voice, and the crowd quietened to hear him.

"I might well condemn you for your words. But I can do better than that. I have a witness who saw you kill the woman Umm Dabbah."

Ghassan the Porter stepped forward, apprehensively. Abu Nuwas struggled to regain his self-control.

"He saw me trying to save her life. Are you suggesting I cut out her tongue with a sword? Do you have any idea how difficult that would be? There was another man there, with a scarf round his face like a bandit. When I surprised him, he mutilated her with a knife, and escaped through the window. I pulled the tongue from her throat in a bid to prevent her choking. If the porter had not intervened, she might still be alive.

"I managed to wound the man, before he fled. There are cuts on his arm, in the shape of the letter Zay."

He traced the curve and dot of the letter in the air with his finger.

"Find the man with the Zay on his arm. He is the killer of Umm Dabbah."

There was a sense of hesitation in the onlookers, as if they were almost convinced. Then al-Shafi'i laughed.

"This is the defence of the child caught misbehaving! 'Another boy did it but he ran away . . .' Is this to become a precedent? Are we to permit any murderer found with the corpse of his victim to escape punishment, if only they blame a mysterious stranger, whom none but they have seen?"

The roar of the mob gave a decisively negative answer to this question. The Qadi stood up.

"The family of Umm Dabbah have until dawn to come forward and claim their blood price. Otherwise, let him suffer the same fate from which he saved the apostate and child-killer Babak ibn Bundar. When the sun rises, the poet Abu Ali al-Hasan ibn Hani al-Hakami, known as the Father of Locks, shall be beheaded. Take them away."

"Might I ask a question, wise Qadi?"

I surprised myself by daring to speak, but my surprise was nothing to the astonishment displayed by my master. Al-Shafi'i acted for a moment as though he were about to ignore me, but something, perhaps curiosity, compelled him to turn.

"What is it?"

"I have not been told whether I am accused, or condemned, and if so of what."

The Qadi waved a hand as if swatting a fly.

"You were present at the murder. You are his servant."

"The porter was also present, wise Qadi. If I am implicated then so is he. And a slave cannot be held responsible for crimes committed at the command of his master."

The crowd had fallen silent, wondering whether there was to be a postscript to the story. Al-Shafi'i realised his moment of triumph was being marred by unnecessary complications, and turned away.

"Let the boy go."

Abu Nuwas watched me walk away, his eyes wide like those of an idiot, his mouth open but empty of words. Then the men who had just released me went over to make the most of manhandling him to the Watch House, expressing their contempt with fists and feet whenever the opportunity presented itself. I kept my head down as I left the masjid, trying to disappear among the masses.

In the gloom I was able to drift with the throng as far as Sharqiya. Slowly they dispersed, returning to their homes and beds. However I kept walking until I was alone. I crossed the river at the Central Bridge, and headed up the east bank until I reached the Palace of the Barmakids.

I let myself into the Hall of the Barid, where a couple of men I did not know dozed on mattresses. I did not stay but made my way into the palace itself. Here I stopped the first servant I saw.

"I need to speak to Ja'far ibn Yahya, urgently. Tell him that the Father of Locks is in danger, and will be dead by morning if he does not help."

I sat where I was, in the middle of a courtyard, and waited. The servant nodded, and left, as if such requests were not unusual in the house of the Barmakids.

I do not know how much time passed, although it felt like hours. Finally I saw a figure approaching. It was not Ja'far, however, but Ilig, the Kazakh bodyguard who had caught me in the Chamber of Ancients. I had assumed he worked for Salam al-Abrash, but I realised now that he must be in the service of the Wazir. I got to my feet as he spoke.

"I bring a message from Ja'far ibn Yahya al-Barmaki, Wazir to the Khalifah Harun al-Rashid. He commands me to repeat his words to you exactly:

" 'I thank you for advising me of the difficulty faced by your master. I am certain your master will appreciate that I am too busy behind closed doors with the Khalifah to offer any assistance at this time. I wish you luck in your endeavours.' "

With that he walked away, leaving me staring at his back, dumbfounded and despairing. At first I did not understand why the Wazir was abandoning us. Then I recalled the off-hand comment my master let slip at the house of Abbas, about Ja'far and Harun:

"Sometimes I wonder about those two; they seem a little too close. If the Khalifah drinks in private, what other sins might he commit behind closed doors?"

Someone must have reported his words to the Wazir. Perhaps it was the poet Abbas, but more likely it was the mysterious woman. Either way, Ja'far had taken offence, and now was leaving Abu Nuwas to his fate.

For a while I stood there in the courtyard, while the household bustled around me. I had no idea what I was to do. I supposed I could return to my original plan of finding a patron for my poetry. Perhaps I could approach Salam al-Abrash. The city seemed different to me though, now that I knew about the missing children and the barbarian spies and the murders in dark places. It was as if someone had lifted a rock and showed me the vile things scuttling underneath, and I could no longer sit on it in comfort.

Then I thought of the last words of the message. They may have constituted a dismissal, but they may also have been a challenge. I had not been discharged from the Barid; or, if I had, nobody had told me.

I returned to the Hall, where I tested my theory by demanding a change of clothes for myself and for a taller man, and supplies for a long journey. I almost expected to be refused, or simply thrown out of the palace. Instead servants arrived silently carrying everything I had asked for, packed into a travelling bag.

I wondered what the limits of this privilege were. Had the servants been instructed to give the Barid anything they requested, or did they go to a shadowy presence for authorisation? However this was not the time to investigate. Rather, it was time to face my fears. I went to the stables.

There are those who claim to find the odour of the camel repugnant, but to me it has a reassuring earthiness. It is the stench of the horse that revolts me. Even walking into the stables caused my gorge to rise.

I think my fear of horses must have begun when I was enslaved by the Badawi. I had very little to do with them before that time. I felt no resentment of the mule, against whose coarse hairy hide my head bounced as we trekked across Ifriqiya. However as I stared every day at the indifferent back of the slaver, it somehow became associated for me with the dung-crusted rear of his stallion.

The ostler assented to my requests without demur. The bay mare had done too much work that day for my purposes, so I trusted him to pick out another steed of similar quality. Then I was forced to choose a pony for myself.

After staring uselessly at a succession of ugly, stinking beasts, I had to admit that I had no idea what to look for in a mount. Eventually I selected a cross-eyed gelding with a face that looked more dumb than dangerous. Leading the two animals at the longest reach I could manage, I left the palace by the nearest gate, and set off westward.

The Watch House in Harbiya was of similar design to al-Takht's in Sharqiya, but located by a canal near to the district's own small suq. I was relieved to see that a light still burned inside. If Abu Nuwas had been taken to the Matbaq, the hulking prison in the Round City where political dissidents were left to rot, there would have been no chance of saving him. Fortunately he was being treated as a common criminal. I tied the two horses to a strut on a nearby bridge, trusting that the proximity of the Watch House would deter any thieves, and cautiously approached.

The door was open. From the darkness of the street I could clearly see the bright interior. A single policeman sat on the ground within, his head hanging down. He looked asleep, and I wondered whether I could simply creep past him. However as soon as I entered his head snapped upright.

"What do you want?"

He was a fat man of middle age, with pouches of skin hanging under his eyes that gave him a dolorous appearance. I had not considered what I would do beyond this point, and now had to weigh my choices quickly. A direct assault was out of the question. Although I would back my knife against his club, he was too big for me to tackle alone. No lies sprang to mind, so I decided to see where the truth would get me.

"I have come to see the Father of Locks."

The policeman got to his feet.

"Have you, indeed? Are you one of his boys? I've heard all about the disgusting things he gets up to, the filthy pervert."

Despite the policeman's words, he did not appear disgusted. His rough breathing was partly due to the exertion involved in standing up, but his wide eyes and leering mouth suggested that he found the idea exciting. With a heavy heart I realised what I would need to do.

251

"Yes, my lord. He is my master, and I must submit to whatever he wishes to do to me. Sometimes he puts his – a respectable officer of the law such as yourself could not imagine the vile practices which I am forced to endure."

His expression suggested he was imagining hard, and he licked his lips.

"Then why would you come to visit him, on his last night on earth?"

I had to think quickly.

"Why would I come? To see for myself that he has truly been incarcerated, and cannot get free to corrupt me still further. Is he in one of these cells?"

I was slowly working my way round the room to the row of doors at the back. Suspicion and prurience battled in the policeman's face, but desire won.

"Don't worry, lad, he is safely locked up in that middle cell there. So does he have many – boys, such as you?"

"Oh, there are many of us. More than I can count. All around his house we stroll and loll, mostly naked, waiting for him to use us as he wills. Some have been so debased by years in his service that even when he is not there they will engage the other boys in debauchery, so that entire rooms will be filled with young men writhing and groaning."

I briefly wondered whether I had overdone it, but the policeman lumbered over to me as I leaned against the cell door, with an uncomfortable gait that suggested his zabb was responding to my words.

"Poor lad. Why don't you come away from that door, and show me what sort of things he forces you to do? I ask only so that I can recognise and catch his kind more easily in future."

"But my lord, is it not better that the poet hears us together? Let him be tormented, in his final hours, by listening to his favourite servant in the arms of another man. It is practically your duty to punish him by reminding him of his sins."

The policeman was as limited in his patience as he was in his intelligence, and fell upon me where I stood. I tried not to choke on his foul stench as he nuzzled and mauled me clumsily, like a garlicky dog. Such was his enthusiasm that he was unaware that my hands were not occupied as his were, but were instead busy behind my back.

The three-pin lock was not a complicated one, but attempting to pick it in such an awkward position was difficult enough without the policeman's clumsy thrusting and groping. I caught two of the pins with a speculative rake, but I could not find the third. I had to let all three drop, then set them again in the opposite order. At last the pins clicked into place, and the barrel turned. I could only hope that Abu Nuwas was alert and awake, and had correctly deciphered the sounds filtering through the door.

By now the policeman was tugging down his pants with one hand and mine with another. I pushed him away.

"Wait – wait."

Managing to free myself, I dodged around him so that he was between me and the cell.

"You must not rush, my lord. We have until dawn to prolong the deviant's misery. Why do you not stand against the door, so that your moans of sweet pleasure assail his ears while I use upon you every trick and technique that he taught me for his own vile purposes?"

The policeman grinned, revealing blackened teeth. He leaned back against the cell door – and toppled over as it swung open. Abu Nuwas, his handsome face battered to a gory mess, leapt upon his guard's chest, and looped his belt around the man's neck.

"Quick, his legs!"

I pounced on the flailing limbs, then noticed the policeman's face turning as blue as his robes. I grabbed a pebble from the ground and hurled it at my master.

"Don't kill him, you fool! He has done nothing wrong, and besides, then you really will be the murderer they accused you of being."

For an instant the poet glared at me, madness in his bruised eyes, and I wondered whether he would turn on me next. Then he released the pressure on the policeman's throat. While the unfortunate guard gasped for breath, Abu Nuwas used the belt to tie him up. I stuffed fabric into his mouth to gag him, guiltily remembering the terror I had felt when ibn Bundar had done the same to me.

Once he had been secured and silenced, we left the Watch House. Outside Abu Nuwas looked to me, and I indicated the two horses. It was only when we were saddled and riding westward out of the city that he finally spoke.

"I must thank you twice, Newborn. First for liberating me, then for restraining me."

I said nothing, and we travelled on until the last houses on the outskirts of Baghdad had disappeared into the darkness behind us.

"I was frightened, Newborn. I did not want to die – at least, not then, and not so stupidly. I was so angry at the pointlessness of what was happening, at the injustice of it.

"Then I heard voices, and the shifting of subtle devices. When I flung open the door and battled for my life, I was not fighting that fat fool, who dreams of pretty boys while he fucks his fat wife. I was fighting the futility, the grief, the violation. I was fighting God."

The next time he spoke, we had left the road, and found our way through the fields by following the black water of the Sarat canal.

"Fear can master us, take away our reason and turn us into animals. But fear can be subdued, it can be defeated by love. When you climbed on that horse, I saw the grimace on your face. I hear how you breathe through your mouth, trying not to inhale the odour of the animal. I feel your body jolt with every step, as you hold yourself rigid in the saddle. Yet you have uttered not one word of complaint.

"You have done it, Ismail. You have done what had to be done. You have done what you chose to do."

I leaned away from my mount and vomited until my stomach ached. Then I cried, fruitlessly straining to weep my soul as empty as my body.

Twenty One

The Tale of the Saint and the Sinner, which includes, The Education of a Poet

We camped that night where the Sarat met the Euphrates, then the next morning followed the river south. There were no signs of pursuit. Ja'far's anger, it seems, was deep enough for him to refuse help, but not so deep that he would have us hunted down. As for the Harbiya mob, I could not imagine them leaving their trades to pursue mounted men beyond the city boundary.

Abu Nuwas was leading once more. I did not ask him where we were going. Once I had told him how the Wazir had turned his back, we had passed beyond words, and rode for most of the day without speaking. I recalled that he had lived for a time in Basrah, and wondered idly if that was our destination. In the end my lack of curiosity drove my master to break the silence.

"Have you ever met a saint, boy?"

I thought about this for so long that he turned to look at me, unsure whether I was ignoring him.

"I do not know, master. I do not know how I would know if I had."

"When you meet the one we are going to see, there will be no doubt. A saint is one without selfishness or hatred, who sees with utter clarity and loves with absolute purity. Such a one is my friend al-Adawiyya."

I nodded but made no other response. Abu Nuwas looked to the horizon, and we journeyed on.

For a second night we camped in open air, but by the end of the third day we had come to the city of Kufah. I hoped that we would seek lodgings, at least for a while. However Abu Nuwas said that he was too well known there. I visited the suq to purchase supplies while he waited in nearby woods, and at dawn the next day we crossed the river by ferry.

Once on the west bank of the Euphrates we no longer followed its course, but instead headed due south. As the river curved away to our left, eventually disappearing, the irrigation canals petered out and the land became increasingly barren. Our water was running out, and I gradually became aware that my master had been more badly hurt during his arrest than I had first realised. His breathing had become noisy, and sometimes he groaned for no obvious reason, although he tried to disguise it as a cough or yawn.

As the fifth day wore on, Abu Nuwas started to mutter to himself. It began with curses, suddenly spat out on no provocation. Later, fragmented phrases dropped from his swollen lips.

"A dozen to the dinar . . . The camel belongs to Abu Yusuf, I swear it . . . Take that milk away. I did not ask for milk . . ."

"What milk, Father of Locks?"

He stared at me through his eyebrows as if deeply saddened by my inability to understand him, then trotted ahead. I was frightened, not least because he was leading me further into empty lands. The ground was rocky, and a forbidding range of hills stretched out ahead. I could not be sure how long he had been irrational. Did he know where he was going? What did he mean about meeting a saint?

When we came near the hills he pointed to some rubble ahead of us.

"There . . . there . . ."

He leaned forward, squinting. I followed his gaze, trying to see what he was peering at so intently. Then I realised he was slowly tumbling from his saddle and falling to the ground.

I dismounted and ran round to him. His eyes had rolled into his head, and he was breathing with difficulty. I had no idea what to do. A brown flicker caught my eye, in the direction he had indicated.

I was alone, and had trusted him this far. I raced across the open ground towards the distant movement.

"Hey! Help! In the name of God the All-Merciful, help us!"

The old woman looked at me in mild surprise as I ran towards her.

"In the name of God, you say? Well, that is different. Had you entreated me in the name of the Devil, I would certainly have taken you to my hut and cooked you for my breakfast."

She was standing by a stream which had been hidden from me by the lay of the ground. She wore robes of rough wool, and in one hand she held a water jug. Her words made me fear she was mad, but then I saw the flash in her eyes that suggested she was laughing at me.

With a farmer's strength she helped me haul the unconscious Abu Nuwas to her hut. This was a low building of mud brick not far from the stream. Inside the hut was virtually bare, containing only a reed mat, a crude screen of wood and cloth, and a prayer rug.

She brought the rug outside and we laid my master upon it. She contemplated him gravely, and sighed.

"Oh, Abu Ali. What have you done to yourself this time?"

The old woman pottered over to what seemed to be a small herb garden beside her hut, and began to pick leaves, while singing to herself.

> "Eyes close, stars open, spark of evening dew
>   The sky above falls silent, below the deepest blue
> You are the Truth that never changes
>   Eternity that is ever new
> The doors of Kings need bolts and guards
>   Your door stands open to let me through
> Each is alone with the one they love
>   I am alone with you."

As I listened to her voice, I understood what Abu Nuwas had meant about clarity and purity.

"My master speaks very highly of you, al-Adawiyya."

257

She looked up from her work.

"Call me Rabi'a. I need no tribe, nor family, so long as I have my Beloved."

She used the same word that the poet had used of his falcon, and it took me a moment to realise she was talking about God.

"My master says you are a saint."

She laughed.

"I am what my Beloved has made me, and nothing more than that. If your master praises me, he is praising God, and I am glad of it."

Rabi'a al-Adawiyya lit a fire and warmed the water in the jug, adding the herbs a little at a time.

"Why don't you see to your horses? I will look after your master. He needs to sleep."

★★★

I too needed to sleep. When I woke, it was dark, apart from Rabi'a's fire, which was still burning, and a distant glimmer I guessed must be the first hint of dawn. Abu Nuwas was sitting up, staring into the wilderness.

"Are you well, master?"

He turned towards me. When I saw the terrible emptiness in his eyes, I thought he had gone for ever, and a shiver convulsed my body. Then he spoke.

"I would be better for a cup of wine."

He smiled cheerlessly.

"The healing of saints is a marvellous thing, Newborn, but their hospitality is meagre."

"And where shall we go now for hospitality?"

The smile faded. I was relieved.

"I don't know, boy. Basrah may be far enough, until it is safe to return to Baghdad. The Qadi's judgement will not stand long, once tempers have calmed, and the Khalifah will already have been asking where I am. Much depends on how the Barmakid answers that question."

"And how will we live?"

"Oh, there are rich men in Basrah, who will pay well for

fawning verse, and for the company of a celebrated wit. Not so well as in Baghdad, but . . ."

His voice trailed away.

"Why are you a poet, master?"

Abu Nuwas was dumbfounded.

"Why am I a poet? Because I can be. Because it is better than selling jugs. Why are you a poet?"

"I am not a poet, master. Not yet. I am al-Rawiya, the Teller of Tales. I thought I wanted to be a poet."

He did not ask me why I used the past tense, as I had hoped he would. Instead he returned to my original question.

"I cannot tell you why I am a poet, but I can tell you how I became one, if you wish."

The wind whipped the scrub, in the darkness beyond the firelight. I nodded, so he did.

The Education of a Poet

Jullaban, my mother, was a beautiful girl in a small town. Fate would have taken her from there, one way or another. She was like a sapphire buried in the silt of a river bed.

When Fate came to Jullaban, it was riding in the baggage train of Hani ibn Abd al-Awwal, of the Hakami clan. He was a dashing, reckless warrior of the southern desert, with an infallible knack for picking the losing side. Hani had fought for the Umayyads against the Army of the Black Flag, and later died in the rebellion of Abd Allah. He was one of few casualties of this uprising. Most of the rebels just surrendered as soon as Abu Muslim took to the field against them.

In between his military misadventures he washed up in Ahwaz, an undistinguished market town in the marches between Persia and Arabia. When he heard of my mother's beauty he paid furious court to her, offering an extravagant bride price. Her family were poor, and could not refuse such glamour.

It was not until they were married that it emerged Hani's wealth was not in his baggage train, but at his estate south of the Empty Quarter. Or so he claimed. A few weeks after the wedding he rode off, promising to return with the gold. Instead he went north to Jazira to join the rebellion, and to meet his death.

Jullaban was left penniless, and, she soon discovered, with child. Ahwaz had little to offer the young widow. As soon as I was old enough to travel, she took her few belongings and moved to Basrah.

Before the founding of Baghdad, Basrah was perhaps the greatest city in the region, a bustling port near the mouth of the Shatt al-Arab. It was, and remains, a place of culture, where the fine arts of poetry and music are treasured. Jullaban took in sewing and sold trinkets carved from bamboo. However the main source of her income was the singing girls who frequented her house day and night.

My earliest memories are of running around the legs of giggling, gossiping women. As in Baghdad, the best singers were rewarded richly, but the demands on them, artistically and sexually, took a heavy toll. My mother's house became a haven, where they could relax and exchange stories without angering their owners, who knew that Jullaban was a respectable widow. An extensive repertoire of poetry was essential for a singing girl, and I memorised my first verses by listening as they taught each other qasidas and ghazals. However, they were often coarse, and I also learned much at a young age about the variety and complexities of love-making.

My mother made enough money that she could afford to send me to study at the masjid. Reading seemed so natural to me that I could not understand why the other boys made such a fuss about it. I wondered whether they all had problems with their sight, that they could not simply look at the page and speak the words. I had committed the entire Quran to memory before my tenth birthday, and my recitations were celebrated, despite my lisp.

I was a devout child, eager to learn more about the holy book which held the answers to every important question. Of course I was also slightly vain, and the praise and attention that I earned for my piety gave me secret pleasure. However, my fame within the city was to attract the attention of a different kind of teacher.

Waliba al-Asadi was a poet from Kufah, who had heard about the pretty young hafiz and came to satisfy his curiosity. I stumbled over my words that day, as he sat brazenly upright at the front of the congregation, blue eyes appraising me. I was twelve years old. The next day he visited my class and persuaded my teacher to send me to his house for the evening. I have often speculated how much he paid, for my virginity.

I was dazzled by Waliba, by his wit, erudition and confidence. He gave me wine, which I had never drunk before, and overcame my virtuous reservations by reassuring me that the Quranic stricture applied only to date wine, grapes having been unknown to the Prophet. I dared to share with him my own thoughts and ideas. He did not mock me or insist that, because he was older, he must be right. Instead he engaged with my theories, challenging them with concepts from Greek and Persian philosophy that were alien to anything I had ever encountered.

My head swam, and I could not tell whether it was the wine, or the intoxicating company of the older man. However I will not pretend that I did not know what was happening. I was not as drunk as that, and the confessions of the singing girls had made me worldly beyond my years. When he suggested that I undress, I knew exactly what he intended to do, and I complied willingly.

Within a week I was travelling to Kufah as Waliba's apprentice. My mother, still easily gulled by a handsome scoundrel, was as overwhelmed by the poet as I had been. Besides, she saw how happy I was, and how much I wanted to go. You may think that Waliba took advantage of me; but at the time I simply thought he was the most wonderful person I had ever met. I wanted to be with him, and I wanted to be like him.

Waliba's circle in Kufah was not unlike my mother's house. At all hours there were visitors exchanging scandal and stanzas. The gossip was wittier and the verse often improvised, or at least original, but otherwise they were similar establishments.

I soon discovered that, despite Waliba's protestations of undying love, he was not entirely faithful to me. Many nights, he was not at home, and I knew that he was spending the evening with friends. Or with friends of friends. Or with boys he had met on the streets.

I did not confront him about this, having spent enough time with his coterie to know that such behaviour would be considered gauche. Instead I gave myself to his closest friend, who forgot any loyalty he might have felt in his slobbering enthusiasm to get his hands on me. Waliba never mentioned my betrayal, although I thought he looked at me differently thereafter.

I took his silence to mean that I was no longer bound to him exclusively. His friends competed for my favours, and I enjoyed the attention. Between the flirtations and assignations I gathered every scrap of knowledge I could accumulate, on history, astronomy, philosophy or jurisprudence.

When I returned to Basrah, I was sixteen years old, beautiful, accomplished and arrogant. I had learned to ensure that my admirers gave me expensive gifts, and was able to live well without the need to work. I offered to support my mother too, but she continued to entertain her singing girls. As her youth faded she needed to be surrounded by gossip and music.

My next tutor was Khalaf al-Amar. This wily fox was an expert on the Jahili, the desert poets from the time before the Prophet. He travelled the land collecting and preserving the ancient lyrics. Sometimes he just forged them. You are familiar with the Lamiyyat al-Arab, the two hundred year old classic rhymed on the letter "L"? That was in fact Khalaf's masterpiece. It was he who told me that before writing anything original, I should memorise one thousand poems of the Jahili, then forget them all again.

I also studied with Abu Ubayda, who taught me the tribal lore, the Battle Days. These accounts of raids and feuds are the oral histories of the Arabs. Abu Ubayda was generous with his learning, but I loved to tease the old sodomite. On one occasion I scrawled a scurrilous verse on a column in the mosque:

    "God bless Lot, and the tribe who love boys,
      And Abu Ubayda, the last of them all . . ."

He is a short, fat man, and could not reach to rub the words off. So he lifted his catamite onto his shoulders, and shouted at him to erase the slander, while a crowd stood round laughing at him.

There were other teachers, and other friends. One was a chubby young man, who sold jugs by day but dreamed of being a poet. He had an embarrassing enthusiasm, like a clumsy puppy, that betrayed his ambition and need to be loved. Half in jest, I called him Abu'l-Atahiyya, the Father of Madness. The name stays with him to this day.

I had many lovers, both boys and older men, but none of them captured my heart. When I fell in love at last, however, it was with a woman. This came as much of a surprise to me as it did to everybody else. Janan was no singing girl, although she came to my mother's house to talk about poetry and music. She was two years older than me, possessed of haughty beauty, and, young as she was, reputed to be the cleverest woman in Basrah.

Perhaps it appealed to my vanity, to believe that only this perfect woman would ever be worthy of me. Certainly it was a very public courtship. I filled acres of parchment with verse in Janan's praise, all of which sold very well. Every rejection became a challenge, in response to which I would devise a lawyer's refutation. When I heard that she had cursed me, I invited her to keep cursing, so that my name would always be on her lips. When she told me that she would never love me, I replied that she could not say that, since only God knew the future. The literati of Basrah followed our romance as others follow horse racing, taking sides and placing bets.

I even followed her on pilgrimage to Makkah. When she kissed the Black Stone, I put my cheek next to hers and my lips to the rock. This was the closest I ever came to kissing Janan. A friend of hers, scandalised, asked me how I could desecrate the most holy of shrines with my lust. I answered:

    "Why else do you think I travelled all this way?"

In the end my persistence won her over. She sent a message saying she would be my lover, but on one condition: that I give up male flesh forever. I spent a night agonising and weeping, and by dawn I had made my decision. I never spoke to her again.

Despite the ostentation of my wooing, my passion had been real, and so was my pain. The obsession with Janan had consumed me so utterly that once it was gone, I lost all direction and purpose. I stopped writing, began drinking before noon and started pointless fights. I might have died before my twentieth year, stabbed in a street brawl or poisoned by wine.

But that was when I met Ja'far ibn Yahya al-Barmaki.

★ ★ ★

I waited to see which way the story was about to twist. However Abu Nuwas spoke no more, but looked away into the darkness. In the end I broke the silence.

"Is that the end of the tale, master?"

"I said I would tell you how I became a poet. How I became a postman – well, that is a different story, for another day. Unhappy is the man with two destinies, for one day they will tear him apart."

"But I thought that Ja'far was your patron."

"Oh, the Barmakid has aided my career. Without his recommendation I may never have been granted audience with the Khalifah, let alone won his friendship. However that aid has come at a heavy price. And now that he has rejected me, my destinies seem to have converged here, in the wilderness."

There was no self-pity in his voice, simply an emptiness that accepted inevitable defeat. Impulsively I moved to sit beside him, putting my arms around him in comfort. I half expected him to lay his head on me, and half feared he would try to kiss me. Instead he continued to stare, as if somewhere beyond the firelight was the answer he was seeking.

"Master, do you know what made me ask you that, ask you why you are a poet?"

He said nothing, but turned to look at me.

"Because all your verse that I have heard dances on the

surface, like those insects that are so light they can walk upon the water. For all its cleverness of imagery and rhyme, you never speak from your heart."

I feared that I had gone too far, and indeed there was anger in his voice when he spoke.

"You want to hear me speak from my heart, boy? Then listen, and I will recite for you a ghazal to my truest and most faithful love, my only source of succour in a bitter world."

I leaned against him, my arms around his waist, and his voice whispered into the night.

> "Stop at the home of those who are gone
>> Cry, if that's what must be done.
> Ask there, "Where have they gone?"
>> We ask, but no answers come.
> Daughter of the Shaykh, bring wine this morning
>> Why do you take so long?
> Lively blood beats in your face
>> Come, dance as you let the wine run.
> From now on I will drink nothing
>> But that which the holy men shun.
> Keep it away from those misers
>> Who make punishing flesh their religion,
> Who sourly await their judging
>> While they sit and watch hours drag on . . ."

I put my hand on his cheek, turning his face. When his eyes met mine they seemed to snap. At that moment I understood, that the brittle glitter of his verse was crafted like a crystal, which invites one to peer into its empty centre. Within is a heartless universe, where our only comfort is a brief flash of light and warmth; where we seek relief in oblivion, from the oblivion we fear.

I pulled his face to mine and pressed my lips against his. His beard felt strange, scratching against my chin. At first he did not move. Then his mouth opened with a kind of sob, and he held my head as we kissed.

He stroked my face. As well as the bitterness of his tongue, I

265

tasted the salt of his tears. I reached down, and wriggled my hand under his qamis, so that I touched the bare skin of his belly. Although I could feel the strong muscles beneath, there was a softness unlike the bodies of the two girls I had held, which reminded me that he was more than twice my age. I was not deafened by my raging blood, as I had been with Hervor in the cedar grove. Instead there was calm, and a serene, almost maternal desire to soothe his pain, in the only way I could conceive.

Pushing further, my fingers closed around the poet's zabb. I had heard so much about this legendary beast, that I was shocked to find it languishing, grey and sickly, in my hand. Some say that the liver is the ruling organ of the body; others say it is the heart, or the kidneys, or even the brain. In the Father of Locks, I am certain that it was his zabb that was pre-eminent, the source and spring of his pride, his desire, his will.

Now, however, it lay dormant and enfeebled. Awkwardly I cradled it, as if it were a newborn lamb unable to suck. Abu Nuwas gave a soft moan at my touch, although whether from pleasure or pain I could not say. I had no map to give me location or direction, so I kissed him with desperate love, and tried to stroke the life back into his limp member. Slowly at first, then more strongly, it stirred, swelled, and raised its head. The poet's breath grew hot and slow against my face.

Just then the voice of Rabi'a penetrated our embrace. Somewhere in the darkness she was singing, in a voice that cut like a diamond.

> "I have loved you selfishly
>   And also loved you truly
> When possessed by selfish love
>   I think about you only
> But when my love is real
>   You free me to see clearly
> And whether true or selfish
>   Love comes from you, not me . . ."

The words were simple, but I could feel Abu Nuwas shift as he listened. Then, slowly, he pushed me away.

"A curse upon you, Rabi'a al-Adawiyya! You are right, as you always are."

He sat back. I was confused, and not a little hurt.

"No, Ismail. For the sake of a few moments of passing pleasure, I will not diminish you forever. And I cannot possess you by fucking you, any more than I can take back my youth, and the foolish decisions I made."

I hugged my knees, still piqued, but conscious now of a growing feeling of relief. Abu Nuwas spat on the ground.

"Thank God the All-Merciful we are in the desert. If this had happened in Baghdad my reputation would be ruined."

He gazed northward, in the direction of his home, and sighed.

"I suppose, now, Baghdad will burn. I only hope the fire is earthly and not infernal."

"But master, is the danger so great?"

"Whatever Abu Murra has, in the Brass Bottle, the Franks cannot be permitted to get their hands on it. Their enemies may be our enemies for now, but diplomacy is a fickle jade, her favours changing with the wind."

"And you really believe we were the city's only hope?"

"Its best hope, perhaps. Ja'far al-Barmaki certainly believed so."

I pondered that melancholy notion for a while, before speaking.

"I would, at least, have liked to save the children; the two that may still be alive."

Abu Nuwas nodded, and we sat silent in the gloom. A flickering light appeared nearby. It was Rabi'a, carrying a torch and a water jug. She did not approach us, but wandered away as if searching for something.

"What is she doing, master?"

He laughed, obviously glad of the distraction.

"She says that the torch is to set heaven ablaze, and the water to put out the fires of hell. Then, free of worry about reward and punishment, free of fear and longing, we can worship God as he should be worshipped: with pure love."

There was a silence. Then he uttered a sharp gasp, and sat upright.

"Fire . . . water . . . water on the fire, fire on the water . . ."

I wondered whether he had been bitten by a snake, or if the madness had returned.

"Can I help you, master?"

He stood up.

"Help me, boy? Yes, you can help me. You can beat me with sticks as punishment for my stupidity. But first we must return to Baghdad."

"Won't they cut our heads off?"

"Possibly, but there are worse fates beyond the firelight. How long have we been gone?"

"This is the sixth dawn rising, master, since we left the city."

"Then we still have time. Fadl ibn Rabi said that he needed a week to raise the gold. If we can find the hooded man before tomorrow, it may not be too late. I know, now, what is in the Brass Bottle."

Twenty Two

The Tale of the Brass Bottle

Abu Nuwas ignored my desperate pleas for explanation, instead busying himself with loading up the horses and filling our waterskins. In a bid to get his attention, I raised the obvious practical difficulty.

"But master, it is impossible for us to reach Baghdad in a single day! It took us six days to ride here."

He grinned at me.

"You forget, boy – we are postmen. Do you still have that pass from the Wazir, which he gave you that first night?"

I did. Although it was now stained and grubby, it clearly commanded loyal Muslims to give me every assistance. Abu Nuwas examined it.

"This may do. If you were alone, the postmasters would be unlikely to trust you. Let us hope my fame, and your pass, will see us safe to Baghdad."

He handed me the bridle of my imbecile pony, and once again I had to overcome my revulsion and clamber into the saddle. I was about to protest that we had not thanked our host, when Abu Nuwas called out.

"Pray for us, Rabi'a al-Adawiyya! We will need it!"

With that he galloped away, and I spurred my horse after him, hanging on grimly.

It was not long before the horses began to tire, but Abu Nuwas did not slacken our pace. I wondered what we would do when our mounts dropped from exhaustion. However I knew better than to ask my master that question when he was in this mood.

We were not retracing our steps, but taking a course closer to due east. When we reached the Euphrates we stopped for a while to allow our panting horses to drink. Then, to my surprise, instead of following the river upstream towards Baghdad, we headed in the opposite direction.

It was not long before we came to a small building outside which tethered horses stood grazing, and I understood my master's plan. A portly man in black robes came out as we approached, and Abu Nuwas shouted a greeting.

"Peace be upon you, Abu Harb."

"And upon you also, Father of Locks. I heard that you had been beheaded for murder."

Abu Nuwas dismounted as he talked to the postmaster.

"Indeed, and it was most inconvenient. Then Isa ibn Maryam flew down from heaven and popped my head back on."

"I see. And these would be the horses purloined from the Palace of the Barmakids, and not returned. What have you done to them? They are half dead."

Abu Harb eyed me suspiciously, clearly holding me responsible for the abuse of the poor beasts.

"I think this pony was half dead to start with. And we are, as you can see, returning them now. We need fresh mounts."

The postmaster looked pained as Abu Nuwas thrust the grubby parchment at him.

"I don't know, my friend. The news from Baghdad has been disturbing. And this pass seems to date from before the Flood."

Abu Nuwas gripped his arm.

"Listen. If you let us have horses and we disappear with them, the Wazir will be angry. He may even dismiss you from your post. But if you prevent us carrying out a mission of critical importance to the safety of the Ummah, then he will have your head stuck on a pole outside your station. The choice is yours, my friend."

Abu Harb peered at him doubtfully, then sighed.

"The sorrel mare and the black filly are the swiftest rides I have. If you are lying to me, poet, I will track you down myself."

After this we had few problems with the postmasters. When

they saw us racing up on horses that they knew to come from a neighbouring station, we needed no dubious passes from the Wazir. Usually they were already leading out a pair of mounts for the next stage of our journey before we had dismounted from our sweating, dusty steeds. I recalled al-Mithaq's boast that he could get to Tiaret in three weeks using the Barid network. As I watched the Black Lands fly past us I realised that, if anything, his estimate was conservative.

The journey was exhilarating but also agonising. I was not riding knock-kneed ponies now, but prime beasts trained for speed. I hung on desperately and followed my master, muscles frozen in terror. To some extent the fear numbed the pain of the long hours in the saddle. However I remember the day mainly as a dizzy haze of sickness and soreness.

The sky was already blackening by the time we reached Kufah, ninety miles from the capital, but we pressed on into the growing darkness. The danger now was real. We could not see the roads over which the horses' hooves thundered, to avoid stones and potholes, and a fall at this pace could be fatal. God, or good fortune, destined us to arrive safely at Baghdad however, as midnight approached.

I expected that we would take our exhausted mounts to the Hall of the Barid, there to seek aid and exonerate my master. Instead we walked the beasts through the streets to the ruckus and rackets of night-time Harbiya, where he was still held responsible for the murder of Umm Dabbah. Abu Nuwas noticed my reluctance.

"By the time we have resolved our little difficulty with Ja'far ibn Yahya, it will be too late. We must act now, and pray that our endeavours meet with sufficient success to placate the Wazir."

"But master, where are we going?"

"We are going to find Abu Murra, and the Brass Bottle. There is only one place they can be. How could a foreigner of distinctive appearance, who cannot speak Arabic, remain hidden in a city full of busybodies? Somebody must be hiding him. Somebody who was holding their own secret meetings with Frankish spies. Somebody who we know was making groping efforts to find out the Name. I believe we will find Abu Murra at the house of Thomas the Syrian."

The leader of the Christian fityan lived north of the Round City, where rowdy Harbiya meets genteel Zubaydiya. His home was a discreet building, lacking in ornament and ostentation, but it sprawled across an entire block. Its only distinctive features were the arrow-slit windows and iron-banded doors that gave it something of the look of a fortress.

We approached cautiously, and were wise to do so. From the shadows of a nearby building, we watched as bands of armed men with torches patrolled the perimeter. Abu Nuwas hissed a curse.

"Well, at least this proves that my hunch was correct. Thomas is a careful man, but I have never known him guard his home so thoroughly. This must be the night when the exchange is to take place."

"What exchange, master?"

"Really, boy, I thought you were cleverer than that. Abu Murra is to sell the Brass Bottle to the Franks. They will pay for it with gold provided by Fadl ibn Rabi. I am not certain what secret the Chamberlain is getting from the deal, but it must be of great significance for him to commit such treachery. And the only way we can thwart the conspiracy is to get into that building."

He was interrupted by a movement away to our right, a looming shape which drifted towards us. It did not approach us, however, but slid ominously in the direction of the Syrian's house. When the torchlight caught the shape I saw it was a boat. Invisible in the darkness, a canal ran alongside the street, presumably connecting the building to the Tigris. Obviously this was how Abu Murra had travelled to his assignation with Brother Catwulf.

A gate creaked noisily upwards, like the portcullis of a castle, and allowed the boat to enter. As we watched it disappear within, and the portal drop down behind it, Abu Nuwas took my shoulder. I sighed.

"Let me guess, Father of Locks. We are going to swim into the Syrian's house?"

"Wrong, Newborn. You are going to swim in, then open the door for me."

"And why do we not both swim in, master?"

"Because, boy, I cannot swim."

There was no answer to that. I considered pointing out that my inability to ride had simply been ignored, but I did not fancy dragging him behind me down the canal.

"Very well then, master. But you must allow me a little time to prepare for our incursion. We might need help from another quarter, if we are to survive this night."

★ ★ ★

I was already shivering when I stepped into the black water of the Tigris. I had stripped down to pants and qamis, with a knife and my lockpicks stuck in the folds of my turban, just in case. The mud closed quickly over my feet, and I began to walk faster, fearing that I would sink into the silt.

The canal ran for some five hundred cubits between the house and the river. Although it did not appear to be guarded, I doubted I would be able to plunge in at any point along its length without making enough noise to raise the alarm. Reluctantly therefore I had agreed to enter via the Tigris.

I made no attempt to swim upstream but waded slowly, water up to my waist, until I was near the mouth of the canal. Then I had to strike out, battling against the current. At times it took all my strength simply to avoid being swept away. Painfully I worked my way to the bank. Here it was too high and steep to climb out, even if I admitted defeat. I clutched at the earth with desperate fingers, and managed to claw myself round into the canal.

The artificial waterway was sheltered from the current, and I was able to cling to the side and assess my situation. Unlike the irrigation channel I had swum in on the day of the hunt, this canal was cut deep to allow boats to pass, and I could not walk along the bed. I pushed off, and began to ease myself along with gentle strokes, as quietly as I could.

That short paddle through the icy blackness felt like the longest swim of my life. Every splash and gasp seemed to me as loud as thunder, and I expected the Christians to come running at any moment. However I reached the gate undetected. Drawing in a deep breath, I ducked under to examine the barrier.

I could see nothing in the filthy water, and tried to feel for the bottom of the gate. We had hoped it would not extend all the way to the bed of the canal. However we had underestimated the Syrian's concern for security. Each dive I went deeper, and resurfaced more noisily. Each time I failed to find the edge of the portcullis.

I found the bottom of the gate and the bottom of the canal at the same time. The portcullis terminated in a row of spikes reaching almost to the mud. Small as I was, there was no way I could wriggle through. I tested the spikes for weaknesses but found none. I broke the surface again, trying to stifle my gasps.

I was alone. Abu Nuwas, I presumed, was lurking near the front door waiting for me to unlock it. I wondered whether I should turn back, clamber out of the canal and seek his guidance. However I knew that if I got out of the water now I could never make myself get back in.

When the light appeared, and the noise, a groaning, slapping sound, my heart almost stopped beating. I was certain that I must have been discovered. Then I realised that it was another boat approaching. The gate began to grind open. I plunged under the water once more, and wriggled beneath the spikes.

I was inside, but exactly what I was in, I had no way of knowing. I guessed that the canal must lead to some sort of boatyard, like a smaller version of that at al-Khuld. I had to assume that the two large shadows above and ahead of me were moored vessels, and swam to their shelter. Then the pain in my chest forced me to surface, trusting to the hulls to conceal my arrival.

In front of me was a wooden boardwalk, to which the boats were tied. Behind it was a brick-built landing, then a wall, with a door which must lead to the rest of the house. I was not surprised to hear voices. Somebody had to be there to open the gate, and to greet the visitors.

I seemed to have got in undetected. Carefully I eased myself between the boats and underneath the boardwalk. Here there was a gap between the wooden boards and the surface of the water, so that I could breathe while taking a better look at the wharf. It was the size of a large courtyard, open to the sky above, but surrounded by walls on all sides. I observed the mechanism of ropes and weights which closed the gate behind the arriving barge. I heard the footsteps of two or three men clattering on the timbers above my head as they came to meet its occupant. And I saw Brother Catwulf standing in the barge, carrying a large sack that I guessed must contain the gold.

Few words were exchanged. There was a boom as the gate closed, and a thud and clink as the Christians helped Brother Catwulf haul the money off the barge. Then the sounds changed as they moved from the boardwalk to the landing. I heard Brother Catwulf's oddly accented Arabic.

"Hey, friend! Don't stand there, give us a hand with the sack."

Finally they banged the door shut behind them, and there was silence.

I waited for a moment, listening in case anyone had stayed behind. When I was certain I was alone, I edged from under the timbers and pulled myself out of the water. The boardwalk was studded with posts, to which three craft were moored. At one end of the landing was a wheel, which controlled the gate, and scattered along its lengths were coils of rope, barrels and other nautical junk. I was approaching the door, when bubbles erupted from the water behind me.

A metal object began to emerge from beside Brother Catwulf's barge. It was dome-shaped and cast from burnished copper. The object drifted to the boardwalk, where two arms shot out and seized the edge. Slowly a figure emerged from the water, human in shape but with the copper dome where its head should be. I was reminded of the old Jewish legends of the Golem, in which statues are brought to life through witchcraft.

Then, as the figure stood upright, it brought its hands to the dome and pulled it off. I was hardly less horrified to see that beneath the shining metal was the head of Gorm the Rus. The dome must been a device to trap air below the water, so that he could breathe as he followed the boat through the gate. He pulled his battle axe from where it hung at his back. And then he noticed me.

Neither of us could cry out; the Syrian's men would have killed us both. Only our footsteps echoed from the walls as I raced for the door, and he blocked my way. I turned around, but there was nowhere to go. Gorm advanced on me while I backed away along the landing. At the end I moved to hurl myself in the water, but a huge hand seized my dripping qamis, ripping the fabric, and lifted me up against the wall.

This time Gorm would not delay, allowing time for me to be rescued. He put down his axe, and his hand closed about my throat, to crush the life from my body. And he looked quite surprised when I smashed him on the head with the belaying pin I had grabbed as I fled.

For a moment I thought I had not hit him hard enough. Then his grip slackened, and we both fell to the ground. I extricated myself and stood up. Blood streamed from his wound, tangling with his red hair, but I could hear his heavy breathing. I contemplated slitting his throat, but could not bring myself to slaughter him like an animal. Instead I left him where he lay and carefully opened the door.

The door led to a courtyard, with a well at its centre. It was difficult to relate the interior of the building to what we had seen from outside, but I guessed that the front door was to my left. Here there were two open rooms flanking a passageway.

I crept out into the courtyard so that I could peer into the nearest room. A torch within illuminated a Christian thug, armed with a sayf. He seemed to be staring at something in the wall. I realised that he was looking through a window onto the passage to the front door. He would see anybody entering or leaving the building before they saw him.

If I was to get Abu Nuwas inside, I had to get rid of the guard. I tugged at my torn qamis, pulling off a strip of cloth which I fashioned into a crude sling. I only had to reach down to find a smooth, hard pebble.

The slingshot is the weapon of the lowest of the low, of the tribe who have not yet developed the bow, of the peasant who cannot afford a knife to cut his bread. When Dawud used one to kill the giant Jalut, he was not a king facing a champion; he was a lone assassin, the shepherd boy lurking in the rocks who dared to take on the oppressor.

He was also very lucky. If the sling was a reliably accurate, deadly weapon, there would be no need for the sword. Or the bow, the spear, the axe, or any other of the myriad tools man has invented to destroy himself with. My pebble missed, rattling against the wall of his room.

The Christian spun round. Recognising the futility of try-ing to actually hit him, I hurled another pebble into a far corner of the courtyard. The second noise confused him suf-ficiently to draw him out of his room. Obviously the enemy he was expecting to fight came waving sticks and shouting.

One more pebble had him sniffing around like a dog. He was close enough now that I could have been on him before he knew, my knife glinting –

Instead I ran for the door. He turned when I flashed past him, but I got to the door before he had started moving. My fingers fumbled with the bars and bolts, and I could hear his feet pounding toward me.

I flung open the door, to see Abu Nuwas thrusting his sword at my face. The blade cut my turban as I dropped just beneath it. It also drove into the chest of the guard who was just behind me, causing his blood to burst across my back.

"Get up, boy. There will be time for prayers later."

We ran into the courtyard. My master headed towards the passage from which I had come, but I took his arm.

"No! Over there!"

A wide double door stood in the wall facing us. We burst through into a chamber hung with rich draperies and strewn with prayer mats. There stood Thomas the Syrian, his deformed face twisting in fury. There, too, was Brother Catwulf, gold dinars spilling from the bag at his feet.

The third man in the room was elderly, with a white beard. He was clearly a westerner, probably Greek, and had odd, bulbous eyes which seemed to stare around us as we crashed into the room. In one hand he held a large flask, fashioned from yellow metal. His skin, however, was not black as Umm Dabbah had described, but fair. Abu Nuwas put his sword to the old man's throat.

"Peace be with you, my friends. Newborn, if you would remove the bottle from this man's hand – carefully! My thanks. Now, this is an interesting gathering. Three Christian conspirators, a fortune in gold, and a mysterious Brass Bottle. Who would like to explain the nature of your business?"

The men were silent. I examined the Bottle, which had a curiously elaborate stopper and a long, thin neck, made from a different material. The old man did not appear to understand what was being said, although his divergent eyes made it hard to tell where he was looking. Thomas smiled and folded his arms. Abu Nuwas continued.

"Nobody? Perhaps I should explain it then. I am sure you will forgive me if I am wrong in certain small details. I have filled in the gaps from my deranged imagination, since I do like a story to be elegantly told. However I am confident that the substance of it is true."

Brother Catwulf was looking around nervously. I realised that he was waiting for Gorm to come and save him. But nobody interrupted my master.

"Very well. I shall take your silence as assent, and tell the tale."

And so he did.

★★★

Once there was a man of Konstantinopolis. I do not know what his name was then, and it does not matter now. He was a soldier, this man, a warrior, and he served his Emperor faithfully. Through courage and diligence he rose to become a General of the Roman Army, and was entrusted with protecting its greatest secret.

Although accomplished on the field of battle, the General

was clumsy when it came to the politics of the Imperial court. He fell out of favour, and his younger, less able rivals were promoted ahead of him. When he was forced to bow to the man who had once been his subordinate, his resentment turned to hatred. He decided to betray his country.

And so the General stole the great secret, which he was supposed to be guarding. He cached it in a Brass Bottle of cunning design, which he had fashioned for the purpose. Anybody who tried to open the Bottle without knowing the proper method would destroy both its contents and himself. With the Brass Bottle concealed in his robes the General fled the city.

Unfortunately his escape plans went badly wrong. He had bribed pirates to take him west, where he hoped to find a buyer for his secret. Once the pirates had been paid, however, they saw no need to make a long and hazardous voyage. Instead they abandoned their passenger on the shores of Syria and sailed away.

The General was now in great peril, alone and helpless in an enemy land where he did not speak the language. He made his way to Dimashq and sought refuge among his own kind there, the Christians of the city. They gave him a new name to conceal his identity. Perhaps there was mockery in the name they chose for him, knowing that he would not understand its meaning, nor recognise it as a by-name for the Devil. They called him Abu Murra, the Father of Bitterness.

However this cursed name seemed to bring him luck. Word came of an embassy heading for Baghdad: a legation from the Kingdom of Frankia, the rising power in the west. Surely their ambitious king would pay well for the contents of the Brass Bottle? Perhaps Abu Murra would be able to sell his secret to Christians after all, and not have to deal with the hated Muslims, against whom he had spent his whole life fighting.

Abu Murra's allies arranged for him to be smuggled to Baghdad, under the protection of their contact in the city: the notorious usurer and extortionist known as Thomas the Syrian. (I see you smirk as if taking pride in that description, Thomas. It was not intended as a tribute.) Thomas sent a messenger to the Franks, who were camped outside the capital. He offered them for sale the Brass Bottle, and the secret of the terrible Fire that lay within it.

The price he asked was extravagant; Abu Murra needed to fund his flight to Christian lands, and Thomas planned to take a generous commission for himself. It was more gold than the Franks possessed, more than any sane man would carry on such a long and dangerous expedition. However the Franks had a secret of their own, a secret that explained their real purpose in visiting the Khalifate.

Far away, in distant Andalus, they had captured a Saracen, a mercenary who came originally from the city of Baghdad. The mercenary sought to bargain with them. In exchange for his freedom, he would tell them a story, one his mother had told him. His mother had worked at the royal palace, and there had seen things she was not meant to have seen. He offered to tell them the tale of the Door That Should Not Have Been Opened; and the Name of the one who opened it.

The King of the Franks, like all sensible rulers, surrounded himself with clever men. When the clever men heard the mercenary's tale, they realised that it had the power to rip the Land of Islam apart. However, they were also clever enough to understand that this would benefit them little. Instead, the King sent his most persuasive diplomat, his wiliest spy and his most fearsome warrior to the court of the Khalifah, to see what their knowledge might buy them.

Now the Syrian's messenger brought a new possibility. If they could sell their story for gold, they could use the coin to buy the Brass Bottle. The Franks turned their attention to finding an ambitious, unscrupulous courtier, with the wealth to afford their secret, and the hunger to use it. They settled on the Chamberlain, Fadl ibn Rabi.

So far luck had been on the conspirators' side. But Abu Murra's suspicious nature was to lead to disaster. He insisted on meeting the spy in person, trusting neither the barbarians nor his host the Syrian. Brother Catwulf resolved that if he was to risk his life sneaking into the city, he would also find the mercenary's mother, and hear her tale for himself.

The old woman had been sworn to silence, at pain of punishment in both this life and the next. She was a gossip by
nature, and to know a secret of such gravity and yet be unable
to share it grieved her sorely. Over the years she had taken to
inventing foul conspiracies and spreading rumours of them,
to stop herself bursting out with the horrible knowledge that
tormented her. Only to her son had she told the real story.

When an exotic foreigner came to her, offering bags of
gold and a sympathetic ear, the temptation was too much for
her. At first she was frightened, but then she told herself that
an oath could not still bind her after so many years, and
besides the foreigner already knew her secret. What harm
could it do, if, just once, she relieved herself of her terrible
burden?

What neither of them knew was that the Father of Bitterness, still suspicious, had followed Brother Catwulf after their
meeting. The priest left discreetly, but Abu Murra's strange
appearance had begun to draw attention from the neighbours.

The Roman General, fearless in war, became confused and
frightened by their stares. Then the widow saw the foreigner
outside her home, and assumed he was an associate of Brother
Catwulf. Boldly she approached him and asked him who he
was. He, accosted by a strange woman and addressed in a
strange language, replied with the only words of Arabic he
knows:

"Abu Murra."

Having just unwittingly told her he was the Devil, he used
the power of the Fire to cover his escape. Now the old woman
was scared. She had broken her oath, and because of her sin
Iblis was stalking the streets. She lacked the imagination to
lie about their conversation when asked, but guilt caused her
to change one crucial detail; instead of the fair skin that she
remembered, she gave him the black skin she believed the
Devil ought to have.

Then her neighbour's son disappeared, and it seemed her
own wicked stories were coming back to haunt her. In desperation she half remembered a fragment of scripture, that an
oath-breaker can expiate his sin by feeding ten needy men.

But there was to be no absolution for Umm Dabbah – at least, not in this world.

Nevertheless Umm Dabbah was the loose thread of your conspiracy, which caused the whole thing to unravel. Now I have the Brass Bottle, and the only mystery left to be solved is the secret for which the Chamberlain risked so much, and for which the widow died. So, Brother Catwulf: *what is the Name?*

Twenty Three

The Tale of the Door That Should Not Have Been Opened

"What a pity. You were doing so well."

Brother Catwulf's sudden confidence was so unexpected that I looked around, thinking Gorm must have recovered. However the warrior was not there, and the spy continued.

"That was entirely the wrong question. The Name itself is not important. In fact you have had it for days. Your servant stole it, but you lack the wit to understand it.

"The Name is useless, without the story behind it. Let me take the Bottle, and I will tell you everything."

Abu Nuwas smiled.

"They say many things about me, brother, and most of them are true. They call me debauchee, deviant and drunkard; libertine and blasphemer; seducer, sinner and sybarite. But my father was a warrior, and no man has ever called me a traitor. If you believe that I would let you walk away from here with what is in that Bottle, knowing the death and destruction which it can unleash – then you are not as clever as you think you are."

"Right then, if I'm not going to learn anything of value, let's make an end to this nonsense."

We had forgotten Thomas was there, and his interruption caused everyone to turn to him.

"I'm sick of listening to this pervert anyway. You can come out now, boys."

Through a door concealed by a wall hanging emerged half a dozen Christians, armed with swords and shields, more like soldiers than street thugs. They quickly surrounded us.

"As they say in the Game of Four Divisions, 'shah mat' – your king is dead. I'll probably find out more from the Frank by torturing him. As for you, poet, you borrow money without paying it back, you punch me in the face, beat up my fityan and now you invade my home. I'm going to make you wish it really had been Iblis that you found here."

Abu Nuwas seized Abu Murra by the arm, and pushed his sword against the old man's neck.

"Tell your boys to drop their weapons, or I kill him. If he dies, you will never learn how to open the Brass Bottle."

Thomas laughed.

"What do I care about his Bottle? I've got the gold, that's all I wanted. Here –"

He snatched a sayf from the belt of one of his men, and thrust it into Abu Murra's heart. As the Father of Bitterness fell to his knees, eructing dark blood, Brother Catwulf's foot flew up. It kicked the Brass Bottle from my hand. The flask soared up into the air, then crashed onto the ground. Its slender neck was broken.

The Bottle seemed to emit a horrific, guttural moan. Then I realised the sound was Abu Murra's death rattle. The fire that began to bubble out, however, was no illusion. A liquid pulsed from the flask, and the rug on which it fell burned with furious, smoky flame.

Amid the chaos I saw that Brother Catwulf had disarmed one of the thugs and was making his escape. I tried to follow him, but a pair of hairy hands grabbed me. Abu Nuwas still had his sword and had felled another of the Christians. Thomas himself blocked the way though, backed by two of his men.

Another of the Syrian's gang had dashed to the well for a pail of water. He hurled it onto the burning rug, but this was a disastrous mistake. The water splashed the liquid everywhere, seeming to enrage the fire rather than dousing it, and spreading the flames across wall hangings and carpets.

Abu Nuwas, faced by three blades at once, was barely holding them off, and it was only because he was trapped in a corner that they had not flanked and overwhelmed him. I struggled, then was surprised to find my captor's grip slackening. I jerked myself free, and looked back to see the thug collapse to the ground.

While I pulled the knife from my turban, I watched another Christian fall. This time I saw the stone that struck him on the head. It appeared that, in the right hands, the sling could be effective after all.

Thomas was consumed by his desire to kill Abu Nuwas, and had not noticed that one of his comrades was no longer by his side. Now, though, a howling arose which compelled his attention. It was high in pitch, but the war cry of the Raiders put fear in the souls of grown men.

The room was full of smoke, and the small figures which darted in seemed like demons, dancing around jabbing at the Christians with improvised weapons. Thomas looked round at the blazing abattoir that his house had become, and Abu Nuwas took the chance to smash the sword from his hand. The poet drew back his arm to strike, but a voice shouted:

"Mine!"

A young man with a birthmarked face walked toward the Syrian. Thomas narrowed his eyes.

"Who are you?"

"I am Mishal ibn Yunus al-Rafiq."

The young man waited until he saw signs of recognition, and they were a long time coming. Then he pushed his dagger into the Syrian's chin and on up into his brain.

I gripped Mishal's gory hand, although I knew that he had been motivated more by hatred of Thomas than by friendship for me. That was what I had been counting on, when I sent a street boy to take him a message. That message was that he could finally avenge his father's murder – if he found the Syrian's door standing open that night.

"Let us get out of here, before the ceiling falls onto our heads."

The words of Abu Nuwas were wise ones, and we followed him into the courtyard. I glanced back at the conflagration that was eating the building.

"Did you really know nothing, master? About the Name?"

"Of course not. You rarely find anything out by admitting to your ignorance. I thought if I showed them I had worked out half of it, they would give away the rest."

"Then you do know what that was, in the Brass Bottle? Was it an Afrit, a Jinn?"

"Yes, boy, I do know. But it was not a spirit. The substance is called Greek Fire, although no Muslim can tell its true nature. It is the reason the Roman Empire still stands in the east, despite nearly two hundred years of Islamic invasions. At sea it is fired by catapult onto the ships of enemies. It decimates navies, and floats on the water still burning. In battle it is sprayed on opposing troops, searing human flesh and causing hardened veterans to run in terror.

"The method of producing it is the most jealously guarded secret of the Romans. With a sufficiently large sample, however, such as the contents of the Brass Bottle, a man skilled in al-khimiya might discover its composition, if he knew how to work with it safely.

"The Franks cannot be permitted to acquire a weapon of such destructive power. The Roman Empire is dying, so slowly it can barely be seen, but dying nonetheless. The west, however, is rising. Some day they will come to take what is ours. And when that day comes I pray they are not armed with . . . this."

Abu Nuwas gestured behind us. Huge ghosts of gold and blood burst out of the crumbling masonry, and the heat scorched our faces like the desert sun. Then the roaring of the flame was echoed by a second roar, from the opposite direction.

Gorm the Rus was stumbling into the courtyard, dragging his axe behind him. One side of his face was covered by streaky lines of blood and caked red hair, and the fire tinted his white skin bronze. He barely looked human at his best, and now his visage was truly monstrous. Several of the Raiders screamed and ran. Others, more courageous, slung stones at him, but their pellets bounced off his skin.

The giant lumbered remorselessly forward, and I realised to my horror that he was walking straight towards me. His blue eyes, so like those of his daughter, skewered me as surely as his hunting spear had done. I hefted my knife wearily, but Abu Nuwas stepped in front of me.

"Don't be silly, boy. This battle is definitely mine."

My master took guard, but Gorm appeared not to notice him. Instead he raised his axe and quickened his pace, emitting the hideous bellow of a wounded, desperate beast.

Abu Nuwas watched his approach carefully. Then, at a few paces' distance, he pounced forward, driving his sword into Gorm's belly. His attack was swift enough that the great swing of the axe passed over him, and the two men pressed closely together, like lovers.

But the Rus did not stop. He walked on, even as the tip of the sword emerged on the other side of his body. He walked on, while the metal slid through his his guts. He kept walking, forcing Abu Nuwas backwards until Gorm could see me. He swung the axe.

I stepped easily out of reach of the feeble swing. Then the warrior and the poet fell to the ground, in a tangle of limbs. I leapt on them with my knife, but Gorm was finally still.

"Get him off me, will you? It is becoming hard enough to breathe round here as it is."

The fire had spread to rest of the building. Smoke drifted across the courtyard, and the air was so hot it hurt the chest. Mishal helped me push Gorm's body away, and we hurried out while the exit was still clear.

We were coated in soot, and went down to the river to wash. Neighbours were beginning to arrive with buckets to extinguish the blaze. Abu Nuwas assured me that the contents of the Bottle would have burned off some time ago, and what remained was just an ordinary fire. Since they were in no danger, we left them to it.

As we splashed the filthy Tigris water onto our faces, blackening them still further, Abu Nuwas gestured behind us.

"Brother Catwulf said you stole the Name. Have you engaged in any unlicensed thievery you have not told me about?"

"No, master. The only thing I have stolen is —"

"The egg! Can you remember the word that was written upon it?"

One who lives by telling tales must develop a reliable

memory. I nodded, and scratched the letters into the mud with my finger. Ghifaha. At. Tighasa. Abu Nuwas leaned over, examining it.

"I think we can assume that we are no longer looking for an occult name, that will summon a demon or Afrit. But what kind of name is this? Ghayn, Fa', Ha' . . ."

He stared at the script for a moment. Then he slapped my back so hard I nearly fell over.

"Atbash! It is Atbash!"

This meant nothing to me at all.

"The Name is Atbash, master?"

"No, boy, Atbash is not the Name. Atbash is the disguise under which the Name has been hiding, laughing at us all this time. It is a trick used by the Rabbis of the Jews, to conceal secret knowledge. Each letter of the word is replaced by its equivalent in a mirror alphabet."

I stared blankly at him.

"See, Newborn. If this were an Arabic name, what would be the most likely first letter?"

"I suppose . . . Alif. Abu, Ibn, Al – they all begin with Alif."

"Indeed. Alif, the first letter of the alphabet, and the first letter of many names. Yet this word starts with Ghayn, the last letter of the alphabet. What was it Isa ibn Maryam said? 'The first shall be last, and the last shall be first . . .' Next we have Fa, which is . . .?"

I counted furiously in my head.

"Twelve from the end."

"Then we replace it with the twelfth from the beginning. Alif, Lam – now a name begins to emerge."

He scratched the letters into the ground with his finger as he worked them out.

"Kha' . . . Ya' . . . Zay . . ."

I knew already what the next three letters would be, without having to solve the puzzle.

"Ra' . . . Alif . . . Nun."

We both gazed at the name he had written, mocking us in the dirt.

"Al-Khayzuran."

It seemed that the Name for which Umm Dabbah had died, the Name of the one who opened The Door That Should Not Have Been Opened, was the name of the widow of the Khalifah al-Mahdi, and mother of the Khalifah Harun al-Rashid: Al-Khayzuran, the most powerful woman in the world.

***

It is unlikely that two more sorry-looking petitioners ever knocked on the door of the Palace of Blissful Eternity at dawn. We were daubed in soot, blood and mud from head to foot, and our clothes were ribbons and rags. However Abu Nuwas would not be deterred, now that the truth was so close.

"My apologies for the hour, but we must speak with al-Khayzuran immediately, on a matter of the gravest importance for the security of the Ummah. We need to talk to her about The Door That Should Not Have Been Opened."

The gatekeeper could hardly believe it when word came back that we were to be bathed, breakfasted, then escorted into the royal presence. As I was being scrubbed and scented, exhaustion hit me like a wave. It felt as though the filth had been all that was holding my body together. However I was determined to see this through.

I had expected to be taken to a grand hall for the audience, but the room in which Al-Khayzuran sat was surprisingly small. A screen hung across the room, but it was a gauze of such fineness that I could clearly see the two slave girls attending her. On our side of the screen there stood a single eunuch guard. We made obeisance, and waited to be addressed.

"Abu Ali al-Hasan ibn Hani al-Hakami, I believe there is a question you wish to ask me?"

My master sat up.

"Yes, o mother of Islam. What was behind The Door That Should Not Have Been Opened?"

There was no movement on the other side of the curtain, the stillness so prolonged that I wondered if she had heard him. Then:

"Who knows about this?"

Abu Nuwas seemed to be surprised by her question.

"My servant and I. The Chamberlain, Fadl ibn Rabi. And, I am afraid, the Frankish emissaries."

"I see. Then there is little point in having you killed. Besides, it would upset my son, who seems immoderately fond of you. Ah, I have always too much indulged his whims."

She seemed deep in thought. My master held his peace, and in time she spoke again.

"I should have told somebody – my husband, or my son. But it was never the right time. There was always peril, conspiracy, intrigue. In the end the only one I trusted to tell was Yahya al-Barmaki.

"I suppose that is why the Chamberlain wanted the secret. If the Khalifah were informed that his mother and his counsellor had kept such dangerous knowledge from him – well, who can say how a monarch will act? However, it will certainly harm the Barmakids. Ibn Rabi's supporters will become the dominant party, and the court will be poorer for it.

"I am a sick woman. The doctors tell me I will recover, but they are idiots. I know that I will not live to see this year's pilgrimage. I am sorry for Yahya and his sons, for they have been good friends to me. But I would like to tell the tale just once, whole and true, if you would like to hear it."

So she did.

★ ★ ★

I was only a slave girl from Yemen, in the beginning. All I knew was the tribe, and the camp, and the animals. I was never brought up to rule the world.

But as I came to my womanhood my master saw that my virginity might be worth a great deal to him, too much to give up for a night of rough pleasure. He sold me to a dealer of Sana'a, who could find a buyer worthy of my beauty.

The dealer, however, believed he could do better, and sold me on in Makkah. There I was displayed in the slave market. I was fourteen years old, and shivered at the stares of the men.

290

God was watching over me though, and made sure that among the eyes fixed on me were those of my prince. Al-Mahdi was a graceful man, cultured, pious and kind. His skin was dark, his mother having been black, but virtue shone from his eyes. I understood immediately that my future happiness depended on remaining in his favour, and used every trick I knew to make him love me.

It was not difficult to distract him from his wife, Rita, a dull cousin to whom he had been married for political reasons. However the real threat came from the endless stream of newcomers, attractive virgins from all across the empire who seemed to arrive almost every day to challenge my pre-eminence.

We lived for a while in Kufah, but did not stay there long. Al-Mahdi was being trained for succession to the Khalifate. As part of his education he was given dominion over the eastern lands of the empire, and sent to Rayy to administer his province. I was carrying my first child, but I was not prepared to be left behind and forgotten. I travelled with him, giving birth to my oldest son Musa along the road. It was a difficult labour, and Musa was born with a hare-lip, which disfigured his face for the rest of his life.

In Rayy we were cut off from many of our circle. We spent our days in the company of a man called Yahya al-Barmaki, whose father Khalid was governor of Tabaristan. His wife Zubayda was of an age with me, and when we fell pregnant at the same time, our friendship deepened. We both bore sons, and often exchanged babies while feeding. I suckled her little Fadl, and she put to her breast my son, who was named after the man who, in Holy Scripture, was brother and successor to Musa: Harun, later to become the Righteous One.

By the time we returned to court, al-Mansur had moved to his new city of Baghdad. To celebrate al-Mahdi's return, his father built him a new palace on the east bank of the Tigris. Al-Mansur loved his son, but they often clashed. The old man had experienced poverty in his youth, and begrudged spending a single copper penny. My Mahdi grew up as a prince. He loved music, dancing and feasting, and would not deny himself any pleasure for the sake of mere money.

But what they argued about most often was me. I had remained al-Mahdi's favourite over the years, and al-Mansur did not approve of a mere concubine being given preference over a legitimate wife of Abbasid blood. When Khalid al-Barmaki fell from favour, I raised money from my own purse to help pay his fine, and this interference also annoyed the Khalifah. Al-Mansur's health was failing, and he was becoming increasingly irascible and unpredictable.

I was therefore terrified when the old man summoned me to speak to him alone. I entered his chamber demurely, eyes on the floor, and fell to my knees before him. He sat with his back to me for a long time before he spoke.

"Do you love my son?"

"Truly I do, Commander of the Faithful."

He turned to me.

"We cannot make choices for our children. When I die, he plans to marry you. My son is no fool, but his heart is soft. As for you, having remained first in his esteem for so long, you must be neither foolish nor soft-hearted. And so I am going to give you this."

He handed me a small iron key.

"Soon I will be going on a hajj, and I do not expect to return. I hope to die in the Holy City, if God spares me long enough. When you are certain that I am dead, open the door that is opened by this key, but do it alone. When you see what is within, you will know what to do."

Later that month, al-Mansur and his household set off on their pilgrimage. I was left behind at the Gilded Gate. Sheer determination carried him as far as the sacred territory, and it was there that his soul finally departed his tortured body. Rabi ibn Yunus, father to our friend the Chamberlain, propped up his corpse behind a screen, and made all the courtiers swear allegiance to al-Mahdi as his successor, before revealing that al-Mansur was dead.

Word came in a matter of days by the Barid, but I waited until the reports were incontrovertible, before I took out the iron key. Al-Mansur had not told me which door it opened, so I had to search the Palace, trying it in different locks. At last I found a storeroom near the stable, which had a heavy door, but within it a lock small enough for the key to fit. I asked the servants, but they shrugged and said they had never seen anyone use the room. I dismissed them, and turned the key. The door swung open.

It was dark inside, and shockingly cold. I called for a lamp, then sent the servant away again. The room was larger than I had imagined. It seemed as if the Palace had been designed in such a way as to conceal the existence of this huge space.

Inside, the room looked like a warehouse, with shelves around the walls. Piled on the shelves were grain sacks. I wondered what manner of grain was so important to warrant all this secrecy. I might have believed that al-Mansur was playing a joke on me, if he had ever shown the slightest sign of having a sense of humour.

I went over and tugged at one of the sacks. It was empty, but draped over a shape below. I pulled the sack aside, to find the body of a child. So lifeless was the flesh that I thought for a moment it might be a statue, before I saw that it had been embalmed. She had been a girl, and from the marks around her mouth it looked as though she had been suffocated. (I know a little about suffocation; but that is a story for another time.)

Something protruded from her ear. I pulled out a tightly rolled strip of papyrus. On it was her name. She was called Mariyah. The rest of her name was there as well, a long one, detailing her parentage back five generations, but I did not take it in.

The next body was a man of middle years. His head was slightly separate from the rest of his body. His face was frozen into an expression of almost comically inadequate disappointment at his situation. I examined the head and found another label, again with a prestigious name.

And that was all that there was in the room: corpses. Old and young, male and female, each victim had been executed with neat precision and carefully tagged with their identity. I did not check them all – the grey faces became monotonous after a while – but I saw enough to notice that all the genealogies ended with the same names: ibn Ali ibn Taib.

The dead were not random victims. They were the bodies of Alids, descendants of Ali ibn Taib and Fatimah bint Muhammad, of the cousin and the daughter of the Prophet. That was all there was, apart from the roll of parchment nailed to the wall at the back of the room. On the parchment was a list of names, updated over time in different inks, but always in the careful hand of al-Mansur, detailing each new addition to the family. Those who had found their way to the room, or met their end elsewhere, were marked with a careful circle after their name.

And that was what lay behind the Door That Should Not Have Been Opened: the evidence of a decades-long, systematic attempt by the Commander of the Faithful to extinguish the bloodline of the Prophet Muhammad, peace be upon him. I burned the parchment immediately, putting it to the lamp again and again until there was nothing left, even though I badly blistered my fingers.

Al-Mansur had told me that I would know what to do, but I think he overestimated my judgement. However I did not weep, or scream. If the Shi'ites learned what was in the storeroom, no army on earth would stop them storming the Palace and ripping us apart. I composed myself, left the room, and locked the door. I told only one person, the serving woman who did my make-up. Her I sent to fetch Yahya al-Barmaki.

He arranged for a large hole to be dug in some land he owned just outside the Basrah Gate. Much of Baghdad was a building site at that time, and there was nothing unusual in their behaviour. However, he waited until the dead of night before getting his most loyal men to remove the bodies and bury them hurriedly. To deter anyone from disturbing the site, he then had a shop built on top of it.

When al-Mahdi returned to Baghdad, I intended to tell him. But he was full of his plans, to build mosques and right wrongs, and I could not destroy his happiness. At times I wondered whether God has cursed me, for my part in concealing the crime. First he took my little girl away from me, my only daughter, my pretty Banuqa. Then my husband died in a hunting accident. It even looked for a while as though ugly Musa might murder my darling Harun.

I freed the slave I sent to Yahya al-Barmaki. Perhaps I should have killed her instead.

Twenty Four

The Tale of the King and Queen of Darkness

"What will happen now, master?"

After her confession al-Khayzuran had risen abruptly and left the room. We sat in confusion for a moment, then a lackey appeared and escorted us, courteously but implacably, from the palace. I glanced around nervously as we went, fearing that she had decided to have us slain after all. However we reached the outside safely, and stood in the square as the first stirrings of the day's traffic hustled around us.

"I do not know, Newborn. The Chamberlain knows about the Barmakids' involvement with the Door That Should Not Have Been Opened. On the other hand, as soon as we tell Ja'far that Fadl has been dealing with foreign spies, they will both have a blade at each others' throats. I imagine they will come to some arrangement. The Khalifah can be unpredictable, and may decide to have the lot of them beheaded if they trouble him with it.

"We must hurry therefore, and bring our news to the Wazir, before Fadl does anything rash."

"But master, what about the children?"

Abu Nuwas gazed at me with profound sadness in his eyes.

"Ah yes, the children. I had hoped to spare you that, Newborn. I hoped that you would forget, or that Ja'far would assign you to new duties, or that you would go back to living with the dolphins or whatever it was you did before coming to Baghdad.

"However, you are right. Ja'far ibn Yahya al-Barmaki can look after himself for a few hours, and if we act now, we may be able to salvage something from this shambles. Very well then, let us see this business through to the end."

He began walking briskly towards Sharqiya. I ran after him, although his words made me shiver as if a chill wind had caught me.

I asked no questions, having grown used to his irritating refusal to share his insights. On this occasion, however, he began to talk as we passed the walls of the Round City. .

"I am surprised you have not worked it out for yourself. I suppose it is understandable in the circumstances. Let us start with what should be clear by now. The abductions have nothing to do with the Brass Bottle or the Name. Umm Dabbah's stories of children being sacrificed to summon demons or Afarit were no more than that: just stories.

"We must therefore look again at each of the disappear-ances, forgetting everything we imagined, and considering only what we know. First, ibn al-Malik, the veteran's grand-son. Had his murder happened at any other time, what would you think?

"He was a young boy involved in a dangerous world he did not fully understand. I am sure your friend Mishal did his best to protect him, but the boy could have met his end in many ways. Thomas may have learned of his true parentage, and had him killed so that he would not grow up to seek vengeance. He may have tried to pick the wrong pocket, and met with rough justice.

"Consider, though, the wound in his throat, too ragged to have been made by knife or sword. I suspect that he simply fell in the river and drowned. I believe the cut happened later, made by debris in the water, or the keel of a boat."

"Then there is no connection between any of the children?"

Abu Nuwas stopped walking for a moment, staring at me in dismay.

"Really, boy, you can do better than that. I think we can discount the veteran's grandson, but the other two are con-nected by the description of the mysterious stranger with black skin. We know that Umm Dabbah was describing Abu Murra, but changed his skin colour to hide her guilt. Who, then, was your friend Layla describing?"

I had thought we were on our way to the house of the

porter, but we continued to follow the walls of the Round City. I struggled to see where Abu Nuwas was going with his thoughts too.

"Ibn Bundar! Is he responsible after all?"

His dismay seemed to change to sympathy.

"Oh dear, boy. Your refusal to see the truth speaks better of your affections than your intellect. There are two possible explanations. One is that Ibn Bundar, or some other black-skinned man, was responsible for the abductions, and just happened to look exactly like the man invented by Umm Dabbah. Or, the person who also claims to have seen him is lying. That person simply heard what the old gossip was saying, and gave us the same story . . ."

"Peace be upon you, Layla bint al-Bazza."

We had arrived at the Basrah Gate, where my master descended upon Layla's shop like a falcon stooping. She seemed both pleased and uncertain at our arrival.

"And upon you also, agent of the Barid. Ismail, good to see you."

I did not understand what he was saying.

"But master, why would Layla lie? She does not need to seek attention, like that old woman . . ."

"No, boy. I know the truth is blinding you, but turn your head and look at what is front of your face. Consider the smell in the porter's house. Then remember that the porter's boy was taken from the street. The merchant's daughter, on the other hand, was taken from a private building. If there was no Jinn swooping from the sky to snatch her, then it can only have been somebody who had access to the house. Or who was already in there."

As Layla listened her face was like butter melting down a stone, sinking and becoming greasier and slower. Abu Nuwas addressed her directly.

"Where are the children, Layla bint al-Bazza?"

I remembered soft whispers in a fragrant garden.

"We all have secrets, deep below the ground . . ."

I could not feel the words leaving my mouth.

"I know where they are, master."

I began to ransack the shop, hurling bundles of cloth to one side. Abu Nuwas watched me intently, as I found the trapdoor for which I had been searching.

"Here."

The trapdoor was heavy and bolted shut. We heaved it open, and immediately the stench assailed us. It was the stink of shit, and blood, and terror. We recoiled from the hole, but a whimper from below startled Abu Nuwas to action.

"A lamp, and flints. There, boy, in the corner. Bring light, quickly."

I lit the lamp, and we peered into the hole. A ladder led down into the blackness. I climbed down first. Abu Nuwas pushed Layla after me, then descended himself.

We found ourselves in a small cellar. At one end lay a rug, stained and smeared with urine and faeces. Two children sat on the rug, a boy and a girl. The boy wore a circlet of corrugated golden cloth, cut into points at the top like the crowns of the Sassanid kings. A wooden sword lay by his side. The girl bore a simpler circlet, and lay with her head on his shoulder, wide eyes staring at us. Both were bound hand and foot.

When he saw us, the boy began to squirm in his fetters. His exertions dislodged the girl, who toppled over and lay on her back, eyes fixed on the ceiling. It was only then that I realised she was dead.

Abu Nuwas leapt forward to set the boy free. I gazed vacantly at the lifeless girl, rather than turn and look at Layla. Now she started to talk, her voice oddly dull in the underground room, yet pounding in my head as if she were not speaking out loud, but directly into my mind.

★ ★ ★

My father was a wealthy merchant of the city of Raqqa, who died before I was born. My mother, having been widowed young, remarried. Her new husband treated me with kindness and love, and I grew up calling him Baba, father.

I remember a happy childhood, roaming around the big house in which we lived. My mother was a sickly creature, often complaining of headaches. However, I was never short of somebody willing to play with me and indulge my childish imaginings. My stepfather was often away for long periods, but there was always my nurse, our cook, and the eunuch.

Then, one day, nurse took me to the river to play. While she was talking to her friend, I walked barefoot along the bank, watching the mud ooze between my toes. A shadow fell across my feet. I looked up, and was surprised to see Baba.

"Come with me. Do not make a sound. We must sneak away without nurse noticing. It is a game."

He swept me up into his arms, and hurried back to the house. Here he opened the door to a room, which I had never entered before. He sat me on the floor.

"Now you must hide, so that neither your mother nor any of the servants can find you. You must not cry out. Can I rely on you to be quiet?"

I nodded, although I was becoming frightened. He stared into my eyes, then said he could not trust me. He stuffed fabric into my mouth, and tied a cloth around it so I could not spit it out. Then he bound my hands and feet, and left me alone in the dark.

At first I kept quiet, thinking that if I was good, he would come back and release me. Then I tried to scream. But even I could tell that my muffled whines were futile.

From time to time he would visit me. When he first took the fabric from my mouth I howled like an animal. He slapped me around the head, and I fell silent. Then he kissed my hair and stroked my head, apologising for hurting me. He said that I could shout all I wanted, that nobody else was in the house.

During these visits Baba made clumsy efforts to clean up the mess that I had made of my clothes. He brought me water, but for food all he gave me was raw meat. I begged him for some bread or rice. In response he shoved the dripping flesh into my mouth.

"Eat, my child. Eat and learn."

Eventually I gnawed at the meat in desperation, and he smiled and called me a good girl.

I have no idea how long this went on for. I took to beating my foot against the ground, in the hope that somebody might hear. Finally, the door burst open, and it was not Baba standing there, but my mother, and behind her, the eunuch.

My eyes filled with tears of frantic relief. Then I tried to shout a warning, as I saw Baba appear behind the eunuch. However my efforts were in vain. Baba cut the eunuch's throat, and it was only then that my mother realised he was there.

He spoke to her, telling her that it was her fault, she had invited the Ghul into her house. I did not understand him, and nor did my mother. She simply stood there, her mouth open, staring at the eunuch's blood as it trickled across the floor. Then he forced the knife into her belly, tugging it up, tearing her skin until the blade snagged against her breastbone.

When he went out again, I lay as still as I could. I could hear my mother struggling for life as she thrashed on the floor, but I listened in silence until her writhing had ceased. Later, Baba returned, and dragged the bodies away. I made no sound, no movement. I did not want to bring anybody else who loved me into the room to die.

The next time Baba came, he sat by me and talked. He told me about the Ghul, which lived within him, as a worm lives in the stomach of a cow. He told me that he had made a pact: that in return for something he really wanted, he had agreed to let the Ghul possess him. The Ghul was a powerful spirit, the offspring of Iblis, the Devil himself. And it needed the blood of children to live.

My stepfather told me that he had planned to sacrifice me, so that my blood could feed the Ghul. However now he understood that the spirit intended for me a greater destiny. I would be its host, when he could no longer nourish it. His duties were difficult and dangerous, he said. Several times he had nearly been caught, and some day his luck would fail him. Then I would carry the burden.

The days in the dark room seemed to have erased my previous life, as surely as the water washed my footprints from the riverbank. Watching my mother and the eunuch die had crushed any last traces of the little girl I had been. Into the emptiness seeped the words of my stepfather, filling my soul, pulsing meaning back into my existence.

Within a week I had been released from the storeroom. I helped Baba clean it out, since he had freed all the household slaves, including the cook and the nurse. We sold the house for a fraction of its value, and left the city.

My stepfather now insisted that I call him by his given name, which was Nuri. We travelled the land, dealing in cloth. The sale of the house had given him sufficient capital with which to trade, and he seemed to be a canny negotiator with contacts all across Arabia.

Two or three times a year, however, the Ghul became hungry, and demanded to be fed. I came to recognise the signs. Nuri would become distracted and irritable, unable to sleep at nights. Then he would go hunting.

When we had been on the road for a couple of years, he asked me to help him hunt. I felt proud and pleased, that I was trusted in a matter of such importance. We were staying in a small town in the plains of Najd. I found some children playing on the street, and joined in their games. Nuri told me I could not be seen leaving with any of them, so I arranged to meet one little boy later. I made him promise to keep the secret, saying I would show him something marvellous.

And I did. I showed him the Ghul, when it emerged from within Nuri, twisting his face and altering his voice to a bestial snarl. At first I was distressed by the boy's screams. But Nuri told me later that they were not cries of pain, but the sound of his soul, his ruh, undergoing purification, so that it could join with God.

As ever when the Ghul had been fed, we left the town the next day. After that day, though, I always joined Nuri in the hunt. We travelled together and slept together, and when I became a woman, he took my maidenhood. He was my father, my lover, my protector and my teacher.

Our life was not without its risks. Although we tried not to return to towns where the Ghul had feasted, it was inevitable that our wanderings would take us back sometimes to places where we had hunted. We were met with suspicion, and a couple of times Nuri was brought before the qadi. However, there were no witnesses or evidence, and they had to release him.

When it ended, it ended quietly. Nuri simply went out one day, and never returned. Perhaps a bereaved parent decided to take vengeance on their own, without going through the courts. I made no attempt to find out. Nuri had instructed me what I should do in such circumstances, even making me repeat his words until he was satisfied that I had memorised them. I packed up our belongings and left immediately, trailing a blanket behind the horses to cover my tracks.

He had told me that the Ghul would possess me after his death, and I wondered whether I would feel it entering my body. However, I felt nothing. At night there were dreams, of blood and shrieking, but I think they had always been there, as long as I had been hunting with Nuri.

For the first time in my life there was nobody to tell me what to do. The nomadic lifestyle had become wearying as well as dangerous, and I decided to settle down. All across Arabia the talk was of nothing other than the wonders of Baghdad, so I made my way to the capital. Here I took the money that we had accumulated in thirteen years of trading, and used it to buy a shop.

My shop prospered, and I began to forget about Nuri, and the Ghul. Then the dreams came back to me. I found myself sitting on the roof at night, staring out across the city, grinding my teeth and tasting blood in my mouth. At last I accepted the truth. The demon was within me, and it was hungry.

I was reluctant to hunt, and risk having to flee Baghdad, and my new life. However the cravings became stronger. I tried to think of a way that the Ghul might be sated, given an offering that ended its hunger forever.

Without Nuri I had nobody to school me in the ways of evil spirits. However I began to conceive the idea of the perfect sacrifice. The children would not be orphans, street scavengers no better than dogs, but instead they would be beautiful, bright and beloved. And there would be two of them, a boy and a girl: the King and Queen of Darkness.

I had always thought of Najida as a princess; she was so pretty and adored. Making her queen seemed like helping her to fulfil her destiny. I was visiting the merchant's wife, but the call of the Ghul rang in my head. When I saw the little girl alone in the garden, I told her that we would play a trick on her mother. With my help she climbed out of a window. I instructed her to run to my shop, where there was a bowl of figs for her, then bolted the shutters behind her.

The boy I found while walking through Sharqiya. I heard about the fire, and the manifestation of the Devil, and was drawn to the neighbourhood. For three days I passed by his house. Every day he was playing outside, and I won his trust with kind words and presents. His mother noticed nothing. When a child disappears, its parents will always claim that they only looked away for an instant. In fact, she was so oblivious that I think she must be an eater of hashish.

When I brought the boy back, I thought it would make Najida happy. However she continued to wail, and beg to be taken home. She even refused her food. The boy was different, quieter, braver. He tried to comfort her, encouraged her to eat. He said that a magic horse with wings of gold and silver would fly down to save them.

I told them about the wonderful destiny I had planned for them: how they would be anointed as royalty, how their innocent blood would transform the Ghul into a beautiful angel, how they would all three fly up to God together. But this did not seem to console them. Even when I brought them their insignia and crowned them King and Queen of Darkness, they did not thank me.

Then you came, Ismail. I knew as soon as I saw you that you would put an end to it. Sometimes I allowed myself to dream that we would fall in love. I imagined us running away together, getting married, and having children of our own, whom you would keep safe from evil spirits. In my clearer moments, though, I understood that you would shine light into my cellar, and make me face what I have done. And

I delayed and delayed, denying the howls of the Ghul as they grew louder in my head.

And now you are here. I am sorry the girl could not wait for you, but at least you have saved the boy. And there is still something you can do for me. I know what must be done next, and I accept it. I ask only that you are the one who does it.

Ah, at last you turn to look at me. Such sadness in your eyes! No, do not speak. Do not ask me to promise never to harm another child, I will only lie to you. The Ghul is still in me, and this is the only way he can be destroyed.

Oh yes, first let your master carry the boy into the light. He has seen enough. That sword seems awkward in your hands, Ismail. Is it the first time you have wielded it? It is heavy, I know. You must put it here, just below my ribs, then push upward. Into my heart.

Don't be weak, Ismail. You will be doing me no kindness, if you do not do this properly, only causing me pain. It is an act of love, Ismail. The last one we will ever share.

I'm sorry. Do –

Epilogue
The Tale of the Boats

Everybody was at the river, that morning. The summer heat had passed, and a brisk wind whipped the surface of the Tigris. Nonetheless the aristocracy of Baghdad came out in all their finery, to see the boats arriving; the boats which carried the treasure of Muhammad ibn Sulayman.

Of course agents and minions would take care of the sordid business of claiming their share. They came merely to oversee the process; and to watch that the agents and minions did not help themselves to a cut of the loot. It had also become a matter of pride, to be seen there. Court gossip would suggest that anyone who was absent was not important enough, or favoured enough, to have been granted a share.

Salam al-Abrash was there. The eunuch had received only a small allocation, but made a great show of collecting it, fussing around his factors and porters. He was interrupted by a tall man with long tendrils of hair falling about his shoulders.

"Peace be upon you, Speckled One."

"And upon you also, Father of Locks. I have not seen you since the day of the hunt- what, two, three months ago? Indeed, I had heard that you were in some disgrace."

"I live in disgrace as the fish lives in the water, my friend. It is my natural element, and therein I thrive."

The two men stood in silence for a while, watching a fat woman arguing with ibn Zuhayr, the Chief of Police.

"But it is written here, in the hand of the uncle of the Khalifah himself – to Umayma bint Abu Isa, five thousands dirhams in silver . . ."

The long-haired man turned to his plump companion.

"What is the cause of all this commotion?"

Salam al-Abrash cast a sideways glance at the man called the Father of Locks.

"You have been out of favour, haven't you? Old Muhammad ibn Sulayman died, on the same day as al-Khayzuran. The Khalifah, deep in mourning for his mother, nonetheless roused himself to send an agent down to Basrah, to ensure that he got his share of the inheritance.

"The agent did a very thorough job. In fact, he took everything of value, leaving ibn Sulayman's relatives with only the rubbish. And rubbish there was, in plenty. The old man was a hoarder, and never threw anything away. Do you know, they found his old school robes there, stained with ink from his childhood? It is said the suqs of Basrah still stink from the hundreds of fish which were rotting in his storerooms, and which they just threw out onto the streets.

"Harun kept the goods for himself: the carpets, the slaves, the horses and camels, the perfumes and spices and jewels. However the money he has divided between his courtiers and favourites. These boats are stuffed full of gold and silver coin, and all those with letters of authorisation have come to take their share."

Now the singing girls arrived, swaying along the waterfront clutching their furls of parchment. The crowds gasped, to see such glamour gathered in a single place. The wives of the wealthy tutted at their innovations of fashion, while secretly noting the trends they would copy. Salam, meanwhile, had more gossip to share.

"Since you have been absent from court circles, you may not have heard about the demotion of your friend and patron, Ja'far al-Barmaki. On the day of al-Khayzuran's funeral, the Khalifah ordered him to hand over to Fadl ibn Rabi the seal ring, and with it control of all the empire's finances. Nobody knows what the Wazir did to so anger his friend, to be stripped of such power, and see it awarded to his greatest rival."

The eunuch broke off when he noticed a slight, pale figure watching from a distance.

"Is that your boy over there? I have often wondered how

he came into your service. One day I catch him breaking into the House of Wisdom, the next he is an honoured guest at the Khalifah's Palace . . ."

"Ah, that is a story for another day. Will you excuse me, Speckled One?"

The boy watched the tall man approach him.

"Ismail."

"Master."

"I have been worried about you. When you ran, after leaving the cellar of Layla bint al-Bazza . . ."

The boy shrugged, and said nothing.

"Where did you go? Where have you been?"

"I have been with Mishal ibn Yunus. The death of Thomas the Syrian provoked a fight for power among the fityans of Harbiya. He gave me shelter, and in return I was able to help the Raiders at a difficult time. The porter's son– is he well?"

The tall man laughed.

"You will never lack for a friend in Sharqiya. I have taken to avoiding the place, so wearying has Ghassan's gratitude become. His wife, though, merely smiles vacantly. Layla was right about her. She has eaten hashish every day, since she used it to relieve her pain after giving birth to the boy."

"And the merchant Imran ibn Zaid?"

"I let al-Takht carry the body of his daughter to him. After all, that is work for the police, not for a poor poet such as myself."

A blast of trumpets broke into their conversation, and black ranks of Guardsmen marched towards the boats. They were followed by a man on horseback, in magnificent robes of scarlet and turquoise. The Khalifah himself, Harun the Righteous One, had come to see the division of the spoils.

A troop of Guards peeled away from the main body, and headed downriver to where the boy and the man were standing. They were escorting a handful of white-skinned barbarians in outlandish garb. One of the barbarians ran from the escort, and approached the boy.

"I had hoped to see you here."

It was a girl, slim, unveiled, with yellow hair like ripe corn.

She spoke to the boy in Greek devoid of inflection or expression.

"You killed my father."

The boy nodded, not challenging the literal truth of the statement.

"He was trying to kill me. You were my first, you know."

The girl seemed surprised at the change of subject. For the first time emotion crept into her voice.

"And you mine. I do not deny that I was trying to distract you from overhearing Brother Catwulf. It was my fault you were there. I heard your master joking about your friendship with the Chamberlain, and gave you the message meant for him. But I did like you. I hoped to save you . . ."

"And now?"

"We are leaving tomorrow."

"Has it been a success, your mission? Have you achieved what you came here for?"

The girl answered as if reciting something learned by rote.

"We are returning with messages of friendship from the Commander of the Faithful. Our embassy has been merely the seed, from which will grow ever greater peace and cooperation between our Kingdom and your Khalifate."

There was an awkward pause, followed by a shout from one of the Guards. The girl touched the boy's face, gently.

"Goodbye, Ismail."

"Goodbye, Hervor. I hope you arrive safely in your own lands."

She looked as if she were about to say something else, but instead she turned and ran back to her escort. The tall man snorted.

"Women! They are always complaining about something. 'You do not bring me gifts, you do not pay me enough compliments, you killed my father . . .' Really, boy, you should stick to your own sex. At least you know what you are dealing with.

"Ah, now here comes our esteemed Wazir. We should pay our respects. He has been enquiring after your whereabouts."

The boy and the man walked towards a handsome Persian, who stood talking to a portly man of middle age.

"Peace be upon you, mighty Wazir! And upon you, Yaqub al-Mithaq. I trust you have recovered from your wound."

The portly man looked suspicious.

"What wound?"

"Oh, I believed that you had suffered lacerations upon your arm, in the shape of the letter Zay. My apologies if I am mistaken."

The man called al-Mithaq bristled, but the Persian intervened.

"Peace be upon you, Father of Locks. I received your message concerning the outcome of your business, for which I owe you thanks. I have been waiting for you to present yourself, and demand a reward."

"I deemed it judicious to absent myself for a while. It seems that I inadvertently caused offence . . ."

"What, for your comments about my friendship with Harun? Great men cannot afford to take umbrage every time they are mocked in private. Besides, it is useful to have a hold on you. Now if you ever annoy me, I shall tell the Khalifah what you said.

"No, I believe that you are most effective in adversity. Also, I wanted to see how the young man would respond. I understand he showed great resourcefulness. In fact, Ibn Zuhayr has been demanding his head, for the assault on his man. I had to convince him that it might not reflect well on the police, that this scrawny youth was able to outwit and immobilise an armed officer."

"I am sorry to hear that our efforts did not prevent the Chamberlain gaining in influence, at your expense."

"Such fluctuations are all part of the game. In the end it was nothing to do with the Name, or the Door. Harun had felt for some time that my family had become too powerful, and it was only al-Khayzuran's influence that had prevented him from acting sooner.

"Besides, one cannot repress the truth forever. Truth is like water: it finds its own level, and will always seep out in the end. One can constrain it with walls and channels, as the miller narrows the river upstream of his mill, and in so doing generate power. But one must tend to the walls constantly, for leaks appear without warning, and a small trickle soon becomes a torrent.

"Yes, careful management of the truth is essential, for those who are responsible for the prosperity of empires. Our lands must be irrigated, but not flooded. We need it to live, but too much of it will drown us. However, there is something more powerful than the truth. Something that, if I must choose, I will take in preference to the truth every time. Do you know what that might be?"

"No, mighty Wazir."

"A sword, Abu Ali. A great big fucking sword."

The Persian turned away. The man and the boy bowed, and walked on up the river. In front of them, a pudgy man with weak eyes dropped a bag of coins, which spilled everywhere. The cream of Baghdad society got down on their hands and knees, scrabbling in the dirt for money. Among them stalked a dwarfish hunchback, shouting like a prophet in the wilderness.

"So the lion has fed, has gorged himself senseless. Now come the jackals and the hyenas, to pick at the remains of the corpse. Once we were men, proud warriors of the desert. Now all that is left is greed, indolence and depravity . . ."

The man and the boy strolled away from the chaos at the waterfront.

"What will you do now, Newborn?"

"I do not think I want to be a poet any more. Nor do I want to be a postman."

"Neither may be matters over which you get any choice. If you are blessed with the rare freedom to decide on your own path, what will you do?"

"I would like to go back to being al-Rawiya, the teller of tales. I have an idea, for a story which will contain all the other stories in the world. It will be the tale of someone who must keep telling stories, or die . . ."

"Is that not what we all do? Tell ourselves, and each other, our stories anew, every day? It is how we know we are still alive."

The two of them walked on, amid the noise and dreams and filth and struggles of the capital of the world. The boy looked up to the older man, with something like sympathy.

"And what will you do, Father of Locks?"

"What will I do? Have no concern for me. I am young, and good-looking, and have a small fortune in gold coins. Well actually, I don't. But that can soon be arranged . . ."

This much I can tell you. Only God knows all.

Historical Note

The Father of Locks is a work of fiction. Although it is based around historical events and characters, I have changed dates, altered facts and frequently just made things up. Anyone seeking to base a political or religious point on information gathered from its pages is duly warned.

However, reality has a strangeness to which the imagination can only aspire. The elements of my story that seem most extravagant or impossible are often those which are rooted in fact. The secrets that lie behind the Door That Should Not Have Been Opened, and within the Brass Bottle, are both taken from the pages of history.

I hope, too, that the story is fundamentally true to the nature of an extraordinary civilisation. While Europe was mired in the so-called Dark Ages, Baghdad was a place of incredible wealth, culturally as well as materially. Poetry and philosophy flourished. The foundations of modern science and mathematics were laid there. Without the Greek and Latin texts preserved in the House of Wisdom, the western Renaissance could never have taken place.

However, the records of this Golden Age are riddled with gaps, inconsistencies and controversies, leaving ample scope for invention. All the previous great civilisations littered the world with reminders of their presence. Virtually no physical trace of Harun al-Rashid's Baghdad remains, neither buildings nor inscriptions nor artworks nor monuments. Bar a few coins and ceramics, all that survives are the stories.

The earliest collection of these stories was made by the scholar al-Tabari (838–923 CE). His masterwork *The History of the Prophets and the Kings* is nothing less than a complete history of the world from the Creation to his own day. Al-Tabari used the methods of Islamic scholarship in compiling his chronicle. He recorded accounts as he heard them, even if they contradicted each other, and made no judgments about their relative trustworthiness. Instead he simply noted who had told him, and who had told them, and so through several generations of oral transmission.

Al-Tabari's history is available in a very readable English translation in the SUNY Series in Near Eastern Studies. However, the general reader who wants to sift fact from fiction is advised to seek out the work of Professor Hugh Kennedy, particularly *The Court of the Caliphs* (also published as *When Baghdad Ruled the Muslim World*). Other important sources for this novel include Andre Clot's *Harun al-Rashid*, and Gaston Wiet's *Baghdad: Metropolis of the Abbasid Caliphate*. I also enjoyed *Harun al-Rashid, Caliph of Baghdad* by Gabriel Audisio, a fabulously over-heated slice of Orientalist melodrama masquerading as history for children.

All the verse in this novel is based on genuine poems by the characters to whom they are attributed, with the exception of Ismail's qasida, which is my pastiche of the form. They are however rough approximations rather than accurate translations. For those who want to learn more, Robert Irwin's *Night and Horses and the Desert* is the best introduction to the literature of the period. *Abu Nuwas: A Genius of Poetry* by Philip Kennedy provides a biography and some excerpts from the work of the real Father of Locks. The truly determined can find a more extensive selection in Jim Colville's *Poems of Wine and Revelry*, although I find his translations functional rather than beautiful.

The most important source for this book, though, is not a work of scholarship but a tour de force of the human imagination. *The Thousand and One Nights*, in its astonishing breadth, variety and brilliance, is the true inspiration and model for my own efforts. My Harun, Ja'far and Abu Nuwas are drawn as much from Sheherezade's stories as they are from al-Tabari's. I make no apology for this. The process of mythologising these figures began in their lifetimes, and was entrenched amid the horrors of the civil war that followed Harun's death. Somewhere between history and legend is where the Father of Locks has found immortality, and that is where my tale is set.

A Note on Names

Arabic names of the Abbasid era do not conform to modern Western convention; they refuse to be confined to the boxes marked forename and surname. They evolved in a world of concentric and clashing social circles, best described by the famous proverb: "Me against my brother, me and my brother against my cousin, me and my brother and my cousin against the world."

To his intimates, his inner circle, a man might be called by his ism, the name given to him at birth. This was usually the name of a holy man or prophet: Nuh (Noah), Yahya (John) or Ali, for example. Sometimes it described a quality his parents hoped he would possess: Fadl means Generous, and Sa'id means Happy.

To the wider world, he would most likely be identified by his family line. "Ibn" (or "bin") means "son of", bint "daughter of." Sometimes the genealogy stretched back several generations. The name of the rebel Zayd ibn Hasan ibn Zayd ibn al-Hasan ibn Ali ibn Abi Talib proudly records his descent from Ali ibn Abi Talib, the Prophet Muhammad's son-in-law.

"Abu" means "father of", but does not always refer to real offspring. If, say, the son of Uthman had no children yet he might be referred to as Abu Uthman, assuming that when he did have a son he would name it after his father. It is also the basis of many nicknames. The notoriously stingy Khalifah al-Mansur was known as Abu'l-Dawaniq, "Father of Pennies" – although never to his face. The name of the poet Abu'l-Atahiyya translates literally as "Father of Madness".

It was only the male line that was traced. Nobody was ever

defined by their mother or daughter, with one notable exception: Isa ibn Maryam, Jesus son of Mary.

Between the intimate and the formal were a variety of nicknames, honorifics and insults. Most began with the definite article, "al-". These names could indicate clan, profession or country of origin. A carpenter might be known as al-Najjar. The historian al-Tabari was from Tabaristan. The name of the musician Ibrahim al-Mosuli started as a joke. Having made one brief visit to the principal city of northern Iraq he became "the man from Mosul" – and the name stuck so fast that he passed it to his son, who probably never went there at all.

We can therefore deduce much about the poet Abu Ali al-Hasan ibn Hani al-Hakami just from his name. His mother, presciently, called him al-Hasan, meaning Handsome. His father was Hani, his son, at least putatively, was Ali, and his tribe was the Hakami. However he was, and remains, best known by a nickname: Abu Nuwas, the Father of Locks.

Glossary

Dates given are Common Era (CE); the definite article "al-" is ignored for alphabetical ordering. All historical characters featured in *The Father of Locks* are listed here. Any characters not included can be assumed to be entirely fictional.

Abbas – (Born c.750?, died c. 810?) – Abu al-Fadl al-Abbas ibn al-Ahnaf was a poet at the court of **Harun al-Rashid**, who specialised in love poems.

Abbasid– Abbas ibn Abd al-Muttalib was the Prophet Muhammad's youngest uncle. His descendants, the Abbasid clan, seized the **Khalifate** in the revolution of 750 and ruled the Islamic world for over five hundred years, although their role became increasingly ceremonial as the dynasty declined.

Abd Allah – (Died 765) – Abd Allah ibn Ali was an uncle of **al-Saffah** and **al-Mansur**, who fought with them against the **Umayyads** but then attempted to take the throne for himself. He was defeated by **Abu Muslim**, and held under house arrest for the remainder of his life.

Abd al-Rahman – (Born 731, died 788) – a prince of the **Umayyad** dynasty who survived the massacre of his family by **al-Saffah** and **al-Mansur**, and escaped to the Hispanic peninsula. Here he established himself and his descendants as **Amirs** of Cordoba, demonstrating a political and military genius that earned him the nickname "the Falcon of Andalus."

Abu Ali – Alternative name for **Abu Nuwas**, used by his friends

Abu'l-Atahiyya – (Born 748, died 826) – Abu'l-Ishaq Isma'il

Ibn al-Qasim, better known as Abu'l-Atahiyya, the "Father of Madness", was a leading poet of his day. He was also called Jarrar, the Jug Seller.

Abu Bakr – (Born c.573, died 634) – a close friend and ally of the Prophet Muhammad, his name means "Father of a Camel's Foal". He was the first **Khalifah**, and considered by Sunni Muslims to be one of **al-Rashidun**.

Abu Hashim – (Died 716) – Grandson of **Ali ibn Abi Talib**, son of **Muhammad ibn al-Hanafiyyah**.

Abu Muslim – (Born c. 700, died 755) – Abu Muslim Abd al-Rahman ibn Muslim al-Khorasani was a revolutionary and military leader, who was instrumental in bringing the **Abbasid** dynasty to power. He is regarded as a national hero in Tajikistan, and there is an Iranian football team named after him.

Abu Nuwas – (Born c.755, died 814) – Abu Ali al-Hasan ibn Hani al-Hakami is widely recognised as one of the greatest poets of the Arabic language. He wrote on many subjects, but his favourite themes were the forbidden pleasures of wine and homosexual love, and as a result he remains a controversial figure in the Islamic world. The nickname by which he is best known, Abu Nuwas, means "Father of Locks" or "Father of Tresses", in reference to his distinctive long hair.

The account of his early life in the chapter called "The Education of a Poet" is largely drawn from historical sources, although with some embroidery on my part. The idea that he might have been a spy, on the other hand, is purely my invention. It may seem implausible that a gay alcoholic poet would be recruited to his country's intelligence service, but the career of Shakespeare's contemporary Christopher Marlowe is at least one point of evidence to the contrary.

Abu Ubayda (728–825) – Scholar of Arabic language and history, and teacher of **Abu Nuwas**.

Afrit, plural **Afarit** – a powerful **Jinn**, particularly one that has been enslaved by a human.

Agathias Scholasticus – (Born c. 536, died c. 582) – a Greek historian and poet.

Aisha bint Abi Bakr – (Born 614?, died 678) – wife of the Prophet **Muhammad** and daughter of his friend **Abu Bakr**.

Ali ibn Abi Talib – (Born c. 600, reigned 656–661) – The Prophet's cousin and also his son-in-law, having married his daughter **Fatimah**, Ali was the fourth **Khalifah** and the last of **al-Rashidun**, the Righteous Ones. Although he is revered by both Sunni and Shi'a Muslims, his place in the succession is the primary cause of the religion's great schism. The historical record suggests he was a gentle and spiritual man, who would be appalled that people are still killing each other over his status.

Alid – a descendant of **Ali ibn Abi Talib**.

Amir – Also spelt Emir or Aamir – a prince. The word originally referred to a military leader. One of the **Khalifah**'s titles is Amir al-Muminin, usually translated as "Commander of the Faithful."

Angilbert – (Born c.740, died 814) – Priest, poet and politician at the court of King **Karol**. There is no historical basis to the suggestion that he spoke Arabic, or travelled any further east than Rome.

An Lushan – (Born 703, died 757) – A Chinese soldier and politician of Iranian/ Turkish origin who achieved great power but rebelled against **Tang Xuanzong**, seeking the Emperor's throne for himself.

Aristutalis – (Born 384BCE, died 322BCE) – The Arabic name for Aristotle, the Greek philosopher who was tutor to Alexander the Great. Aristotle's wide-ranging curiosity and logical approach were hugely influential on the philosophy and science of the Abbasid era.

al-Asha – (Born c. 565?, died c. 625) – Maymun ibn Qays al-Asha was a blind poet of the early Islamic era. It is said that he was prepared to give up fornication in order to become a Muslim, but when he heard that he would have to give up wine as well, he decided to have one more year of drinking before converting. However he died before the year was up.

Banuqa – (Born c. 767, died c. 783) – Daughter of **al-Mahdi** and **al-Khayzuran**. She was her father's favourite, and her early death was greatly mourned.

Barid – The postal service of the Khalifate, which doubled as its spy network.

Barmakid – The al-Barmaki clan, **Yahya ibn Khalid** and his sons **Fadl** and **Ja'far**, were the dominant political force at the court of the **Abbasid Khalifahs** for nearly half a century.

Bashshar – (Born 714, died 784) – Abu Mu'adh Bashshar ibn Burd was an innovative poet, who was a pioneer of the Badi ("avant-garde") style of verse perfected by **Abu Nuwas** and his circle. Although blind from birth, pox-scarred and extremely ugly, Bashshar was a notorious womaniser.

Bon – The shamanistic religion of Tibet before the coming of Buddhism. Buddhism spread mostly by absorbing local traditions rather than replacing them, just as early Christianity adapted Christmas and Easter from pagan festivals, and Bon is now considered to be one of the five schools of Tibetan tantrism. Its original beliefs and practices are difficult to disentangle from Buddhist reinterpretation, and the description given here is largely speculative.

Catwulf – (Born c.750?, died c.800?) – The Irish priest Catwulf appears only briefly in the pages of history. In 775 he wrote a letter to King **Karol**, saying that God had raised him to the throne "for the greater glory of the kingdom of Europe." His subsequent career as diplomat and spy is wholly fictitious.

Cubit – The distance from a man's elbow to his fingertips, around 18 inches.

Dinar – derived from the Roman denarius, the dinar remains a unit of currency in many Islamic countries. During the reign of **Harun al-Rashid** it was a small gold coin weighing one or two grams.

Dirham – a thin silver coin worth one twentieth of a dinar.

Eggihard – (Died 778) – The office of Mayor of the Palace was an important one at the Frankish Court, and the death of the holder of this title in the battle of **Orreaga** would have been a significant loss.

Fadl ibn Rabi – (Born c. 755, died 824) – The son of **Rabi ibn Yunus**, Fadl ibn Rabi was **Harun**'s Hajib, or Chamberlain, and arch-rival of the **Barmakids**.

Fadl ibn Yahya al-Barmaki – One of the **Barmakid** clan, son of **Yahya ibn Khalid** and brother of **Ja'far**.

Farsh – A large, thick rug, used as both seating and bedding.

Fatimah – (Born c. 605?, died 632) – The Prophet's daughter, and the only one of his children who lived to bear children herself. The account of her death given here is based on Shi'a sources and is hotly disputed by Sunni Muslims.

Gao Xianzhi – (Died 756) – a Chinese general of Korean origin, who led the Tang army at the battle of Talas River.

Ghazal – a love song.

Ghul – an evil spirit in Arabic folklore. The Ghul inhabits graveyards and eats human flesh. It can live on corpses but will also take on the form of an animal to lure children to its lair. In some accounts the Ghul is a **Jinn** fathered by **Iblis** to prey on mankind. The word is the origin of the English "ghoul".

Hadith – The Hadith, or "Sayings", are accounts of the life of the Prophet **Muhammad** and records of teachings attributed to him. After the Quran they are the main source of Islamic law and theology.

Hajj – the pilgrimage to Mecca which every adult Muslim is expected to perform at least once in their lives.

Hani ibn Abd al-Awwal – (Died c.755) – Father of **Abu Nuwas**.

Harun al-Rashid – (Born 763, reigned 786–809) – Fifth **Khalifah** of the **Abbasid** dynasty, he was the son of **al-Mahdi** and **al-Khayzuran**, and succeeded his older brother **Musa al-Hadi**. Despite a relatively undistinguished reign, he became the subject of innumerable stories, as the model of a wise and just ruler.

Hashimiyah – A political and religious sect, who believed that the true **Khalifate** passed from **Ali** to his grandson **Abu Hashim**, and then to the **Abbasid** family.

Hisham – (Reigned 788–796) – **Umayyad Amir** of Cordoba, son of **Abd al-Rahman**.

House of Wisdom – As with so much about the early Abbasid era, there is debate and controversy about the precise nature of the Bayt al-Hikma, the House of Wisdom. It seems to have been either a library or a university, and may not have been founded until the reign of **Harun**'s son al-Mamun. Nearly every detail concerning it in this novel, including the Chamber of the Ancients, is invented.

Hruodland – (Died 778) – Very little is known about the Governor of the Breton Marshes, who died in the Battle of **Orreaga**. However both he and the battle must have been remembered, either by oral transmission or, as I have suggested, in Latin verse. Four centuries later, with his name and most of the historical facts altered, an unknown author made Hruodland the eponymous hero of the first great work of literature in the French language: La Chanson de Roland.

Husayn al-Ansari – (Died c. 782) – Husayn ibn Yahya al-Ansari ibn Saad al Obadi was the **Wali** of Zaragusta (Zaragoza) from 774–781. He eventually surrendered his city to **Abd al-Rahman,** but was later murdered by him anyway.

Iblis – The Muslim equivalent of Satan, also known as **Shaitan** and Abu Murra.

Ibn Kulthum – (Died 584?) – Amr ibn Kulthum Ibn Malik Ibn A'tab Abu Al-Aswad al-Taghlibi was a poet and warrior of the **Jahili**. Among the tales told of him, it is said that he killed the King of Hira who murdered Tarafah, the King having insulted ibn Kulthum's mother, and that he died at a great age after drinking too much wine.

Ibn Salih – (Died c. 770?) – Ziyad ibn Salih was the leader of the Muslim army at the Battle of Talas River.

Ibn Shaddad – (Born c. 525?, died c. 615?) – Antarah ibn

Shaddad al-Absi was the son of an Arab tribesman of the Banu Abs, and an African woman. At first he was not accepted by his tribe, but he won their respect through his courage and his talent for verse. An epic poem from the time of the Crusades describes his heroic deeds and his love for his cousin Abla.

Ibn Zuhayr – (Born c. 730?, died c. 790?) al-Musayyab ibn Zuhayr al-Dabbi was a veteran of the Black Flag revolution, and was head of the **Shurta** under three different Khalifahs. He was twice awarded the prestigious governorship of Khorasan, but does not seem to have been as successful an administrator as he obviously was as an enforcer.

Ibrahim al-Imam – (Born c. 701, died 749) – Head of the **Abbasid** family, older brother of **al-Saffar** and **al-Mansur**.

Ibrahim al-Mosuli – (Born 743, died 804) – a musician and poet, father of **Ishaq al-Mosuli**.

Ibrahim ibn al-Mahdi – (Born c. 780, died 839) – son of the **Khalifah al-Mahdi**, younger brother of **Musa al-Hadi** and **Harun al-Rashid**.

Ibrahim ibn al-Walid – (Reigned 744) – an **Umayyad Khalifah**.

Ishaq al-Mosuli – (Born 767, died 850) – a musician and poet, son of **Ibrahim al-Mosuli**.

al-Iskander – (Born 356BCE, reigned 336–323BCE) – the Arabic name for Alexander the Great, King of Macedon, who extended his empire as far as India before his early death. Some believe that he is Dhu al-Qarnayn, the "Two-Horned One" mentioned in the Quran.

Ja'far ibn Yahya al-Barmaki – (Born 767, died 803) – Ja'far was the youngest member of the influential **Barmakid** family, son of **Yahya** and brother of **Fadl**. He was a friend as well as courtier to **Harun al-Rashid**, until his mysterious and fatal fall from favour.

Jahili – An Islamic term describing Arabs before the coming of the Prophet, it implies an ignorant, primitive way of life.

Janan – (Born c. 757?) – a singing girl, beloved of **Abu Nuwas**.

Jinn, plural **Jinni** – a fire spirit, a "genie".

Jullaban – (Born c. 740, died c. 820) – Mother of **Abu Nuwas**.

Ka'bah – A small building in Mecca made of black stone which is the most sacred shrine of Islam, and forms the focus of the **hajj**.

Karlo, King of the Franks – (Born c. 747, reigned 768–814) – The Franks were a Germanic people who, by the late 8th century, occupied most of what is now France, Germany, Italy and the Low Countries. Their military and cultural dominance came to a peak under a king who was known in his own language as Karlo or Karol – it is not certain which – but is recorded in the Latin chronicles of his time as Carolus Magnus, Charles the Great. He is best known today by a mediaeval French version of that name: Charlemagne.

Over the course of his long reign Charlemagne laid the foundations of modern Europe, and also of the Roman Catholic church as we know it today. Contact between his court and that of **Harun al–Rashid** probably began in reality some ten years later than I have suggested, but seems to have been largely cordial. Harun is said to have sent Charlemagne an elephant, of which the Franks were very proud.

Khadijah – (Born c.555, died 619) – First wife of the Prophet **Muhammad**, and mother of **Fatimah**.

Khalaf al–Amar – (Born 733, died 796) – Arabic writer, collector and alleged forger of **Jahili** poetry, teacher of **Abu Nuwas**.

Khalifah – The word "khalifah", traditionally written in English as "Caliph", means "successor", and became the principal title of the leaders of Islam after the death of the Prophet. The events surrounding the creation of this role remain the source of bitter dispute; the conflicting accounts of Sunni and Shi'a sources is only the beginning of the controversy. It does, though, seem to have been a pragmatic response to political realities, rather than a planned succession.

Kharijite – "One who walked away", a member of a dissident sect of Islam who did not recognise the authority of the Khalifate.

al-Khayzuran – (Born c. 740, died 789) – al-Khayzuran, whose name means "The Reed", was the mother of **Harun al-Rashid**. She was a Yemeni slave girl, tall, slender and beautiful, who was a concubine of the **Khalifah al-Mahdi**, then scandalised the court when she became his wife. Al-Khayzuran was a friend and ally to the **Barmakids**, and her political influence was a source of increasing resentment to her older son **Musa al-Hadi** during his brief reign. It has been suggested that she had him killed so that her favourite **Harun** could succeed to the throne. However even he seems to have tired of her interference in the end.

Labid – (Born c.560?, died c.661?) – Abu Aqil Labid ibn Rabi'ah was a poet, and author of one of the **Mu'allaqat**. He gave up writing after converting to Islam, although his work was praised by the Prophet **Muhammad**.

Li Linfu – (Died 753) – Chancellor to **Tang Xuanzong** for 18 years. For all his political astuteness, history has judged him harshly; his ruthless elimination of all his rivals left no competent officials to take the reins after his death, and this is seen as a significant cause of the anarchy that followed.

Li Siye – (Died 759) – Second-in-command of the Chinese and Farghana troops at the Battle of Talas River.

Mahakala – Buddhists regard Mahakala, which means "Great Black", as a "Dharmapala", a Protector of the Way. However, his fangs, claws and crown of skulls betray the Tibetan demon from whom the Buddhist deity was developed.

al-Mahdi – (Born c. 740, reigned 775–785) – Third **Khalifah** of the **Abbasid** dynasty, son of **al-Mansur** and father of **Musa al-Hadi** and **Harun al-Rashid**.

Malik ibn Anas – (Born c. 715, died 796) – Malik ibn Anas ibn Malik ibn 'Amr al-Asbahi is regarded by Sunni

Muslims as one of the most important interpreters of scripture and holy law. The Maliki school of juris-prudence, one of the four recognised by most Sunnis, was founded on his studies. The story of his clash with **al-Mansur** is an interesting reflection of the balance of power between state and scholarship in the **Abbasid** era.

al-Mansur – (Born c. 712, reigned 754–775) – Second, and probably greatest of the **Abbasid Khalifahs**, and the founder of Baghdad. He succeeded his brother **al-Saffah**, and was succeeded by his son **al-Mahdi**. Nearly all the stories told about him in this book are drawn from historical sources.

Maria al-Qibtiyya – (Died 637) – "Maria the Copt", a Christian woman who was either wife or concubine to the Prophet **Muhammad**.

Marwan ibn Muhammad – (Born 688, reigned 744–750) – Marwan II was the last **Khalifah** of the **Umayyad** dyn-asty. He took over in a period of chaos, and rarely knew peace during his brief reign.

Masjid – a mosque.

Mazdaist – a Mazdayani, a follower of the teachings of Zoro-aster. Zoroastrianism was the main religion of Persia until the Islamic conquest, and survives as a minority faith in the region. Zoroaster or Zarathustra was a poet who wrote hymns to a benevolent creator God called Ahura Mazda, some time between the 6th and 4th centuries BCE. His monotheism seems to have been a significant influence on the development of the Abrahamic religions.

Mizmar – a reed instrument, similar to an oboe.

Mu'allaqat – The Seven "Hanging Odes" were considered to be the finest examples of pre-Islamic Arabic verse, although there is (inevitably) disagreement about exactly which poems they were. They are said to have been written in gold and hung in the **Ka'bah**, but this may be a retrospective explanation for a name of which the true meaning had been forgotten. The traditional canon includes works by **al-Qays, Tarafah**, Zuhayr, **Labid, ibn Shaddad, ibn Kulthum**, and ibn Hillizah. **Abu**

Ubayda, however, produced a list which featured poems by **al-Nabigha** and **al-Asha** instead of the last two.

Muʿawiyah – (Born c.602, died 680) – Fifth **Khalifah**, and first of the **Umayyad** dynasty.

Muhammad – (Born 570, died 632) – Abu al-Qasim Muhammad ibn ʿAbd Allah ibn ʿAbd al-Muttalib ibn Hashim is accepted by all Muslims as the final Prophet of God. It is customary to follow his name with the phrase "Peace be upon him", as a mark of respect. All the stories relating to his lifetime included in this book are based on early Islamic accounts.

Muhammad ibn al-Hanafiyyah – (Died 700) – Son of **Ali ibn Abi Talib**, father of **Abu Hashim**.

Muhammad ibn Sulayman – (Died 789) – An **Abbasid** prince, first cousin to **al-Mansur**. The account of events after his death given here is based on historical sources.

Muhammad of the Pure Soul – (Died 762) – Muhammad ibn Abd Allah, known as al-Nafs al-Zakiya, the Pure Soul, was an **Alid** rebel in the time of **al-Mansur**.

Musa al-Hadi – (Born c. 760, reigned 785–786) – Fourth **Khalifah** of the **Abbasid** dynasty, and oldest son of **al-Mahdi** and **al-Khayzuran**.

al-Nabighah – (Born c. 535, died c. 604) – al-Nabighah al-Dhubyani was a Christian poet, one of the most celebrated writers in Arabic of his day.

Orreaga – The Basque name for Roncevaux or Roncesvalles Pass, scene of a notorious massacre of Frankish troops in 778.

Otsoa – (Died c.778) – Otso in the Euskara language means "wolf", and the Basque leader Otsoa was known to other peoples by a translation of his name: Loup in French or Lupo in Gascon. It has been suggested but not proven that he was responsible for the ambush of **Hruodland**.

Qadi – A judge.

Qamis – A light shirt.

al-Qays – (Died c. 550) – Imruʾ al-Qays ibn Hujr was the earliest poet whose work is included in the **Muʿallaqat.** He is credited with the invention of the qasida.

Qin, qanun – stringed instruments of the zither family.

Rabi ibn Yunus – (Died 786) – A freed slave who became one of the **Abbasids'** most trusted servants, although according to some accounts he was murdered by **Musa al-Hadi** after an argument about a slave-girl. His son **Fadl ibn Rabi** inherited, and built on, his position.

Rabi'a al-Adawiyya – (Born c. 717, died 801) – Rabi'a al-Adawiyya al-Qaysiyya, also called Rabi'a al-Basri, was a poet and mystic, considered to be a Sufi saint.

al-Rashidun – The "Righteous Ones", a Sunni term for the first four **Khalifahs,** who were chosen from among the Companions of Muhammad, the Sabaha. They were **Abu Bakr, Umar, Uthman** and **Ali. Harun al-Rashid** was given his epithet in tribute to these early leaders.

Rita – (Born c. 745?) – cousin and wife of **al-Mahdi**.

Roman Empire – The division of the vast Roman Empire into western and eastern halves began as an administrative convenience, but by 395 the split had become permanent. The western half collapsed within a century, when Rome itself fell to barbarian invaders, but the empire survived in eastern Europe and the Middle East for nearly a thousand years afterwards.

   This eastern Roman empire, with its capital in the city variously called Byzantium, New Rome, Constantinople, and now Istanbul, is usually referred to as the Byzantine Empire, but this name is a later invention. It was a Christian state, and its language was Greek not Latin, but its citizens considered themselves the heirs of Augustus, Vespasian and Marcus Aurelius. To its people, its allies and its enemies it was known only as the Roman Empire.

al-Saffah – (Born c. 720, reigned 750–754) – First **Khalifah** of the **Abbasid** dynasty. He came to power as a result of the Revolution of the Black Flag, and cemented his position by massacring members of **Umayyad** family whom he had invited to a feast; his name means Shedder of Blood. He was succeeded by his older brother **al-Mansur**.

Sayf – a sword. The word is usually associated with the

curved "scimitar", but in the 8th century it would have been a straight blade.

Salam al-Abrash – (Born c. 750?, died c. 820?) – a eunuch courtier, who served three generations of the Abbasid family.

Sappho – (Born c. 620BCE?, died c. 570BCE?) – A Greek lyric poet. She was held in high regard by later generations of both Greek and Roman writers, but very little of her work has survived. Much of her love poetry was addressed to other women, and her name and birthplace are the origin of the words "sapphic" and "lesbian".

al-Shafi'i – (Born 767, died 820) – Abu Abdullah Muhammad ibn Idris al-Shafi'i was a scholar of fiqh, the process of establishing Islamic law and custom from interpretations of the Quran and **Hadith**. Although he studied under **Malik ibn Anas**, his own work was of such significance that a separate school is based on it, and the Shafi'i school is one of the four recognised by Sunni Muslims. Reality and pious myth are hopelessly entangled in accounts of his life and character, so that it is hard to say what the real man was like. However the portrayal of him here as pompous and dogmatic is not founded on anything but my feeling that clever men need to learn humility before they become wise.

Shaikh – Also spelt Sheikh or Shaykh – a term of respect, meaning tribal leader or elder. It can also indicate a man of learning.

Shaitan – the Devil, **Iblis**.

Sherbet – a cold, spiced non-alcoholic drink often flavoured with rose petals or liquorice.

Shurta – the Baghdad city police. Their function and organisation remain uncertain, but they seem to have been of low status, and as likely to start riots as to prevent them.

Span – The width of an outstretched hand, considered to be half a cubit, or around nine inches.

Sulayman al-Arabi – (Died 780) – Sulayman ibn Yaqzan al-Arabi was a **Wali** of Barsalona (modern Barcelona) and

Girona, who sought an alliance with the Franks to resist the rising power of **Abd al-Rahman** in the region.

Surah – A chapter of the Quran.

Tang Xuanzong – (Born 685, reigned 712–756, died 762) – The longest ruling Emperor of the Tang dynasty in China. In his youth he was a dynamic leader, but his grip on affairs loosened as he aged, and his reign was to end in tragedy.

Tarafah – (Born 543, died 569) – Tarafah ibn al 'Abd ibn Sufyan ibn Malik al-Bakri was one of the most celebrated pre-Islamic poets, and his ode was the longest of the **Mu'allaqat**. According to some accounts he was buried alive as punishment for writing a satire about the King of Hira.

Thalaba ibn Obeid – (Died c. 780?) – A friend and ally of **Abd al-Rahman**.

Tunbur – a long-necked lute.

Umar ibn al-Khattab – (Born c.586, died 644) – A companion of the Prophet **Muhammad**, and close friend of **Abu Bakr**. On the latter's death he became the second **Khalifah**.

Umayyad – The Umayyad clan ruled over Islam for nearly a century (660–750), between the Righteous Ones (**al-Rashidun**) and the **Abbasids**. At their peak, the family did much to stabilise the Muslim empire, but in a two year period from 743 to 744 there were five different **Khalifahs**, and the chaos left the dynasty's last ruler, **Marwan II**, in charge of a fatally unpopular regime.

Uthman ibn Affan – (Born c.580, died 656) – The third **Khalifah**. Although he was from the **Umayyad** clan, he is considered to be one of **al-Rashidun**, and was not succeeded by a member of his family but by **Ali ibn Abi Talib**.

Wali – The governor of a city.

Waliba al-Asadi – (Died 786) – A poet and mentor to **Abu Nuwas**.

al-Walid II – (Reigned 743–744) – an **Umayyad Khalifah**.

Wang Wei – (Born 701, died 761) – A poet, painter and

musician, who also had a successful political career, rising to become Chancellor. Although he was a remarkable polymath, a knowledge of Arabic is not recorded as being among his accomplishments.

Yahya ibn Khalid al-Barmaki – (Died 805) – Head of the **Barmakid** family, father of **Ja'far** and **Fadl ibn Yahya**.

Yang Guozhong – (Died 756) – An official at the court of **Tang Xuanzong.** Despite his drinking, gambling, and incompetence, he was promoted to Chancellor through flattery of the Emperor and the influence of his cousin **Lady Yang**.

Yang, the Lady – (Born 719, died 756) – Yang Yuhuan, usually known as Yang Guifei or Lady Yang, is considered to be one of the Four Beauties of Ancient China, although she was apparently plump by modern standards, and according to some accounts suffered from unpleasant armpit odour. Her life and death are the subject of innumerable plays, novels, operas and films.

Yazid III – (Born 701, reigned 744) – An **Umayyad Khalifah**.

Zindiq – A general term for a Muslim whose beliefs are regarded as heretical by mainstream Islam.

Zubayda – (Born c. 740) – Zubayda bint Munir was the wife of **Yahya ibn Khalid al-Barmaki**.

Recommended Reading

If you enjoyed reading *The Father Locks* there is one book on our list, which is perfect for you, *The Arabian Nightmare*.

The Arabian Nightmare – Robert Irwin

"Robert Irwin is indeed particularly brilliant. He takes the story-within-a-story technique of the Arab storyteller a stage further, so that a tangle of dreams and imaginings becomes part of the narrative fabric. The prose is discriminating and, beauty of all beauties, the book is constantly entertaining."

Hilary Bailey in *The Guardian*

"Robert Irwin writes beautifully and is dauntingly clever but the stunning thing about him is his originality. Robert Irwin's work, while rendered in the strictest, simplest and most elegant prose, defies definition. All that can be said is that it is a bit like a mingling of *The Thousand and One Nights* and *The Name of the Rose*. It is also magical, bizarre and frightening."

Ruth Rendell

"... a classic orientalist fantasy tells the story of Balian of Norwich and his misadventures in a labyrinthine Cairo at the time of the Mamelukes. Steamy, exotic and ingenious, it is a boxes-within-boxes tale featuring such characters as Yoll, the Storyteller, Fatima the Deathly and the Father of Cats. It is a compelling meditation on reality and illusion, as well as on Arabian Nights-style storytelling. At its elusive centre lies the affliction of the Arabian Nightmare: a dream of infinite suffering that can never be remembered on waking, and might almost have happened to somebody else."

Phil Baker in *The Sunday Times*

£6.99 ISBN 978 1 873982 73 0 266p B. Format